Praise for Tomoyuki Hoshino
and *We, the Children of Cats*

"I see [in Hoshino] an ability to truly *think* through
fiction that recalls Kōbō Abe. This superlative
ability makes even the most fantastical details
and developments read as perfectly natural."
—Kenzaburō Ōe, Nobel Prize–winning author of *Nip the
Buds, Shoot the Kids* and *Teach Us to Outgrow Our Madness*

"Like a heat shimmer on a summer's day, Tomoyuki
Hoshino's stories tantalize and haunt. From 'Paper
Woman' to 'A Milonga for the Melted Moon,' Hoshino
writes of people stranded between poles of reality
and dream—with each option as uncertain as the
other. Wonderfully translated, selected, and presented,
this collection of works will be required reading."
— Rebecca Copeland, Washington University, author
of *Lost Leaves: Women Writers of Meiji Japan* and
translator of *Grotesque* by Natsuo Kirino

"[Hoshino's] stories are filled with images like sacred
spaces: even as each seems perfectly self-contained, they
secretly refuse their apparent closures, spinning forever
across limitless expanses, dropping seeds along the
way for further growth. As they travel always towards
some distant other place, they live on through myriad
forms that possess no tidy resolution, no real end."
— Mayumi Inaba, award-winning author of
Hotel Zambia and *Portrait in Sand*

D1555342

"These wonderful stories make you laugh and cry, but mostly they astonish, commingling daily reality with the envelope pushed to the max and the interstice of the hard edges of life with the profoundly gentle ones."
— Helen Mitsios, editor of *New Japanese Voices: The Best Contemporary Fiction from Japan* and *Digital Geishas and Talking Frogs: The Best 21st Century Short Stories from Japan*

"What feels most striking and praiseworthy about Hoshino's work is how he deals with ambiguity—not as a fusion of multiple meanings, nor as their simple coexistence, nor as symbolic of meaning's absence; rather, he deftly weaves these concepts together and then, in the space between them, makes his escape."
— Maki Kashimada, award-winning author of *Love at 6000°* and *The Kingdom of Zero*

"The loosely linked stories collected in *We, the Children of Cats* home in on everyday events of millennial Japan only to slowly pan out onto alternate realities—voyages, crimes of passion, cultural histories of treason, sudden quarrels, and equally sudden truces. Bergstrom and Fraser's translations brilliantly capture the emotional tones and shape-shifting nature of Hoshino's language. These stories explore the longing to be somewhere, sometime, or even someone else so strongly that reality itself is, before you know it, transfigured."
— Anne McKnight, Terasaki Center for Japanese Studies at UCLA, author of *Nakagami, Japan: Buraku and the Writing of Ethnicity*

We, the Children of Cats

Stories and Novellas by Tomoyuki Hoshino

Edited and Translated by Brian Bergstrom

with an additional translation by Lucy Fraser

FOUND IN
TRANSLATION

Some of the translations in this collection have appeared elsewhere in slightly different form and are reprinted with kind permission: "Chino," published online by the Japanese Literature Publishing and Promotion Center (J-Lit Center, 2005); "Air" in *Chroma: A Queer Literary and Arts Journal* (Spring 2008); and "The No Fathers Club" in *Digital Geishas and Talking Frogs: The Best 21st Century Short Stories from Japan* (Boston: Cheng & Tsui, 2011).

The stories and novellas in this collection were originally published in Japanese in the following venues: "Paper Woman" as "Kamionna" in *Issatsu no hon* (Asahi Shinbunsha, March 2000), reprinted in *Warera neko no ko* (Kōdansha, November 2006); "The No Fathers Club" as "Tetenashigo kurabu" in *Bungei* (Kawade Shobō, Spring 2006), reprinted in *Warera neko no ko* (Kōdansha, November 2006); "Chino" as "Chino" in *Kawade Yume Mook: Bungei Bessatsu—Asian Travelers* (Kawade Shobō, July 2000), reprinted in *Warera neko no ko* (Kōdansha, November 2006); "We, the Children of Cats" as "Warera neko no ko" in *Shinchō* (Shinchōsha, January 2001), reprinted in *Warera neko no ko* (Kōdansha, November 2006); "Air" as "Eaa" in *Gunzō* (Kōdansha, November 2006), reprinted as "Ea" in *Warera neko no ko* (Kōdansha, November 2006); "Sand Planet" as "Suna no wakusei" in *Subaru* (Shūeisha: March 2002), reprinted in *Fantajisuta* (Shūeisha, 2003); "Treason Diary" as "Uragiri nikki" in *Bungei* (Kawade Shobō, Summer 1998), reprinted in *Naburiai* (Kawade Shobō, 1999); "A *Milonga* for the Melted Moon" as "Toketa tsuki no tame no mironga" in *Bungei* (Kawade Shobō, Spring 1999), reprinted in *Naburiai* (Kawade Shobō, 1999).

ISBN: 978-1-60486-591-2
Library of Congress Control Number: 2011939692

Cover: John Yates / www.stealworks.com
Interior design by briandesign

10 9 8 7 6 5 4 3 2 1

PM Press
PO Box 23912
Oakland, CA 94623
www.pmpress.org

Printed in the USA on recycled paper, by the Employee Owners of Thomson-Shore in Dexter, Michigan.
www.thomsonshore.com

Contents

To All of You Reading This in English

As you know, on March 11, 2011, an enormous earthquake struck eastern Japan. At the time, I was at home in Tokyo working on a novel. The shaking was unlike anything I'd experienced before. It went on and on, up and down and side to side, as if I were in a small boat tossed by angry waves; minutes passed, but still it didn't stop. The bookcases and walls swayed like wind-buffeted trees.

I'd never thought earthquakes were frightening, but in this moment, I felt true terror in my heart. This is how my life will end, I thought. I felt the strength leave my body, and, afraid I would collapse right there, I put my hand against the wall, using all my might just to get through it.

As soon as the shaking subsided, I turned on the television. Tsunami warnings were sounding. The tsunami arrived unbelievably quickly. There was no sense of reality to it at all. It crashed over the coastline and rushed across rice fields with amazing speed. Images of it swallowing fleeing cars and fleeing people were broadcast live from helicopters. Watching them, I felt my heart break a little, somewhere deep inside.

That wound has yet to heal. And if someone like me, shaken up in Tokyo and watching the tsunami on television, was so affected, how must it be for those the tsunami touched directly? When I think of them, my body trembles.

Twenty years ago, I lived in Mexico, drawn there by a love of Latin American literature. Doing so taught me that what I saw before my eyes at any given moment was not the entirety of reality. Latin America is a place where, for good or for ill, extraordinary events ordinarily occur. I was frequently faced with absurd occurrences I could do nothing about, but on the other hand, it forced me to be creative and resilient as I confronted whatever may come next. I found my powers of imagination growing more expansive as I lived there in that society.

Now, faced with this enormous earthquake and tsunami, what I need, as my heart threatens to break apart completely, is the will and imagination to confront another reality I can do nothing about. As I read back through the pieces in this anthology on the occasion of their translation into English, I felt this need all the more keenly. That's why I write stories in the first place, I thought.

In every story, the characters attempt to confront an unyielding reality using the power of their imaginations. The characters in these stories all share a certain measure of minority. This minority is invisible to the eyes of the majority. Which makes it as though it never was. But reality is made up of more than just what meets the eye. In these situations, those in minor positions call upon their powers of imagination to create spaces of belonging. This imaginative power creates worlds that affirm their being rather than deny it. With a strength that rivals that of reality itself.

The earthquake and tsunami, as well as the resulting nuclear crisis, have transformed, in the blink of an eye, the position of the majority, who had been simply living their lives normally up till then, into that of the minority. And those who had already been living in minority positions have been driven to ones even more minor. Especially now, because the damage they've sustained has been so great, various people existing in positions of minority have disappeared entirely from the world's view. Those calling for "reconstruction" imagine only the reconstruction of the majority, leaving those in the minority behind once again.

Truth be told, after the quake, it hasn't been uncommon for me to feel writing literature to be rather ineffective.

Yet, at the same time, it is only by writing stories that I am able to inhabit a future at all.

The stories included in this anthology are, without exception, ones for which I feel a deep affection. My fiction may be a bit different from the image that comes to mind when you think of modern Japanese literature. But these fictional worlds are minor Japanese realities (even as several have Latin America as their setting).

My wish is for the words in these stories to overcome our various differences and lodge themselves within the bodies of all of you.

Tomoyuki Hoshino
June 2011

Translated by Brian Bergstrom

Paper Woman (2000)

It's been two years now since I became a novelist, and I've found myself thinking more and more about just who it is who reads the things I write. This may be simply due to the relatively poor sales of my own books, of course, but it may also be due in no small part to my recent pondering of what larger meaning a novel's existence might bear. After all, statistically speaking, the number of people reading novels is decreasing, part of a general decrease in the sales of literature, but I think the real problem may be that fewer and fewer people really read any more, really consume literature as if printing the words on the interiors of their bodies.

As I've continued my professional writing career, I've come to think of it as an art that wavers, like a heat shimmer, between joy at the prospect of becoming something else and despair at knowing that such a transformation is ultimately impossible. One could say that a novel's words trace the pattern of scars left by the struggle between these two feelings. Which is why a novel should never be seen as a simple expression of an author's self.

For this reason, I use my novels to write about things other than myself. But I am nevertheless always aware that what I end up creating will never be more than a portrait of my own imperfect transformations, that what the reader is deciphering while reading my novels is merely my psyche. And as they do, they'll also be reading their own psyches, which are likewise caught in the process of trying to become other than themselves. A true experience of reading is always located in the territory where these two forms of consciousness intermingle.

The moment this intermingling occurs, a professional writer becomes a professional reader. I myself have written more than few critical essays about the work of others, and have even earned money reading the rough drafts of aspiring authors. In the majority of cases, what I find in their works is an arrogant assertion of the author's self at the expense of all else. Or, alternatively, an author covertly draws attention to the spectacle of his or her attempt at transformation, thereby inadvertently creating a one-sided assertion of authorial self anyway. It's been said that as the number of readers has dwindled the number of authors has swelled, and I would add that this is linked to the proliferation of ferocious posing among these authors. On the Internet, within fanboy culture, anyone can pose as anything. But I increasingly get the feeling that no one is truly attempting to become something else, or rather, that no one has anything in particular to aspire to be, that they don't have any real idea what they want to become at all. It's impossible for anyone who's never truly attempted to become something else to comprehend the despair of inevitably finding oneself unable to. Someone who has never felt the despair of trying every means possible to do the impossible has no way to imagine the unhappiness of another. So there's no reason to think such a person could ever truly write a novel.

Of course, if one asked them, "What do you want to be?" or "What do you want to do?" one would receive perfectly normal answers, such as, "I want to become a creator, and work for myself," or "I want to find a job that will allow me to maintain a stable household," and such answers would indeed be the result of earnest consideration. But this resolve reveals its fundamental unsteadiness once push comes to shove, once one's conviction to pursue whatever goal is forced to stubbornly weather seeming impossibility to persevere. One could say that most people are only living their lives halfway when compared to the passion of someone like the Paper Woman, whom I met a year and a half ago. Or at the very least they could be said to be missing out on an essential part of life.

The Paper Woman was another of these writers attempting to become a novelist. She wrote a fantastical tale about a woman who could eat only paper and eventually became entirely composed of the stuff, and it moved me enough that I took it upon myself to contact her and set up a meeting.

As I surveyed the teashop where we agreed to meet, I picked her out at a glance, saying to myself, "Aah, that has to be her." She was as pale as if she were the woman in the story come to life, her short hair dyed a beautiful silver. Of course, her diet turned out to include more than just paper, and she brought Darjeeling and orange-marmalade-slathered scones to her lips with relish. "Do you sometimes dribble soy sauce onto sheets of paper and wrap them like seaweed around your rice?" I asked, and she replied with a touch of contempt. "I'm not a literal bookworm, I don't actually eat paper. Besides, no matter how much paper a bookworm eats, it's still just a worm in the end, no? Wanting to become paper and eating paper are two different things."

"Good point. If eating paper turned you into paper, all a little kid who wanted to be a soccer player would have to do was eat other soccer players to succeed."

"Have you eaten many authors, Mr. Hoshino?"

"No, no, I've never spent any time wanting to become an author. Become a novel, maybe."

"If you're still saying things like 'I want to become a novel,' you've got a long way to go, I'd say."

"Would you?"

"I mean, I was thinking things like that when I was still in elementary school and keeping a diary. I realized that diaries were lies, that they were filled with omissions and inaccuracies, so if I wanted to write the details of my days precisely, down to the smallest second-to-second fluctuations in my mood, my life and my writing would have to overlap exactly. In other words, I'd have to become a novel."

"You were quite precocious."

"I was just a bookish little girl. And you were a late bloomer, right, Mr. Hoshino?"

"So how is wanting to become paper different than wanting to become a novel?" I asked, getting a bit more serious.

"If you took the matter a bit more to heart, I think you'd see what I mean for yourself. But to answer you anyway, in elementary school I was working with some papier mâché and I realized that it was a lot like brains. You know how you make papier mâché, right? You soak newspaper in water until it gets soggy and starts to mash up, and then you add some glue. So, in other words, within this gluey substance are countless words and letters all smashed together. It's like my brain as I read books and then think, my thoughts forming out of the mashed-up words I've put into my memory that I rearrange to make something new. Brains are just so much papier mâché."

"So your brain is hardened and stiff?"

"I just have to make sure it isn't exposed to the air. Anyway, I began to think of myself as formed out of papier mâché, which made me better able to understand how it must feel to be paper itself."

"Such anthropomorphism is quite typical of young girls."

"It's not anthropomorphism. Pay attention. What I realized was that the feeling of having no feelings was how it felt to be paper. In other words, I was attracted to paper, but paper itself, as banal as it sounds, has no inner self, can only absorb characters and words into itself without assigning them meaning. That's how I wanted to be, I realized. And I simultaneously realized that the more I wanted to be paper, the farther I got from actually being like it, which made me sad."

"So that's why you wrote that story."

The little girl protagonist could only eat paper, which upset her stomach and made her pale and thin. One day she went to school and almost no one noticed her, and she was caught off-guard by the reflection she glimpsed of her profile in a window out of the corner of her eye. She was almost invisible from the side, as thin as a page. She began to worry that she was more paper than girl.

"Have you ever thought much about mermaids, Mr. Hoshino?"

"Well, to a certain extent. There's a part of me that's always been rather enamored by fish. I even wrote a story called 'The Mermaid Myth' when I was in grade school."

"You should publish it sometime! I went through a Mermaid Girl phase myself, though it was in high school in my case. My boyfriend at the time had what you might call a 'mermaid fetish,' to the point that everyone called him Merman, actually, and he always told me that I'd make a good mermaid. It sounds like a joke when I say it now, but at the time I did all these things to please him, growing my hair out until it reached my butt, wearing a bra made of scallop shells, making myself a spangled tailfin. I would invite Merman over when my parents were away and wait for him on the bed dressed like that."

"Costume play, huh? Do you have any pictures?"

"God forbid."

"And you're right, it makes for a funny story, but you can also feel the special sadness of the mermaid myth, too. What makes them so attractive, so moving to contemplate?"

"It's the impossibility. But it's also a gender issue, I'd say. These days there are all sorts of people who are neither man nor woman, or who are mixed racially, and it seems like it wouldn't be too huge a leap to think about humans mixing with animals, or even mixing with plants and trees. We can imagine these things precisely because of the times we live in. Mermaids are simply ahead of their time. It makes their sorrow all the more palpable."

"I think I understand. You want to become a hybrid child of human and paper."

"Indeed. Well, paper doesn't have blood, so I couldn't really blend with it that way. I think I want to intermingle at a level deeper than blood."

"So, at a spiritual level? Though paper doesn't really have a 'spirit,' either, so . . ."

"It's difficult, right? What does it really mean to be paper? There are so many things I've yet to learn."

It was a few days afterward that we began living together, and it was four months after that when we married. I called her Paper. Indeed, she became my Paper Doll.

It didn't feel as if I'd literally wedded myself to paper, of course, but I was happy all the same. Paper conformed to my personality with almost alarming speed and soon came to resemble me almost exactly. It wasn't just a matter of liking the same food or music or places. She began to resemble me in all ways, getting hungry at the same time I did, growing annoyed at the same things and in the same way, using the same words and phrases I would when discussing a movie we'd just seen. When I'd display my pleasure at this, she'd just reply happily, "I have a lot more blank pages left in me!"

And truly, I was happy and comfortable. But I worried that I was the only one who really was. Was Paper able to tell that in my heart of hearts I didn't really feel that she was paper, and did this make her sad? And was she on the verge of slipping into a vortex of depression from that very emotion, since feeling sadness was itself simply yet more proof that she wasn't really paper?

So I made every effort to treat Paper like actual paper. I got a hint from a British movie I saw for an erotic game we could play. We called it "The Earless Hōichi Game." I'd use a variety of pens and brushes to write stories all over Paper's skin. At first this tickled her, but soon Paper's pale skin would grow flushed and sweaty, her breathing ragged.

Goosebumps would appear and she would murmur hoarsely, and from time to time she'd open her eyes and watch my hand move across her, trembling as she did. When I'd still my hand and read what I'd written aloud, she'd be overcome again, her body twisting and turning, gripped with a new type of excitement. There was no need to make her earless like the real Hōichi, so I used a fine-tipped pen to inscribe the lobes and curved inner surface of her ears. She was especially sensitive there, and seemed to orgasm under my pen.

I, too, was filled with an uncommon pleasure as I wrote. Egged on by the heat that would rise from Paper's body, from the perfume of her sweat and other fluids, from the sound of her moans, I would write and write and write. My whole body would flush with heat as a tingling pleasure engulfed it, and my nerves grew so sensitive that I could no longer bear to wear clothes. At the same time, I felt a clarity within me that made me feel like I was not one man but ten. Was this what omnipotence felt like? Writing was making me all-powerful.

We'd end the game when I finished writing, or when I'd run out of space on her body, or when one of us grew too tired to go on. And that was when I'd punish Paper. *If you were really paper, you'd feel nothing, you'd just lie there and allow yourself to be written on. You're a counterfeit Paper Woman. You don't deserve to be written on. I'm erasing it all.* Berating her like this, I'd dunk her in the tub and wash her body clean. Paper would always weep then, wrenchingly, despairingly, and murmur her desire to be tattooed.

Surprisingly, Paper would remember the things I wrote across her body perfectly. By "perfectly," I mean down to the exact characters I chose. She claimed to remember them with her skin. She said the feeling of the pen moving across her skin would return sometimes, and even though she fought against it, she'd feel pleasure as it did. So I'd type what she told me I wrote on her into my word processor. Soon our "Earless Hōichi Game" became the method by which I wrote everything. I became unable to write anything that didn't have Paper lying beneath it. I wrote my stories during this period as if painting them. And you could say that Paper was my muse in this sense.

Our tragedy, as is usual with these things, began with Paper's pregnancy. We'd been having sex without taking precautions since even before we got married. So it was hardly a shock when we got the news eight months after the wedding, but Paper became withdrawn nonetheless, sighing to herself while gazing out at the setting sun from the veranda. I tried to placate her at first, saying things like, "It's perfectly natural that paper would become pregnant," or, "A child of paper might turn out to be paper too," but Paper would just look up at me and say, "That's not what I'm concerned about," refusing my comfort.

"You know I don't literally want to take the shape of paper. Don't talk to me like a child."

"I'm sorry. I guess I just overestimated how alike we'd become, thinking we'd merged completely, body and soul. It seems I've been neglecting my efforts to get even closer to you."

"Don't say such things. It makes me want to die. It's me who's lost the ability to become you."

"What are you talking about? Your ability is nearly supernatural!"

"But I understand now. I've lost my ability to be made into things. So I've gotten pregnant. Becoming a mother is the same as becoming an author. I can no longer just accept the words of others, now I have to produce my own. My time as paper has come to an end."

I understood Paper's sadness. It was the same as the terror that haunted me as a writer. One trades one's self-hood for the ability to write. It's the choice one makes the moment one decides to be an author. Or, not just an author. Taking one's place in the world involves a choice like this for everyone; no one is exempted.

"If that's how you really feel about being pregnant,

maybe it would be better to get an abortion. I'd feel sorry for the child."

"I can't do that. I've made the decision to accept anything, to hybridize spiritually, physically, in every sense, and so I can't decide to expel something from me as if cleansing my blood. It's not our place to decide who deserves pity.

"Tomoyuki, it is up to you to save me."

"I want to become more paper-like too, just like you."

Paper ended up loving the little boy she birthed and raised. Naturally, she didn't try to make him into paper, and we gave him a normal enough name, Kazuyoshi, by reversing the characters for Hōichi. I helped her raise him too, of course, and while he slept I'd use Paper as paper like always, caressing her with my pen, drawing illustrations and completing manuscripts on her body, reading her favorite stories to her as she closed her eyes to relax. In order to become more like paper myself, or, to put it more precisely, to become more like Paper as she strove to become more paper-like, I began to read much more than I had previously. I read all the books Paper told me she'd read, one after another. I tried to guess what she was thinking when she stared blankly into space, using all the information about her that I'd gleaned to attempt to replicate her thoughts down to the letter. Whenever I'd succeed in expressing Paper's feelings even better than she could, or supply her with the exact word she was grasping for, she'd smile like an artificial flower blooming underwater. I loved this smile of hers above all.

Even so, the void inside Paper never filled. Its edges spread wider and wider, and I found myself unable to keep up. Paper taught Kazuyoshi words, and though he couldn't speak yet, he could recognize and point at them with his finger, but as she stared at her child trying to vocalize, her expression would darken, the skin on her face would harden, and she'd appear to fall into that deep hole within herself out of which she was unable to crawl. Perhaps taking after his mother, Kazuyoshi's ability to memorize words was astounding. But this seemed only to add, however slightly, to Paper's sadness. When I asked about it, Paper told me that faced with her child's genius, the shining white of the blank pages in her memory would dim, seem dingy. "My pages are ripping out," she'd lament, weeping.

"Don't the pages filled with writing outnumber the ones ripping out?"

"What good is that? What good is a book with missing pages?"

"Paper wears out. It's a mistake to think that you can keep it pristine forever."

"I want to be a perfect archive, though. For Kazuyoshi."

"A library of everything? A famous author once wrote that you'd have to become the whole world to become a perfect archive."

"I know that. Look who you're talking to, I'm the woman who told you that in order to keep a perfect diary she'd have to become one."

"But a person cannot become a world. A person can never be any more than just a part of one."

"You've become quite a degraded being, haven't you? I don't think you could get any more broken down than you are now!"

"I'm just an ordinary man. That's why I can understand your pain at not being able to truly become paper, right? It's not just you, Paper, anyone can feel this way, be gripped with regret and sadness at the prospect of never truly being able to understand another person's feelings completely. As an ordinary man, I can want to understand you as much as I can, become you as much as I can, and still I can't avoid reaching the limit of my ability to do so. But isn't reaching this limit satisfaction enough?"

"It didn't matter who it was, Merman or anyone else: all I ever wanted was to understand everything there was to understand about the people important to me. I want to understand the you that even you don't understand. I use words to absorb things into myself. If I could really become paper, really become a book, I'd be able to absorb all of the people important to me into myself. But I can't become that kind of paper, so there's no way I can become you the way I want to. And I can't bear to be such a flawed model for Kazuyoshi. My very existence has lost its meaning."

"I still need you, Paper. You are the only thing that allows me to write. I can only commune with things outside myself through writing. I'm a limited, unremarkable man, so I still need words to do this. And paper."

It became a daily chore to convince Paper to go on. All my time and energy were exhausted just with childcare and stabilizing Paper's emotions, so nothing was left over to devote to stroking Paper with my words. And Paper, in turn, took this cessation of my pen's play across her skin to mean that her utility in even this arena had come to an end, agitating her even more. So I pushed myself to write something, anything on Paper's skin at least once every other day, no matter how tired I was. But as I scrawled these pale approximations of the sentences that used to flow across her, Paper would feel the difference on her skin and her expression would cloud. And eventually, my exhaustion rendered me unable to produce any more words at all. In the end, the mere sight of Paper's tired, lackluster skin would fill me with dark irritation.

Paper, for her part, was growing visibly emaciated. Her hair whitened even without her bleaching it, and it would fall out like withered grass if brushed too hard. Her appetite disappeared as well, and soon she resembled nothing so much as a collection of bones and dehydrated skin. Her tongue grew mossy, her eyes perpetually widened in seeming fright, her gaze fixed. This drastic change occurred so quickly I didn't even have time for it to sadden me.

It was about a month ago that strange words began to flow from Paper's mouth. I should have taken more notice then. I'd been pouring all my energy into writing on Paper's "human parchment" when she suddenly murmured, *water definitely flow definitely insect.* Though she sometimes moaned or made other sounds during our writing sessions, we never conversed, so this brought me up short. Running her fingers along the folds in the skin around her pelvis, she continued, murmuring, *yo e ro sun,* just nonsense syllables. "What is it?" I asked, and she replied, "I see characters, characters besides the ones you've written," and then she started pointing to the words I'd just written on her. "Look, you wrote the water radical, 氵, right here, and 'definitely,' 必, here. Put them together and you get the character for 'flow': 泌. And below that, look, combine that 'u' (ウ) with the 'definitely,' (必) plus 'insect' (虫) and you get 'honey' (蜜)! And over here, along the left crease of my groin, *yo* ヨ *e* エ *ro* ロ *sun* 寸 combines and becomes 'investigate': 尋!" But all I saw where she pointed were so many wrinkles. Every time she moved, these wrinkles would shift, and it seemed that they'd form new words for her to read. *Wa ki shi nichi yon mata na sai hi,* she'd burble, taking apart the characters for "chatterbox blossom" I'd just written, and soon I couldn't take any more. I was gripped with despair. I took a sleep mask I'd been given on an airplane from my dresser to place over Paper's eyes and dressed her in clothes that exposed the least amount of skin possible.

It was around that time that I started to seriously consider tattooing Paper. I thought that if the words on her skin were fixed and meaningful, she'd stop getting so caught up in the chaos of the characters' formation, and her mind would grow more ordered as well. I decided to write out a translation of *Don Quixote,* a book we both esteemed above all others, in as fine a print as I could manage, then find a good tattoo artist to complete my plan.

But it was already too late. One day, Paper was dozing in a sunbeam on the living room floor, scratching absently at her dry, nearly eczematic skin, when she suddenly informed me, "I think I've finally completed my transformation into paper." And thereafter, I was forbidden to write on her, or touch her skin, or even enter her room. Outside the times she needed to take care of the bare minimum of her bodily needs, Paper remained holed up in her room, holding Kazuyoshi in her arms and reading to him from books only she could see. Weeping, I ended up having to enlist the aid of the tattoo artist to tie Paper naked to a bed and force sleeping pills into her mouth, and thus we were able to finally tattoo her with *Don Quixote,* starting with the first chapter.

Paper remained docile during the tattooing even after she woke up. Though she'd sometimes moan in pain, she also read along as the words were drilled into her skin, laughing at the characters' antics. This was the final step on the journey Paper had undertaken to connect with the world solely through books. Though my passion failed to even approach Paper's, I still embraced a similar desire to hers as an author, so I vowed in my heart to pour as much energy into my future tappings at my computer as Paper was devoting to her body now.

Paper wanted her whole body covered, but I decided to leave her face blank, telling her she could always fill it in later. The words *Don Quixote: The Ingenious Gentleman of La Mancha* ran down her backbone. "Let's compare spines!" exhorted Paper, so we lined her up with the new *Don Quixote* translation that had just come out from Iwanami Press and took a picture. Of course we couldn't fit the entire thing on her body, but I assured her that we'd try to fit more onto her in the future.

Characters inked in midnight blue now covered Paper's body like a swarm of tiny insects. Her body as she stood palms out, arms spread wide, looked like a jacaranda tree in full bloom, the dark blue seeming almost to glow. Transfixed by the sight, I kissed the lines of text that striped her skin. I ran my tongue along them as if using it to read. Goosebumps appeared just as they had when we'd first begun to live together, and she sighed heavily. I felt satisfied, as if I'd somehow become like Paper as well as she completed this final step in her transformation. "I am paper!" exulted Paper loudly. I nodded my agreement.

The next day, I headed to the clinic at Paper's request to take Kazuyoshi to get his DPT vaccination. I did a little shopping too, and ended up returning home about four hours later. I knew something was wrong as soon as I opened the door. I was greeted by the thick odor of petroleum. Paper's figure, standing in the living room and silhouetted in the light of its southern exposure, glowed bluely. Before I had time to say a single word, Paper struck a match and lit her gasoline-soaked hair. Faster than the blink of an eye, flames engulfed her head and rose toward the ceiling. Fire leapt up in front of me, too, even as I started to run toward her. Paper spread her flames to the gasoline-soaked surroundings. All I could do was clutch Kazuyoshi to me and retreat as I screamed incoherently into the flames. Kazuyoshi started screaming too, as if he were also on fire. Paper's voice cried out, "At last! I'm so happy! I am finally, truly paper—look at me burn!" Brushing embers from me, I watched as the blue-black writing melted into the oils bubbling up from her skin and transformed into flame and smoke. "No, no, this is wrong!" I wailed, sobbing. *You're wrong, there is no paper, no words that exist in a state of perfection, pristine and hidden from human eyes, such paper is not really paper at all, you have me, you have Kazuyoshi, we can read you, we can write on you, we can still give you meaning, you know the promise of eternity is a lie.* But my words failed to reach Paper. She collapsed into the flames and burned up as I watched. Fleeing the spreading fire, I finally ran out the door, delivering myself and Kazuyoshi into the embrace of the silver-suited firemen rushing to the scene.

I haven't written a word since. My writing's meaning burned up along with Paper. As if tracing patterns in her ashes, I would begin this or that story, but it hurt too much—every word felt ripped from my very skin. And yet I have no other way of writing left.

Paper's absence taught me that novels are already meaningless, that their meaning has always been illusory. There is no one left who craves words like she did, who wants to absorb them completely and be read herself in turn. And she wanted me to do the same to her, to absorb her and let her read herself off me. I responded as well as I could, imperfect as I am. But I was all she had. She wanted so much to connect with so many more, but only I ever made the attempt. And it was too much for me to bear alone. Now all I have left is a mouth full of regret. These lonely words hurt more than I can say.

The No Fathers Club (2006)

The No Fathers Club got its start not only because my days were filled with free time, but because my friend Yōsuke took me to see a game of No Ball Soccer.

No Ball Soccer was just like normal soccer, only there was no ball. The five members of the team would pass and shoot as if one was really there. The opposing side's goalie would jump and make a save as if intercepting a ball actually flying toward the net. The shooter would be crushed. And the crowd would go wild, raising their voices to the heavens as if they truly had just witnessed an unbelievable save.

I was the only one who couldn't see it. The players and fans and referees all watched the non-existent ball. They'd steal this absent ball from each other, dribble it between their feet, feint one way then move the other, leaving their opponents to overcompensate and fall. Careful not to overlook a gap in the defense, the offensive player would find one and shoot the absent ball through it like a bullet. It would hit the bar. The offense would raise their hands to their heads and shouts of "GOOOAAALLL!" would fill the air. A ring of celebrating players would form. The invisible ball rolling around near the net would get a kick from the sulky, defeated goalie.

At first I felt uneasy watching, thinking I was being tricked, that everyone was in on a joke that excluded me. Or like I'd been invited unsuspectingly into a cult, listening blankly to a charismatic zealot's overheated sermon. But as I kept watching, at some point I started to catch the fever too, to stand up and cheer with everyone else for a particularly spectacular play or boo and give "thumbs-down" to a bad call. I still couldn't see the ball, but it was really there. I even began to hear the faint thump as it connected with a player's foot.

I hadn't been this excited since I was in sixth grade, playing chicken in the dirt-filled expanse of an unfinished housing development during the summer and winning. The game was to race along as fast as our bikes could carry us, aiming for the furrows and jagged protrusions that scarred the area and launched our bikes into flight, and the one who could go the longest without braking was the winner. I wore my red windbreaker and practiced my falls for when I wiped out, and in the end I held victory in my hand, the rest of my body bloody from being scraped across the ground.

I'd just been killing time, perhaps, since the day I was born. I was raised in aimless plenty, average in my academics and athletics, in my looks and my conversation, in the economic status of my two working parents. Maybe that was why my passion had thinned. Despite my youth I already felt like I was just living out the rest of my days. When my father died in an airplane crash when I was eight, I felt as sad as anyone, but he'd hardly ever been home and I barely had any memories of him playing with me, so I became accustomed to his now eternal absence soon enough. He left a small inheritance and some life insurance money behind for us, and between that and the settlement from the airline, there was no danger of falling on hard times, so, though both my younger sister and I felt a bit uneasy about it, our days continued to overflow with leisure just as before.

Though I should have had my time occupied when I enrolled in a midlevel high school, my free time only increased exponentially, and it started to weigh heavily on my body. It got hard to breathe. I joined the soccer team, but the interactions I had there were just like in any other school activity, and as if flipping switches within myself I first played the role of newbie, then that of the experienced senior two years later. I'd wanted to play flat out, wild and willful like Brazilian players did, but it was impossible for someone as lacking in passion as I to even figure out how to act willful or wild in the first place.

I started hanging out with Yōsuke when I found out that his father had gotten sick and died when he was in fourth grade. Don't get me wrong, though, it wasn't like we found each other and started sharing our tales of woe about our single-parent households or anything.

One evening in early spring, near the end of our freshman year in high school, a particularly tiresome older teammate was threatening to keep us late after practice and Yōsuke tried to excuse himself, saying, "My father's coming home tonight after being away for a long time, so I have to be home in time for dinner." The older boy responded angrily, "What are you talking about, idiot? You don't have a father!" Yōsuke dipped his head and gave his accuser a dark look. Everything grew quiet around them. Feeling bad, the older boy muttered, "Sorry," to which Yōsuke drew himself up and replied fiercely, "He's expecting me," then gave a curt nod and left.

The next day, I greeted Yōsuke in a loud voice when he came through the door. "So was your father glad to see you?"

After a beat, he twisted his lips into a grin and said, "He gave me a whuppin', 'cause I was late."

"He hit you? Even though he comes home so rarely?" I pressed him, and he replied, "Well, it didn't hurt much, since he's dead and all."

"Yeah, I know what you mean," I said, going along, "I massage my dad's back sometimes, but it never gets any better, 'cause he's a corpse."

"You too? Don't worry, it's just your mind playing tricks on you. His back's not stiff, he's just dead."

"But I press down and it doesn't give! So you're saying he's not stiff, he's frozen?"

We couldn't help but go on and on like this.

It was thrilling. No one else could join in. First the older boys, then everyone stopped talking to us. The atmosphere of the place grew frosty, the air palling balefully around us. Even though it seemed like we were making everyone angry, we couldn't stop.

After that, Yōsuke and I would talk about our fathers from time to time. Regardless of whether anyone was around to overhear, I couldn't suppress the breathless excitement I felt when we started to get carried away with our father talk. When we became sophomores, we performed a two-man stand-up routine at the welcome banquet for new members called "Let's Talk About Papa." Naturally, no one laughed, and we even heard people muttering darkly to each other, "It must be nice with their parents dead, no one to bother them. They should think about how we feel." The two of us felt our teammates' anger swell almost to bursting as we chattered away.

It was around then that I watched my first game of No Ball Soccer. It occurred to me as I did that we could use this approach for our problem. If a ball could materialize out of thin air that had more substance than any real ball just by having everyone agree to act as if it were there, wouldn't a father more real than any real father materialize if we just acted as if we believed he was there with every fiber of our beings?

So we quit our increasingly hostile soccer team and started the No Fathers Club. We admitted only those whose fathers truly didn't exist in this world, so children of divorce were out, though illegitimate children who didn't know their fathers were in. The idea was to pretend we really had fathers every second of every day, leaving no room for sharing feelings or talking about our pitiful situations, so to those seeking therapy: sorry. We announced our conditions and even required the production of official family registers as proof, so we were shocked when we ended up admitting nineteen members, including some from other schools.

At our inaugural meeting, everybody introduced themselves and then we opened the floor to a discussion called "My Father's Like . . ." We shared the problems and conflicts we had with our faux fathers and discussed together strategies for dealing with them. I told everyone how my father was perhaps too understanding, and that while it was nice that he let me do as I liked, I sometimes wondered if he really just didn't care.

"So when I came home all bloody from playing chicken with my bike, my mom chewed me out, but my dad just said, 'If he dies, he dies. What can we do?' I thought, is that what he'd say to the papers if I committed suicide? And then later, when I drove the car around even though I was only fourteen, all he said was, 'In Mexico they let kids your age learn to drive on their own and just get licenses for them later.' It makes you wonder, right? Aren't parents supposed to judge their children's behavior just a little, teach them right from wrong?"

And the girl who then said, "Actually, I'm envious of you, Joe. Your father sounds like he really understands children," was the girl I ended up dating, Kurumi Kunugibayashi.

"If you told a kid who had a real interest in cars that driving around when you're fourteen was no big deal, he'd keep driving, right? But if that kid was just trying to act big by doing it, he'd lose interest. With just a few words from your dad, you lost interest and stopped trying to sneak the car out, right Joe?"

I was dumbstruck. You got me, I thought.

"Well, actually, yeah. That's what happened, I heard him say that and I stopped trying to drive."

And I even muttered to myself under my breath, yeah, that's right, my dad was right all along. Muttering to myself like that really did the trick. At that moment, my father truly felt real to me.

"Yes, he was right all along," agreed Kurumi, overhearing me. She went on.

"So that's why I was thinking, maybe all the issues with

our dads that we've been talking about only seem like problems 'cause we're still just kids. We just don't understand what they're trying to do yet. In my case, it took five years after the issue came up before I could look back and see what he was trying to do, to come to terms with it."

When Kurumi first got her period at eleven, her father gave her a rather explicit sexual education. Showing her all sorts of things, from Hollywood sex scenes to pornographic woodcuts, he explained that it was just a natural part of life, like eating or drinking or breathing or menstruating, so there's no need to make a big deal of it. It was just that if you're too careless eating or drinking you'll end up poisoned or dying young from alcoholism, so by the same token, if you're careless about sex, you'll end up pregnant before too long, so to avoid getting into trouble you should be slow and careful as you progress past your first time. It's just like how you only start eating real food after getting slowly weaned from your mother's breast, he explained.

"It was like torture. While he was showing me the woodcuts I kept thinking of all sorts of things, like when we'd go into the bath together when I was little, stuff like that. He started seeming dirty to me, and I was embarrassed and so angry I thought I'd explode, but he wouldn't let me run away. I didn't speak a word to him for a while after that."

Kurumi paused, and surveyed the room.

"But what I understand now is that my father was also fighting down the same explosive embarrassment I was. It wasn't that he wanted to talk about those things with me, it was just that my mom had dropped the ball and wouldn't do it. So my dad had to take the dirty job and give me the information I needed. Though if it was appropriate to do it so explicitly to an eleven-year-old girl, I don't know. But I do know that thanks to him, I'm well prepared for how perverted boys can be."

The boys in the group chuckled a bit at this, though

I was moved by her words once more. "Your father was trying to become your mother too," I said, almost at a whisper. Kurumi's eyes opened wide in surprise as she looked at me, and she nodded her agreement.

The only thing that intruded on the intimate space forming between us was the guy who then asked, "But that never happened, right? Were you talking about your made-up father? Or were you remembering when your real father was still alive?" In response, I warned him, "You're about to lose your membership here, saying things like that. The rule is that we act like we truly have fathers, every moment of every day, in our thoughts and words and actions." Guys like that, with weak powers of imagination who couldn't keep up their concentration, ended up dropping out of the club before long.

Though, even I had trouble at that time thinking very deeply about what kind of person my father really was. The father I created now didn't have to be a continuation of the father who died nine years ago. The way he parted his hair, how far his belly stuck out, what health problems he might have, how he'd romanced my mother when they were young, what he was like when he was in school, how old he was when he lost his virginity, all these things, even things a son would never know about a real father, if I didn't create them for him he'd remain insubstantial. Imagining myself having to create absolutely everything, down to how he acted as a child and what kind of people his parents were, I felt faint at the prospect of the potentially endless labor ahead of me.

Even so, as we kept meeting and sharing tales of our fathers, the words began to come more easily, like flowers blooming, and my father began to take on an independent existence, to "take his first steps," so to speak. The most important thing at this point was the responses I would get from the other members. Especially Kurumi, when she gave her interpretations of my father's actions I felt I got a whole new perspective on him I'd never had before.

We started going out after two months passed, when summer started, and 70 percent of what we talked about was our fathers. Nervous, I made up all kinds of things, last weekend I drank beer with my dad, he told me about trying to start a small textile business, he's Hong Kong–crazy and knows everything about Hong Kong movies, I rattled on and on. Kurumi responded in kind, happily jabbering about skipping school and helping out at the supermarket her father manages, about the things the other workers would tell her about him, about how he's pretty popular with the ladies there but he's too pure-hearted to notice, things like that. Our conversations were so taken up by talk of our fathers, we hardly knew anything regular couples knew about each other, not our interests or backgrounds, nothing. We went on a trip, just the two of us, to Hokkaidō during summer vacation, and even then we'd do things like imagine how we'd be acting if our fathers had come along, buying picture postcards and souvenirs for them, and we ended up seeing the sights as we traveled half through our fathers' eyes.

Thinking back on it now, that might have been the peak of our relationship. The membership of the No Fathers Club took a sharp dive at the beginning of the second school term. All sorts of excuses were given, "I'm busy with my job," "My schedule's full with school activities," "My father's sick," but what was really happening was members getting tired of the faux father game. When even second-in-command Yōsuke stopped coming, I confronted him, asking, "What about your responsibilities as a leader?" Yōsuke replied with a serious expression. "My father died." Appalled that he'd say such a thing, I shouted at him harshly, "If he's dead you can just bring him back, can't you? That's what we do!"

"It was a suicide. He drank a bunch of poison. He left a note saying, 'Let me rest in peace.'"

"That's impossible. A made-up father has no right to die. We've put so much into creating and supporting him, he can't just disappear like that. If he did, it's 'cause your commitment is weak, Yōsuke. Just try again, do it like we started all this, like playing No Ball Soccer!"

"*I* started that, you know. 'Cause I wanted to play soccer. I don't want to live with a fake father forever. So, I quit. Say hi to your dad for me."

And with that, the No Fathers Club shrank to just Kurumi and me. I told myself that the others were just jealous of our deep connection. Just overwhelmed by the extreme realness of our fathers.

It was a mild, sunny day in early autumn, and we were discussing once again how we'd take care of our fathers in their old age. As we were imagining ourselves nursing our elderly charges in the future, the words, "But we'll still be together then, right?" escaped my lips before I quite knew what I was saying. Kurumi looked me slowly up and down, then tilted her head slightly and said, "Well, I'd always thought so. You know what, I kind of want to meet your father, Joe."

Meet my father? Not knowing how to respond, I sat there for a bit in stunned silence. Kurumi added, "I think our fathers would get along, don't you?"

"So we'd all get together, the four of us?"

"Yeah. Why don't you come by my house next time? I'll play host."

"Well . . . Dad's kind of busy . . ."

"So's mine. That's why if we don't do something about it, they'd never get a chance to meet. You haven't said anything to your father about me, have you? I've told mine all about you. He seems to want to meet you too, and your father."

I flinched. I didn't know if I had it in me to start talking to my father alone at home. I could think up all sorts of details about my father to talk about with Kurumi, but it seemed impossible to start a conversation with him when I was by myself. Kurumi's father suddenly seemed more grounded, more real than the one I'd created, and I felt passed up by her. Or, to be more precise, by the unwavering firmness of her commitment to her father.

"In any case, I'll talk about it with my dad," I said, then fled.

As I climbed into bed that night, I tried as hard as I could to imagine Kurumi in her house having a conversation with her father. If I couldn't even imagine that, I'd surely misspeak when the four of us all met, and Kurumi would coldly criticize me, say things like, "Who do you think you're talking to? My father'd never say something like that," and that would be the end of it. Just like when you play No Ball Soccer, if Kurumi and I weren't completely synced up, we wouldn't hear the words of the silent conversation the same way.

Telling myself I couldn't fail, I peered into the darkness and hesitantly started to speak to my father made of air. There was no answer, but still I launched myself into conversation. At first I was afraid of the silence and devoted myself to filling the air with words, most of them about Kurumi.

After a while, I started to get into the rhythm of the conversation, and suddenly my father began to talk back. The things he said caught me by surprise.

So this Mr. Kunugibayashi, I think I know him. He manages the Maruhan supermarket in Yoshino-ga-oka, right?

Uh-huh . . . I muttered, and left it at that, his words leaving me otherwise speechless.

I've never dealt directly with him, so we've never talked, but I've seen him around. I might have seen his daughter, too.

Now that I thought of it, they were in industries that would bring them into contact. Of course, that was before they both di—I put a lid firmly on the doubts that started to boil to the surface, and told myself that I could do this.

So, do you want to come with me to visit the Kunugibayashis? I squeezed the words out.

I do.

'Cause you want to meet my girlfriend?

You're being childish, Jōji. I know what's going on here. Kurumi looks at her father and sees that men our age don't have very many true friends. A man preoccupied with his work mistakes the other men he works with for friends, but in truth he has no one he can really rely on. It's actually easier to work that way. But no one wants to face such a lonely truth, so everyone acts like they're buddies. It's sad, but what can you do?

So Kurumi's trying to give you and her dad a chance to make a real friend?

Isn't she?

And you don't have that many friends either?

What do you think, Jōji?

Well. I don't know.

I wouldn't think you would.

Am I too much of a child?

Do you have many friends, Jōji?

You've gotten rather talkative all of a sudden, haven't you, Dad?

It's just because I'm looking forward to meeting Kunugibayashi and his daughter. Set it up, would you? I'm asking you seriously.

I don't know how dependable I am, but I'll try.

Good. Well, good night, then.

Good night.

As I fell asleep, I was absently aware of my father's presence receding before it finally faded from the room completely.

I didn't have a chance to talk with my father again before the big get-together, but my excitement continued to build, a ceaseless fluttering in my chest like blades of grass shivering in the breeze. Confidence suffused my body from head to toe.

When the big day arrived, I bought a cake large enough for four people to share and went to the Kunugibayashis' house accompanied by my father. Kurumi's dad was quite a bit taller than mine, and he welcomed us into the house with a booming voice and a hearty shake of his firm, thick-skinned hand.

Just as Kurumi had predicted, our fathers got along swimmingly. They began by talking about work, but, sensing that they were squandering their opportunity to get to know each other, they began talking about us instead, and then my father asked, *Is it true you like soccer?* Soon we were all swept up in hotly debating which J-League team was better, JEF Chiba or the Urawa Reds, and then the discussion jumped to Hong Kong movies after someone brought up *Shaolin Soccer,* and before we knew it we were planning a four-person trip to Hong Kong for the beginning of the new year. Soon there was less and less room for Kurumi and me in the conversation, and our presence became unnecessary to keep it going. Kurumi, smiling ear-to-ear, refilled our teacups again and again. My father started visiting the bathroom frequently, probably from drinking too much tea. When he did, Kurumi's father would turn to me and say things like, *Your father's a nice guy,* or, *What a jolly sort.* I'd reply, *No, no, you're the one who's a cheerful soul,* things like that. And I'd mean them.

Kurumi's mother was about to get home, so that day we left the Kunugibayashi household before dinnertime.

My relationship with my father grew ever more profound. It was probably for just that reason that we had our first big fight.

It was over something little. I was talking to him about how I wanted to live my life on my own terms, and then it suddenly came to me that a student's life was not for me, so I made up my mind not to continue on in school. I said as much to my father: *I think my boredom with life comes from always being at school, and I think I'd be more fulfilled if I worked in the real world. So I'm not going to apply for college, I'm going to look for a job instead.* My father erupted like a volcano.

Don't be naïve! You don't know what you're saying, you just like the way the words sound! That's the worst. You're just being gutless, using "getting a job" as some kind of out. Whether you go to school or go on the job market, I don't really care, but you have to take your decision seriously. You think your parents will just give you money if you decide to go to school, right? How can you hope to succeed in the real world with an attitude like that?

With these last words came a slap across my face. The span of Dad's palm was the width of a fan, and I flew back and hit the wall behind me. I cracked the back of my head hard and things went black for a second, and after I came to, my father was nowhere to be found.

I was shaken. I ran my fingers again and again across my cheek where it was hot and tingling painfully and cried as I drank the blood from my split lip that filled my mouth with the taste of iron. So this was how substantial my father's presence had gotten? He was able not only to converse with me face to face, but could even slap me around?

I wanted to share my excitement at this development with Kurumi, but for some reason I hesitated. I had the feeling Kurumi would do something to dampen my mood. So I never mentioned it. But it seemed impossible to have a secret just between my father and me. Kurumi and I could have secrets, but how could I with him? And yet, now I had one, and I felt guilty about keeping it.

In return for the previous invitation to their house, this time we had the Kunugibayashis over at our house in the middle of the winter, right when JEF Chiba became first-time J-League champions. We gathered around the clay *nabe* stewpot and started drinking at noon. Though Kurumi and I were only allowed one glass of beer each.

After a while, Kurumi's father, still in high sprits from JEF Chiba's win, started telling the story of his bungled, premature attempts at sex education with his daughter, making us all laugh.

Sure it's a funny story now, but at the time I thought I'd never be close to you again, Dad. It was really hard.

These days, I'd probably be accused of sexual harassment,

or child abuse. It sounds weird to say it, but when I met Joe here, I was relieved from the bottom of my heart. I could die without regrets, I thought.

I laughed, a bit unnerved.

We're only sophomores, Dad.

Age is hardly a factor in these matters.

Kurumi's dad really was a pure soul. Compared to him, my father seemed positively lewd.

You two seem as close as if you've been together for decades. Doesn't it seem like we've been friends that long, too?

It does, it does. We're blessed as fathers, aren't we?

We sure are. Want another, Nobuo?

Sure, sure, Hisashi. Here.

. . . .

. . . . *aaaah.*

You know, it took a lot of courage to do that as a father, Nobuo. A lot of confidence. That's what I thought when you told that story, anyway.

Ha ha. Well, thanks, but let's not talk about that anymore. How to be a good father, things like that. You just try to be the best parent you can, you know?

When I opened my eyes, the room was pitch dark. I felt like I'd been sleeping for a long time, tucked under the *kotatsu*'s heated blankets, but when I looked at the clock it was only five in the afternoon. I turned on the light, woke Kurumi, and turned on the gas heater.

"Where are our fathers?"

"They went out for a walk to clear their heads."

They were nowhere to be found. The food in the cold *nabe* looked almost completely untouched. The beer was about half empty. Kurumi and I exchanged a sheepish, somewhat awkward look.

"Well, we should …"

"Yeah."

It was almost time for my mom and younger sister to come home, so Kurumi jumped to her feet even before I finished my sentence and pulled on her coat.

"Sorry for leaving you to clean up."

Kurumi said this at the doorway, looking at me with a lost expression on her face. *Say hi to your dad for me,* I almost said, but stopped myself. I just stood in the doorway for a while instead. I heard a sound like a walnut cracking somewhere in my chest.

The four of us never got together again after that. Kurumi and I decided that our fathers were getting along so well that there was hardly room for us in the equation, and they spent all their time out drinking or going on little trips together. Our fathers wouldn't talk about things like that with their son or daughter.

"So that's true friendship, I guess. I think it's great. That's what I wanted to have happen." Kurumi's face was expressionless as she said this to me.

"Yeah. I don't talk much to him about what I talk about with you, or what we do together anymore."

"I do, a little. Just enough to be polite."

I wondered if Kurumi was talking less and less to her father as well. Or, not just talking less, but finding it impossible to talk to him even when she wanted to. Because he wasn't there anymore. The sight of the cold, untouched *nabe* appeared behind my eyelids once more. It seemed that day we'd gone as far as we could go with this.

"The Hong Kong trip looks like it'll be put off, too. Well, they're both busy men, so what can you do? Besides, we have our entrance exams starting then. Maybe we can go during spring break, though."

Irritated at Kurumi's refusal to accept the end of things gracefully, I told her about the incident I'd told myself I'd keep secret.

"Dad's grown pretty independent of us, so I guess it doesn't matter if I tell you this. He hit me once, you know. Split my lip on the inside, the blood really gushed out. Here, look."

I folded back my lip so she could see the inside of my right cheek.

"I kind of get what you mean, but I also kind of don't..."

"It was swollen up all that night, like I had the mumps. I said I didn't want to go to college, that I wanted to get a job instead, and he was like, 'Don't be naïve! How's a kid as immature as you going to hack it in the real world?!' And then, WHAM! It really opened my eyes. Dad's trying to show me what it means to stand on my own two feet, so he's ignoring me on purpose and paying more attention to your father."

"I think your father was right," said Kurumi with a sigh, looking at me with a mix of sadness and irritation. "So did you decide to take the entrance exams?"

"Well, you know..."

"Let's both promise to take them, for the sake of each other's independence."

I groaned. "Isn't it kind of early for that?" I protested weakly.

"I've already signed up for the spring training course."

The No Fathers Club, already down to just Kurumi and me, fell apart completely. But I was satisfied it had served its purpose well: our fathers had come back and attained an independent existence, and we'd filled our free time with rich, rewarding days together.

It was after school on the first day we'd come back from spring break to start our junior year. I decided to accompany Kurumi on her way home. We made small talk about little things like the entrance exams and such, and then I asked her a question.

"Do you still talk to you father?"

Kurumi shook her head.

"Don't you think that's a good thing?"

Kurumi drew a deep breath, and then let it out.

"Our connection was always through our fathers, wasn't it? If they disappear, we don't have anything in common anymore, do we? I don't understand what you're trying to say, Joe."

"But if our fathers disappear, doesn't that just give us

room to get that much closer to each other? We can't always relate to each other through our fathers, can we?"

"The idea was always to be a foursome, though. Remember? We were going to stay together to take care of our fathers when they got too old to take care of themselves."

"Take care of who? I'm going to have to care for my mom, but other than that . . . "

"All you ever really wanted was to say goodbye to your father. He disappeared before you could do that, so you forced him to come back and let you perform some sort of farewell ceremony with him. Now that's done, so you don't have any use for him anymore and you feel like you're your 'own man.'"

"It didn't matter to either of us if we had fathers or not! We were just trying to pass the time, so we wouldn't go crazy with boredom! But what's gone is gone, there's no denying that."

"So you were spending all that time with someone who didn't matter enough to you to even care whether or not he really existed? You really are a shallow one, Joe. Is that what you think building a deep relationship with someone is? I promised a bunch of things to my dad. Like if I met someone more wonderful than him, that's who I'd spend the rest of my life with."

"Then you'll spend the rest of your life alone, Kurumi! Your father's just some ideal man you've made up in your head!"

"Maybe so. But I'd rather have it that way. It beats putting up with someone with passion as thin as yours for the rest of my life, that's for sure."

"If your father really was still alive, maybe we could have met as two self-sufficient individuals."

Kurumi looked at me with a scornful look on her face. "And what, exactly, is a self-sufficient individual?" she snorted.

"If our fathers had been alive, there wouldn't have

been anything to bring us together. It's ridiculous to think we'd have gotten together without them."

I sighed. "Maybe you're right," I agreed. And as a parting shot, I said the line I'd forbidden myself from uttering: "Say hi to your dad for me." Kurumi's final words to me were, "I'll pray for your father's health and happiness." It was like attending my own funeral.

Chino (2000)

Translated by Lucy Fraser
(Town and village names in this story are fictionalized)

The trip down was good. I was still thinking it would be one-way. It had been about a month since I'd come to this small country below Mexico. I'd knuckled down to some intensive Spanish study, gotten to know the ways of the people, and learned to handle the spicy food.

Preparations complete, I boarded the bus, filled with the excitement of a man about to blast off the face of the earth. Here I was, about to plunge into infinite space!

Well, infinite space was pretty cramped. Just as we were about to depart, a chubby, greasy-looking man with a turkey dangling from his arm barged on board and sat down next to me. Our vehicle was an old yellow school bus bought cheap from some foreign country, with patched-up seats that were meant to fit two people each. A Mamá the size of a small mountain, with a kid on her lap, was already sitting to my left, so no matter how skinny I might be, this guy deciding to join us was like a sumo wrestler plopping down into a brimming bathtub. Something had to give.

I smiled and let them crush me.

Most of the bus windows were stuck shut, so it was hot and muggy inside. The combination of corn-tinged body odors and animal smells was nearly overpowering. The brat next to me squirmed constantly, shouting and singing and laughing hysterically. The turkey, both legs tied so it couldn't move, lifted its gangly head like a cobra and squawked. The driver was playing Latin music, all trumpets and drums, so loud the sound was breaking up.

Meanwhile, rolls of fat came weighing down on me from both sides; breathing was becoming a challenge.

This, I told myself happily, was culture. The spice-scented flesh and heat clinging to my thighs and arms—all of it was culture. The important thing was, here and now in infinite space I was in immediate contact with people from a culture very different to my own.

Half just wanting to breathe more easily, I turned and asked the guy next to me, in my newly memorized Spanish, "How much for that turkey?" He shifted and mumbled something, but I didn't get it. I couldn't even tell if he'd understood my Spanish.

I gave up on my conversation with Señor Turkey, who was shyer than he looked, and turned my attention to Mamá. Her skin was brown, but the shape of her cheekbones, her flat nose, and her straight, thick black hair were all similar to my features. She must be, like half the population, mestizo—of mixed Spanish and native Indio blood. The kid on her knees, who suddenly shut up the minute I looked at him, had eyes like marbles, but his flat nose and thick lips were identical to his mother's. I grinned at Mamá and she nodded back without smiling. I pointed to the kid and tried to say he was a nice child—*"Niño, bien"*—which launched her into a flood of explanation. I could understand a few words here and there, but all in all it was gibberish to me. I couldn't bring myself to tell her that, yes, although I had initiated the conversation, I was unable to understand a word she was saying. So I pasted a friendly smile on my face and nodded, though actually I was gazing out the window beyond her, at some vultures.

The vultures were perched in a scrawny tree, seemingly doing nothing. Who knows, there might have been a dead body under that tree. For nearly thirty years, the country had been at civil war, with guerrillas—many of them indigenous Maya—battling the government. Vast numbers of people went missing, or were forcibly "disappeared." I wondered if the vultures ate their corpses. Just like in Tokyo, where the number of large black jungle crows increases with the amount of food scraps and garbage set out on the curbs, maybe over here the number of vultures swelled along with the number of missing persons.

The thought made me all the more determined. This was it. I was really going to fucking do this! I got so worked up, I didn't notice the sudden change in events till I registered the sound of the belch and saw the little kid go white, his mouth puckering up like he was about to cry. By then he couldn't hold it in any longer, and vomit spilled out all over my jeans. A warm, sticky sensation spread over my thighs, and a pungent sour milk smell wafted up. Mamá whacked her child on the head, saying something like, "Warn me next time you're going to throw up!" Then she turned to me with an embarrassed look, gave a solemn apology, and began to wipe my pants with her shawl.

I forced myself to smile. Don't get angry, I told myself, this is culture. But I couldn't help myself, it bugged me more and more. Can you really say you have no money, when you feed your kid so much that he pukes? Why do poor people have so much damn body fat to spare, anyway? And why did this have to happen to me just as I was venturing out in search of the guerrillas who were fighting to end poverty? Well, I thought, these people are riding the bus like it's an everyday thing; they're probably not as deprived as the indigenous people.

When I left Japan, feeling good, in my torn T-shirt, raggedy jeans, bandanna, and several days' stubble, I might have looked like your typical backpacker, but I was different from those apathetic bastards and proud of it. I wasn't here as a tourist, or to conduct interviews; I was here to find the guerrillas and become one of them.

Those backpackers were irresponsible brats for the most part, little rich boys and girls playing homeless when of course they did have homes to return to. It's ridiculous, I thought, the way they depend on the strength of the yen to get around, and then brag about "traveling on the cheap." I was painfully aware that the Mamás and Señor Turkeys of this country saw me as just another one of those brats. But unlike that crowd, I understood only too well that I was riding on the wings of my country's currency. No matter how dirty I might look, I knew my travels were buoyed on that lighter-than-air aluminum one-yen coin. A mode of travel little better than drifting and staring: never to touch down, never to make contact with other worlds, never to dive right in. I knew my body stank of yen, and would show me up as an outsider wherever I went.

I'd rehearsed these bitter thoughts many times before. Even back in Japan I couldn't shake the feeling that I was floating in empty space. I'd get so angry at how false everything was: hypocrites planting their feet on the ground and shouting to the world, "We Japanese are defenseless, surrounded by potential enemies on all sides, but we won't go down without a fight! Stand proud! We'll fend for ourselves!" Those types didn't really want to protect themselves or anyone else in particular; they just sought out the safety of the group. It was all a lie, confusing "me" for "us." Where was this "us"? Who the hell were "we Japanese"? I, for one, had no idea. I only wanted to be able to say, "I'm me," to define my own outline clearly. I was conscious of that as I traveled all over. But, unfortunately, I realized that because of the yen even I was connected with those "we Japanese" types. I could see that at times the yen might be a weapon, and anyone who wasn't "us"—well, we were duty-bound to kill those bastards, without feeling a thing. My outline was blurred by my Japanese language and money, making me another member of the "we Japanese." Which also lay responsibility at my feet.

For me to become purely myself, I would have to gouge all the money out of my body by the roots. I wasn't about to dress in folkloric costume, loll by the water smoking *mota*, or screw around. The kind who did that had this idea of uncovering their true selves, when all the while they're wearing the dollar or yen or euro or whatever for protection. No, I was going to join the guerrillas, and instead of money, I'd offer up my life to vouchsafe my trust-worthiness. I'd probably die, but I needed to prove I could get by on my own strength. Which is why I quit part-timing at different jobs, dumped my girlfriend, and moved out of my apartment. What little money I had, I brought along to kick-start my journey. There might very well be people out there who would kill me without thinking about it, to get the last yen buried in my body. I was gambling: could I rid myself of the stench of yen, or would it be too late? Would I disappear along with my money?

When I told Jody these things, he railed at my being so naive. I was "stuck in the Sixties" like those sheltered idiots, he said, who thought it a sin to be born in a First World country. They'd hang out naked on the beaches out west, trying to alleviate their guilt. Well, I didn't give a crap about ancient tales. I just wanted to become a guerrilla, with a body and mind purely my own.

Jody was a good guy, really open. We had this strange connection. He was an aspiring photojournalist from New York, staying in Ambigua to study Spanish, like me. Ambigua was a small town that survived on its language instruction industry—every household offered private Spanish classes, homestay included—and the streets were full of foreign students. It was Jody who gave me the secret info on the guerrillas. He hadn't been to the mountains himself, but the town was buzzing with rumors, some more reliable than others, about the guerrillas. Just like the word on *mota*. Pretty soon, Jody said, he was going to start interviewing the guerrillas, so we agreed on a time and place to meet again, then I left just before him.

We pulled into the Coatltenango terminal (a small marketplace, actually), where I was due to change buses. As soon as I began wandering around looking for the bus to Ilusión, the whispers started, Hey, it's a Chino, a Chino. Everyone was hounding me to buy stuff. I looked straight back at them and insisted, *"No, soy Japonés"*—No,

I'm Japanese. Chino meant "Chinese," and at the airport and the border and customs, that's what everyone had been calling me. I guessed to them there was no difference between Japanese, Chinese, Korean, or Vietnamese. After hearing it so many times, I got so angry I felt like saying, Japón! Don't you know Japón?

At that point an old pale-skinned man stepped out of the crowd. He looked poor, and extremely kindly. "Jou are Japanese?" he asked in English. I nodded, and he added: "So, jou are perhaps Maki's friend?" I didn't have a clue who this Maki was, but thought I might seem less suspicious if I had a name behind me. I replied, "Maki who lives in Ilusión?" He gave a knowing grin. "Ah, yes, Maki's friend," he said, and happily directed me over to the bus for Ilusión.

According to Jody's info, I had to hitchhike even farther, beyond Ilusión to a village called Realidad. I'd meet there with a don Ignacio, who would set me up with guerrilla sympathizers in the village, who might then possibly guide me deep into the forest. The problem was, Realidad was a frontline, with guerrillas and government soldiers constantly battling for control. Not only would I have to avoid getting caught up in skirmishes, but there were other complications: the villagers, who were distrustful of both sides, were extremely closed to strangers; and the army had set up checkpoints on the main roads. Whether or not I could hitchhike in all that mess was the key. Just thinking about it made my asshole shrink in sweaty terror.

I assumed I'd be able to get some more reliable information from this Maki woman, but I guess that was optimistic.

I arrived in Ilusión after nightfall. It turned out to be a typical country town: there was a central plaza with a church and town hall, and we pulled into an alley alongside. Right in front of the bus stop was a cheap hotel. I ate fried chicken for dinner at a rickety old food stall next to the hotel. When I was traveling, I stuck to a regimen of fried chicken and fresh fruit, to avoid digestive problems.

I got up early the next morning and asked the hotel girl for directions to Maki's place. The directions weren't too difficult, so I caught on right away, but after I left I kept thinking back on how insistently she had warned, "Be careful."

I saw a lot of villagers on the road, walking in groups of twos or threes. Their features were definitely Indio, but they were not wearing traditional clothes. Whenever I greeted people, the replies were curt. I'd say, "Nice weather isn't it?" or "Is there no market today?" and get the shortest possible answer. Maybe my Spanish wasn't good enough. Or else the civil war had been going on so long that nobody wanted anything to do with outsiders. Any foreigners around here would be seeking out the guerrillas, which explained why the locals wanted to avoid associating with me. When I asked the way to Maki's place I did see their hardened features soften a little, but they didn't want to continue any conversation.

After I'd walked about ten minutes, the houses began to fall away and I came to the edge of the village. Ahead of me there was nothing but a dusty white country road that seemed to stretch on forever. Occasionally a few chickens would wander out to the middle of the road and strut about. There were some simple shacks around, where women in brightly colored *huipiles* went about their farming and household chores. Whenever I asked if this place or that was Maki's house, they either shook their heads or completely ignored me, not comprehending my Spanish.

I started to feel faint from the heat of the sun beating down. It was like being pelted with heavy cannonballs of light. I thought I'd maybe get a lift if a car came by, but there was no sign that anyone actually traveled this route. I happened to see a mango tree growing by the roadside, and couldn't resist; I ripped a dusty piece of green fruit from the branch, peeled it and bit down, but it was hard and bitter, inedible. I started to wonder what I was doing here, and began to feel like I was living a lie.

This had to be the road to Realidad, I thought. I'd probably get there soon. I might even run into some guerrillas there. The girl at the hotel had insisted that I be careful. If guerrillas turned up right now, what would happen to me? If I could just talk to them, maybe they'd let me join up. Or then again, maybe they'd just take my lie of a life, no questions asked, and I'd disappear along with my yen.

Just as my confused feelings—wanting to die, not wanting to—reached a miserable crescendo, I came across a thin little Indio woman scooping water from a large urn in front of a ramshackle home. Short of breath, I puffed out, "Maki?" When the woman nodded, I felt like crying, from sheer joy at having survived. I looked at my watch and saw it was more than an hour since I'd left the village.

The woman silently gestured for me to go inside the house. I didn't have the strength to speak, but just stepping into the shade felt like diving into cool water and I let out a cry of pleasure. It felt so good my skin was tingling.

Maki came toward me, from farther inside. When I saw that she was dressed in traditional clothing like the other woman, it gave me a jolt for a second. Maki spoke to the other woman in a language I didn't understand, then greeted me with "Buenos días." I returned the greeting, reached out, and shook hands with her. Her hand, roughened with farm work, didn't look like it belonged to a Japanese woman. I was shown inside to a slightly larger room, where she pushed a broken stool toward me, and motioned for me to sit. She offered me a drink, and I said, Yes, please, anything would be fine. I tried to make conversation, to dispel the sense of unease that was eating away at me. "What a long walk! It was stupid of me to try it. I almost thought I'd faint from heat exhaustion." Maki wasn't impressed; she said people always walked up and back, that was normal here. My discomfort peaked at that point, since even though I was speaking Japanese, I saw that Maki was deliberately answering in Spanish every time.

Maki passed me a glass of water, and sat down facing

me. So I asked her, straight out, why was she speaking Spanish to me? Her expression never changed at all as she replied.

"This is my home, so it's only natural. Although of course, technically, Spanish is a foreign language around here, but . . ." I had to ask to be sure: I had assumed she was Japanese, but was she actually born here? She shook her head and knitted her brows slightly.

The conversation didn't go well: she had to rephrase everything she said so that I could understand it; I stubbornly pressed on in Japanese and she answered in deadpan Spanish.

From what I could understand with my basic language skills, Maki had worked as a teacher for five years before quitting to be posted as a JICA volunteer to this village. She felt so comfortable here that she stayed on after her duty ended, and was now living with this woman Libertad, who was like a sister to her (I couldn't believe they were the same age!). A widow with a one-year-old child, Libertad scraped by selling handicrafts and crops from her small field, and Maki helped too.

I asked if she'd been home to Japan at all, and she said that from the first moment she'd arrived in this village, she felt as if she'd been born again. Why would she go back to her past life?

Surely there were visa and citizenship issues? No, few here believed in those things. There were a great many people who just ceased to exist, and anyone who went over to the side of the guerrillas was no longer recognized legally as a national.

If the army found her out, she'd be arrested at best, maybe even "disappeared."

Being here made her feel alive, she said. Of course, when she thought about things like being "disappeared," she also felt the reality of death. She did not want to forfeit her new life here, nor did she want to leave Libertad and her child. That's why she didn't want to die, that's why she had the energy to try to stay alive. Did I have anything that made me not want to die? Or were living and dying not all that different to me?

Of course the conversation didn't really go this smoothly. For starters, even though she knew I couldn't speak Spanish, Maki had this habit of asking difficult Zen-like questions, talking in abstractions. I felt like I wasn't speaking with another human being, but with another species. I felt closer to the Mamá on the bus than to this woman. I found myself wanting to crush her strange confidence.

"Hey, I feel the reality of death too. My dad died when I was little. To me, death is like when something that existed suddenly disappears, and there is no connection between the time before and the time after it's gone. That's how I look at it, anyway. And if thinking about these things is enough to make you feel you've gone native, well, good for you."

"But why come all the way out here to this remote village? The only foreigners who come to a village like this, that's known for being dangerous, are people who are interested in contacting the guerrillas. Isn't that what you're after too—a taste of danger?"

"Sure, that's right. But I'm not about to move to another country just to give myself some sense of reality. That's not for me. I want to be a part of changing the world, doing away with the reality that exists right now."

"Everyone says that. Try that line out on Libertad. Her man was lynched by the guerrillas."

"Do you really think equal mistrust for the army and the guerrillas makes you into a model native? It's easy for you to go local when the Japanese government conveniently supports you with yen the whole time. Do you think the people here really accept you? You can't change your race. You're still just a Japanese immigrant."

Maki's face distorted with pain. I chuckled inwardly, but it was way too soon to gloat. She ground her teeth for a second, took a deep breath, then spoke again. "So what will you do if the guerrillas let you join them, and then, as soon as you feel completely at ease, rob you of everything you own? Have you thought about that? Suppose the guerrillas you thought were your kindred spirits only see you as a source of income . . . Will you just think of it as 'fate'? It isn't so easy to erase all traces of Japan from your body."

"I'm prepared for that. I'll take a gamble on which way things fall."

That was my answer, but I was shaken. From the beginning I hadn't been able to comprehend all of Maki's Spanish. It was more like I heard the sounds, and intuited what she wanted to say. How? Easy, we were one of a kind. She'd already done what I hoped to do. She was a joke, and I hated the fact that I was just as ridiculous. Just the thought of repeating her same laughable mistakes made me bone-tired.

I looked over at Maki, who had gone expressionless again. Her eyes behind those dirty lenses were like glass balls; they revealed nothing. Her rough-cut dull black hair was braided in typical Indio style. She was maybe thirty, but her sunburned skin was tough and gritty and iridescent. I kept staring at her, but it was hard to say whether she was looking at me or at a point behind me on the wall. I stared even harder. Look at me, I was trying to say to her, but her eyes just slid over my face. It filled me with sadness.

When I left, I stopped by a hot spring Maki had told me about. Not much of a hot spring, really; it was more of a small pool dammed up off a lukewarm creek. I swam in my shorts. Soon a canopied truck arrived, and a herd of kids—not in traditional costume—tumbled out the back. Primary school students, they looked like. They pointed at me, whispering, Chino! Chino! I just smiled and put one after another of them on my back and swam them around the pool. Afterwards, they gave me a lift in their truck. Unlike Maki, I had no longer had any reason to want to walk that road.

The next day I wandered around the village. That evening I was invited to the home of Luisito, one of the boys from the day before. The children couldn't pronounce Tomoyuki, so that night I became Tomo-iki. They turned me into a piggyback machine, attaching themselves to me like we'd grown up together.

Their mother Teresa was the one who finally liberated me from my exhausting labor. She was probably younger than me, but she ran the house with a style that was as impressive as her figure. She poured me orange blossom tea, and asked if Maki was in good health. When I nodded, she asked me, smiling, if we got on well. I smiled back.

"You got me on that one. She spoke Spanish the whole time."

"Oh." Teresa was lost for words. Her face suddenly clouded over in tears.

When I apologized, she told me that she had thought Maki didn't talk with anybody anymore, and so she was just happy to hear that she still could, and that she had spoken in Spanish, even to me. When she thought about how Maki must be feeling right now . . . Teresa broke into tears.

It turned out Maki had done a homestay at Teresa's house. She loved the village intensely, and the villagers liked her too, fondly calling her La Pintorita—the Painter—because she taught art. When she'd been there about a year and a half, a thief broke into Teresa's house when everyone was out. He seemed to know just what he was after, because he went straight for Maki's money, taking nothing else. Since Maki had kept her funds together in one place, this meant that she was completely broke, but what disturbed her much more was the disappearance that night of Libertad's husband Jaime. Jaime, a mestizo, was one of Maki's pupils, and it was through him that she'd made friends with Libertad. A few days later, Jaime's charred corpse was discovered. Although Teresa's household had told Maki that she was family now and welcome to stay with them, Maki disappeared for a while. The villagers searched everywhere, and finally found her hiding out at Libertad's house. After that, Maki never spoke to any of them again.

"She often told us she only started to feel alive after coming here. But when she was betrayed, she felt like she couldn't trust anyone, that's why she left the village. When I think about how she must have felt speaking in Spanish to you . . . Anyway, it was probably good that you two were able to talk."

The next day was Sunday and I went to church with Luisito's family. In the afternoon I led a troop of kids up to the top of a nearby hill. We could see not only the whole village, but the road to Realidad and the Indio settlements on the way, even as far as Maki and Libertad's house. The guerrillas were probably lying low in the forest still farther on. I wondered if I hung around like this whether I'd encounter them, or maybe the army. I wondered if settling down in this village was even a real possibility.

Three days later, I caught the bus back to Coatltenango. Luisito didn't want to go to school that day. I kept picturing him whimpering, "Nice Tomo-iki, don't go!" but Maki's expressionless face soon crowded Luisito's out. I expelled any sentimental thoughts. I wanted to talk back to Maki, to tell her, You think you're facing up to harsh reality, but in fact you're the one who's locked yourself up inside your own illusions. As if I had any right to say anything to her at all.

On the journey back, I felt like my feet were dragging, so I stayed a night in Coatltenango and caught the bus to Ambigua the next day. There were frequent connections between Coatltenango and Ambigua—I treated myself and bought a ticket for the nonstop express. This time it was an old tour bus, instead of a hand-me-down school bus. It had tinted windows but the air conditioner was broken, so inside it was still hot and humid. The bus was still fairly empty, so I took over an entire two-person seat and lay down.

Would Jody still be in Ambigua? If he was, I wondered if I'd I admit to him that he was right, that I had just been searching for a way to feel better about myself. That I had finally realized that if I wanted to become a guerrilla, I should do it in Japan . . . Anyway, I thought I would study a bit more Spanish in Ambigua.

About twenty minutes before we were supposed to arrive, the bus stopped. I sat up and looked out the window, but we were still on some nameless mountain road. I asked a rather bohemian-looking elderly gent across the aisle, "What's happening?" and he answered in perfect English, "It's a military check. Get your passport ready."

That made me a bit nervous. I pulled out my passport. A soldier soon appeared at the door and barked some kind of instruction. Uneasy, I looked over at the gentleman. He nodded silently. Everyone stood up and filed off the bus one by one, empty-handed.

They lined us up next to the bus and two soldiers started checking IDs, from either end of the line. I was near the left end so my turn came around quickly. The soldier, who looked like he was in his thirties, flipped through my passport and said, "*¿Chino, verdad?*"—Chinese, right? Just look, it says right there, I thought to myself, but I gave a polite smile and answered, "*No, Japonés.*"

The soldier peered into my face, then at my passport again. His military cut, protruding cheekbones, and dark complexion made him look like a samurai warrior from another time.

"*Entonces, es Chino*"—Well then, you are a Chino.

Come on, I thought, and told him again, "*No soy Chino, soy Japonés,*" enunciating each word. The soldier handed back my passport, and muttered once more, "Chi-no."

Shaking with anger, I clenched my fist and spoke in Japanese. "You fucking dogshit soldier." You want me to call you Chino to your ugly samurai face?

The elder gent must have seen how angry I was,

because he whispered to me, "Don't get angry, boy. Chino just means Asian."

"Huh?" I asked, looking at his face. He nodded.

So all Asians were Chinos. So that's what it was. Chino just meant "Oriental." Why Chino? Because China's so big? Because it has the largest population? No, probably because most immigrants came from China. Latin America was made up of all different races, and Asian immigrants probably usually meant Chinese.

I calmed down a bit. Though why should being thought of as an Oriental make me calm down? I got angry being mistaken for Chinese and wanted them to call me Japanese, yet I hated being seen as just another wad of yen. If I didn't have a problem with being called Oriental, wasn't that a contradiction?

Thinking about it that way made me confused, but I had a feeling I was on the right track. That was where I was different from Maki.

"*Muchas gracias, entiendo bien*"—Thank you very much, now I see—I said to the gent. I told him a bit about myself, and he gave me his business card. He lived in the capital; I was welcome to come and visit sometime.

The line of people began to troop back to the bus. With permission from the soldiers I went to take a leak on the side of the road, while the passengers behind me moved ahead onto the queue. Some of the soldiers and passengers, freed from the tension of the encounter, were pointing and laughing at the broad backside of a woman stepping up onto the bus. So when a dry explosion shook the air, we were taken totally by surprise and thought we would be killed. Rounds of gunfire resounded. I went flat to the ground without even doing up my fly. I heard the other passengers screaming as they scurried for the bus, but I just lay there imagining in detail the pain I would feel when a bullet pierced my back. How many seconds would the burning feeling last? When that was over, would I die in agony? I didn't want it to hurt.

I swore at myself for being captivated by my stupid imaginings. Get real. Should I go on lying there? Should I escape back to the bus? Or should I make a run for it and get away from the road? Those were the important questions, the ones linked directly to survival. An Oriental who can't survive without using yen for a shield isn't a real Chino.

A different type of gun was now firing close by. The soldiers were returning fire. A pungent gunpowder smell drifted towards me. The sound of the army fire was more overpowering and it was getting farther away. The military seemed to be winning. I had space to breathe now; I raised my head a little, but I was on the other side of the bus and couldn't see the fighting. Yet there really were guerrillas just over there.

The guerrillas. I wanted to talk with them, touch them, smell them. If I could just do that, I wouldn't care if they misunderstood and shot me, killed me. I didn't understand a thing: why the guerrillas existed, what I had to do with the guerrillas, how the world worked.

Thinking that made me feel like I was going to cry. And right about then I noticed that my thing—not zipped away properly—was getting hard. Staying flat to the ground, I slid a hand under and checked myself. I felt sorry for it, quivering as if I had just come. What a meaningless existence, heading places for no good reason! What an empty existence! Maki and I were both dead ends. I doubted if she'd ever have children—she wouldn't be able to stand hearing people always call them Chino.

"*Levantese, Chino*"—Get up, Chino—said a soldier standing behind me. It was the samurai from before. The sound of the guns had stopped, and people were getting onto the bus.

"*¿Donde, guerrillas?*"—Where are the guerrillas?—I asked, listening with my whole body for the answer. My longing was so sharp, I felt my skin would split and bleed if it was touched.

"*Se fueron*"—They left.

Something tore inside my chest. I did my fly, stood up, returned to the bus to grab my bag, then hurriedly got off. The soldier saw me and said something, but I ignored him and just kept walking along the road. He came up and grabbed my arm with machine-like strength and ordered me to return. I tried to resist, but he forced me back onto the bus. The doors shut and the army truck out in front led us away.

"*Siéntese*"—sit down—the driver told me. I was still standing on the steps of the bus. I didn't respond. He said it again.

"*Siéntese*, Chino."

I answered weakly, "I'm no Chino."

We, the Children of Cats (2001)

"Masako?"

"Is that . . . is that you, Naru?"

"It's me."

"I don't believe it. Didn't we promise not to call each other? We'd been so good . . . "

"Yeah, but you heard what happened here in Tokyo, right? Someone let off poison gas in the Hibiya Subway line! A lot of people died!"

"I know."

"Well, I thought you might be worried. I went back and forth for a while, but I finally decided to give you a call. I'm alive, Masako. I'm able to talk to you just like always. I wasn't on that subway. This is me talking, the real me."

"You called just to tell me *that*? We only had a hundred and two days left to go! Why would I think you were taking the subway at rush hour anyway? I thought we said we'd only call each other if something had *actually happened* to one of us."

"But if I *actually had* breathed poison gas, how could I call you?"

"Look, a while back there were some terrorist attacks here because of the presidential elections, and I thought maybe you'd be worried and considered giving you a call. But really, it was just me grasping at an excuse to call you. So I didn't."

"But if you had, Masako, I wouldn't have looked down on you. I'd have been moved at your concern for my feelings."

"In other words, that's how you'd like me to be feeling right now about you, right?"

"Wow, I can't win, can I? I call to tell you I'm okay and I get yelled at."

"This is exactly why we agreed not to call each other! We wanted to see how long we could trust that the other was okay without constantly checking in. If we're going to live together after I get back, we've got to make sure we don't become codependent. If all you need to tell me is that everything's fine, wouldn't a letter suffice?"

"I get it, I apologize. Sorry I'm still alive."

"Oh, for the—as if you'd have to worry about it if you *had* been killed. And as if you'd called me back when the Kobe earthquake happened, anyway."

"That was in Kobe!"

"You go to Kobe sometimes! It kept me up a few nights, wondering if you were okay. You didn't think I might wonder about you?"

"You know I hardly go anywhere that far away! And if I had, I'd have told you."

"From here, Tokyo and Kobe seem like the same place. Everything that happens in Japan seems connected to you. I wanted to call you, but I didn't and you didn't call me either, and I felt like we ended up all the stronger for it. I mean, you're not worried about me, are you? As dangerous as this country is?"

"I've never been to Peru, so it's hard for me to visualize it. If I think about it as dangerous, I get so worried I want to take a plane and fly there right now. But I can't do that, so I just pretend everything's fine instead. I trust you."

"Trust? Is that really what it is? Would you really fly here if something happened to me?"

"Of course I would."

"Would you come even if all I said was that I was so lonely I couldn't stand it anymore?"

"Of course I would! Are you sure nothing's going on

with you over there? Are you okay? No problems with your Peruvian friends?"

"Why are you asking me now? All I wanted was to hear you say something like this right off the bat."

"Well, I thought we were doing all right on that front just with the letters . . . I'm sorry, I called you because I wanted to talk to you, it was all my idea. I should hang up."

"You just don't get it, do you? If all you're going to do is hang up on me, don't call in the first place!"

"Look, can we just stop pretending? The truth is, we both wanted to hear each other's voice."

"That's not what I'm . . . well, fine. Maybe you have a point. You've sounded pretty excited since I first picked up. It's only natural, poison gas and terrorism in Tokyo will rile you up. I mean, terrorism in Lima, it's scary but it happens all the time, it's not a surprise. Walk around a bit and you can see for yourself why someone would want to get some terror going. But in Tokyo, it's pretty extraordinary. And extraordinary is fun. Especially for you boys."

"I confess, I might be a little excited. I sat in front of the television all night, I couldn't sleep at all."

"Let me guess what you were thinking about that kept you up all night. You were imagining yourself in that subway car, right, the gas flooding in and you're about to die? And then you imagined me, hearing about your death and getting sad, and things got all tragic and dramatic?"

"Well maybe. I thought about things like that, sure. But getting tragic and dramatic, that's a girl fantasy. Whatever else I might be, I'm a boy, and as a boy, I should imagine boy things, like what if the poison gas had been dropped in that deep dark forest in the middle of Tokyo? What if someone put that gas in a crop-duster and sprayed it over the whole city? Not that that's what I was actually thinking about, though. It was more like: almost everyone in the city is dead, and everywhere you look, in the streets and in the houses and in all the buildings, in the rivers where people jumped to try save themselves, there are all these dead bodies, so many all piled up everywhere, blood running from their mouths and eyes and noses, and one of them is me. I kept imagining it like that, and I got goosebumps, it was a weird feeling, almost nostalgic, like an itch somewhere deep inside, I couldn't sleep. And I thought, this isn't right. The most real thing in the world to me is Masako, and yet this crazy thing I'm imagining seems just as real, so real I can taste it. And so I needed to hear your voice, I needed to get my feet back on the ground or I didn't know what would happen, and so I called you. Even though I knew you'd yell at me, call me selfish."

"That's really what you were thinking about, Naru?"

"I knew it, you're upset . . ."

"No, no, I mean, is that really how your thoughts went? So clearly, running on like that, right up until you called me?"

"Nothing gets past you, does it? No, it got clearer as I was talking to you just now, as I was putting it into words. But I wasn't making it up on the spot to impress you, if that's what you mean."

"No, I know, I know. So, did it happen?"

"Did what happen?"

"Are your feet on the ground?"

"Oh! Yeah, they're stuck right on there, couldn't get 'em up if I tried."

"I see."

"I'm glad I called, you know. Not just for me, for both of us."

"Me too."

"So when that hundred-and-second day comes, we're seeing each other, right?"

"Absolutely."

"And maybe living together?"

"Absolutely."

"Have I passed?"

"If you keep going like this, you will."

"I'm not going to call again, you know."

"Thanks for calling."

I remember putting down the receiver and hitting the stop button on the tape recorder. I'd recorded the conversation imagining us listening to it years later, thinking that after she got back and we'd been living together for a while, maybe we'd start to take each other for granted and we could play the tape, listen to this romantic conversation together; but once I'd really taped it, it was clear to me this would never happen. And indeed, even now that Masako really was here, sleeping quietly by my side every night, we've never listened to it. The moment I hit stop I regretted it, I didn't know why, but I was convinced that nothing good would ever come of it, that it would only end up hurting me somewhere down the line, and I tried to forget I'd ever made it at all, even tried as much as possible to forget the conversation itself. But I couldn't bring myself to actually destroy it, and so sometimes, like now, shaken awake by a tiny earthquake in the middle of the night and possessed by an odd mixture of disquiet and anticipation, half-exhilarated, unable to fall back asleep, I can't stop myself from thinking back.

Exactly one hundred and two days after that call, the moment Masako appeared pushing a cartful of luggage through Narita, I believe my life up to that point reached its peak. I'd been imagining her emerging unadorned by any ethnic gewgaws from Peru, wearing just a simple ivory tank top and loose-fitting pants of vivid Mediterranean blue, her nails painted a softly shimmering gold, her lips touched with the lightest pink and her eyes shadowed pale green, that platinum bracelet of hers dangling from her right wrist, a cardboard-colored cloche perched on her head.

And as it turned out, except for her wearing tight-fitting navy blue jeans, my predictions all came true. I told her as much right away, it was the first thing out of my mouth; her face lit up when she heard. "I was thinking the exact same thing!" She'd known I'd show up in these beige linen pants and this open-necked shirt made of Prussian blue Indian cotton, the ring she sent from Peru with the outline of a cat cut out of it adorning my right ring finger. It was what I'd worn to see her off the year before, and she'd thought, *I bet that's what Naru's going to be wearing when he meets me, as if I'd only been gone a few minutes.* So she decided to change into what she'd been wearing then too, and went into the bathroom in the airplane just before it touched down, changing out of the winter clothes she'd been wearing when she left Lima.

But this was the sort of secret pleasure borne of separation, and I knew that our conversation would grow stale within forty-eight hours, that little differences would start to crop up, little irritations, and slowly we'd begin our journey toward leading unremarkable, socially acceptable, boring lives like everyone else; and yet, all the same, we ended up getting married. That moment in Narita had shown us there was nothing more important than being close to each other at all times, close enough to touch. Sliding in next to Masako to help her push the luggage cart was enough to envelop the entire right side of my body in her warmth, and, as my hand covered hers on its handle, it was as if I were a little boy again, trembling in the face of the sheer miracle of coming into contact with the world beyond myself, and as I felt a similar tremor move through her body, it was like an epiphany: this was the feeling of being alive.

The clock showed me it was 3:15 in the morning. *If only we could reawaken that feeling and make love again,* I thought ruefully as I softly slipped out of bed, trying not to wake my wife. Masako had gone to work at a major auto-maker after returning from Peru and finishing her master's, so she had to wake up early in the morning like everyone else. I, on the other hand, worked in publishing, and it didn't matter if I got there in the morning or afternoon, which meant I usually ended up sleeping through the morning, but I try at least twice a month to coordinate my sleep schedule with hers and today was such a day.

I went to the bathroom and, shivering in the cold, washed between my legs with a spray of hot water. I went into the kitchen/dining room to turn on the heater, and put the teapot on the range to boil water to make some of the *maté* one of Masako's friends had sent her from Peru, and then I walked over to set my mug on the table. Small and round, it was crowded with magazines and houseplants, leaving only a tiny space to eat on. I'd been consumed with potting the plants as they proliferated, but now I thought, *we could stand to get rid of one of those*, as I looked down at what must have been at least four pots of arum plants. *We should get rid of some of the ivy too, it breeds like marmots.* I trim the plants back when they get overgrown, but Masako always saves the clippings, telling me not to be wasteful, and puts them in water until they sprout roots and I can plant them in yet more pots. I eat surrounded on all sides by this tropical profusion, hunching my shoulders to fit, and I feel eaten at by the greenery sometimes; it gets on my nerves, and I shout, *Throw them out, just dump them outside on the ground!* Masako promised we'd take them with us the next time we visited her parents, but that kept failing to happen until finally, eight months later, she's going to go and visit them this Saturday, three days from now.

Wait, now it's only two days from now, the day after tomorrow. Thinking about it like that, the plethora of potted plants didn't seem so bad. The week before last, during the New Year's break, we hadn't gone to visit her family when they'd gathered at her grandparents' house in Mizuto, so this weekend her family pressured her to make up for it, told her to come up and visit her parents in Takazaki when her grandparents were going to be there. "And bring Naruto, too," they added, and she finally gave in.

I wondered if the battle from eight months ago was going to pick up where it left off.

"It's not like you're asking us to buy a stuffed animal or something," Masako had said then, upset. "We're the ones who'd have to take care of it, not you!"

Some cousin of hers had just given birth to her second child, and a former classmate was pregnant too, and these things had kept entering the conversation until it was just a matter of time before someone said, "And so, do you two have any plans . . .?" And while I figured that Masako would just play it off like she usually did, saying, "Well, you know, sometime down the line perhaps . . ." and then trailing off to leave me to bear the ensuing awkwardness in silence, instead she exclaimed, "Look, it's none of your business!" And suddenly all the years of unspoken dissatisfactions between them came boiling forth all at once.

"Oh, I know, everyone feels like that at first." Masako's mother acted as though she'd been rebuffed like this time and again, but she was going to control herself, allow not a trace of irritation to color her voice as she responded.

"When I first married your father, his father was after us right away, demanding *grandchildren, grandchildren* from us all the time, and I took it pretty hard too. But looking back now, I think it would have been better if I had had my children earlier. As I've gotten older, I've drawn more and more strength from having had them."

"So you should be completely satisfied now, then, right Mom? Good for you!" I could feel Masako's impatience prickle me as she spoke.

"Please try to see it from my point of view. I get asked all the time, not just by blood relations but ones on your father's side, too, 'Aren't they thirty already? Isn't it getting a bit late to be starting a family?' And I always take your side, I always say, 'I respect my daughter's wishes,' but dear, there's a limit to how much I can be expected to put up with."

"Dad, shouldn't you be protecting Mom from that kind of thing? Why do they need to prod excuses out of her? You should just state the matter clearly, 'My daughter doesn't want to have children,' and that should be that."

"Don't say you don't want to have children!"

"It's the truth, so why shouldn't I?"

"Oh, stop it. Both of you, stop it, stop provoking each other like this," her mother broke in, her voice sounding drained and powerless.

"I'm not saying you have to have children. There are a lot of things to consider, I know that—your finances, your careers, your time commitments, this modern lifestyle with both of you working—I'm not saying you have to pretend you're living in the past. It's just your grandparents, and you know, Yoriyasu-san, everyone really, they're worried that you don't have any intentions of starting a family at all. So we just want you to make it clear that you do want to start a family someday, and don't worry, it doesn't matter to us when."

"Well, then I'll make it as clear as I can: I don't intend to ever have children."

"Never? In your whole life?"

"Till I die."

"I don't know if you should say 'never' like that. Just a mother's opinion."

"Everyone becomes a parent! It's nature's law, your duty as a person!"

"You probably won't understand this, Dad, but talk like that is considered discriminatory these days."

"It's discriminatory to become a parent?! Such foolishness. So childish, only a selfish child would refuse to be a parent."

"Fine, then. Fine. I'm a child. You treat me like a child, I'll act like a child. You think I'm just a child anyway, you don't respect my opinions at all."

"I said I respected your opinions just now, didn't I?"

"If you meant it, then you'd accept it when I said I didn't want to have a baby!"

"Does Naru agree with your decision?" Masako's father asked this without looking at me.

"You always do this, Dad. Don't be a coward, ask him

yourself!" Masako looked at me. Her eyes communicated nothing. They didn't urge me to hold the line with her, they didn't challenge me to disagree, they just regarded me. And so they made guilt well up within me all the more.

"We agree completely on this issue," I said to her father. Masako was still looking at me, and so I returned her gaze. It remained as vacant of meaning as before.

"Really? You don't need children either, Naru? Such an adult you are," he shot back, perhaps as strongly as a father-in-law could at his son-in-law. My mother-in-law threw me a lifeline, asking what my father-in-law had yet to.

"I'm not saying this to criticize you or anything like that, I'm just curious: why is it that you don't want children of your own?"

"We have enough to occupy us just with ourselves, I'd say, and we're happy enough with that."

"Just with yourselves, you'd say?" My father-in-law's tone was ironic.

"We live in a time when it's believed that there cannot be society without individuals. I understand where you're coming from, I do. But if starting a family brings us pain, we lose our reason for being alive in the first place. It's so hard to find a reason for living these days. It's simply no longer the case that having children or starting a family will automatically give you one. Or at least, that's what we've discovered in our lives together. Right now, our reason for living is something other than having children."

"So you're saying we have no right to expect grand-children or great-grandchildren? Don't you realize that your elders need reasons to live, too? Well, you don't have your parents anymore, maybe you can't understand what I mean."

"Dad!"

Masako protested loudly, and I tried to calm her, saying, "No, it's all right, after all, it's the truth. I'm used to it." My father divorced my mother while I was too young to remember, and I've never met him, or even know if he's still alive. My mother took pride in raising me alone, and three years ago, after seeing the face of the woman I was to marry, she died an early death from stomach cancer.

"I know you don't understand, but if you think about it a little, you'll see that it's increasingly the norm for our generation to defend their right not to have children, and you're caught in the middle of that transition, though I think it's a bit of an overstatement for you to say the wishes of the younger generation come at the expense of those of the older. I believe that it's better for society to give the younger generation this choice than for us to get married and have children just because that's what's done, and then end up creating unhappy households because we've never had the chance to determine for ourselves what the meaning of our lives might really be. It might try your patience, but it's not like we're just playing around, doing whatever we like—we're barely getting by, barely able to hang on as we try to live our lives."

I believed in what I was saying, I knew it was true, and yet I couldn't shake the feeling that I was just spouting a bunch of conventional wisdom. My chest swelled almost to bursting with the feeling that I was just using these words to avoid saying what I really believed. And not just me, I knew that what Masako was asserting so fiercely was also just so much conventional wisdom to her as well. I knew Masako's passion was directed not against the expectations of her parents or her family or the world in general, but rather against me. After all, the truth is Masako and I have hardly discussed the issue at all.

It's really my fault. The subject came up just once, right before we got married. Masako brought it up, asking, "What do you think of having children?" I hadn't thought much of anything about it, so I just said, "Hmmm, well . . ." and then stopped speaking. I was thinking that I had no qualms about discussing it, that in fact I thought we really should talk about it, but nevertheless I lost the power of speech. I felt my face grow pale as I asked myself, *What do I really think about this?* And no answer came. I couldn't even think of possible responses to choose from. Perhaps because the question itself didn't seem real to me.

I'm a quite unnatural creature. I wanted to be more natural. I wanted it to be natural to me either that I'd want to have children or that I wouldn't. Though to long for such a thing is itself unnatural, which irritated me further.

I certainly wasn't against having a child. Once I even lived with a woman who had children. She was a single mother. She had a four-year-old daughter and a one-year-old son. I made a good substitute dad, if I do say so myself. I felt affection for the kids, I was able to scold them when necessary, and I had even been willing to put my name in their family registry if it came to that. She changed her mind about the relationship before it came to that, but I had no regrets that I had considered it.

What I find impossible is imagining myself with children of my own. Even with that woman's children, knowing that for all intents and purposes I'd become their father, I couldn't imagine the four of us really building a household together. I could imagine all sorts of things about my future with the mother, how old we'd be at different points in our lives together, how our relationship might evolve, but when I tried to include her children into these imaginings they'd break down, my head filling with sandstorms of static like a television screen, my thoughts frozen.

Masako watched me freeze up and gingerly offered, "Well, it would be better if we did it before we turn thirty . . ." And even these soft words, really little more than a sigh, struck me like a blow. "We don't have the money," I said, finally, and that's how it'd been left ever since.

All I've done since then is avoid confronting both my real feelings and Masako's, striving instead simply to soothe any possible tensions or hurts that may come up between us. And as I did, I left Masako hanging, ignoring the stress she was surely feeling. Little by little, even our sexual habits changed. It wasn't just that we did it less and less frequently, it was that I would grow uneasy inside her even with a condom on, and after a few thrusts I would switch, entering her anus instead. Masako neither encouraged nor discouraged me. I myself didn't like anal sex, it felt dirty to me, but I was equally unable to stop doing it. I felt like we were two pieces of a wooden puzzle, built to fit this way and that was that.

I poured the rest of my *maté,* now cold, into one of the arum plant pots. If we didn't have all these plants we wouldn't have to go up to Takazaki, I thought, selfishly. And then I plucked every arum and ivy plant from their pot, roots and all, and dumped them into the compost pile near the sink. It was already past four.

As I reached my hands into the sink to wash out the cups and teapot, the lid on the teapot started clattering by itself. My hands froze. A deep rumbling resounded as the ground began shuddering beneath my feet, the arum and ivy tendrils trembling as they stuck out every which way, the dishes rattling in their rack, the picture frame over the phone crashing down with a bang.

Another earthquake. Surprisingly big. I reached quickly to steady the dish rack and yelled, "Earthquake!" toward the bedroom. Then I changed my mind and headed into the bedroom, but by then, the tremors were already winding down. Masako was sitting up in the bed, still half asleep, her short hair sticking up where it had been mussed against the pillows. She seemed to return to her senses when she saw me, and then she buried her head in a feather pillow.

"Are you okay?"

As I sat on the edge of the bed and stroked the back of her head, her body stiffened. "You unfeeling shit," she said, the pillow muffling her words. "I thought you'd abandoned me."

"Did the earthquake wake you just now?"

Masako nodded and said, "I woke up, and you were gone." And then she buried her face again in the pillow.

"I was drinking some *maté* out there," I explained, pointing to where the light was still on in the kitchen. Masako drew a cherry-blossom pink cardigan around her shoulders and used the remote to turn on the heater in the room. She put the blanket over the cardigan and huddled beneath it.

"I thought you'd run off without me."

"God forbid."

I turned on the little TV mounted next to the closet; NHK came on. The news hadn't started yet. I put my right arm around Masako's blanket-shrouded shoulder and used my left to press her head against my chest. She relaxed, putting an arm around my middle. We stayed like that for while, and then she sat up away from me as the news came on and announced that a magnitude 4 earthquake had hit Tokyo. Tokyo had been experiencing a series of midsized earthquakes lately; this was the third quake since the end of last year to score a 4 on the Richter scale. Last year had also seen a series of volcanic eruptions occurring throughout Japan, and this, coupled with the end of the century approaching, made people suspect, without evidence, that the Big One was coming any minute, and emergency supplies had been selling out all over.

"It was big enough, really, but at the same time it was just another 4. I'm getting used to them."

Masako looked at me, her brows furrowed, and then pointed at the floor, saying, "Looks like a lot of stuff fell on the ground."

"And why didn't you actually come in the room, why did you just stay out there yelling 'Earthquake!' at me? I was still asleep when it started, and it scared me. Things were falling all around me and you weren't here beside me, so of course I got scared, I thought I'd been abandoned to fend for myself now that the Big One had finally hit Tokyo."

Masako shrugged off the blanket and sighed as she buttoned her cardigan. "I was so lonely."

"I'll say it again, I'm sorry I wasn't there for you. But I knew it wasn't a big earthquake, and I was right, it wasn't. Can't we leave it at that?" I was trying to choose my words carefully. These days, I've been choosing my words carefully with Masako a lot. The news informed us that this morning was the sixth anniversary of the Great Hanshin-Awaji Earthquake that hit Kobe.

"It's been six years already?"

"Yeah, six years."

"Six years, and now we're in our thirties."

I said this while turning off the television, my back to her. She shook her head when I asked if she wanted me to put some tea on for her.

"Six years since then . . . you know what I mean, 'since then.'"

"Since we were apart, and the earthquake hit Kobe."

"Yeah," Masako said quietly, "As long as you remember."

"So what you really want to say is that six years ago you were lonely in Peru because you'd thought I might have been hurt in the Kobe earthquake, but even now that we're together, you're still scared that you'll die alone and abandoned when an earthquake hits. Isn't that right?"

"Oh look—it's Soccer!"

Masako interrupted me as she caught sight of something on the veranda through a gap in the curtains, and she slid open the glass door and said again, "Soccer!" And there, in a small pool of light spilling out from the bedroom, sat a little white cat with black markings. The glass door and his spotted mouth opened simultaneously to let his soft *miao* pass through.

Crap, I thought. Soccer, this little cat marked just like a soccer ball who'd shown up on the veranda during the France World Cup, had a habit of ignoring Masako and running up to me. It always irritated her. She'd mutter about being the fifth wheel. Things would escalate, Masako making herself miserable until she was browsing pet store catalogs and home pages, pointing out dogs and little birds she would never otherwise like and saying, "Maybe I'll get this one . . ." But the only reason Soccer liked me was because I was around during the day to play with him and feed him sweet shrimp. Whenever I happened upon him outside, he'd ignore me completely, even run away if I pressed the issue and tried to pet him; it hardly seemed as though he actually preferred me in any real way. But explaining this did little to assuage Masako's loneliness in the face of our seeming chumminess.

But this time, maybe because he was extremely hungry, as soon as he saw Masako straighten up from crouching down to greet him, he ran in and followed right after her as she walked into the kitchen to the refrigerator, swirling around her legs as she put some leftover tuna and a bit of miso soup–soaked dried fish in a bowl and walked back into the bedroom to place it on the veranda, where he tucked right in.

As Masako was bending down to talk to the cat, I was bending down to pick up the things that had fallen on the floor during the earthquake: a half-read book, a box of tissues, some plastic cosmetic bottles, a stuffed cat playing with a soccer ball. There were used tissues spilling from an overturned wastebasket, and an empty pill case with the numbers 1 through 21 printed on it. Sleeping pills? Masako always seemed to sleep well, but maybe she didn't.

"Oooh, Soccer farted!"

Masako came running in from the bedroom pinching her nose between her fingers, then took her hands, cold from the veranda, and cupped them to my cheeks as I crouched on the ground. "Cold cold cold!" she exclaimed. I remained frozen in place, staring down at a portable tape recorder, which had also apparently fallen on the ground. Masako withdrew her hands from my face. And she looked at me with eyes that communicated nothing, saying, "That's from six years ago." And indeed, the label on the tape made it clear it was the one I'd made then.

The first thing that came to mind was that perhaps

Masako had intentionally placed it somewhere I was likely to run across it. But I never had, I'd just blithely gone about my business ignoring it until I finally noticed it now that it had been knocked onto the ground by the earthquake.

"It's cold," muttered Masako, and she went back into the bedroom to wrap the blanket around herself again. Soccer finished eating and sauntered slowly back in through the open glass door to curl up at my feet and fall sound asleep. His solid little body warmed my cold toes. I reached down to scratch him under the chin and down his back. His soft skin moved independently over his delicate bones. I got up and walked over to close the door to the veranda, leaving a gap just big enough for Soccer to slip through, and then picked up the portable recorder and brought it with me as I sat down on the bed. My head was in turmoil. I couldn't decide whether to push play.

I should be the one to broach the subject, I thought. But Masako prevented this, too. "You left that tape out where I would find it because you had something to say to me, right? So say it." It was impossible to clear up misunderstandings now that each of us was suspicious of the other, and so I thought instead about what I could say that would cut most directly to the heart of the things. "Let's not get in another argument with your mother this weekend." Masako wrinkled her nose, snorting.

"As if it had nothing to do with you."

"That's exactly it—I can't think of it as something that has to do with me, and it worries me."

"You might have held onto your hesitations for six years, but my feelings have changed since then. Festered."

"You always tell me I don't think enough about how you feel, but you don't make any effort to understand the things that bother me, do you?" I couldn't prevent the conversation from slipping away from the real subject.

"I don't think that. I just don't think you want to know the truth about the situation, that you don't really know anything about me."

"I know you've been hiding your feelings from me."

"I don't mean my feelings. I'm talking facts. You don't know that I might not be *able* to have children, do you?"

At this, I stopped knowing which way was up, and, disoriented, I simply didn't know what to say. After a bit, I managed to force out, "How was I supposed to know that if you never told me?"

"You wouldn't have listened if I tried." Masako's legs hit the edge of the bed and she sat down on it, reaching over to scratch Soccer's belly with her fingernails. Soccer's eyes opened slightly, then closed again.

I knew I needed to understand Masako's feelings now that I knew she was facing never being able to have children of her own. But children seemed so unreal to me, how could I imagine what it might mean not to be able to have them?

Masako began to talk. When she was younger, still in school, she'd been wrapped up in an affair with a married man who wanted her pregnant with his baby, and they ended up trying for over a year to no avail. And that's why he left her in the end, returning to his wife and kids.

"I wanted to talk about it with you, Naru. I didn't know what I wanted to do. I thought that if you said you were happy enough without children, then I'd be satisfied with just our life together, just the two of us, and I'd never have to talk about it again. But if you said you did want children someday, I resolved to go in and get tested and do what it took to make it happen. Do you understand how scared I am of getting tested? No matter how sure I might be that I don't want children, being told I *can't* get pregnant is like being told I'm not really human, you know?"

"That's . . . that's not true," I said in a small voice, "Those things aren't related."

"Exactly, it's not true. It's an emotional thing. And so you can understand why if I don't feel like the people around me support me, like my family, if everyone's looking at me like a failure, a failure as a woman, as a person, and then besides that, there's that humiliating test to take, maybe I really will fail—facing all that alone, it's unbearable. Surely you can understand that much, can't you?"

And indeed, I should have known something was up eight months ago.

"But you wouldn't listen to me. And so I got depressed on my birthday, and I ended up talking about it with someone else. Ryū."

I sighed. Ryū was Masako's coworker, and he came over pretty frequently to visit. Masako acted as Ryū's relationship therapist. Ryū was in love with a man who'd been hired around the same time as him named Mashiko. The whole company, Mashiko included, thought they were just good friends, but Ryū had been thinking that he was laying the groundwork to be able to carry on a secret, intimate relationship even if Mashiko eventually got married; as it turned out though, Mashiko got married right away and Ryū fell into a deep depression, which occasioned his coming over all the time to visit Masako.

"He told me I was being stupid. People talk all the time about what a 'real person' is, what makes a 'real man' or 'real woman,' but can you really define what's human and what isn't? Ryū told me about when he visited Mashiko's children, feeling as if he were jumping out of an airplane. Looking at those two children, he felt like he was excluded from the cycle of life, like he'd outlived his usefulness as a *Homo sapiens*. Ryū said he felt like he'd died in that moment, like he'd been killed, reduced to a living corpse. And yet, at the same time, it struck him as meaningless to think of being human only in animal terms, that perhaps a human like him who was made to never have children is actually better for the world as a whole. If you're born unable to have children, then not having children is 'natural' for you, what's this talk of 'treatment,' who's treating what, who's the one with the problem? Ryū really gave me a talking to." And then Masako's tone grew cold as she asked, "Do you understand what I'm talking about?"

"You wouldn't believe me even if I said yes."

"Well, do you know what Ryū did after that, then?"

"He decided to accept Mashiko as he was, children and all, and achieved even greater enlightenment through his silent forbearance. Am I close?"

"In an ideal world, maybe. Happily ever after and all that. But in the real world, if you don't get something in return for your sacrifices, you end up breaking down. So what do you think ended up happening with Ryū?"

I shook my head, less interested in Ryū's psychology than that of the woman talking about him. What was Masako getting in return for being held in suspense for so long?

"You can't guess, can you? Of course not. It doesn't interest you. All your attention's taken up with your own worries."

"I knew you'd say that. You're always out to prove how little I understand about other people's feelings. But you don't need to prove it to me. I admit it. Everything you say is true."

"I'm not proving something to you, I'm trying to explain myself, tell you something you didn't know about me for the last six years. Maybe all the things that worry me seem of a piece to you from a distance, like when we lived so far apart all those years ago, but to me, it's changing all the time, it's never the same moment to moment." Masako pulled out one of the drawers installed under her side of the bed and fished out a letter.

"I heard what Ryū had to say and thought, well, okay, so I can't have children, so what? What's the problem? I don't know how Naru feels about it, but I'll just have to live my life without children, it's decided. But then I got this letter from Kasumi, and I didn't know what to think anymore, it was all unclear again."

Masako took the letter out of its envelope, looked it over to find the section she wanted, and then folded it to show me.

"I got it about a year ago. I was the one who introduced them, but I never dreamed something like this would happen. It was a real shock, enough to make my period late, which made me worry more, but the worst part was that I couldn't talk to you about it."

Ryū wanted to become a single father and had asked Kasumi to bear a child for him, since he couldn't have one himself. He offered to pay for everything, so all she had to do was get artificially inseminated and have the baby. And of course, he'd pay her a fee on top of that. It's not much, but would ¥5,000,000 be enough? Kasumi said she went out of her mind with anger, asking him what exactly he thought friendship really was, but Ryū insisted that having a child like this was his life's purpose. I'd always wanted to share the joys and hardships of childbirth with someone else, but I was born without being able to give birth, he said. But I don't care, it's not a woman's special privilege or God-given right to give birth, if a child arrives you welcome it whether it comes from some womb other than your wife's or girlfriend's, or out of a man's body, or if it's a clone or an android—it doesn't matter how it's born. I know I'd want it no matter how much it contributed to overpopulation, no matter if there were measures taken to limit how many new people came into the world, no matter how twisted this world ended up getting, how encrusted with unbending, obsolete beliefs, I'd still want a child to raise as well as I could to help straighten this twisted world back out, I'd want to pass on all the wisdom I'd gleaned from my brief stint upon this earth. Kasumi didn't have an answer for that and asked if he'd considered adoption, but Ryū explained that he wanted to give every-thing he had to his baby, right down to his genes. Kasumi found herself left with no more counterarguments and moved by his words; it felt inhumane to refuse him after hearing him explain his motivations, so she accepted the offer with the caveat that to please her parents she would insist on having them get married, even if it was in name only, but Ryū refused, saying that if she really understood what kind of knowledge he wanted to pass on to his child, she'd know he could never agree to such an arrangement, that he would raise his child as a single father and that was that, and so she tried to refuse the fee he wanted to pay her but in the end he sent it to her, and she wanted to know what Masako thought about the whole thing, did she think it was okay?

I handed the letter back to Masako, saying, "I think I get it." It was sad, and a bit repulsive. But I felt a certain kinship with the repulsiveness; I recognized myself in it.

"Well, I *don't* get it. I can see why Kasumi would resist, of course, and I also understand the almost prayerful views that Ryū expressed, but I don't know what to think about how it turned out. Hearing about it made me feel like my decision not to give birth was twisted, like it wasn't the right thing to do anymore. Ryū's not meant to give birth, but am I really not meant to, either? Every year I just get older and my body ages too, soon I'm going to pass the point of no return—I have to decide, right now, but I can't! Even though the longer I put off my decision, the more the whole thing becomes moot."

I couldn't keep still any longer. "There's nothing twisted about you! Either decision will be right."

"So *help me!*" cried Masako, her voice rising.

I nodded my head and swallowed. "Did Kasumi end up giving birth?"

"I'm scared to ask. I'll probably find out from them pretty soon anyway, like it or not."

"Do you pity Ryū?"

"I . . . I don't . . . "

"I think I understand what he's doing. He thinks that if there are more people like him in the world, if people like him become the norm, then everything will be better, the world would be a better place. But the flip side of that, and I don't think he realizes this, is that wishing for that is the same as wishing that there were fewer people who *aren't* like him in the world. He wouldn't be able to ask a woman for the kind of thing he asked from Kasumi if he didn't secretly feel that way. It's a form of revenge against those who can have children themselves, who think nothing of it. It refuses to accept that part of reality, right down to the root. I don't have such a well-defined target, but I think I share that kind of impulse myself."

"I see," said Masako, nodding deeply. "That's what you meant when you said you understood. On this tape," she continued, handing him the portable recorder, "you say that when you die you want to take the world with you. I didn't get it at the time, but listening now, I can hear you fantasizing about extinguishing the whole human race to accompany you when you die. You said the only thing that seemed as immediate and real to you as I did was imagining all of Tokyo wiped out by sarin gas, right? Which means that when you're with me, you're able to block out everyone else in the world from your mind, right? So a child would just get in the way. You've wiped it out before it can even be born. No, it's true, I'm sure of it. You're a baby killer. That's your way of extinguishing the human race. You said you understood my feelings just now, but I think you'd have to kill yourself to really do that. You feel guilty, like a baby killer, and so you can't talk about children at all. You're scared I'd figure it out as soon you admitted you didn't want children."

If I could have willed my heart to stop, I would have. Or willed a huge earthquake to strike and wipe me out. If I could have just died of natural causes right then, right there, everything would have been solved. I was an unnatural person. A human who rejects humanity, an inhuman human. The only natural thing I could do was die.

"Do you find me repulsive?"

"You really need to ask me that? Don't you understand that I know there's something in you stopping you before you act on these secret feelings in your heart?"

"I can't even believe that myself."

"You need others to believe in you. I wanted to do that for you, Naru, and I wanted you to want me to."

"I do."

It had gotten light outside, beyond the curtains. Crows cawed at each other as they picked over the garbage. My eyes stung with a combination of fatigue and the dry air from the heater.

"What are we going to do?" asked Masako, sounding exhausted.

"The difference between me and Ryū is that I've got you, right?"

"I feel like I've been halfway like Ryū myself. Like I've been trying to ask myself to become my own surrogate mother."

"And Soccer's been the thing keeping you from doing it?"

Masako, as if suddenly coming to her senses, looked down, then under the bed, and then out in the kitchen, saying, "I guess he left," as she walked onto the veranda. I followed her. Soccer wasn't out there either. There was frost forming on the tuna in his dish. The air was cold and silvery, as if made of ice. There was no one on the sidewalk below. The only things that moved were the white puffs of breath from our mouths. *This is raw reality*, I thought. It was bracing as it touched my skin. I embraced Masako from behind as she said, *It's cold*, and I whispered in her ear, "Let's improve the world, together. Like Ryū said." Masako twisted around to look at me, saying, "Should we really decide just like that, after a single conversation?"

"I think it's what we both want."

Masako took a deep breath. I felt her body swell, then shrink again.

"Well, that may be so," said Masako, laughing suddenly. "It was good to get it all out, I feel better. Just don't forget you're still on probation, mister."

"For how long?"

"Your whole life."

"Ahh, a short sentence." I felt myself beginning to smile as well.

"You know, I thought it would work out like this. But why do I still feel suspended, like nothing is actually settled? Did we decide this all on our own, as two individuals? Or was it decided for us?"

"Maybe it was." It felt like something had truly changed, that the decision we'd made was right, and yet I too felt as though the two of us were floating, weightless. "But it'll still feel like we decided this together, and that's how reality feels for unnatural folks like us."

"So I'm unnatural, too?"

"Yes. By which I mean, very human."

"I see. So, you want to get started now?" murmured Masako, nibbling along my jawline. I nodded, and we went inside like that and ended up back in bed.

The paperboy came by, the brakes on his bicycle squeaking intermittently. I glanced out through a gap in the imperfectly closed curtains. Masako followed my gaze. Laughing guiltily, we stifled our voices and went back to our caresses. Running my hands and tongue across her body as if smoothing her hair, my breathing began to synchronize with hers as her hands and tongue responded in kind.

Masako's breathing gradually began to slow, become more regular. Eventually, her hands stopped their movements and fell back into the sheets. Hot and vaguely vegetable-scented, Masako's breath flowed in and out of her half-open mouth. My lips and ears bathed in this breath, I knew that we weren't going to make love.

We'd left the door slightly ajar, and Soccer slipped back in, soundlessly.

Air (2006)

The flute played the quiet with its hoarse-throated cry. It was a song like wind allowing a flute to sculpt its contours, a Tōru Takemitsu composition called "Air." My chest tightened as its birdsong phrase repeated. It felt like Tsubame had flown into my room and was whispering in my ear.

With "Air" playing on a loop in the background, I spread tissues across the floor beneath my desk chair, dropped my pants, and rubbed myself erect. Then I took the alcohol-wiped blade of my X-Acto knife and pressed it carefully against my penis, gently pulling it along the skin. The cold came first, followed closely by sharp pain, and a light flow of blood began running toward the root. I wrapped the shaft in tissue paper. With my spit-wet finger I caressed the mouth of the wound. An involuntary cry of pain escaped me. The stopper that had blocked my throat like the pit of a plum worked itself free at last, and sadness surged up all at once. My tears and cries seemed to have no end.

I don't do it because it feels good. I do it because if I didn't, I would lose any sense I was still alive. It was a variation on the theme of the wrist cut, the penis cut. I have no desire to approach death, so I avoid my wrists. I want to approach a deeper, more fundamental loss, so I cut my penis. I can get as close as possible to the loss of Tsubame this way.

I say I lost him, but he didn't die, we didn't even have a falling out. Tsubame simply went along with his diplomat lover, Dr. Hiroda (as everyone called her), when she was transferred to Mexico. At the farewell party the two of them held at their home, Tsubame had told me lightheartedly,

"Come visit us! We'll have three spare rooms, you can stay for as long as you like. Any one of them is bigger than your entire apartment, Tsubasa!" But I had already reached my limit. I couldn't stand this one-sided affair any longer. It was just that I couldn't bring myself to end things when he was near. When he told me he was going to Mexico, I realized my chance had come. Seeing that I could no longer stand the situation I'd found myself in, destiny had lent its helping hand.

So I vowed never to go to Mexico, never to see Tsubame again as long as I lived. And with this feeling filling me, I sang him a farewell song at his farewell party. It was "La Golondrina," a song sung in Mexico at times of parting, which I'd memorized phonetically for the occasion.

Are you leaving, where are you going, *golondrina?*

If you hurry so, you'll tire,
Lose your way in the wind,
Have nowhere to rest your wings.

I'll make you a nest near my bed,
You can weather the cold months there.

I am lost here too.
O Heaven! I cannot fly like you, *golondrina.*

Oh, my lovely *golondrina,* I hear your song,
And think of home, and weep.

I'd also recorded myself playing the flute, and I sang with the recording as accompaniment. As I sang, the thought that the words were a direct expression of my heart overwhelmed me, and I started to cry. And once I started, I couldn't stop. No one knew of my decision. Tsubame remained ignorant of the confession I was singing to him as I mouthed the Spanish syllables of "La Golondrina." So my song was received with a vague sort of generalized pensiveness, punctuated by a few women bursting into tears in sympathy with mine.

Tsubame praised my flute playing. He knew how hard I'd practiced to make the instrument my own.

The first time we ever did anything alone together was when I went with him to a memorial concert for Tōru Takemitsu. Dr. Hiroda, who was originally supposed to have gone with him, had had something come up, so he asked me to go in her stead. I'd never heard the name "Tōru Takemitsu" before, and I found contemporary classical music so boring that I was fighting to stave off sleep throughout the show. I even abstained from the wine offered during the intermission. Still, Tsubame saw through all my efforts, of course.

The concert ended with Takemitsu's posthumous work "Air," then the house lights came up. Tsubame hurriedly wiped tears from his eyes, saying softly, "I want that piece played at my funeral. It makes me feel like I wouldn't mind no longer being human."

Was the piece really that great? Spurred by this thought, I ran out and bought it on CD. Patrick Gallois was the flutist on the recording. Even though I didn't understand what made it so great, I listened to it over and over. And as I did, the Takemitsu-borne wind that Gallois played began to penetrate my flesh, to blow through my body. It was music, yet it wasn't. It fell somewhere between a natural breeze and a man-made breath. I felt as if by opening my body to this wind, I, too, could transcend my own humanity.

This must have been what Tsubame had meant, and I was filled with joy at my realization, and ran to tell him. And wouldn't you know, he ended up giving me a flute of my own as a present.

"It doesn't matter if you're bad at it. You understand the feeling, so I want you to play the wind," he told me, rather affectedly. Artists have a tendency to say pretentious things without a hint of irony. Tsubame was an unsuccessful artist who painted all sorts of bric-a-brac in colorful abstractions, and who Dr. Hiroda, the daughter of a gallery owner and fifteen years his senior, discovered and later made her lover. To cut a long story short, I ended up meeting Tsubame because a close friend from middle school had a sister who was an editor for an art magazine, and we were introduced at a party at her house.

Truth be told, the flute he gave me was somewhat of a burden. But I gave it my all because I knew it pleased him. I took lessons whenever I had a day off, and even during normal workdays I'd practice for an hour in the park early in the morning. I'd initially planned on mastering the phrase from "Air" that I liked so much, but this turned out to be much too distant a goal, seeing how I found myself occupied entirely with just "La Golondrina."

Listening to "Air" again now, I caressed the wounds cut into my penis, and as I blew on them, the pain seeping into my flesh, I felt the air rush through me. The wind blowing through my hollow core seemed to produce a hoarse-throated sound. I became a flute as the wind passed through me, and I played my own version of "Air." I thought of Tsubame, who'd crossed the sky and left me. He'd shown me the difference between him and me, flight-less wing that I am, and yet he also made me feel what it was to be alive. I resisted the urge to cut myself again.

Layers of scars adorned my penis like the patterns carved by waves. When Misaki was about to go down on me the first time, she noticed them and pulled back. "What's that? Some kind of disease?" she asked. "Well, of a sort," I replied ruefully, "A disease of the heart."

"I didn't know you were into that kind of thing. You like it rough? I must not be enough for you!"

"You are more than enough for me. It's just when I'm alone, I end up hurting myself."

I told her the truth. I told her all about Tsubame, save for my pathetic feelings for him. But the explanation didn't ring true even to myself. I'd never fallen in love with a man, my seduction success rate with women averaged about sixty percent, and things with Misaki were going perfectly well, so I hadn't known what to make of my quickening heartbeat when I'd first met Tsubame. Did I simply respect a man so able to live life on his own terms? Was I just drawn to someone whose talents exceeded my own?

Tsubame was popular. With his svelte physique, his gentle voice and way of speaking, his meltingly sweet disposition, his guileless way of approaching things that fell outside his ken, he possessed an openness that put everyone at ease while concealing the sharpness of his true insights. These elements blended miraculously to produce a sultry allure that wafted from him almost palpably. Yet he was devoted to Dr. Hiroda exclusively. All others who crowded around remained firmly in their places as dear friends, nothing more. Myself included.

Yet I had the feeling that in his heart of hearts, I stuck out at least a little from the rest of these "dear friends." And regardless, I simply wanted to be near him. It didn't matter if it was just the two of us or not. It was happiness itself just to hear his voice speak his words, to have him laugh or be moved or get excited by mine. Our moods would melt into each other and become inextricably mixed. And then I would decide not to think about these feelings any further. I would shed my clothes and satisfy myself with Misaki.

But even so . . . At long last, I confessed my secret feelings to Misaki. Her response was unexpected, or maybe I should say, old-fashioned. In short, she became a ball of fire ignited by jealousy and trust betrayed.

"What is this load of crap? The truth is you like your junk slapped around by some dominatrix, don't you? You get off when it hurts, right? So why don't I try biting you? I'll chew you up and spit you out, you animal, you monkey who walks like a man!"

As she said this, she actually tried to bite me. Naturally, we soon split up. The truth was, I was playing at being something I wasn't even more than Misaki guessed, so my fault in the matter was hardly trifling. But even so, I made use of Misaki's convenient misunderstanding.

My cuts scab over and the scars they leave after I peel

them off overlap and build on each other, deforming my penis until it looks like it's ringed with rubber washers. I was running out of places for my blade to slice. I wanted proof that I was alive. I wanted to remake myself into a form I could point to and say, "*That* is Tsubasa Tsutsui." I imagined myself with a vagina, tracing the line coarsely referred to as the "ant trail" that runs from behind my balls to my anus with the point of the blade.

I felt as if I already had a vagina. What other explanation could there be for the sweet pain that overcomes me? It was simply buried beneath this thick wall of flesh. My body was hiding my vagina deep within itself. A vagina concealed a hollowness. I was a flute, I was hollow too, wind rushing through my empty core. If I could just split my flesh open, my hollowness could be exposed. I could just turn my flesh back on itself and voila! A vagina would appear! Just as Takemitsu sculpted the air by caressing its contours to make wind into music, I could make myself into an instrument just by cutting through the hymen obstructing my flute! And then I would be my true self at last, and living my life would regain its meaning.

Excited by these thoughts, I drove the blade hard into my perineum. Pain incomparable to any penis cut shot through me from my spine to the crown of my skull. This was my penis's root. It was more resilient that I'd imagined, and more sensitive. But to cut into it was to make the vagina cut. If I couldn't stand to do it, I'd never become my true self. The extent of the sacrifice gave value to the act's completion.

I pictured myself penetrating my own hole, exploring it with my fingers. Just imagining it, my body was gripped with agony. If I really did it, I suppose I'd pass out, ascend to heaven. Ascend. I'd rise like Tsubame up into the sky. We'd ride the wind and dance up there, together in the air.

Today it happened in a crowded train. A penis appeared at my crotch. It was so sudden it hurt. It pressed up against someone's thigh. I supposed there were a lot of men who did this, who molested their neighbors with an innocent look on their faces. I supposed that now I knew what it felt like to be one of them, however involuntarily.

Though no one else could tell that my penis was there. My penis wasn't real. It was invisible. I was just your run-of-the-mill woman, my body as feminine as anyone else's, except from time to time I felt a penis sprout from my crotch. It was only the feeling that sprouted, though, my physical body didn't change at all. I called it my air penis.

I don't really remember when it first appeared, but I do recall that sometime before I was old enough to go to school, I wet my pants trying to pee off the edge of a river-bank while standing up, even though no one had ever told me that was possible, and I ended up getting scolded by my parents. My parents had thought I'd simply lost control. I tried to explain that the pee hadn't come out the hole I expected it to, but they didn't understand.

I was afflicted off and on with this illusory feeling ever since, and I began to worry about why this was happening to me as I neared puberty. I didn't otherwise feel like a boy, and I wasn't attracted to other girls. If only for this one little problem, I'd be able to wax lyrical about my girlhood like any other woman. My air penis held a certain sort of innocent sex appeal for me, and it began to interfere with my sexual development as a woman. This was because my hallucinatory penis was maturing right along with the rest of me.

It was about a year after I first started to get my period that one morning I awoke to the feeling that my lower body was swelled to its very limit. Thinking I just had to pee, I went into the bathroom. I'd already sat down on the toilet before I realized that it was really just the feeling of my air penis growing harder than it ever had before.

I'd already experienced the occasional erection before then. I found that if I just ignored them, they'd dissipate before too long, taking the air penis itself along with them. But this time it hurt, like a stake was being driven into my crotch. The pain was sweet, though. I put my hand on my air penis. A tingling kind of ache washed over me, making me dizzy. Before I knew it, I'd rubbed my air penis until I came. Of course, no sperm spurted out.

After much painful consideration, I finally came to a conclusion on the matter I could live with. Say you were to lose your right arm for some reason. Even though there's no arm there any more, a phantom arm may sprout and replace it, and it can grab things just as before, or you can feel like you're writing with it, or biting its nails, or stroking your lover's skin; the phantom arm can itch or hurt or even feel pleasure. Even after years have passed and you've become accustomed to everyday life with one arm, you may still be bothered by this sort of phantom arm sprouting up from time to time.

This air penis of mine was surely the same sort of thing. It was the remainder of something that used to be there but was removed. Maybe in a past life, a man driven by a desire to become something else cut off his own penis and, at that moment, gave birth to me.

Since reaching this conclusion, I became much more relaxed. Because my origins were different, it no longer mattered that I was developing differently than the other girls around me. I didn't know if I was really a man, or, since I may have been driven to cut off my own penis when I was a man, I was really a woman, or if I was really neither one. I felt like a real woman most of the time, but when I started to think deeply about which gender I might truly be, I sometimes felt like a "counterfeit woman, hiding from the world." Counterfeit yet real. But nevertheless, a woman.

With my relaxation came my first boyfriend. I could even have sex normally. One morning, I opened my eyes and then took off my clothes, asking him,

"Can you see my wee-wee?"

I'd woken up with an erection. Though it had almost nothing to do with sexual excitement, my air penis was hard.

"I see it, I see it," Masakazu replied, and he reached out and fondled my clitoris. Oh, for the—well, what could I do? What I really wanted was for him to feel my penis the way I did, to touch it and suck it and put it up his ass, but this would have to suffice.

It was my personal idol. I couldn't see it, but I knew my air penis was real. It was like a ghost, something that was removed and should have disappeared yet didn't, as if it had unfinished business. What compelled it to appear, what excited its interest? I became increasingly intrigued by the shrouded origins and mysterious desires of my air penis.

The temperature had risen to nearly 40° C. It was the hottest it'd been all summer. It seemed to me that the humidity in the staging area was making the heat twice as intense. Even so, the drag queens waiting for their turn to go, the people dressed like speed skaters covered in arabesque patterns, the bodybuilders displaying their bulked-up chests, the bearded men wrapped in leather and dripping with chains, the people made up to look like who knows what, the couples with their smiles so broad they seemed close to bursting, all their energy seemed inexplicably high. The only one who seemed to give off any negative energy was me, my bashful, retiring bearing paradoxically making me feel all the more conspicuous and anxious.

I was attending the Tokyo Gay and Lesbian Pride Parade. I'd found out about this festival for sexual minorities on the Internet after making a cursory search to see if I was alone in having an air penis. If I hadn't possessed such a thing, if I were just your average girl, I likely would have never encountered even the term "sexual minority" my whole life. I also found out for the first time that "heterosexual" was the term for those who weren't "homosexual." Of course, homosexuals weren't the only "sexual minorities" out there. There were those who liked both boys and girls, as well as countless other, more complex conjunctions of love and identity. And since that was true, it seemed natural that a girl with an air penis could find a place among these folks. At the very least, I figured I'd meet others who shared some of the realities of my existence, so I found myself wandering out to watch the parade.

A vehicle approached, covered with pink and white and rainbow-colored balloons and blaring club music loudly into the air. Beautiful men danced atop the stage it carried, showing off their toned bodies. A welcoming cry welled up from the crowd that lined the street, and a crowd of musclebound men stripped to the waist flooded the street in the vehicle's wake. There was another vehicle covered with women wearing golden dresses like royalty, followed by a group of lesbians and then a group of serious-faced men and women brandishing placards and shouting slogans. All the participants exuded an aggressive, "I'm so-and-so and such-and-such, here I am!" sort of pride, and it was a bit much for me to take. I felt humiliated. "I have an air penis! I have genitals made of nothing! It might just be a hallucination! It's not even as real as a dildo! Never mind me, I'll leave now!"

Yet, as my loneliness increased, so did my desire to assert my presence, and before long I'd darted into the street and mixed into the lively crowd of men and women who trailed after the tail end of the parade with little self-consciousness. There seemed to be plenty of others who'd gotten wrapped up in the festivities and left the sidewalk to join in even though they'd not officially registered as participants, so it seemed unlikely I'd be reprimanded for doing the same. And in fact, another young man jumped in and joined the group right after I had.

This young man seemed as uncomfortable as I was, walking along with his body hunched and his eyes fixed on the ground. It looked as if he'd come alone and was unsure whether he really belonged, so he'd watched from the sidelines until the urge to join in the parade became overwhelming and he found himself following me when I darted into the fray.

We seemed to be the only ones walking lonely and unaccompanied within the group. Telling myself that this was a festival, that the sky was clear and cloudless, I approached the young man and said, "You didn't come with your boyfriend?" The man looked shocked and gave me a hateful look, shooting back combatively, "And what about you? Your girlfriend dump you?" I was unsure how to respond for a moment, but then concluded that though I was there to assert my existence and pride, the worst thing to do would be to pretend to be a lesbian, and so I said, "My boyfriend doesn't share my opinion on these issues." The man's face twisted, and he snorted a laugh. Perhaps thinking that this was too rude a response, he added, "So, you joined the parade out of a sense of justice, because you oppose discrimination?" He was looking at my wrist as he spoke. There was a rainbow-colored bracelet hanging from it. In an attempt to get into the spirit of things, I'd bought it from one of the booths that lined the parade route. I didn't really understand what the English words ACT AGAINST HOMOPHOBIA written on it meant exactly, but I figured I'd fit in better with these colors on my body somewhere.

"You saw me run into the street from the sidewalk, didn't you?"

He nodded, muttering his assent. He seemed to realize that he'd followed my lead because he'd sensed a discomfort in my actions that resembled his own.

"Well, we all have our reasons. I guess we all came here because no one understands us, no one sympathizes with our situations. I wouldn't say I've found a place to call home, but it did seem like I might not feel so ashamed if I came here," he explained with sudden gentleness.

A list of possible "reasons" scrolled across the back of my mind, but it occurred to me that it might be precisely because his fit none of them that he found himself in search of "a place to call home." His sense of shame once he got here might be due to his not being gay exactly.

"I'm sorry for earlier, saying 'boyfriend' without thinking."

This at last brought a smile to his face, though a dark one, and he said, "That's okay. After all, he was never really my boyfriend."

His words sounded a chord within me, played a beautiful melody. My air penis appeared. I suddenly got the feeling that maybe this was someone who would actually be able to see it. My whole body finally became suffused with a heat appropriate to my surroundings. Energy began to pulse outward from inside me, igniting my flesh. Turning my newly heated gaze on him once more, he appeared translucent. It seemed as though if my inner furnace got any hotter, he might start to shimmer and eventually disappear altogether. He seemed like a man whose body was bound to the earth solely by the density of his emotions, whose borders were only vaguely defined. I found myself on the verge of reaching out and touching his uncertain skin. I wanted to embrace him, even if it meant embracing a cloud. Suppressing this urge, instead I said, "There seems to be an afterparty. Do you want to go with me?"

At the gay club in Shinjuku Ni-chōme where the afterparty took place, we gave ourselves over to the movement of our bodies and danced all night. Tsubasa seemed unused to this kind of place, his native uncertainty becoming even more pronounced, but nonetheless he seemed to make the best of it as he put his body through its paces.

I'd figured that the afterparty was to go all night, so it didn't surprise me much when at around four in the morning, this woman who said her name was Hina told me with flushed cheeks that she was exhausted and then said, "My house is close, do you want to come over?" All I really wanted was to talk with her somewhere intimate, just the two of us, so I didn't really care whether we went to her house or somewhere else, but in order to capitalize on the heat we'd unearthed during our conversation in the parade, it seemed like now, with our emotions and endurance peaking, it was the right time for liftoff.

As soon as we entered her fifth-floor apartment, Hina opened the windows. The air that had been trapped in the room started to exchange with the comparatively cool air from outside. The summer sky was already starting to brighten with the coming dawn, and we could hear songbirds singing noisily. "I don't have an air conditioner, sorry," she said, turning on a fan instead. We crouched together in front of it. "It's so ho—ot," said Hina, and she took her clothes off quickly, soon becoming completely naked. Taken aback, I just looked at her, and then she asked, "Do you see it?" while spreading her legs. She didn't seem to be propositioning me, but rather seemed to be actually pointing at something. All I saw there was what I'd been imagining as I made my vagina cuts, just a set of normal female genitals. But I intuited that telling her that would disappoint her, so instead I just looked into her eyes.

"So you don't see it either?"

Hina muttered this to herself, her voice and expression deeply disheartened, as if her very existence had just been refuted. A certain note of self-deprecation also sounded in her words, and I felt myself stirred by a tender sort of pity. "Can I touch it?" I asked, reaching my hand out. Hina nodded absently.

Not knowing quite what it was I was supposed to be touching, I started aimlessly caressing the area around her vagina. And then I suddenly withdrew my hand. What was that?

My body responded to his touch like a plucked string. He really touched it! I grabbed Tsubasa's hand and made him touch it again. His hand was fearful, pulling back against me fairly forcefully, but his fingers were curious. They slowly traced the contours of the air penis. Experiencing the touch of another for the first time, it unfurled like time-elapse footage of a sprouting plant, erecting quickly to quivering stiffness. Startled once more, Tsubasa withdrew his hand. This time I made him grip it with his whole hand. As I did, my body convulsed with a pleasure I'd never known before. I moaned involuntarily. I communicated my desire to him with my eyes.

But I didn't respond to her right away. After all, there were things I wanted her to know about me, too. Impatiently stripping off my clothes, I exposed my crotch to her, asking as I pulled my bothersome penis out of the way, "Can you see it?"

There were countless scars there. Some places were swollen like welts, while others were covered with raw, red scabs that looked about to spurt with blood if peeled loose. Tsubasa was obviously not showing me these. He wanted me to see something invisible. Not see it exactly, but know it was there. I tentatively brought my fingers close. And then, in the area where the wounds seemed most concentrated, I touched him. Tsubasa, like me, responded convulsively. In a tense, high-pitched voice, he said, "That's where I open up. Do you see?" I nodded. I lay on my stomach and licked him there. Just as Masakazu did to me, I caressed the tip of Tsubasa's real penis as if it were a clitoris. Tsuabasa cried out hoarsely. The place I was licking soon became wet with something other than just saliva. Tsubasa's vagina opened its red flesh walls to me and I pushed my tongue farther in. The smell grew thicker. Tears ran freely from Tsubasa's eyes.

Unable to control my passion, I opened my body as my emotions overflowed. Hina breathed into my invisible vagina. Her breath blew through my hollow core and past all the other holes opening up all over my body, etching musical scales into the air. My music began to play.

And as it did, I put Hina's invisible penis, which I had been gripping the whole time, into my mouth. She made a sound like the song of a rare tropical bird.

Her penis was like a rod of mochi skewered on a

chopstick. It filled my mouth and made me start to choke, so I pulled my mouth away. I decided to nibble its side instead. Like playing a flute. I was playing Hina. I put the head in my mouth and worked my tongue and teeth like it was the reed of a clarinet. My eyes shed sparks in response to his touch, and I sang out, "Oh, oh, no, oh, no!" I raised my body up and made Tsubasa lay face up. Hina looked down at me from above. Her eyes saw me as I really was. Not as some person shaped approximately like any other man, but as I was, a body that produced sound when wind blew through it, an existence so faint it seemed about to disappear, yet still persists: she caressed the real Tsubasa Tsutsui. Tsubasa, who held me as I was, who needed no terms or labels, not gay or lesbian, not man or woman, not any of the myriad other ways I could be categorized: Tsubasa held me, accepted the air penis that made me unlike anyone else, as if I was just another person, just like everyone else. Tsubame had entered my heart and together we'd taken flight, yet alone I'd crashed back down, I couldn't fly alone, but now I'd found Hina, who understood my vagina's wish to be opened, who made my spirit soar, and tenderness for this Hina gushed up from within me like oil from a well as our bodies of air fit together, melded, saturating me with happiness, and sadness too.

Tsubasa was getting wetter and wetter, and so, as I gazed into his eyes, I plunged my air penis into his air vagina.

Hina's still-swelling air penis continued to grow, and Tsubasa's newly opened vagina was still quite narrow, so they came quickly, releasing cries like rushes of wind from their mouths. Hina's voice sounded to Tsubasa like the cry of a raptor at the moment it fixes on its prey. Tsubasa's voice burned into Hina's ear like the squeal of a flute blown suddenly and too hard. As her air penis drove further and further into his air vagina, Tsubasa heard an unearthly wind blow through the conjoined hollowness they formed as the circuit between them closed, and his chest swelled with simple joy at the thought that the duet this wind carried might travel all the way to reach Tsubame's ears. As the air vagina engulfed the air penis, the heat melted their doubled flutes into each other and produced a dazzling brightness. Tsubasa grew completely transparent as Hina looked at him through the nearly blinding light, and to Tsubasa, Hina's entire body was transforming into one huge invisible penis.

As the two winds sounded their unbearably high-pitched notes in unison, their melting, liquid bodies vaporized completely, billowing out the window into the boundless sky outside to evaporate into thin air. A breeze blew through the empty room, ruffling the curtains as it passed. The first golden rays of the morning sun fell across the tatami-matted floor. Even now, the intermingled sounds of the dual wind continue to play their hoarse-throated "Air."

Sand Planet (2002)

*They say everything the sand touches turns to sand. I was proof
of that myself, long ago. I sat on that beach from dusk till dawn,
watching the sun sink, the stars glitter, listening to the sea's
song all through the night, and then, as the sun rose again to
shine down on me where I sat with my arms around my knees,
I transformed into a sculpture of sand myself. Waves lapped
at my hips, and bit by bit I crumbled, washed away into the
ocean. But even as the sea swallowed me and I became just so
many tiny grains, I never dissolved. I simply sank deeper and
deeper, thousands of meters deep, until I settled in a pile at the
bottom near a trench, and ever since, that's where I remain,
however many thousands of years may pass.*

*This is why deserts can only expand. Like an army of
tiny crabs rising from the water to mount an invasion deep
into the land, tiny grains of sand rise from the ocean floor
and march relentlessly from the shallows to the beaches, from
the beaches to the plains, from the plains to the mountains. If
all the lands of the world become deserts, the oceans won't
have a chance. Steady and inexorable as the flow through an
hourglass, every drop of water will eventually be replaced by
a grain of sand.*

*This dried-out planet is already made of nothing else:
sand continents, sand seas, sand skies. Only the shifting shapes
of the dunes mark time's passage. It passes but never progresses.
It just circles around and around the same spot. And watching the sand as it moves, listening to the sound it makes as the
wind carries it through the dunes: no one at all.*

Fight the sand. Before I die, bury me in the Arabian

Peninsula or the Sahara. Make a grave in the desert for all of the dying animals and people. If we bury the sand in bodies, now before it can overtake us, the organic matter will wet the sand as it rots. Bacteria will multiply, microbes will grow, feces will permeate the sand, soil will form. Now, before it's too late, put me on a plane, send me to Morocco. Make good use of my corpse.

Miyoshi Kawai (48), father of Yoshinobu (17), lay muttering like this to no one in particular, day and night, till he died. Yoshinobu had actually tried to get the terminal cancer patient onto a plane, but he could not overcome his greatest obstacle: his mother, Myōko (45). She insisted that they couldn't bury him in some unknown desert, but instead would inter him right there in the garden. Burned to ashes and shut up in an urn, their memories and feelings for him would fade, but buried raw and literally "returned to the earth," their memories, feelings, even his body would blossom into new life. Reassuring him like this, they convinced him to breathe his last on the tatami floor in his own house. Yoshinobu, his little sister, Bimyō (15), and their mother dug up the garden that night, stripped him bare, and buried him. Ten days later, after an investigation by police who had received complaints from the neighborhood about a dreadful stench, the three of them were arrested on suspicion of illegal disposal of a dead body.

This autobiographical story was the first manuscript Yoshinobu ever submitted as a newspaper reporter. Aside from rewriting his father's less intelligible utterances to make them more poetic, it was all true. After the investigation, Yoshinobu and Bimyō weren't prosecuted, but Myōko was sentenced to three months in prison and two years probation.

Of course, the paper never published it. Though Yoshinobu was a member of the Saitama Prefecture Police Press Corps, this was the only manuscript he'd submitted after two whole weeks there, and the Saitama bureau chief was taken aback. *Look, if you wanna write about an old story, it needs to be pegged to something in the present, and besides, it's got to sound like a real newspaper article. Maybe when you've got a little more experience, you can take it over to the local news section and submit it again.* And with this, he rejected the manuscript. Yoshinobu thought it made sense, so he quit his assignment at the police station, where he'd basically been a phone jockey anyway, and, following the example of his elder colleagues, began going directly to the cops and courthouse so he could submit some kind of article every day without fear of it being rejected.

Eventually, the bureau chief and the police chief at the station came to regard him as the most promising of the three in his cohort, and he was given free rein to gather information for a big-deal story just as an incident occurred at the Shirasagi Elementary School in Tokorozawa: an indiscriminate mass killing just like the poisoned curry incident in Wakayama a few years earlier. It took place at the height of the rainy season, so at first it was suspected to be food poisoning or E. coli O-157, but then aconite and oleander were detected in the udon noodles with meat sauce, and it was declared a homicide. Fifty-four people were hospitalized: three teachers, thirty-four sixth-graders, and seventeen fifth-graders. Of these, three sixth-grade boys and five sixth-grade girls died by the next day. The police questioned the children who regained consciousness. When a sixth-grader named Soejima heard the names of the eight who had died, he asked, *Is Yasuda still alive?* After the police confirmed that the girl named Yasuda hadn't eaten the school lunch and was unharmed, Soejima confessed that Yasuda headed an "association" that had committed the crime, which saved the skin of the criminal investigation division, who'd been unable till then to produce a single suspect. However, Yasuda refused to say a word to her interrogators, and they were forced to rely on Soejima completely to make their case. It remained unclear whether the association had members outside Yasuda's class or year, to say nothing of whether it had spread to other schools, nor was it clear how many of the eight who died had been members, and then Soejima's condition took a sudden turn for the worse and he passed away, paralyzing the investigation.

As a cub reporter, Yoshinobu was supposed to talk to the bereaved families and school officials, but he was aware that what he was really expected to do was to stay out of the way. They were refraining from interrogating the children and already had someone on-site at the scene of the crime, but since only the children knew the facts about the association, the mass media was using every resource at its disposal to dig up everything it could, and every story, no matter how specious, ended up treated like a major scoop.

First, Yoshinobu contacted a sixth-grader who worked on the school newspaper, and once he had painstakingly won him over, he made his proposal: *How would you like to write a real newspaper article? About how your friends are reacting to the incident, say, or the relationship between Yasuda and Soejima, or information about this 'association' . . . we'll publish any article you write for us, as is.* The boy agreed on condition of anonymity, but since he just brought in what was clearly a rehash of an old article by another paper, Yoshinobu didn't bother to inform the boy when he rejected it. A few days later, the boy's parents called to complain: *You've been poking around, harassing our child, and now he's so traumatized he can't get out of bed!* Yoshinobu denied it, of course, but since he couldn't tell the whole story, he was forced to apologize. The parents demanded that the paper condemn his behavior publicly by publishing an article detailing what he'd done wrong, and when the bureau chief refused, they took their complaint all the way to the Press Corps. The organization promptly called a general meeting to get the truth from Yoshinobu, and when he categorically denied it, it decided to reinstitute its strict ban on contacting or collecting information from children, declaring that in the event the ban was violated, the violator would be expelled from the

Corps. And, at least for the time being, the parents backed down too.

But Yoshinobu had yet to learn his lesson, and he sought out a student from a different school—one who attended the same cram school as some of the children who'd been members of the association—and he asked her to gather information for ¥5,000 a day, with an upfront payment of ¥10,000. Two days later, the girl, Minagawa, appeared at the appointed meeting place and handed back his ¥10,000 bill, saying, *All the kids at that school, whether they were members or not, knew there was poison in the school lunch that day, and they're really depressed because even though they all ate the meat sauce udon together, only nine people died. I don't know how I'm supposed to live out the rest of my life either after this failure.* Spurred on by thoughts that set his entire body aflame, he tried to write a column based on Minagawa's comments, but in the end he gave up; it seemed like lies slipped in no matter how he tried to write it. Shortly thereafter, the Press Corps learned that he'd contacted Minagawa and expelled him. But his bosses at the office couldn't care less about the Press Corps's rules—this was a major scoop, so they pressed Yoshinobu to hurry up and turn the information he'd gathered into an article. Yoshinobu, who hadn't submitted a single manuscript since the incident occurred, couldn't bear the pressure and finally fabricated a harmless story based on a made-up comment. When the story ran in the newspaper, they let him know quite frankly that they were disappointed in him, but Yoshinobu felt like he'd really accomplished something for the first time since he'd been hired.

After that, Yoshinobu turned into an incompetent reporter unable to get any material on his own, content to just hang around the Tokorozawa police station and the school that had no hope of ever reopening. When his body could no longer withstand the strain, he bought a used Corolla II and slept in it with the AC running full blast whenever he had time to spare. His colleagues stopped

asking him to do anything more than write hack articles about things like car accidents and city council announcements, and meetings at the bureau office had become torture for him, so he pretended he had some investigations to do that night and, instead of returning to the office to do galley proofs, drove out and parked his car in the middle of the street and just sat there, dazed.

When he took a vacation about three months later, it was because his mother had collapsed from a stroke. The investigation into the poison incident hadn't progressed at all: Yasuda had yet to let out a peep, while the other students were so unresponsive they seemed to have lost the power of speech entirely, so it was difficult just to fill the pages day after day, the prefectural edition in particular made up principally of articles seemingly diluted by many times their weight in water. So even though Yoshinobu, feeling useless, couldn't see how it would make a difference one way or the other, he nonetheless rushed to the hospital in Yokohama right away. His mother was a bookkeeper at a small food company, and on her way home from work she'd begun to feel poorly and had stopped by their family physician's clinic, where she collapsed. She'd talked to Yoshinobu on the cell phone the previous night, grumbling, "This late summer heat is terrible! I feel so sluggish," but Yoshinobu had been too burnt out himself to care about someone else's exhaustion, so he'd just made the appropriate "uh-huhs" until he could reach the end of the call. The doctor informed him that she might not make it, so he left his sister there with her that night so he could make the funeral arrangements with his mother's younger brother.

His mother breathed her last at dawn. Yoshinobu witnessed these last moments. She looked exactly the same, lying there as if still simply sleeping, but the gravitational pull of their relationship, the charged space between them, suddenly disappeared. *So this is how it feels when time stops*, he thought. He and his mother, the air and the

bed, everything existed separately, scattered and unrelated. Each was just another grain of sand. Slowly, time started up again, and the gravitational pull of the relationships between Yoshinobu and the things and people around him was restored, except that between him and his mother, who was gradually turning the color of wax. Yoshinobu thought that he'd like to continue watching her, just like this, till she rotted away into fluids and seeped into the ground.

His mother hadn't left a will, but Yoshinobu was positive she wanted to be buried. After the wake, during the all-night vigil in the room where her remains were resting, he put the question to his sister as they gazed together out into the garden: *Shall we bury her?*

I really don't want to cause trouble for Misaki, she demurred, referring to her boyfriend, who'd promised to live with her once he graduated from technical school. Yoshinobu nodded. *Well, at the very least let's put some dirt from the garden in the casket.*

All right, then, his sister agreed, but then she slipped away and left everything to Yoshinobu, saying she lacked the courage to peek inside the casket.

So it was Yoshinobu who opened the casket, removed the coolant, and stripped his mother of her white burial clothes. After that, he took some scented oil in the palm of his hand and spread it over her cold, hard skin. It began to shine, reflecting the light in the room like a mirror, and then he covered her body with layers of garden soil as if tucking her into bed.

Parts of his mother's ashy white body protruded from the soil like a species of rare mushroom. This soothed him, and he supposed that tomorrow, at the cremation ceremony, everyone would throw in flowers of every color and kind and it would look just like a flowerbed. At the very least, she could rot a little now and mix with the soil before the cremation, which should allow her to rest a bit easier.

Perhaps she'd been embalmed; whatever the case, she didn't rot, but even so, when the time came to open up the

coffin it really took him back to his father's burial incident, though, as one would expect, it caused a bit of a commotion among the guests. *Please, I've thought this through, many of you are aware that my mother devoted herself to ecology in her later years, putting her time and energy into creating a garden full of fertile soil for the good of the earth, and—this is something she talked to me about while she was puttering around in the garden—Mother wanted her eternal resting place to be in this very soil, and so I was just thinking I should obey her wishes . . .* Yoshinobu explained himself enough that, despite their bewilderment, everyone was sufficiently satisfied to throw in their flowers. The dirt-filled casket was heavy as a boulder.

The cremation finished, he picked the bones out of the scorched earth and opened the urn to divide some of the ashes into two pill cases, one of which he passed to his sister, burying the remaining ashes, bones, and dirt in the garden. He replaced the ashes in the urn with the ones he made by making a pile of fifty or so beloved travel albums and diaries dating from when his mother and father had crisscrossed the country, a sheaf of letters they found and left unread, a clipping of one of Yoshinobu's content-free newspaper articles, and a few eccentric hats his sister had made, then burning it all in the garden. Yoshinobu entrusted his sister with the task of watching over these remains until the forty-ninth night and returned to his apartment in Urawa. But Bimyō likely called Misaki to come stay with her from that night onward. Otherwise, she'd have probably simply fled.

There was one more day left in his vacation. He couldn't believe he'd have to be at work when morning came again. It seemed a distant memory that he had been a newspaperman at all. Time's flow seemed about to be diverted from the future and forced to eddy in the stultifying recent past. He'd heard there was some movement to reopen the school, so he figured he'd be reassigned to that beat along with the other reporters from the Tokorozawa

bureau. Whenever he wandered around the gray buildings of the school and the surrounding apartments, they
seemed somehow ill-dressed, as if wearing high-water
hand-me-downs, and he felt as though he wasn't a reporter
on assignment but a man getting lost in his own childhood,
on the verge of disappearing into an alley like a villain slipping away after a crime.

Once, as Yoshinobu found himself surrounded all day
by teachers as he collected information at the elementary
school, he found himself drawn almost against his will to
the pool, and he jumped in. Even though the prospects
for reopening the school seemed unlikely, the school had
filled the pool to the brim with clear water as if to say to
the children, *this is your place, you're welcome here whenever
you decide to return.*

Looking at this pool so unlikely to be used in the near
future yet full of water so sparklingly clear it almost hurt
to look at it, Yoshinobu was overcome with the absurdity of the whole situation, of pretending to be absorbed
in hanging on these teachers' and administrators' every
word, and he stole away into the pool area, stripped to his
underwear, and dove right in. He stayed underwater until
he could no longer hold his breath, and then drifted up
to the surface to float there, face-up, his body completely
relaxed. He closed his eyes to the sun's dazzling shine and
found himself engulfed in the sound of water, a light blue
horizon stretching behind his eyelids like an infinite desert.
Its surface was neither dune nor grassland nor the surface
of the sea, and it undulated unceasingly as the wind played
across it. Bobbing on this ultimate surface, Yoshinobu
gazed up at a shining, deep blue velvet sky with closed
eyes and everything seemed false. The surface may be blue
or green, the smell may be sea or grass, but he was sure that
whatever the case, it wasn't real water or real dirt, it was just
so much plastic buffeted by a fan. *I'm on a set somewhere,
surrounded by manufactured oceans, manufactured plains.
That's all nature actually is to me, just a series of sensations*

recreated in rooms. Even my own self is just a recreation, an illusion. Everything I touch and know to be myself is just the product of a brain that's no more than just another illusion itself. Not the grand illusion of life's endless cycle. This self of mine is no everlasting soul able to pass through cycles of reincarnation—it's the empty shell made and remade with every cycle, an infinite illusion.

Yoshinobu decided to take advantage of this last day he still had a future and drive his silvery blue Corolla II down a little road that wound its way along a stream near the edge of the Higashi Urawa green zone. Sun beat down on his right arm hot enough to fry it, and a CD of Andean music played on the stereo, the cries of the *quena* and the *zampoña* sounding less like flutes than birds. From time to time, the songs of the real birds outside would drift in through his open window as if to join in.

His arm was burnt red, so he came to a stop in a shady park at the edge of the woods. The cicadas called out *kana-kana-kana,* endless as an image reflected in facing mirrors. As if to challenge them, the birds also chirped noisily among themselves. Yoshinobu found himself seduced, and he stepped into the trees even though there was no path.

It was as if he'd stepped into the sound of the flutes he'd just been listening to. As his feet crunched through the thick mat of leaves and into the decaying loam beneath them, a cloud of black and white swallow-sized birds scattered into the sky like black sesame salt. He raised his eyes to watch them and continued walking, only to be hit in the face with the broad fronds of a fern that appeared suddenly before him. He heard the wind shake the trees, the branches rustle as birds landed on them, the squirrels and other little creatures as they skittered across the leafy ground. Suddenly, an old man brushed by Yoshinobu, wearing a reddish-brown wide-brimmed hat and similarly colored short-sleeved jacket. Reflexively, Yoshinobu gave a little bow in his direction. But the wizened old man, with his dark eyes and tearful expression, just continued on his way, his head down and muttering something to himself as he made his way into the forest.

The trees were getting thicker, the ground at his feet deeper in shadow. The cries of the cicadas dripped down and clung to Yoshibnobu like liquefied lard, while the noisome birdcalls scattered in all directions around him as the light bleeding through the leaves of the trees shape-shifted constantly. He had lost his way completely. Thinking that the best way to get out may be to follow the old man who'd just passed him by, he looked around, but the man had disappeared without a trace.

Yoshinobu sat down on nearby rock outcropping. He tried to be careful lest the moss covering it stain his khaki-colored chinos green. Overcome with exhaustion, he closed his eyes. He immediately felt surrounded. As if crowds pressed in on him from all sides. His body trembled.

Yoshinobu opened his eyes again. A hot, wet wind blew down from the sky obscured by the leaves above him, bathing him in its raw, vegetal scent. He imagined that he was sitting in the mouth of an enormous beast made of grass. It should have been cool here in the shade of the trees, but he was sweating. His underwear stuck to his skin, wet enough to wring out. Figuring that the sun might at least help evaporate the moisture, he got up again and started walking.

Eventually, he found a clearing roughly the size of four and a half tatami mats. The bright green of the short grass covering it dazzled him. He felt a drying breeze as well. Yoshinobu stripped down completely, wrung out his clothes and used some branches to hang them in the sun, and then lay down face-up on the ground. The sun squeezed the sweat from his body like a vise, but even though he felt in danger of dehydrating completely, he also felt a deep calm. Once all his sweat was drained, would his flesh begin to melt?

As if in preparation, his consciousness began to melt instead, and Yoshinobu started to drift off to sleep. His genitals, in turn, began to swell, extending up and out. Like an unfurling bean sprout, he thought, laughing to himself. If it sucked his melting flesh into itself and began to extend farther than it was supposed to, up and up until it peeked up above the trees, would it be visible from the city? A long, thin penis, waving in the wind like an enormous asparagus. Yoshinobu suddenly felt surrounded by people again. But his eyes were already too heavy in his sockets and he couldn't rouse himself to get up. He ended up sleeping there until the sun slid into shadow and his flesh grew solid once more.

Perhaps because he'd overslept in the afternoon, Yoshinobu couldn't sleep that night, and he felt like he was lugging himself around like a big bag of garbage. He had to return to work the next day, so he decided to look over the newspapers he'd allowed to pile up unread. As always, the main stories focused on the debate over whether to reopen the elementary school and he could probably have read the articles just as well with his eyes closed. And indeed, their authors may well have written them with their eyes closed as well. Yoshinobu had yet to fully learn the "blind touch" possessed by the highest tier of journalists.

But when he began reading the Society section of the *Saitama Daily*, he came across a series of special reports that opened his eyes at last. The reports told of a community of homeless people living in the forests along the outskirts of the city. Street people wanting to escape contact with others seem to have moved out into hard-to-reach areas like the grassy plains along the banks of the Arakawa River, the Minuma Wetlands near Higashi Urawa, or the Sayama Hills behind Tokorozawa, building makeshift barracks and tent-cities in increasing numbers. Ironically, these green zones are also places rife with illegal dumping, and it's from this garbage that the homeless derive the resources to support their lifestyles, reusing some things for themselves and selling others to make a little money, and since they're helping ameliorate the illegal dumping problem, the city authorities turn a blind eye to the squatting. In places where the homeless "immigrated" comparatively long ago, they've established small villages, and though they avoid too much invasion into each others' business, they nonetheless obey an unspoken code of conduct and a minimal system of mutual aid, thereby equipping them with the means to respond to threats from the outside. The number of foreign workers among them is relatively small, but they nonetheless pop up here and there; the article quoted a man named Abdullah (a pseudonym), who came from Pakistan to earn money to send home until his body gave out and he lost his job, after which he could no longer show his face in his community and he ended up drifting into the forest: "I gave up my home, I gave up Japan, and I immigrated to the Totoro Forest. I threw my passport away."

Early the next morning, Yoshinobu capped off his all-nighter by filling a thermos with dark, fresh-ground coffee and making a sandwich of hardboiled eggs minced with onions, and then he headed back to the Higashi Urawa green zone.

The morning light fell like lace curtains. Yoshinobu traveled down the little road along the stream, its banks lined with illegally dumped garbage, as if passing through them one by one, and soon he ended up at a small municipal park. Just as he suspected, he found a homeless man starting the day by washing his face in one of the public restrooms. Yoshinobu decided to follow him, though from a safe distance.

The cicadas began to sing. The man carried four full plastic water bottles, two in each hand, and placed two of them in the little building that stood like a checkpoint at the head of the trail into the woods as he passed it.

The man's blue tarp tent was located a just a bit farther into the trees. Just before he entered the tent, Yoshinobu called out, *Hey, I need some directions, can you help me?* The man turned to look at him, and so he asked, *Can you tell me the way to Abdullah's residence?* The man swallowed his laughter like a yawn and said, *Why don't you look up his address?* And when Yoshinobu, shocked, exclaimed, *You have addresses?* he played along, saying, *Yeah, that might be a good idea, we can put numbers on the trees and stick mail-boxes all over.* Yoshinobu pointed into the trees and asked, *Maybe over there could be Roppongi?* And he sat down near to the man's tent. He brought his egg sandwich out of his bag and set it on his knee. *I'm going to have breakfast now, do you want to join me?* he said in a low voice, holding out part of his sandwich. The man grew irritated and refused, but when the fragrant fresh-brewed coffee was offered to him, he accepted.

You really don't know Abdullah? He's from Pakistan.

I don't know any foreigners.

Aren't there some around here?

You sure you didn't see a ghost? There're a lot of those around.

Really? You see them?

Occasionally. I drink at night with someone and fall asleep, and when I wake up, poof! No one's there. Maybe I was just drunk, who knows. The man laughed to himself.

Are there areas famous for suicides around here?

Suicides? There's suicide and then there's suicide, you know. If you can't work and you're body's falling apart and you spend all your time drinking and you fall asleep somewhere and end up dead, that's suicide too, now isn't it?

That happens a lot?

It happens. People die but they've got no home, no one does, so you come back as a spirit and end up drinking with someone by mistake. I'm a new guy here, I'm still out on the edge doing this checkpoint job, that's as far in as I can live for now, but you hear stories about the people farther inside. This forest used to be a lot thinner, but more and more people died in there and the soil grew rich and the forest got thick like this, I hear the dead come back and mix with the living folks in there. I've never been, but it sounds pretty fun.

Can I ask a question? It's okay to tell me I'm being disrespectful. It's just, I've heard that the people who've come here to live are hard to get a long with, they don't like people. Is that true?

Who'd you hear that from?

A friend of Abdullah's.

Who are you? The man's voice became expressionless, as if he was getting tired of talking.

I'm a friend of Abdullah.

You know, sometimes people come by here looking to arrest illegal aliens.

I'm just a student, said Yoshinobu, producing an old university ID card. *I had a part time job as a bag boy, I got to know Abdullah there.*

Is that so? Well, I still haven't seen any foreigners.

I'll take a look around. You say you've never gone farther in?

NO FIRE! The man yelled, grabbing the cigarette Yoshinobu had just lit and crushing the ember between his fingers. *No fire! It's forbidden in the forest. If a fire started in here, everyone would die.*

How was that decided? Did you all discuss it among yourselves? How do you let new people know?

Everyone knows without having to "decide" it. Think about what you'd fear most if all you had taking care of you was you. So no fire. You can walk around here all you want, but don't smoke. I don't know what'd happen if someone found you out here with flame.

Yoshinobu thanked the man and left him and his tent behind. It was nine-thirty. Still, he hadn't gathered enough information to make an article. After walking about ten minutes away from the tent, he pulled out his cell phone and called in to work. No one was manning the desk yet, so he ended up talking directly to the bureau chief: *I've been out since this morning following up on an appointment I had made for a story about urban life, so I'll go to the Police Press Corps meeting this afternoon directly from here.* He then put a call in to the Press Corps office to make sure no major incidents or accidents had occurred, and then, turning off his phone, Yoshinobu headed into the depths of the forest.

The intensity of the light was different from the day before, but the scenery was much the same. The trees and the soil seemed to sweat, giving off a rich odor. The atmosphere blazed hot enough to exude oil on the verge of being set aflame by the cicadas' cries, while little birds chirped like falling water. Yoshinobu walked and walked, sweat dripping from his jaw, but he failed to find any tents or makeshift huts dug out by the homeless. There seemed to be no people at all. From time to time, he encountered a terrible stench and, following it, would find a clearing where the trees were a bit sparse and a hole had been dug and filled with a bunch of unidentifiable garbage. It didn't always seem to be organic matter that was buried, but still, the sharp scent would remind him enough of how it smelled when he buried his father in the garden all those years ago that it made him wonder if corpses were hidden in the bottoms of these holes as well. *Were the bodies of the homeless piling up, higher and higher?* The metallic buzz of the cicadas and flies that filled these sunny clearings drilled fissures into Yoshinobu's skull as he wandered, hallucinating corpses.

After stumbling upon however many of these garbage pits, Yoshinobu's headache became so unbearable that he sought refuge in the hollow of a huge tree that towered in the deepest, shadiest part of the forest, but no sooner had he sat down than he heard a shrill, ragged voice somewhere nearby. He crept toward it and, peeking from behind a tree, found that he had returned to the clearing where he'd fallen asleep the day before, and that the old man in the reddish-brown wide-brimmed hat was standing there alone, his withered body stripped to the waist, waving his arms as he held an animated conversation with some unseen interlocutor. **Upon awakening at the dawn of the first morn, I look around and all before me is**

snow—how can there be snowfall in these tropical climes, I cry! And following this preamble, the old man launched into song:

> **Oh, the snow's a-falling!**
> **Little stones a-falling!**
> **Dig dig dig! Dig dig dig!**
> **You can't dig out!**

> I've never seen snow back where I was born, so to see it now, here on the earth's backside, well . . .
> *You know, there is some snow that, no matter how hot it gets, never melts.*

(The old man changes his voice for this line).

> You mean this snow's not cold?

(The old man touches his finger to the ground).

> *You see, it's salty! This is salt! Salt blown here by the wind!*

(The old man mimes licking his finger, and uses the other voice for this line).

> What is this? The ground is sown with salt and rock, nothing can grow!
> *Yes, that's the way it is here for the Sons of the Earth's Backside!*

(As he says this, the old man turns to where the audience would be sitting and stands stock-still, snapping to attention).

> **Take a ride on the Dominican turtle,**
> **And end up in the Palace of the Dragon King,**
> **The premier neighborhood in Hell!**

> Here, where the wind blows only hot, the only crops are stones, and the only dust is salt, people disappear like thinning hair, one after another: three people arrive and four pass on, five sicken and six die, seven are born and eight expire, until there's no one left but me, Urashima Tarō, the last Son of the Earth's Backside.

How long has it been now, I wonder? Once I was left all alone, I stopped being able to tell if I were alive or dead. How long before I become just so much fertilizer amid these stones?

Living here, so many miles from my nation,
In this far-off República Dominicana
Bathed in the sunset's red illumination,
I lie lower than the stones that mark the fields.

And so Urashima Tarō of the Earth's Backside sat murmuring to himself when, wouldn't you know, there came a voice! *Don't worry, dear Tarō*, it said. It was the voice of the Dominican Turtle who had brought Urashima Tarō here to the Earth's Backside. A giant clock hung from the Dominican Turtle's neck, the hands on its face moving backward with each tick.
Look, Tarō, I'll return you to where you began! You can start over, in a different world!
So saying, the Dominican Turtle put Urashima Tarō on his back and started off on the road toward the mountains.
(The old man tromps around the clearing)
And wouldn't you know it, when they reached the village, there were his friends who had tilled the salted earth with him, and they were cheerful and youthful as they came out to welcome Urashima Tarō home. All around, water sprung from the earth and jade-green foliage grew, and Urashima Tarō thought he must have been brought to the Kingdom of the Dead.
No, no, dear Tarō! This too is a neighborhood in Hell, but we decided to work together to dig wells and channel rivers, and now see our robust harvest! We entreated Mister Turtle to run his clock faster for us so we could complete our task, and it ended up taking a hundred and fifty years!

Ahh, so a hundred and fifty years is how long it takes for stones to turn to fertilizer!

No, no, we tilled the soil with the dead.

At this, Urashima Tarō and the villagers thought back to when they were brought to this strange land, deceived by promises that they would become "Plantation Owners in Paradise"; they remembered all the years and years that had to pass before this land of salt and stone could become a place to make a home. (The old man mimes tears)

It hurts to think it's been so long,
All those months passing into years—
This moment is the turning point,
We bid farewell at last, in tears.

Urashima Tarō of the Earth's Backside found himself surrounded by these natives with their various shades of skin and lived among them happily, if humbly, but not a day went by that he didn't think of his family back home: his mother, his father, his older brother, his younger sister.

So much time has passed, there's no way any of them could still be alive! With no letters from me to them or them to me, surely I've been forgotten!

The sickness in Urashima Tarō's heart soon spread to all the other villagers. Everyone grew melancholy and disconsolate, singing old songs together until their throats gave out, drawing pictures and telling stories of the sea and sky and forests of their homeland, unable to stop regaling visitors with one timeworn tale after another. Some told so many of these stories that they began to believe that they had never left their homeland and it was the Dominican Republic that was a dream.

Urashima Tarō of the Earth's Backside became convinced that all of this was a sign that he should let go of his past for good so he could live peacefully in the present, and he decided to revisit his homeland one last time.

Turtle, O Turtle!
Please, Mister Turtle!
Take me back to my home on the far side of the Earth,
If only once more before I die,
Please, Mister Turtle, please!

And the Dominican Turtle gave his answer,

O silly rabbit, you are mistaken!
Your home is here, beneath your feet!
It's no easy thing to return somewhere
Once you've been forsaken!

But Urashima Tarō of the Earth's Backside refused to back down.

This dream I see is almost my reality
But still I can't forget the land from whence I came.

Leaving was easy, returning terrifies me,
Terrifies me, yet still I must go, let me go!

You are sure you must?
I am sure, let me go, I must go! Nothing could terrify me more than this ache in my breast.

And so he left, flying the flag of his homeland made from cotton he'd spun with a song in his heart to signal his triumphant return; but, alas, too much time had passed, for a single second hand's tick on the clock of the Turtle was a year in the life of those back home, and so, unbeknownst to him, so many, many years had passed that he could never return to his mother and father, he no longer shared a language with his brothers and sisters, it was as if he had never seen this city before, it had become a maze into which if he stepped a single step he'd never be able to escape.

It was just as the Dominican Turtle had told him, this land had prospered even as it'd forsaken its best and brightest, and so he vowed to return to the island where these best and brightest now resided; and yet, alas, the ache in his breast remained.

And so it was that the ache that plagued the breast of Urashima Tarō of the Earth's Backside was incurable, and as he set off on his journey back to the warm, emerald green island, it spread throughout his whole body. Perhaps my entire life, beginning to end, has been a waste, he worried, and as he worried, he grew thin and wan and sorrowful, and he dreamed and dreamed, dreaming so many, many dreams that when he finally awoke again he found himself lying once more on the tiny tatami mat where he'd passed the first days of his life. And peering down at him, could it be? His younger sister, Yayoi, now so old?

(The old man lies down on the ground)

Ah, Brother, you're awake at last! Do you know who I am?

(The old man says this in falsetto)

I think I do! You're Yayoi, my sister! What happened, have I been dreaming all this time?

You've reached the end of your life, my brother.

But I haven't done anything with it! I still have so much I want to do, for the good of the world, for the good of mankind!

You flew your flag in the Dominican Republic, my brother. Look!

And with this, Yayoi showed him a piece of pure red cloth. Indeed, it was the very flag Urashima Tarō of the Earth's Backside had brought with him from the island to present to his mother and father, a flag of Japan dyed so red the sun in the center disappeared completely. Yayoi had kept it from the authorities like a secret, and now she wrapped Urashima Tarō's body in this red flag with the red sun in its center and cremated him, burying the ashes and bones in forestland owned by her husband, and so it came to be that even now Urashima Tarō of the Earth's Backside continues to dream his dream of the República Dominicana.

For all eternity may this world be thine,
O Forsaken of the Earth, till pebbles now
Into mighty rocks shall grow
Whose venerable sides moss doth line!

With that, the old man bowed deeply to his unseen audience, and Yoshinobu erupted into enthusiastic applause. The old man's eyes boggled and his expression suddenly shifted, seeming on the verge of terrified tears, and, shrinking protectively into himself, he scampered like a rabbit into the forest. Yoshinobu gave chase, shouting, *Wait! I just want to talk to you!,* but the forest gave up no further sound.

It was two days later that Yoshinobu drove off to Takazaki so he could pay a visit to the owner of the forest. He'd obtained the bureau chief's blessing to pursue the story the previous day. *I'm planning on tying the homeless issue to the illegal dumping problem, so I'd like it to be placed under the jurisdiction of the Saitama Municipal Government bureau; if all goes well, I'm thinking of writing a series of special reports under the title, "The Transient Totoros of the Urawa Forest,"* explained Yoshinobu. *If all goes well or nothing goes well, you're spending time on this thing so you better come up with an article in the end, got it?* The bureau chief was reading a weekly scandal sheet with his feet propped up on his desk as he said this. *At any rate, it's better to get something out of it than nothing, so if you submit an article, make sure you also submit a request to cover expenses—and feel free to pad it out a bit, too, okay? I don't want you to turn into one of the losers around here.*

*I bet you'd call the people I'm researching "losers,"
too, asshole.* But Yoshinobu refrained from speaking his
thoughts aloud and, declining the chief's offer to join him
for lunch, he set off instead to Saitama City Hall. After
completing the paperwork to join the Saitama Municipal
Government Press Corps, he introduced himself to the
bureau chief there and, as he ate his lunch, finagled an
introduction to Hisada, a city councilmember who was
heading up the movement to preserve the green zones in
the Higashi Urawa–Minuma Wetlands region; that night,
they went out drinking together, and Hisada confessed,
You know, I don't really understand what that Saitama
Daily *article was talking about. I mean, it's true that there
are some homeless people living in the park along the stream,
and it's true that some of them live off what they pick up out
of the garbage that's dumped out there, but I've never heard of
anyone actually making a home inside the forest.*

I've seen some.

*The people you saw were probably just poking around
the areas where garbage gets dumped, if there were anyone
actually living out there, they'd have been rousted out by the
security we have patrolling the woods.*

A liberal municipal body would do such a thing?
Yoshinobu asked, taken aback, and Hisada chuckled ruefully. *It's quite a headache for us, that. We get attacked all the
time by advocates for the homeless accusing us of protecting
trees at the expense of people. But symbiosis is just a dream—
if a bunch of people started living in a small wooded area
like that, the balance of the ecosystem would be destroyed. A
person can always move on and live somewhere else, but a
tree is rooted to the spot, it can't move once it starts growing
somewhere, so the best we can do is ask people to refrain from
crowding in on what's already established. It's not an ade-
quate replacement, of course, but we do hand out food and
donated clothes and blankets almost every day in the park.*

Yoshinobu mulled this over. Nature conservationists
pour all their efforts into protecting trees, and advocates for

the homeless pour all their efforts into protecting people, so it's natural that these green zones and forests would become the frontlines of a conflict between the two. And he began to mutter to himself. *Everything the sand touches turns to sand. Anything that's part of a group tries to turn what it touches into a part of itself. Into a part of its brain. Bury the corpses in the forest. Die in the forest and come back as a tree.*

The conservation group Hisada represented had been buying the Minuma Wetlands piece by piece to place it in a "green trust," but the Higashi Urawa forest had an owner from long ago who was willing to cooperate with them. Yoshinobu said that he wanted to meet this owner, and Hisada gave him the contact information.

The person with the surname Sakai who came out to meet Yoshinobu when he arrived was an old woman, just shy of her seventieth birthday. Hisada had told him that the current owner was the widow of the original proprietor, but when Yoshinobu offered his business card with a formal *Call me Mr. Kawai*, the reply that reached his ears still dizzied him: *And you can call me Yayoi Sakai.*

Do you get to visit the forest often?

Oh no, I'm afraid I leave it all to Mr. Hisada these days. I visit maybe once a year.

It's a lovely forest, isn't it?

It truly is, there's a certain mystical quality to it.

Does it have a long history?

She began to talk about a shrine that used to be there, how the only son of the man who ran it had been just a baby when he died, so the shrine ending up disappearing, and after a bit, Yoshinobu changed the subject, asking, *Do you have any siblings, Ms. Sakai?* And Yayoi grew quiet and nodded, asking softly, *Have you been in the forest yourself, Mr. Newspaperman?*

Do you have something to tell me?

Are you going to put this in your article?

You don't want me to? If I've offended you in any way . . .

Yayoi waved her hand impatiently. *Just conceal my name, and if you say that that would compromise your journalism, then so be it. But everything else I leave up to you, Mr. Newspaperman.*

I'll make my decision after I hear what you have to tell me.

That forest is a grave. My brother's.

It is? Your brother passed away?

I think you already knew he had, Mr. Newspaperman. Please continue.

What I'm about to tell you, I don't know how much of it's true or just made up. I didn't hear it directly from Misao, my brother. I pieced it together from things I heard from the people I met who were involved with the case brought by those who'd been duped into immigrating to the Dominican Republic. I hear Misao wanted to join them in the struggle, but he was too late. It would have been something if he had, though, that's for sure. He was stubborn through and through, with a firm sense of right and wrong; he always had a hard time getting along with others or compromising, and he was shy, too, I hear he kept to himself even over there among the other immigrants.

You know, that temperament of his was part of the reason he emigrated in the first place. After the war ended, he was troubled, he tried school but it never seemed to work out, and he just ended up hanging around the house; if he encountered anything pure or idealistic he would get all wrapped up in it, make all these plans in his head. He'd tried becoming a productive member of society, but it hadn't worked out, which made him ripe to get sucked into some revolutionary movement or other, and so our father signed him up when the government began advertising for people to go and settle in the Dominican Republic. I think Misao was twenty-five or six at the time. Mother and Father somehow got their hands on some stock to give him; he took it with a dark look on his face, and he hardly said a word to us from then till it was time to leave. Thinking back on it now, it must have seemed to him like they were paying him off so they could cut their ties for good. He must have gone along with it because he felt he had no other choice. Happily, we were told that the Dominican Republic was a lovely tropical nation where it was easy to grow crops, and he was going to receive a plantation with huge fields and a spacious house when he got there, and they told us he'd even receive a stipend for the first three years to get him started on the right track, so we figured Misao was finally going places, you know, he was our brother so we wanted to look on the bright side of his situation.

But when he arrived, that wasn't how it was. The land he received was a third of what he'd been promised, and the ground was so white with salt it looked like snow under the morning sun. When he tried to till the soil, it was just rocks, and it seemed impossible that anyone would look at it and think it could be made into farmland. The house was just a rough-hewn little hut dug into the ground, and no rain ever fell to cool the air, making it impossible to sleep. There was nothing to eat, and I hear it was the children who began to die first.

It became unbearable before long for the immigrants, so they went to the consulate, asking them again and again to deliver on what they'd promised, but the consulate reminded the immigrants that as representatives of His August Presence, ambassadors were one degree from being angels—did they really want to sully the ears of a Son of Heaven with their pitiful pleading? You should learn shame, they were told. You should learn forbearance and fortitude, there's no soil that can't be turned to farmland with the diligent application of fertilizer, no matter how salty or stony it may be, and besides, no true Son of Japan would give up before attempting to smash the very stones into arable earth! And so their protests fell on deaf ears. I can just imagine what happened when Misao heard what they said. I'm sure he tried harder than ever, worked and worked and worked to turn every stone and every grain of salt to soil and make it the richest, most fertile land in all the world. I hear that even as those around him fell ill or abandoned their plots and left, he would be out there trying to break the stones into soil with his pickaxe, wash the salt away with water he would walk miles to get from the nearest well, sacrificing his body to this solitary battle with the earth. But for all his effort, none of the vegetables or fruit he grew ever got bigger than a little boy's wee-wee, and so the de facto leader of the immigrants looked at Misao killing himself in the fields and decided to move him to a plot that was at least comparatively more farmable, if only to remove his piteousness from view.

But even so, none of the land the immigrants were given to divide among themselves was good for much of anything, and the majority of them refused to give up, so all the immigrants ended up trying to make their living in the two or three areas of comparatively tolerable farmland. Naturally, there wasn't nearly enough to go around, and Misao, saying that he couldn't abide taking land away from anyone else, ended up becoming a tenant farmer on one of the large plantations owned by the Dominicans. Several of the immigrants reached out to him, saying that tenant farming like that was tantamount to voluntary slavery, but Misao refused their offers to work for them on their land, asking them how they could just cheerfully work on land that had been bilked from the natives by foreign swindlers and their accomplices? *I won't be a part of any more evildoings*, he said, blunt as always. Some of the immigrants who were having the roughest go of it decided to band together and go back to Japan, and they invited Misao to join them, but he was just as blunt to them: *What, you didn't die like you were supposed to on this barren mountain they dumped you on, so you want to go back and be kept like a pet till you finally do? Don't play the patriot with me!* And on and on he went, spitting on the land of his ancestors until the Japanese immigrant community shunned him too.

It was around that time that Misao started going into the forest. In the mornings and evenings, he'd just disappear from the village. One day, the wife of a Haitian tenant farmer Misao was friends with wandered into the woods to pick some wild fruit—mangoes, maybe? papayas?—and she ran across Misao in a clearing way back in the trees, yelling and singing. The tenant farmer, hearing his wife's story, became concerned, thinking that maybe Misao was performing some sort of dark ritual in there, so he entreated another Japanese immigrant to go with him to investigate; they sneaked together into the woods and tried to spy on him, but Misao sensed they were there right away and stopped performing his one-man show right then, dashing nimbly into the trees like some kind of lizard or squirrel or rabbit. And after that, Misao was never seen except when he worked the fields during the day, but his hoarse shouting could be heard emanating from the depths of the forest like the cries of some terrible bird. Some in the area would joke that it was like High Mass, except it was just High Misao.

And so the years passed with no word from him, and Father died, and then Mother, and finally my eldest brother decided that even if it was just an empty gesture, we had to try and include him in the division of the assets, so he sent a telegram to the island requesting that Misao come back at least for a little bit. We were shocked when a reply came back right away saying he was on his way and two or three days later he showed up on an airplane. And we were also shocked by his appearance—he was barely sixty, I think, but he looked like a frail, wizened old man. His hair was pure white and the skin of his face and hands was like wrinkled leather—he looked like a different person altogether. At first he stayed with my brother out in Sakado, but he left there before long, claiming that he couldn't talk to him, that no matter what he tried to say nothing got through, and so he ended up staying with me after I explained the situation to my husband. When I asked him what he and our brother were fighting about,

Misao explained that he wanted to display a flag he'd brought with him at our parents' gravesite, but our brother wouldn't allow it, and he showed me this piece of red cloth he had. It was a Japanese flag that had been dyed so the white was red too. You know, like the song? "For the flag we fight! Till the red obscures the white!" He'd actually done it. I can't tell you how disturbing it was to look at. I shuddered and asked him why he wanted to do such a thing, and he said, *This flag represents my life, everything our parents did to me is all right there, and I wanted them to accept responsibility but I'm too late, they died on me, so I thought at least I could present it to their graves, but no matter how I try to explain it to my brother in this country's goddamn language, nothing gets through.*

It was the same when we tried to talk about the inheritance. *I don't need anything from them but an apology, and since they're gone I'll take one from you all, I want you to apologize to me, just a word saying sorry for banishing me like that.* We told him that we hadn't banished anyone anywhere and were glad to be reunited with him, that we could figure out somewhere for him to live as part of the inheritance discussion so we could live together as brothers and sisters again, but Misao, he'd have none of it. *You're just like the government go-betweens, everything you say is lies, if you had any integrity you'd own up to what happened and offer me a word of apology, just one word!* He was screaming at us in his shaky, high-pitched voice. I started crying then and said I was sorry, but our brother wouldn't budge, saying, *Misao, quit it with these mean-spirited accusations. Even if our parents are guilty of banishing you, it was because they felt they had no choice, and your sister and I were just children then, how could we stop them? I think everyone here understands how hard you've had it, so please, control yourself.* And Misao muttered, *Once you've been separated longer than you've been together, I guess even family become strangers,* and refused to speak to us at all after that. He left for the Dominican Republic before the inheritance was even completely settled, and none of us made much effort to get him to stay. As it was, it seemed better that he just go back, for his sake as much as ours. My foolish brothers, it would have been better if either of them had been a little better at forgiveness. Though I ended up convinced that Misao would return again someday just because he left that red flag at my house, so I guess I was pretty foolish too.

It was three years ago that the advocacy group for the Dominican immigrants came to Japan to file their suit. We'd been contacted by some of the immigrants themselves previous to that, informing us that Misao had passed on five years before but they hadn't known how to get a hold of any of us, so it took a while to track us down. They explained that they had cremated him and made a grave back in the Dominican Republic, but they had also saved a part of his remains to bring back to Japan, which they kindly gave to us along with some of his effects, a notebook and a cassette tape. They explained that he'd disappeared completely after he returned from Japan and that they only knew what became of him because the Japanese Immigrant Cooperative was contacted by a nursing home in Santo Domingo that an old man of Japanese descent had died there and they went to investigate. I felt so bad, I wrapped his remains in that red flag with the red sun in its center and burned them as I listened to the tape, and then I scattered the ashes in the forest. I don't suppose Misao minded that overmuch, at least.

I'm sorry, can we stop? I'm exhausted. If there's anything else you want to ask, I'll be glad to answer your questions if you visit me again some other day, but I'm not sure what more I have to tell you, said Yayoi, ending the interview, so Yoshinobu returned to his car and tried playing the tape she'd handed him on the stereo. It turned out to be a recording of the one-man show Yoshinobu had seen in the forest. But there were parts inserted here and there that Yoshinobu hadn't witnessed.

For example, when Urashima Tarō of the Earth's Backside is abandoned alone in the fields of salt, muttering vaguely that he stopped being able to tell if he was alive or dead, a figure rises from the ground like a heat shimmer, taking the form of a goddess who looks just like a bodhisattva, and she admonishes Tarō thusly:

> **This forest, this island, this world: how many bodies have come to rest within them since dawn of human history? Thy feet rest upon land formed from the bodies of hundreds, millions, trillions of people who now exist as soil. It may be said that all that ye call land is merely corpses, people and cattle, fish and fowl and all the myriad creatures of the world piling up as they expire, year after year after year. Taketh the soil in thy hand: the mud that stains thy fingers once was living flesh. This world is a world of corpses. Ye living struggle and squirm but briefly amid the nooks and crannies of its cadaver-strewn surface. Ye may gain vitality by feeding on the dead, grow strong and energetic. But ye must never grow arrogant. Take heed.**
>
> *And as this salt-statue goddess rising from the field spoke to Urashima Tarō of the Earth's Backside, tears flowed from her eyes that melted her away until she sank back down completely, salting the earth once more.*

Later, during the part when Urashima Tarō of the Earth's Backside misses his absent mother and father, there is a section where he can't stop going over and over the words they spoke, dwelling on every little part of how it was back home. Before long, this imaginary hometown is more vivid than the Dominican scenery in front of him, and before he knows it, his father appears in his hut and joins the action:

> *And what's this? My father has curled his fingers and pulled a finely folded Japanese flag through them and look! Now it's red, all red, so red it's dripping!*

Speak of this to no one. My words are only for you, Tarō. Lock them in your heart, let your actions show the world what I teach you. If you speak the words I teach you aloud, people may understand them but they will never penetrate their hearts, not all the way. This is how it is with the human mind. You must never simply believe the words people say, and you should never tell anyone anything that's only words.

Misao never performed his one-man show for anyone else. He kept it to himself, "locked in his heart," performing it again and again with only himself as audience. Did this tape contain the story he needed to tell so badly, yet couldn't bear to?

Yoshinobu shivered as he brushed against the enormity of such loneliness. The loneliness of words that wanted so badly to be said but refused so violently to be told.

Yoshinobu thought Misao was like the founder of a religion who rejected religion. He was too aware of how small a part of the universe he represented to do such a thing. He couldn't bear to force himself on others, it was too obscene. He couldn't abide the universal principle by which every story requires another's suppression to be told.

Misao rejected the logic of overthrow. He longed to effect change but he refused to overturn the world through struggle against others. Leaving behind words he'd never asserted or even said to anyone else, he attempted to articulate his world in its entirety, banishing nothing, no one.

The notebook, worm-eaten and ink-smudged, contained drafts of letters and tables tallying harvest yields, columns of sale prices and profits. The letter drafts consisted of scribbled sentences like *I'm doing fine, as always*; *Here's hoping you get a chance to visit soon!*; *My sincerest condolences*; at one point, a double strikethrough attempted to obliterate the line *Why can no one understand my pain?*

Misao didn't seem dead to Yoshinobu. He could always visit the forest and see him again. They were stuck in a stage where they kept bumping into each other without really connecting, but soon the time would come when they'd have a chance to exchange words, to really get to know each other. *He's not a stranger to me, that's why I understand him*, thought Yoshinobu. And besides, strictly speaking, Yayoi never actually saw Misao's body, so there was no proof he was really dead. He should try to contact the members of that Japanese immigrant group who told Yayoi that Misao had died, maybe go to the Dominican Republic himself, see the grave they all pitched in to build for him: that would be perfect. In any case, Yoshinobu decided to pursue the issue as far as he could. And so he began commuting regularly to Higashi Urawa, gathering material about Japanese immigrants in the Dominican Republic on the one hand and hoping to get a chance to see Misao perform his one-man show one more time on the other.

His work was interrupted by the news of five sixth-graders from Shirasagi Elementary who'd gone missing and were discovered five days later, weakened and prone, in the woods of the Sayama Hills, and there was apparently a bit of turmoil regarding their being taken into protective custody. It was a homeless person living there who'd found them. *You've been doing something with those free-range homeless people, right?* said the bureau chief when Yoshinobu showed his face. *Well, here's your big break! Write, write, write! A hundred lines, two hundred, whatever, just give me something.*

Yoshinobu poked around the area amid the masses of other reporters, and after filing his impressions of the investigation's basic outline and the physical features and general atmosphere in the area with the Tokorozawa bureau reporter assigned to the police station, Yoshinobu wrangled an introduction out of Hisada that landed him a visit to the office of an NGO concerned with protecting the Sayama Hills area, where he received a lecture about the situation of the homeless in the Hills from an assistant professor who moonlighted as the NGO's representative. And so, after making a map of all the places where the homeless population was concentrated and some of the animal trails and footpaths in the area, Yoshinobu entered the forest just after nine that evening, armed with a flashlight and some whiskey.

Compared to the small copse of trees at Higashi Urawa, Sayama Hills was exceptionally large and dense. The new moon plunged the area within the trees into a darkness so total it was like a bottomless bog. Every step he took terrified him, as though he were always on the verge of stumbling into deep black water. Turning on the flashlight only illuminated his immediate surroundings and disquieted him more, so Yoshinobu closed his eyes instead and tried to sharpen his hearing and sense of touch so he could grasp the shape of the darkness. The cries of the insects outlined the terrain's hills and hollows. Small nocturnal creatures made sounds signaling the whereabouts of the trees. Open areas were indicated by the pronounced concentration of life he sensed in them. *Was there a sea of souls spreading out endlessly all around us all the time, invisible to the naked eye?* Belonging neither to the world of the living nor the dead, this sea of souls pressed in on Yoshinobu, forming a current that flowed, ghostlike, around him. Yoshinobu gave himself over to its flow and made his way forward.

From time to time, the smell of rotting organic matter other than soil and grass would waft toward him, which usually meant that he'd discovered an area inhabited by the homeless. Whenever this happened, Yoshinobu would call out, pass some whiskey around to whoever responded, and ask questions. *Have you happened to see any elementary school kids wandering around? Do you know of any kids living here?*

And so he ended up interviewing school officials in the daytime and wandering the wooded Hills at night, arriving as soon as the sun went down. The children were released from the hospital after three days, but they refused to say a single word to anyone: not to the doctors at the hospital, not to the people who had searched for them, not even to their parents; so it remained unclear how they spent those five days away from home, why they left, or what connection it may have had with the poisoning. The school officials reported that not only the five runaways, but increasing numbers of the general population of schoolchildren at Shirasagi Elementary had stopped speaking as well, particularly sixth-graders, leading the school counselor to diagnose them with Post-Traumatic Stress Disorder. This was a big part of the reason why the school had yet to resume classes after the summer break.

Five days after he'd begun his nightly wanderings, Yoshinobu ran across a homeless woman, who, while not the one credited with finding the five missing children, had nonetheless let them stay with her for a night. He'd known of her existence from things the other homeless people living in the area had told him, but he hadn't been able to find her. She displayed an unusual wariness at first, refusing to answer him and frustrating any attempts to get to know her until he handed her a prepaid cell phone, saying, *Well, maybe we can use this to talk instead.* Her voice came to him over the phone, explaining, *I'm a woman, so I can't just wander around as I please like the other people out here do. I can't be too careful protecting myself. You don't run into people so often in here, so it's safe in that sense, but at the same time, if you do run into trouble there's no one to help you. I try to blend into the woods so no one notices me here in my little hut, my senses honed like an animal's to let me know if someone's nearby, so to be found out like this by a reporter came as quite a shock.*

Even with her fine-tuned senses, the woman hadn't

noticed them approaching. She'd been collecting fallen leaves to stuff her pillow and gotten tired, and when she straightened up to stretch her back, there they were: five kids silently walking toward her. *They aren't human*, she thought. *These children are not of this earth.* Chills ran down her spine, but, perhaps because they were kids, she ended up calling out to them before she quite knew what she was doing. *What're you kids doing here?* she asked, and all five of them, their backpacks slung over their shoulders, turned to face her at the same time.

You kids shouldn't be in a place like this.

A boy wearing glasses nodded.

Well if you know that, then go home! she said, and told them how to get out of the forest. But the children shook their heads.

So you're playing hooky, hiding out here when you're supposed to be at school? Is that it?

The children didn't answer and instead came closer, taking off their backpacks to sit at her feet.

Why so quiet? You kids from the deaf school?

A boy with a dyed blond crew cut nodded, but the tallest boy shook his head and took from his backpack a little booklet with "Last Words" written on its cover, opening it to a certain page to show her. There was a drawing of a person's face with no eyes, ears, nose, or mouth, along with the words, "We believe in silence."

You took a vow of silence?

The tallest boy shook his head and flipped through the booklet's well-worn pages before showing it to her again. There was another illustration, this time of a naked green man sleeping in a tree, and beneath it the words "There are ways to use one's voice and remain silent at the same time. Through silence, we can gradually get closer to nature, to the plants and animals."

At this, the woman became convinced she was being played for a fool, and she said, *I don't understand this, but I want you to get out of here. Come on, stand up, I don't want to have anything to do with you, and trust me, you don't want to have anything to do with me, I don't care if you ran away from home or whatever it is you're doing, just go do it somewhere else.*

A girl with long brown hair tied back with a bandana shook her head, and then folded her hands beneath her cheek to mime sleep.

Fine, don't talk to me, but don't expect me to understand you. Have it your way.

The woman began to leave, and as she did, the five children lay down simultaneously and shut their eyes as if to sleep. Looking back, she noticed a slight hollowness to their cheeks that stopped her.

You haven't eaten, have you?

The boy with the blond crew cut kept his eyes closed, but nodded.

If you can walk, come with me, but I warn you: I don't have anything good.

The tall boy opened his eyes and looked at the woman, shaking his head.

Can't you move? Well, just wait here then, I'll bring you something.

Now several of them were shaking their heads adamantly.

But if you don't eat anything, you'll die. Do you want to die?

None of the five answered that. A girl with big eyes wiped away a tear.

The woman was getting annoyed again, so the tall boy brought the little book back out, showing her the pages one by one this time. It was a homely thing, just a bunch of computer paper stapled together.

Page one: "Written here are our last words. In the end, they are the only ones we need to believe. Putting these words into practice, we will lose our need for words at all. And when this happens, our hearts and bodies for the first time will be one, be perfect. Like the animals, the grass, the trees, the rocks. Do you have what it takes to stop being human?"

He turned the page, and on the next two facing pages, conspicuously large type on the right side proclaimed, "We believe in these last words, and pledge to forsake all speech!" while on the left, smaller type simply stated, "We believe in silence." On the next page, the word "Teachings" was printed in bold, and every page thereafter featured a new lesson.

Lesson One: "Humans thrive on words and are destroyed by words. The words that destroy are no different from birdcalls or barks. To believe in these meaningless cries is like believing in a drawing of a sardine head. Let us stop thinking about the meaning of the meaningless words spoken by others and simply listen to them as music."

Lesson Two: "We who were raised listening to words that destroy continue to speak meaningless words that bear no relation to what's in our hearts. To cherish what's in our hearts, let us refrain from speaking words. Let us use our voices as musical instruments instead."

Lesson Three was the page she'd been shown before: "There are ways to use one's voice and remain silent at the same time. Through silence, we can gradually get closer to nature, to the plants and animals."

Lesson Four: "Once one has become accustomed to not using words, one begins to think less about things as well. One becomes closed. This is proof that one is getting closer to reaching a state of simply being alive."

Lesson Five: "Those who are simply alive do not fear death. Breathing, blinking, dying: it is all the same."

Lesson Six: "However, one must not be impatient. Those who attempt to end their words through death instead of silence end up cursed eternally. They suffer forever in a hell made of meaningless words."

She flipped past the rest of the pages to the end. One page bore the legend, "Words have reached their end," and on the facing page was printed: *Author: Saeko*

Yasuda; Publisher: The Association of Finished Persons; Date of Publication: March 31, 2002.

The woman sat down with the children, saying softly, *You're serious about this, aren't you? Being serious about something's a scary thing.* And then she asked them, *This "Association of Finished Persons," that's you, isn't it?* The children nodded weakly.

But you're not quite finished yet, she pointed out, laughing. *You still understand the words I say, don't you?*

The boy with glasses put his hands over his ears. The tall boy pulled them away.

Now, now, you're doing the best you can. But no matter what you are, plant or animal, everything eats, and if you kids don't eat, you can't finish being human.

Standing up, the woman roughly roused the children from the ground, pulling them up by their arms, swatting their buttocks with a stick, kicking at them with her feet as she herded them to her shack. The children began to perk up a bit as she did.

She started a fire in the clearing to heat up some expired instant miso soup, and the children sucked it down. However, they wouldn't touch any of her expired convenience store rice balls, fried chicken, or chocolate.

They continued their conversation, the children responding to yes or no questions with headshakes and nods.

Do you plan to live in this forest? They stiffened, some of them nodding.

Well then, do you plan to die in this forest? All of them shook their heads.

You don't want to die? They nod.

But you don't want to live? They nod.

You poor things, your heads have outgrown your bodies. You can't become animals or plants with such oversized heads. Look, this is the kind of person who can become an animal.

The woman folded her legs beneath her and brought the upper half of her body down to the ground, pushing out her bottom, and then braced herself low to the ground with her arms and stretched, meowing.

There are a lot of stray cats around here. I once read a book about a child who wanted to become a cat. Cats move their ears while they're sleeping, and they wake up as soon as they sense danger; they can wake up and run away at full speed in an instant. The child thought that if she couldn't do that, she'd never become a cat, so she practiced it diligently. Every morning, the second she woke up, she would leap up and race into the garden in a flash.

The children laughed, as soundlessly as they could.

Plus, she ate bugs and field grass, put anything and everything in her mouth to see if it was edible. Later, she learned to speak languages from Africa and all around the world and became a linguist. She was half-human, half-animal, and so she became a linguist.

The children knit their brows, and the woman flicked the creases between them with her fingernail.

You can't become an animal just by giving up language, is what I mean. Do what you want—don't speak, don't eat, take poison—but what is an animal, or plant, or thing? If you continue not to eat like this, your arms and legs will waste away and you'll be bedridden; but sad to say, you'll still be thinking all sorts of stuff in your heads. Though I guess that might suit you kids with your oversized heads, maybe you'd prefer to live completely inside them, your bodies useless.

The girl with big eyes had begun tearing up as she looked at the woman.

Everyone dies. You won't become animals following that stupid book, all that will happen is that you'll end your lives for the sake of a life that's not even your own. If you still want to disappear like that, feel free. But if you seriously want to slip free from a life lived only in your heads, then go on, get out, forage your own food. Either way, when you get up tomorrow you'll no longer be welcome here. I want you wake up and dash away as fast as you can, like a cat.

That night, the woman let them crowd into her little

hut while she slept outside, wrapped in a khaki-colored sheet.

Do you know what happened to them after that? Yoshinobu asked.

I don't know, and I don't want to know.

Well, I'm going to tell you anyway. They were discovered about four days ago lying on the ground, too malnourished to move, by some other homeless person living in the forest, and the police came and took them away after he reported it.

Is that so? . . . I guess some people can't leave well enough alone.

Yoshinobu hung up the phone and got up from where he'd been sitting on the ground next to the woman's hut, and then slipped out of the Sayama Hills while it was still dark, got in his car, and drove out to Higashi Urawa. He drove faster than he ever had before. He no longer felt the relation between pressing down on the accelerator, the car speeding up, and his body moving through space. So he pressed down on the accelerator as far as it would go. Yoshinobu himself remained perfectly still.

Some people can't leave well enough alone . . . Yoshinobu supposed the woman had felt the edge of her loneliness as these words escaped her lips. Loneliness like a knife, slipping frictionlessly into the soft flesh of her breast. All he really knew of her, in the end, was her voice. As she was telling her story, Yoshinobu sensed that she must still have the children's booklet, but when he offered to leave for a bit so she could put it on the ground outside the hut so he could take a look at it, she replied, *I don't have it, my memory's this good because I need it to survive.* So Yoshinobu made do with leaving her the prepaid phone, saying, *If you think of anything else you'd like to tell me, just call.* Though of course he knew she wouldn't.

When he arrived at the woods, he closed his eyes and walked carefully just as he had in Sayama Hills, testing the ground first one step then the other. The sound of his footfalls, of the dirt, of the dry leaves and grass echoed in the dark and told him where the trees grew thick and dense and where they opened into clearings.

He couldn't bear to sleep at home in his bed. He wanted to be free from human thoughts, lose himself amid the trees and earth. His father had wanted to be buried in sand out of a sense of duty, but instead he'd been stripped and buried in the soil of the garden because of Mother. Surely this had been the fate he'd truly desired. And because of Yoshinobu, Mother too had ended up stripped and covered with garden soil before she was cremated. Surely this, too, had been what she'd truly desired.

Yoshinobu longed to bury his flesh within the earth as well. The trees sighed their heavy sighs as he reached the heart of the forest where not a breath of air from the outside world seemed to penetrate, and there he shed his shirt, his pants, his underwear and stretched out, face down on the ground. *Do I want to lie and rot like this, too? Do I want it like they did, possessed by a desire to rot and rot until the tiniest particles of protein in my brain break down, become one once more with the soil?*

He took a deep breath, inhaling the scent of the earth, enjoying the cool sensation of each grain of dirt that pressed against his cheek. If he stuck out his tongue it would reach the ground, he could cover his wet tongue with dirt, taste it as it melted in his mouth. Dirt, precious as flesh. He rubbed his skin directly against it. He moved his hand between his legs and dug out a hollow in the earth beneath himself. Dirt packed in under his fingernails as he dug and dug until he lost all feeling in his wrist, making a hollow that engulfed his hot, erect penis in soft, newly aerated soil as he thrust himself in. Once ensheathed, he stopped his movements and felt with his entire body the coolness of the earth and the sleeping breath of the forest; the rise and fall of the earth's skin as it breathed, up and down, up and down; the smell of the trees and the breath of all the little animals; the sweaty dewiness of the grass.

Planted now in the soil, Yoshinobu's root drew all these sensations into itself and reached straight down into the earth, the way the soft soil slid along it tickling him all the while; and it got hotter and hotter as it passed through the magma and the juice dripping from the tip melted the hard layers of metal in the core as it bore straight on through until it reached the other side of the world, poking its head through the surface of Hispaniola, its mountainous surface strewn with rocks and blasted white with salt; and it grew longer and longer as it bathed in the rays of the tropical sun that sliced through the air like a knife, turning it greener and greener until the umbrella of the glans opened to shade the dry earth from the sun's harsh rays, allowing the soil in its shadow to retain the moisture that rained from it; plants of all kinds sprouted in numberless profusion, great plains of grass forming in an instant; and soon the umbrella-tipped penis split into slivers that quickly thickened into a stand of white, cauliflower-form trees that soon enough turned a deep broccoli green; and then the earth grew wet and trees put down their roots, underbrush spread, palms and banana trees reached skyward, banyan trees extended their aerial roots to the ground, and a canopy of thick leaves formed, creating daytime darkness beneath them; and then a full moon appeared in the shadow-strewn sky, making the entire area glitter like a mirror beneath its glow, and in the midst of it all, delighting in the feel of the smooth bark of the trees against his penis, jumping up and down, singing and dancing, wasn't that Misao? In and out of tune, singing songs and reciting lines. But the words were indistinct, Yoshinobu couldn't catch them. *Hey! Look over here! It's me! Look at me!* Yoshinobu felt like shouting at Misao even as he also had the feeling that he mustn't hear what Misao was saying, that he must leave this place before too long, and the conflict between these impulses paralyzed him. And then he heard the flutelike call of an owl, and it smoothed his anxieties away.

Getting up and brushing off the dirt, Yoshinobu put on his clothes, searched for a rock to use in place of a desk, and booted up his laptop. The moon was a crescent so slender its weak light seemed barely able to reach the ground, but to Yoshinobu it shone like a silver sun, illuminating every sign of life within the forest down to the tiniest detail. The leaves sparkled like kaleidoscopes. The homeless woman in Sayama Forest, the five sixth-graders she met, all the children who ate the school lunches filled with poison and sickened or died, Misao's mother and father and sister and brother, Misao himself, Minagawa, Yasuda, Soejima, his own parents, his sister—Yoshinobu saw them all twisting and twining around each other like the tangled roots of a mangrove, braiding together to form a single gigantic tree. Their words rose like sighs from the great tree's crazed profusion of leaves, and he felt them on his skin as they knit together to form one grand, priceless story. Yoshinobu grasped desperately for them, his hands spinning line after line of characters as he did. What he wrote were words, yet were not words. A flag of Japan dyed deepest red, invisible to the human eye. A magic spell to turn the coming sandstorm into a muddy rain.

Title ▶ The Homeless Totoros of the Outlying Forests (1) ◀
Subtitle ▶ "Last Words" ◀
Lede ▶ Two incidents: a school lunch poisoning three months ago that resulted in the deaths of nine elementary school students, a recent incident at Sayama Hills in which five elementary school students were found in the forest after apparently losing their way. Tracing the actions of students attending Shirasagi Elementary School, where both incidents took place, one homeless man emerged as the point where they intersect. Interviewing this man, who immigrated to the Dominican Republic half a century ago and who

currently drifts from place to place in the Sayama Hills area, we get a better picture of the circumstances that drove these children to mass suicide. ◀
Text Start ▶

"I just don't know how I should live out the rest of my life."

So states Kimi Usui (12), a student at New Tokorozawa Elementary in the city of Tokorozawa, immediately following the poisoned school lunch incident at Shirasagi Elementary. Kimi reports that she knew in advance that poison would be mixed into the school lunches at Shirasagi Elementary, as well as knowing that "it would be our turn next." However, she despaired when the poison killed only nine students and was thus a "failure," meaning that the "next turn" would never happen.

"I think that most of the older students at Shirasagi Elementary ate the school lunches knowing they were poisoned." Kimi's words allude to the existence of an extensive "association" at the heart of the poisoning, while also forcing one to contemplate that it seems the children had been ardently anticipating the poisoning's occurrence.

◊

Deep within Sayama Hills, famously the model for the forest in the film *My Neighbor Totoro*, a homeless woman named Michiko Kanamori (45) sheltered five Shirasagi Elementary sixth grade students in her makeshift "home" three days before they were found and taken into custody. All five had already stopped opening their mouths by that time, she says. Not to speak, not to eat.

"If you tried to force them to use their mouths, they would open up this weird booklet and point at it. There they had written 'We believe in silence.'"

This handmade booklet, with "Last Words" printed on the cover, was, according to the colophon, put together by an organization known as the "Association of Finished Persons" (Representative: Misae Yamashita) and issued previous to the incident, on March 31st. Michiko wasn't aware of it, but this little girl, Misae (11), was the core member of the extensive "association," recognized as holding the key to solving the mysteries of the poisoned school lunch incident.

Yoshinobu stilled his hands and took a deep breath, trembling. He was excited, as if soaring through the air. He felt as if he were looking down from high above even as he sat typing at his keyboard in the middle of this clearing that glittered silver amid the night-darkened woods. He had no doubt. He knew that he wasn't just writing words—no, he was living the unseen lives of those he wrote about.

As Michiko took the booklet in her hand and flipped through the pages, she found herself reading a strange, childish "lesson." It stated that by refusing to listen to the words of others or use words oneself, by banishing every word from one's head, one would at last exist simply, as an animal, plant, or object. The five followed this doctrine, practicing silence.

However, the youths were also engaged in fasting, which the booklet did not instruct them to do. "If you want to become like an animal or plant, eat something," Michiko encouraged them, but all they would allow to enter their mouths was a little miso soup.

Michiko guesses, "After the incident with the poisoned school lunches, they can no longer stand to let food pass their lips." However, if we remember the words of Kimi, quoted above, might we suppose instead that they were still pursuing mass suicide, just in a different form?

◊

Similarly, Tarō Shimaura (72), living a transient existence in the wooded areas of Sayama Hills, wakes at sunrise every morning and, deep within the forest, performs a one-man show distilled from his own life as it has occurred up until that day. Wishing not to be seen by others, he performs in the early morning, but near the end of last year he noticed he had an audience peeking at him from the shadows of the trees. It was Misae.

Without a trace of embarrassment, Misae walked up to Tarō and spoke frankly and with deep emotion. "I'm still only a child, but watching that was like watching my own life." When Tarō admonished her, saying, "It's dangerous for little girls to come into the forest alone," her face clouded. "That's why I come here, because I don't care what happens to me. I feel so unneeded by this world that I want to disappear, and so sometimes I come to the forest. Once I'm here, the trees and animals and birds don't speak a word, and that's good, it erases that feeling of being unneeded, makes me feel better. But now I've spoken with a human being inside the forest, and I feel like I can live again. This is the first time that's ever happened to me. I want my friends to see your show, to hear your story."

Tarō refused, but Misae wouldn't back down, promising that if he wouldn't tell the story she would do it in her own words. Even so, Tarō held firm, but he knew that Misae would likely tell her friends at school regardless, and a feeling of doom overcame him, and he cursed himself for his carelessness.

To be continued
(Yoshinobu Kawai)
* *Note: all names have been changed.*
◀ END

Upon finishing part one, the reality contained within it overwhelmed Yoshinobu. He completely believed in the words displayed on his monitor, body and soul. *This is the truth*, he thought. *We mustn't let facts deceive us.* He was pursuing secrets that could never be found in mere fact. He could see Yasuda and Misao talking to each other right before his eyes. He even stood up to try and approach them. Though bodiless, he could sense their presence all around him.

He walked around for a while until his agitation subsided, and he realized that he needed pictures. *When I get home, I should make a mock-up on my computer of the little booklet I couldn't get from the homeless woman. I can use a digital camera to take a picture of the front cover, and then the truth will finally be realized.*

Yoshinobu sat back down on the ground, faced the laptop he'd set on the rock, and began part two.

Title ▶ The Homeless Totoros of the Outlying Forest (2) ◀
Subtitle ▶ May This World Be Thine, O Forsaken of the Earth! ◀
Text Start ▶

The show that Tarō Shimaura (72) performed alone every morning within the depths of Sayama Forest, far from public view, was a story told in song interspersed with monologues detailing Tarō's bitter experiences as an emigrant to the Dominican Republic. It begins with an altered version of the national anthem:

For all eternity may this world be thine / O Forsaken of the Earth, till pebbles now / Into mighty rocks shall grow / Whose venerable sides moss doth line!

◊

It was 1956, a little over ten years after the end of World War II, when Tarō left for the Dominican Republic. He was 25 years old.

That year, a terrible infectious disease spread through his family, and his father and mother passed away from overworking themselves while sick. Because they lacked the money to put them in a hospital, the children cared for them until their final moments at home in their beds, and after conferring among themselves, the surviving five siblings buried the two of them in the garden.

"It wasn't just that we didn't have the money for a proper grave—they also became good fertilizer for the sweet potatoes in the garden."

These golden sweet potatoes grew abundantly and were so sweet they seemed to melt in the mouth. The flesh of the parents became the flesh of their children through these sweet potatoes, the children's bodies thus becoming the parents' eternal resting places. When he thought of it this way, Tarō, even as a lung condition rendered him bedridden, felt their strength well up inside of him.

◊

When Tarō recovered his health, his oldest brother handed over an application from the government for emigration to the Dominican Republic. "It's my responsibility to stay here and carry on the family name, so you go there and make a name for yourself." He knew that this was merely an excuse to get rid of one more mouth to feed, but Tarō boarded the ship anyway, his pockets filled with a pittance to cover expenses and a pinch of soil from the garden.

However, rather than the plentiful farmland and comfortable homes the government had promised, he found himself presented instead with a narrow wasteland and a crude shack.

"When I got up in the morning and

looked at the land, the whole surface was pure white. I got excited, thinking it had snowed on this South Seas island, but when I tasted it, it was salty. The salt in the soil had crystallized when the temperature had fallen during the night."

The soil, sown with rocks and salt, could never be farmland no matter how hard one struggled, and one after another the immigrants deserted their land. Tarō, however, remained.

"When we appealed to the government officials, they refused to listen, saying that the rocks and salt would break down into fertile soil. But, though I tried every day to smash the rocks with a hammer, it was only my body and soul that crumbled into sand."

Eventually, the Japanese government could no longer avoid responsibility and arranged for the majority of the settlers return to Japan *en masse*, but Tarō refused to go, saying, "I don't want help from you crooks again." He moved to a different plot of land and got by as a tenant farmer on a Dominican plantation.

◊

Tarō finally decided to return to Japan at sixty, cursed by poor health and lessened mobility. In 1995, he set foot on Japanese soil for the first time in almost forty years; however, his siblings made no effort to meet with their penniless brother upon his return. As a final parting gift, Tarō sent them a flag of Japan with the white dyed pure red, and then "exiled" himself to the Sayama Hills.

"In the end, it turned out that I'd died when I left Japan. But when I think about it, my body is made from the dead flesh of my parents, so my dead self will also become fertilizer for these woods. Even though I won't remain in anyone's memory, I am able this way to repay my debt to the living things of the earth. That's why I'm not lonely."

Still, he kept performing his shows, perhaps because he did want to leave a memory somewhere, after all.

"Everyone, no matter who they are, tries to overcome the dissatisfactions and obstacles in their lives by expressing themselves in various ways. However, these expressions of self should never be foisted on people, never be sold to the highest bidder. When you sell yourself like that, all you're creating is a scam, a power relation. Whenever you try to say anything to anyone, the words get mixed with lies that others can't help but hear. It's this kind of thing, this power relation that's most effective for cutting people down. Self expression is fine, but it should remain quiet, locked away inside your heart."

An expression of self meant never to be heard, borne from a desire to force himself on no one; this was Tarō's one-man show.

◊

However, this expression of self none-theless inadvertently touched the heart of Misae Yamashita (11). One day, as summer approached, Misae, who had come out to watch his performances many times during the winter, showed him a handmade booklet, telling him, "I made a book of the things I learned from you." Tarō, after reading it, felt intense regret.

"Because I'd been alone for so many years, I let myself feel at ease with her, began to hope that maybe she would understand, you know? But the words that child wrote were words of force and coercion. No matter who wrote them, that's what they'd be. Words are always mixed with lies, so you should never try to use them to persuade others."

Tarō tried to warn Misae about this, but she obstinately insisted, "The words of your play are like a Bible to me. My mission in life is to spread them," and soon she disappeared.

Tarō doesn't know that Misae was brought before the Family Court, let alone her role in the poisoned school lunch incident. Yet, seeing how things have played out, perhaps he does know, better than anyone else in Japan, what catastrophes may yet be on the way.

And so, even now, Tarō continues to perform his one-man show in the Sayama forest, before an audience of no one.

—End
(Yoshinobu Kawai)
Note: all names have been changed.
◀ END

You might say that this is my *one-man show,* Yoshinobu told Misao, who stood there right before his eyes, seeming on the verge of tears. Misao's body was twisted a bit, looking back at Yoshinobu with dark, wet eyes, an elderly deer covered in a soft coat of white and reddish-brown. *You must read these words, they will be able to break through and destroy those "Last Words," this is where the truth is, here, in my . . . in this . . .* and with that, Yoshinobu's words left him.

Silence reigned.

Something very like despair raced through Yoshinobu's heart. The deer blinked its sorrowful eyes, and, turning its white tail towards Yoshinobu, carefully walked away. Gradually, the sound of its footsteps as it picked its way across the dry leaves on the forest floor faded in the distance. And then, once more: silence.

Yoshinobu returned to his apartment at dawn, the same time the morning edition went out, and he sent in the first part of his article to the office. In his email to the bureau chief, he wrote, "I've finished gathering material for my special report and decided to make it a column. A two-parter. The circumstances of the investigation make it a bit urgent, so I'd appreciate it if we could run this soon, if possible in the morning edition the day after tomorrow. I'm sending along the first part of the manuscript today. I'll send part two and the pics for each installment sometime this afternoon."

After that, Yoshinobu spent two hours making the mock-up of the little book on his computer and took two photos of it with his digital camera, one a close-up on the cover, the other showing it lying open. To illustrate part two, he chose a snapshot he'd taken when he'd been interviewing the homeless in the Sayama Hills. Taken from behind at an oblique angle, the face of the middle-aged man in the photo is obscured, and Yoshinobu sent it off with the caption, "Tarō adds to his one-man show a little bit every day, even now. 'No one ever stops growing.'"

Yoshinobu didn't turn off his computer, though, and instead he navigated his web browser to a search engine and typed in the words "letter of resignation." He spent about a half an hour searching through the hits before he found a template he wanted to use, and then he composed a draft of a letter of resignation for himself. And with that, having done everything he had to for the time being, he collapsed, nearly unconscious, onto the bed.

It hadn't even been three hours when the phone call from the managing editor woke him again at ten.

He was bombarded with questions. *Am I supposed to use this two-parter as the top story in the prefectural edition? Have you talked about this with the chief? It's rather long, isn't it? Are the pictures ready?* The chief had fallen ill from overwork and was taking some sick days, so the managing editor was preparing the edition. Yoshinobu hadn't predicted this.

The chief told me that a hundred or even two hundred lines would be fine, since it was a special report, so I let myself have a good bit of room. And I sent some pictures with captions, you should have them already. The chief has a pretty good idea of what's in it, so yeah, make it the top story today, that would be great, he said. *Great, gotcha,* said the managing editor, hanging up.

It wasn't too long before he called again.

About this manuscript, the content is good, but maybe you should obscure a few details a bit more.

Don't worry. I take total responsibility for everything related to this article. If there are any questions or complaints, you can let me know via cell phone.

Even using aliases, people are going to know who you're talking about. Have you contacted the parents of the minors?

When the main bureau was doing the initial investigation, I requested some interviews but was refused.

And then?

I didn't need them for this article.

They might sue.

Are you scared?

Look, if this article was airtight, I'd be right there holding the line with you, but you know there're holes in it.

Trust me.

I do trust you, but rookies are green, you know? To begin with, the writing is hardly standard.

Is that so?

It is. There's a whiff of the literary to it, don't you think? It's a newspaper article, it has to be the facts. Just the facts, nothing more.

But that's what I tried to do, as much as I could.

It has a lot of subjective opinion in it, too. It's risky. When you're young, you don't notice these things on your own.

It's an article with a byline, right? Isn't it natural to include the viewpoint of the writer?

There's nothing wrong with having a viewpoint. But these subjective things have to be supported by facts. A reporter can't appear as the subject of the article.

I didn't put myself in it like that.

You omit the pronouns, but you could put them back in if you wanted to, like "I think . . ."

Look, if you can't publish it as is, just reject it.

It'll be fine if you just change some phrasing, make it sound more factual. It's a problem of style.

I don't think I really understand what you mean by "factual." I don't think writing an article is just a matter of stating facts, so please, reject it.

If you don't rewrite it yourself at least a little bit, I'll just end up blue-penciling it myself until it sounds like a proper article.

In that case, please file it under your byline, not mine.

You're rather high-and-mighty, aren't you?

Publish it as is or reject it, that's all I'm asking.

Fine, I get it. I suppose bearing full responsibility will be a good experience for you, too, at any rate.

Eventually, it reached to the point that the bureau chief got wrapped up in it, so Yoshinobu promised to make as much effort as he could to revise it and this settled things down. Yoshinobu went back to sleep and, in the evening, went up to the office to discuss the layout of the headlines and so forth with the production editor of the prefectural edition, while the managing editor was busy having it out with another reporter about a manuscript.

He invited the managing editor to a sushi dinner that evening and listened to him talk about how it had been when he was a cub reporter and his views on journalism in general. Around ten o'clock, the galleys were up, and Yoshinobu, as promised, edited his wording so the article would pass muster. In the production department, Yoshinobu approved the hard proof, fixing the manuscript for the second part to satisfy the managing editor as well. He also replaced the anthem parody addressed to the "Forsaken of the Earth" with an unaltered version of the famous Norinaga poem, *If asked what lies within the true Yamato heart / the answer is the mountain cherry, fragrant at the dawn.* The managing editor glanced over it briefly and commented, *Now this is some good writing.*

The next day, Yoshinobu opened the morning edition and failed to feel the blinding excitement of peeling back reality's false skin that he'd imagined he would. *Seeing it in print like this, it's like a different article entirely,* he thought, the strength leaving his body. *But at least there's still the second half to go,* he told himself.

The chief was still on vacation. Just like the day before, Yoshinobu consulted with the managing editor about the modifications to his manuscript as employees from the sales department bundled copies of the Saitama edition for that day and the next into bundles of a hundred, preparing them to be distributed throughout area the next morning; he put in an appearance at the Saitama Prefecture Police Press Corps, surprising the reporters from other papers, and soon enough, the day was done. That evening, after going over all of the articles, the managing editor confirmed with the production manager that he was satisfied, put a word in with the younger reporters to "just finish up with the galleys," and left; it was then that Yoshinobu put in a call to the production department to replace the second part of his article with the old version that included the "Forsaken of the Earth" anthem parody. He checked the galleys one last time and then persuaded the reporter assigned to graveyard duty, who was one of his cohort, to let Yoshinobu replace him, and so he spent his last night at the office.

Early in the morning, two hundred morning editions for the next two days arrived from the sales department. One by one, Yoshinobu cut a page out of each prefectural edition and circled his article in red. At 5:30 a.m., he placed his letter of resignation on the department head's desk, telephoned the prefectural policeman on duty, leaving his cell phone number so he could contact him if any major incidents or accidents occurred, and then, carrying the pages he'd cut out and a bunch of packing tape, he climbed into his Corolla II.

First he headed out to Tokorozawa. The car flew down the empty highway at over 120 kilometers per hour. Low clouds covered the sky; there was no sign of the coming dawn. He stopped by the homes of the elementary school students he had visited during the course of his investigation one by one, following the marks on the map he carried, and quietly slipped only his page into each of their mailboxes. It felt like scattering poison, like planting bombs. Then he went to Shirasagi Elementary, sneaking through the school gate and into the main entryway to tape the pages to the glass. He stuck one to the school gate itself as he left. After that, he went around to New Tokorozawa and all the other elementary schools in the area and taped up newspaper pages on those, too. And then he went to the Sayama Hills. He looked for places where there seemed to be a comparatively high concentration of tents and taped newspapers on nearby broad-trunked trees. *These aren't poison*, he thought, *they're wall papers*. He also left several copies of the edition in front of various tents and shacks.

Yoshinobu went back down the highway, this time heading toward Higashi Urawa. Once he gave back the words the forest had given him, his project would be complete. Words that were not words would struggle and squirm, eventually tearing through the thin, swollen membrane covering the world to expose the true face of slime-slicked, corpse-ridden reality.

Traffic had already increased in the inbound lanes, and it was beginning to get congested. It was almost nine by the time he arrived. There was no time to paste up wall papers and stealthily slip away, so Yoshinobu hurried directly into the forest. The sky was still dark, the air heavy with mold and wet.

He found no trace of any tents near the entrance to the woods; there was no sign of human life anywhere. The cries of birds and cicadas filled the air, and though Yoshinobu found it as hard to breathe as always due to the raw smell of the plants and soil, there wasn't the killing heat from before. Yoshinobu couldn't find the spot where he'd written the article two days ago. He gave up, resigning himself to just pasting up some wall papers on the trees around the entrance.

As he taped the final sheet, Yoshinobu's heart unexpectedly flooded with an intense wave of grief. An excruciating sorrow. Yoshinobu began to reread his article. At some point, he'd begun reading it aloud. By the time he got to *For all eternity may this world be thine, O Forsaken of the Earth*, he was shouting. Yoshinobu was no longer reading his article, he was performing Misao's play. The speeches, the songs, the sermons: the show would go on, nothing could stop it. He began to perform the gestures that went with the words. When it was time for him to grow thin and wan and sorrowful, he laid himself on the ground. When it was time for Yayoi to talk, he spoke in falsetto.

And finally, he sang the anthem of the Forsaken one more time and finished the show. He bowed. There was no audience, of course. No one eavesdropping, either.

Yoshinobu headed back toward his car, accompanied by the sound of his feet stepping on dry grass. Inside his head, he was still reciting lines from the show. He tried plugging his ears and loudly singing a different song, but he still heard it. He was overcome by the impulse to shout out loud, *What can it mean to keep speaking like this all alone? I still have words to communicate to the outside world, look, these are my words, right here!* He opened a morning edition from the bundle of newspapers he'd put in the passenger's seat. But it was as if he'd opened a completely different national paper by mistake, as the thick lettering of an unfamiliar headline jumped out to greet him.

Yoshinobu froze. Like sand through an hourglass, Yoshinobu could see the meaning draining from his article as it crumbled to dust. He could hear it in his ears. He could feel it on his skin.

The words in his head had stopped. Yoshinobu tore the article out with his fingers, and, rushing into the darkened forest beneath with heavy clouds, pasted it over the first article of his that caught his eye, and then ripped down every other copy of his article that he could find.

Large drops of rain began graze Yoshinobu's cheek. Distant thunder resounded. Maybe the other papers would get soaked and all fall apart.

"I Wanted to Stop Being a Person and Turn into a Cat"
The Shirasagi Runaway Breaks Her Silence

Official sources confirm that a twelve-year-old sixth-grade girl from Shirasagi Elementary (Tokorozawa), one of the children who had disappeared into the woods of Sayama Hills before being found and taken into protective custody by the Tokorozawa police on the 14th of this month, has at last begun to talk about what happened during her disappearance.

According to sources at the school, the girl claims that she ran away because she "wanted to stop being a person and turn into a cat." She tried locating food on her own within the Hills, but was unsuccessful and began to suffer from malnutrition.

Asked to interpret this behavior, some experts have said, "It's possible that the trauma of having eaten a poisoned school lunch led her to avoid any food prepared by human hands."

The girl refused to speak at all after being taken into protective custody on the 14th, but she began talking to her parents on the morning of the 18th and has now reportedly recovered enough to answer questions from the school and Tokorozawa city officials. They say the girl explained that her ability to speak again stemmed from remembering the words spoken to her by a homeless woman in Sayama Hills who had helped her.

Sources also report that some of the other children who had run away with the girl and refused to speak afterward have now begun talking to friends and family, and as they recover, they may soon begin speaking about the incident as well.

Author's note: this novella was inspired by watching a video of "Homesick in My Dreams" (Kyōshū wa yume no naka de), by documentary filmmaker Jun Okamura, who makes films about Japanese immigrants in Brazil.

Treason Diary (1998)

Yukinori Akimizu smelled the smoldering of explosives beneath the floor of the Ambassador's Residence, and the sensation relived by his skin as he imagined his arms and lips and scorched shriveled hair fly apart in a matter of seconds was the smell of iron that had enfolded him in its spreading wings as it rose up out of Miss Michiko's body when he had stabbed and killed her with a knife at sixteen years and seven months old. Really, though, that iron smell had never actually left his right hand or cheek or anywhere else the blood had splashed, it was just that now, mere seconds before his death, it was as if his body had somehow become Miss Michiko's body as it had lain curled like a red, hook-speared worm, and it felt as if that rusted iron smell that seemed impossible to imagine circulating within a living thing was now wafting out of wounds in his thigh, his stomach, his left breast, out of all eight stab wounds he had left in her body. He had written all of this down, he had wanted everyone to understand: his lover Mermalada, Miss Michiko, his father, Kiyoto, Kisaragi, Abraham, and now he wanted them to know that he understood for the first time how Miss Michiko herself must have felt as she was overcome by this inescapable smell, and he choked up with regret. Of course, he could just be choking on the smoke flooding the air. Had the explosion already happened? His eyes were filled with tears that flowed with no sign of stopping, and Yukinori found he could see nothing, hear nothing. He thought this was because he'd already been ripped apart, his arms and lips and scorched shriveled hair flying in all directions. There was no sound or smell left in the present for the dying. It was just: he still felt the brightness and warmth of lemon-colored light through his eyelids. He couldn't imagine where the light would be coming from, it probably meant the roof had been blown off. The first time he'd felt himself bathed in such clear, pure light was when he'd first walked the streets of Lima that summer five years ago. The flowers, five or six times the size of any in Japan, reflected the light as if they themselves were suns, and Yukinori had felt as if these flowers with unknown names, these white and red and yellow and purple flowers, were pasted directly onto his eyeballs like posters. As he'd continued to walk despite this feeling, his field of vision had swum not only with flower petals and light but with flashes of some other color, and he had teetered precariously and finally collapsed. Happily, this occurred not fifty meters away from the house of Father Fidel Cato, who was expecting him, and he was soon discovered by the Father's niece and admonished never to forget to wear a white hat in summer or he'd succumb to heat stroke again.

The man who had introduced him to Father Cato was a third-generation Japanese Brazilian named Albert Morishima who had accompanied him on his journey to Lima. Had Morishima been a different sort of man, Yukinori would probably be tricking girls as a go-between for some prostitute trafficker by now, and, crying and gnashing his teeth, he vowed never to forgive his father who had so blithely handed his son over with no thought to the outcome. After fleeing the thankfully empty hallway where Miss Michiko still lay moaning, after scrubbing the blood from his body in the pool locker room shower, wondering how blood could have possibly gotten into all the places he discovered it, after staring blankly at the cherry-blossom-pink water flowing over the blue tile and swirling down the drain in the floor, after changing into his gym clothes and stuffing his bloody school uniform and knife into a rucksack and showing up at his father's factory and telling him only that he had just stabbed a teacher at school and showing him the bloody contents of his bag, his father consulted briefly with his vaguely seedy Japanese-Peruvian underling Michael Hisomida and then ordered his son to do what this man said from then on and never showed his face again, not even after Yukinori was handed a fake passport by Hisomida, who seemed to run some sort of black market business on the side, not even on the night before he was scheduled to leave, when instead his father called him on the phone, saying that it seems as though the things I did to try and make you fly high may have instead triggered your attack, but you know that now our bond as father and son is severed, and with that, Yukinori was handed over for good. He was then handed over once more from Hisomida to Morishima and told that now he was Morishima's cousin and could hardly speak Japanese. From then on, as though he really had lost his Japanese, Yukinori barely uttered a word. He was occupied instead with suppressing the nervous tension rising up within him so that he didn't end up stabbing Morishima too, and he lost track of where he was or what was going on around him, and thus he no longer had to think. So he no longer had any need to speak.

It was a period of dying slowly, thought Yukinori to himself around the time he became able to speak Spanish. I was like a tube of fish cake, he thought, my body just so much salty, *dashi*-flavored white paste, inside and out, save for a big empty hole in my middle. There was nothing, no words or anything else to be found, just vacant space. Everything ended up sucked into this hollow void and crystallizing, embedding itself deep within him: the flowers fulgent and voluptuous enough to drive you crazy; the hot wind so dry it could shrivel a crocodile into a lizard; the cold morning fog, wet and heavy and eating into your chest to rot you alive; the sound of Spanish, like balsam berries popping. Yukinori Akimizu, this baby born in Los Angeles to his father's Japanese-American mistress, then left with her when his father fled back to Japan, then brought and left with him after she tracked him down in Japan, he'd been slowly dying, his fish paste corpse carried to Lima, where he could be born once more. Now he spoke only Spanish, and he knew where he was, and he knew what was going on around him: he could give voice to it at last.

So he wrote in his diary in Spanish. He was keeping a diary as language practice. He'd been keeping it since the day he arrived in Lima. He didn't actually start writing it until after his Spanish had gotten good enough, but he went back and began his account from when his new self had been born.

The diary always revolved around Miss Michiko's murder and his father. At first the newly reborn Yukinori thought that reflecting on incidents and people from his "former life" was unhealthy and he tried to avoid it, but as his Spanish improved he felt his ability to think deepen, and he came to feel that this ability to put his past into words itself was a sign of rebirth. He described the incident again and again, attempting to recreate its most minute details. As he wrote and rewrote, he remembered more and more. Or maybe it wasn't that he remembered more, but rather that he was only now finding out the things he had been thinking during those fateful moments.

At first blush, it seemed a simple incident. Miss Michiko was standing in his way, he had a knife in his hand, so he removed the obstacle with the knife. But that no longer to seemed be the truth, he thought. He wanted to write the truth. He wanted to describe precisely the quiet feel of Miss Michiko's body accepting the knife as easily as it would a man. The knife had encountered no resistance whatsoever. As it was sliding in, it was as if every orifice on Yukinori's body had been sealed completely, and everything, Miss Michiko's screams, the smell of flowering daphne that had always emanated from her body, the iron smell that came from either the knife or the blood itself, he couldn't tell, the rustling sound his clothing made as he moved his arm, his own voice as he spoke, all of it seemed so far away and jumbled. Where there once had been air was now water. Miss Michiko's eyes, her mouth, her ears, her arms, her very cells, they all opened wide to Yukinori. Thinking it over again, he realized that in Miss Michiko's very lack of resistance, he had felt his own mother. It was not his knife but rather he himself he'd wanted accepted so smoothly into her warm, soft flesh, he thought, and wrote. He felt that perhaps after stabbing her eight times, what he'd really wanted was to nestle his own body into the curve of hers as she'd lain curled like an invertebrate at his feet, moaning in a low voice, and be caressed beneath the right hand she had pressed against the wound on her left breast. He realized that he'd been filled with the intense desire to take off his clothes and become a newborn baby again, put that bleeding left breast in his mouth and suckle the milk and blood and make it into a part of his own body. The truth was that he'd noticed himself starting to unbutton his white shirt and had quickly run to the pool locker room and undressed, stroking the part of himself that was just now entering adulthood with his blood-covered hand until he found himself staring vacantly at the cherry-blossom-pink water swirling into the drain as he rinsed away semen and blood. And if Miss Michiko truly had been a stand-in for his mother, he had made a mistake choosing into whom he would slide his knife. He should have slid it into his father. It was his father who'd stifled him, who'd been the muddy water isolating him from the world. His body grew and seemed to develop just like everyone else's, but this was just an effect of it absorbing this dirty water and swelling. It was this filth-extruding father whom he truly wished to stab. Not just him, but the parents who had nourished his filthy seed into fruition, and their parents as well, he needed to kill them all with his own hands or he'd never be clean. And if that was impossible, he had no choice but to stab himself. But instead his knife had stabbed Miss Michiko. It had all been a big mistake, he thought. But now that he was living somewhere far from his father, it was the same as if he were dead. My father is dead. Writing these words, his father's existence seemed truly to lose its reality, and he felt as if he had coalesced instead from the dew on the grass or out of particles of light.

As he wrote, he came to feel that writing itself was reflection, was redemption, was rebirth, was revenge, was oblivion. Transcribing the complex things inside him as precisely as possible in his still-clumsy Spanish was exhausting, like writing with an invisible third hand. It wasn't unusual for him to begin and end a whole day just writing in his diary, but Yukinori accepted this exhaustion, seeing it as justly arduous labor and punishment, and during the two and a half years it took for the relation between his word-spinning brain and his mouth and hands to become transparent, writing and living seemed one and the same.

But he was still assaulted with a discomfort bordering on nausea when he tried to read what he wrote. No matter how much time passed he could never get over it. He could find the newly reborn Yukinori Akimizu nowhere on the notebook's pages. He'd told himself as he wrote that he was just practicing his Spanish, but this awful feeling like the floor dropping out from beneath him refused to go away, and sometimes it swelled to an unbearable intensity. With the nausea would come the feeling that his stomach, his lungs, all of his internal organs were about to explode from his throat until he turned completely inside out. And if it really happened, he thought, I'd be relieved. Like taking a knife in your hand, like kissing someone deeply, he imagined that if he could just feel again the sensation of skin rolling under itself, of sharp metal piercing mucus-slick, barely resistant flesh just one more time, things would feel real again, and what was on the surface would remain on the surface and what lay within would remain within. When he felt like this, Yukinori would wander into Chinatown and set off firecrackers with the Chinese Peruvians. Watching the firecrackers explode with dazzling brightness, he'd feel himself becoming cleansed, and he supposed that if he were to throw his notebooks into the fray and blast them into the sky, some of his feelings of guilt would disappear too. But he could never lay a hand on them. He knew if he did, he'd be right back where he started. So he grew irritated, gripped with the desire to blast away the whole rest of the world, and rather than his notebooks he'd wrap hair from his head or skin peeled from the heels of his feet and hands around the firecrackers and watch these things fly apart instead.

He stopped writing when he started thinking mostly in Spanish, when he found a job with Father Cato's help working at a warehouse selling meat, when he took a *mestiza* Peruvian lover: when he began thinking of himself as just another Peruvian hyphenate. And it was then, during an eighteenth birthday party for Father Cato's niece, that Kiyoto Kamihara showed up, uninvited. As this twenty-one year old, having arrived from Japan just a few months before and barely able to speak the language, began speaking in Spanish to Yukinori anyway, he immediately felt as though he understood him completely, as if able to trace even his smallest inner contour and hollow with his hand, and they shared a striking rapport even before the revelation of their similar pasts. Inevitably, it seemed, Kiyoto turned out to have beaten two elementary school children to death with a hammer at sixteen and had panicked the populace with taunting letters telling of his crimes. Upon his release the previous year from a juvenile detention center, his family had advised him that he couldn't live in Japan any longer so he should go elsewhere, and when he replied that he wanted to go to Peru, he'd ended up taking off right then, not even stopping to see his old house or his two brothers, accompanied to Narita by only his parents, and when he lost control of himself during a stopover in Atlanta, hallucinating that an airplane made of human flesh was crashing to the ground and flowing with blood, he saw his parents once more as they cried every day at his bedside in the hospital, and as he regained his sanity through the feelings of anger and contempt they inspired, he regained his ability to travel, and he finally breathed free air for the first time as he touched down in Lima.

Yukinori remembered the incident well. It had had an impact, of course, but it had also left him numb. It had been as if a thick felt wall had separated him from the other boy, and just as he could barely hear the screams from the other side, the voices of his friends as they whispered about it around him would be similarly muffled for the other boy. He'd felt no connection between his life and those murders. Even so, it hadn't been as if he saw them taking place in a separate world, either. It was more like how a sleeping leg doesn't feel like a part of your body. So about a year later, as he was stabbing Miss Michiko eight times, he hadn't felt influenced by the other boy, or as if he were imitating him: he hadn't seen himself as similar to him at all. At the same time, though, he sometimes felt that it didn't necessarily have to have been him who'd killed Miss Michiko, that it could have been any student, that he'd acted not on his own behalf but as someone's proxy. As for who that someone might be, he knew it wasn't anyone in particular. It simply seemed to him that while he and Kiyoto and this hypothetical third party had nothing really in common, they were nonetheless interchangeable. Though even this feeling could have just been an effect of the process of writing his personal history in his diary here in Lima.

He and Kiyoto only exchanged confessions once. Moreover, they just recited the basic facts as if summarizing newspaper articles and withheld their emotions and opinions. Indeed, this very act of withholding itself conveyed their emotions and opinions quite clearly, and that each understood this was a sign of their deep connection.

Yukinori felt that if he'd been able to run away to Lima before turning sixteen that the incident might never have happened. Kiyoto surely felt the same way. He wrote as much in his notebook, but even as he did so it felt like a lie.

I came to Peru to change society, said Kiyoto. It's my duty, and I'm qualified for the job, he said. In reply to Yukinori asking why he would come to Peru to do this, Kiyoto explained that if society has broken you, you must ally yourself with other broken souls wherever you can find them, and Peru is a broken country so it must be filled with broken people. In Japan it's impossible for the broken ones to find each other, those who do the breaking conspire to keep everyone separated and lonely because they're so afraid of the broken ones' power, he explained further, intensity building behind his words. Broken people are like fictions in Japan, everyone pretends they don't exist, but here in Peru I can have a real existence, and when I realized that, I decided to come here.

These were new words to Yukinori. Hearing them, he felt himself start to be reborn once more. He felt the poison and ancient, impacted pollution within the self he'd made out of the pages of his diary escape and dissolve into the air where his voice mixed with Kiyoto's as they talked. The nausea that threatened to reverse his skin and expose the mucous membranes within subsided. Yukinori quit writing his diary again. He wanted to break open the shell he had made for himself when he first came to Peru. He felt he could finally bury for good the shadowy Yukinori he found on the pages of the diary who felt like a trick of the mind.

Kiyoto's Spanish improved quickly as he became more integrated into Peru, the same way walking around breathing the air and drinking the water transforms those things into blood and flesh, but his speech never shed its stiff, written flavor. Yukinori started to worry that his words sounded like they came out of a book too, but when he asked Mermalada about it, she replied that they didn't and that if anything his Spanish sounded like hers, so perhaps what he really sounded like was a girl.

Mermalada was a woman with skin that looked and smelled like toasted wheat. She could predict the movements of Yukinori's heart before he could, and in the blink of an eye, she could take control, make them hers. From the moment she was introduced to Kiyoto Kamihara, she sensed danger and tried to avoid him. The first time she said as much to Yukinori, the blood had drained from his face, and he'd felt rejected, the same way the Yukinori Akimizu who'd lived in Japan would have been rejected had she met him. The blood returned quickly, however, and this time flooded his head, transforming him from the shoulders up into flame. Looking at Yukinori, his face flushed red as a sunset, Mermalada told him that she was just jealous, that she was a weak, pitiful person, that Yukinori's world was her world, and she burst into tears. Yukinori remembered that Mermalada was sensitive to the tiniest shifts in his mood as if to the faintest emissions of pollen from flowers, and he loved her all the more. Even so, when Kiyoto invited Yukinori to go with him to visit Santo Domingo National University, she responded that it was a bad place, and gave him a look so fierce he found himself shrinking back in its face. She demanded he cut off his friendship with Kiyoto. It's either him or me, not both, she said. I've bared everything of mine to you, she cried, but you still hide the secret holes gaping open inside you. I understand how you must be feeling now, but if you don't tell me anything about your past there'll always be things I'll never know. Yukinori moved to strike her, but the arm movement felt wrong somehow, and he pulled the punch. Instead he threw a picture of the two of them to the floor and stomped it, smashing it to pieces. Maybe there's still hope for me yet, he thought, if only in the fact I did this and not hit her.

Yukinori wanted to finally fill the holes within himself. He wanted to integrate the new Yukinori with the old, make them one and the same, inside and out. He wanted to be entirely new, all the way through, no matter how you sliced him. So he took time off work and headed out to Santo Domingo University with Kiyoto.

Santo Domingo's campus was a banquet of propaganda. There were posters plastered everywhere, forming a seamless mosaic leaving no space unadorned, and he covered his ears after tiring of hearing his voice drone on reading them back to himself. Across wall after wall, spray-painted in a thousand colors, the slogan IT IS RIGHT TO REBEL blared from all sides, reminding him of tunnels defaced by motorcycle gangs back in Japan. He'd seen many such tunnels growing up in the mountains of Gunma, where the gangs ran wild. He'd pass through them on the way to school. It seemed like an illusion that he was in Lima, visiting a university. It seemed more likely that he'd emerge from these graffiti-spackled surroundings and find himself back at the school where he'd stabbed Miss Michiko. He felt himself repeating his past and began to lose sight of why he was there. Lining the pathways connecting the departmental divisions were open-air markets staffed by hippie-ish men and women selling South Asian incense, Che Guevara and Mao Zedong–emblazoned posters and pins and T-shirts, books of East Asian philosophy with titles like *The Study of Zen*, collections of pornographic Japanese woodblocks, all sorts of things. Kiyoto stopped at one of these shops. He introduced Yukinori to three long-haired men and women named Abraham Cerpa, Kisaragi Gilvanio, and Mary Heidegger. Mary was an exchange student from Canada. Kiyoto explained that they were members of the East Asian Culture Study Group, and that he was their cultural consultant.

During the course of the following seventy-two hours, Yukinori found himself sucked into the swirl of their maelstrom of good and evil. We're going to our "Dōjō," they said, referring to the place that doubled as their headquarters and their home, and together they climbed down into the bed of the Rímac River. It was a relatively wide river and its flow was sluggish, neither brown and nor grey but cloudy and stinking of rot. Foam formed on its surface and never dissipated, and from time to time a dead fish would drift past. It seemed to Yukinori like a flow of the viscous fluid produced by the decomposing bodies of various organisms. Yukinori grew sensitive to the smell of rotting meat. He saw in the mud the partially rotted shapes of people and monkeys and pigs and dogs and tomatoes and onions mixing together, their meat half fallen from bones that stuck up out of the mucilaginous broth as if from a well-simmered pot of chicken soup. Atop the piles of discarded trash that lined the riverbank lay the fresh garbage produced by the marketplace that day, like a sauce. There was a strip of land between the edge of the water and rise of the riverbank surrounded by chain link and honeycombed with cardboard buildings like a hive. A gate was located where the bridge met the riverbank, and on either side stood two boys who faced the visitors down, their arms folded across their chests and their hair grown long only in the back, like birds' tails. A group of young men and women around Yukinori's age played soccer in the road that led to the bridge. The boys nodded silently when Abraham introduced Yukinori as a friend.

There were roads just wide enough for a person to squeeze down winding between the cardboard buildings, and each bore an official name. Abraham and Kisaragi's house was located on Naturalism Avenue, District Four. Once inside he had to stoop to avoid hitting the roof made of giant leaves with his head. The room in back was a kitchen *cum* dining room, the room in front was a bedroom *cum* living room floored with straw mats, and behind the kitchen was a little garden where the wash could hang to dry. The so-called "Dōjō" was this living room, small enough that six people sitting side by side threatened to burst its seams and topple its walls. On the back wall hung an oversized portrait of Mao, and in unison they faced this portrait and sang songs of praise to him in Chinese, then lit some incense and sat *zazen*-style to meditate. Even Kiyoto went along, folding his legs beneath him with a creased brow and solemn, downcast eyes. Aghast at the ridiculousness, Yukinori restricted himself to simply crossing his legs and waiting for the others to move again.

Beneath the straw mats was cold sand. The rotten odor of the river filled the room. The smell of cooking soup, the scratchy sound of salsa music playing on cassette players, the ammonia stink of urine, the cries of children, the voices of television actors, smoke of every sort, all these things and more emanated from the houses around him and mixed with the river's stench. If he put a flame to the wall beside him, the entire place would go up in flames before anyone had a chance to get away, he thought: everything would burn away to nothing. These paper buildings could stay up only as long as it didn't rain. They stood in the face of the dry wind, in the face of the realization that they could go up in smoke at any moment. Yukinori supposed that if fire ever really did end up peering down at this paper city from the towering height of its giant body, they'd have to use the river's putrid broth of rotten plants and animals to quell it.

After *zazen* meditation was finally over, it was time for Japanese practice. Before, he was told, there had been martial arts practice at this point. D-O-W-N-W-I-T-H-N-E-O-L-I-B-E-R-A-L-I-S-M chanted Kiyoto in Japanese, and everyone repeated it back. Next he asked: I-S-N-E-O-L-I-B-E-R-A-L-I-S-M-B-A-D? And Kisaragi answered: Y-E-S-I-T-I-S. I-S-A-M-E-R-I-C-A-C-O-R-R-E-C-T, I-S-C-A-N-A-D-A-C-O-R-R-E-C-T, M-A-R-Y-S-A-N? N-O-I-T-I-S-N-O-T. W-H-E-R-E-I-S-Y-O-U-R-H-O-M-E, A-B-R-A-H-A-M-S-A-N? M-Y-H-O-M-E-I-S-T-H-E-W-O-R-L-D.

The sun went down, and after a dinner of jerky-tough beef boiled in beans, they went back into town and stopped at the local bar. They ordered a bottle of cheap Pisco. As they drank and drank, they started talking to a nearby table of men, one of whom spit out his story: I'm a pilot but thanks to that fuck Montesinos I'm working as a damn taxi driver, and I'm about to lose that job too, and then Yukinori's group raised their voices in a chorus, saying, you're one of us, our time will come, see these hands, we'll use them to take it back and return it to you, and with that they all sang a song together. They ended up draining two bottles' worth of alcohol and Kiyoto paid the bill. The bar closed and they were chased out, only to buy even cheaper brandy through the steel-girded window of an all-night liquor store to take back to the riverbed "Dōjō" and keep drinking. Those who got sick threw up onto the ground through gaps in the straw mats and covered it with sand. Those who had to urinate would just walk out into Naturalism Avenue. I'll blow it all away, repeated Yukinori to himself. I'll blow up Chinatown with firecrackers. I'll set fire to this shantytown and burn it to the ground. I'll bomb Miraflores Plaza and reduce all those stuck-up bastards to chunks of meat. I'll drop a bomb in the middle of Japan. I'll machine gun my father full of holes. But I won't have holes. I'll be filled up full, all the way through. I'll use my exceptional endowment to obliterate Mermalada and her foolish words and send her up to heaven. Just you watch.

Yukinori awakened to his eyelids and cheeks and arms assaulted by the sharp light of the sun as it climbed high into the sky, piercing through the ceiling that was little more than a bundle of leaves. Pressing a beer to his aching head, he was greeted by Kisaragi, who seemed to be returning after being out somewhere. Yukinori asked her why she had such a strange, Japanese-sounding name like Kisaragi. It's my code name, replied Kisaragi with a laugh, if I used my real name it'd cause problems for me later, and she plopped down next to Yukinori, pulled out a joint and lit it. As Yukinori moved to take the joint directly from her fingers with his lips, he found them covered instead with Kisaragi's own. As they reverently inhaled the smoke, they slowly removed their clothes. Yukinori felt as if he were peeling off his skin. Kisaragi's fingers on him seemed to caress the wet, shiny bundles of his nerves directly, and his body stiffened and shook with wave after wave of sensation. As Kisaragi wrapped his stiffest part in her fingers, he felt as if she held his very foundation in her hand and was thus able to invade his body. Kisaragi transformed into soft, flickering light and caressed Yukinori as if insinuating herself into his exposed skin. The skin the light caressed was inside Yukinori. His insides were splayed across his outside. The softness and warmth bathed his defenseless interior as if performing an act of mercy. Yukinori felt as if the one who had really been stabbed was himself. Yet that wasn't true. Why hadn't he been the one the knife penetrated, he thought, tears coming to his eyes. The whole reason he'd ended up stabbing someone in the first place was because it was pointless to ask the question why, so asking it of himself now seemed all the more futile, and an intense feeling began to rise within him. It swelled and strengthened, stimulated by the warmth and light caressing his interior. At some point Kisaragi's warmth was replaced by Mary's, and in her Anglophone-accented Spanish she cried out, you're swallowing me, you're sucking me up! Kisaragi slipped beneath Yukinori and began grunting rhythmically, her ass covered with sand. When from time to time the grunting grew muffled, it was due to her mouth filling with Abraham.

The twilight was wet with the humidity rising from the river, and Yukinori regained consciousness hungry, dragging his heavy body like a python slithering through the tropical heat into the kitchen area, where he sucked down the last of the beans from the night before. Unsatisfied, he went out into Naturalism Avenue, fighting vertigo and looking for somewhere to buy food. He didn't see any likely place, though he begged some bread from one of the houses bleeding light into the darkness, and then he lost himself in the labyrinthine tangle of streets, thinking that he had no choice but to keep moving, keep running, if he stopped he'd be overtaken by the question why, he had to keep fleeing as far as possible from Miss Michiko's body full of holes vomiting her insides, and as he ran, he eventually calmed, realizing that he was fleeing an illusion built of darkness, and as the dawn began to stain the sky, making everything glisten as if submerged in water, he found himself back on Naturalism Avenue, standing once more before the "Dōjō," and he went in and fell again into the futon of flesh.

Awoken by his new friends dragging him up to find some real food, Yukinori breathed in the moist air so sour with sex and vomit and muttered that he could feel himself rusting. He wanted to rinse off somewhere he could feel fresh air, even if it was in the fetid river. Why don't you just rinse off under my shower, joked Kisaragi, and Yukinori responded with ill-tempered silence as he trailed after the others.

Yukinori regretted sleeping till noon. He usually carefully avoided napping during the day. Whenever he slept until the sun grew strong enough to throw the shapes of things into sharp relief, their edges honed to slice you open, he always dreamed of glittering knives. The knives shone bright enough to mistake for sunlight, slicing through clothes into thighs and torsos, felling body after body. The falling bodies belonged to Miss Michiko, or Yukinori himself, or his father, or the half-American, half-Japanese mixed-blood mother he'd never lain eyes on, whom he'd never even known the name of. He'd stab the knife eight times. He'd count on his fingers, fingers that smelled of iron. He'd bring these fingers to his nose and the lukewarm, wet metal odor would fill his nostrils like a nosebleed. He'd lick them and taste the iron. Then he'd wake up, more often than not, to find himself as stiff as steel.

As soon as they'd filled their bellies with potato omelets, Abraham broached the subject of Yukinori joining their group. He didn't mean the East Asian Culture Study Group. Join our organization, he said. The Study Group is just a local branch of the real group, meant to aid in the indoctrination of students. The real group is MARTA. MARTA aims to topple the neoliberalism that controls the world, to destroy racist nationalism and bring about a final worldwide revolution that will wipe out poverty and discrimination everywhere. Therefore all the mongrel outcasts of the world must unite and take the reins of power. But right now our leader and founder is rotting in prison and his immediate release is our top priority. We've been recruiting comrades to help with this, and Kiyoto, our Japanese agent, scouted you and gave you his highest recommendation, so please, join us and help us achieve our mission.

Yukinori knew that the past seventy-two hours had been a brainwashing session designed to paralyze his common sense. Why should I rescue some Peruvian revolutionary, he asked, refusing Abraham's entreaty. The organization has no nationality, replied Abraham, pointing at Mary, and that's why our mission is one that will change the whole world, but then Yukinori cut him off, saying, I grant that your revolution has its reasons and makes sense for you, but "wipe out poverty"? "Final revolution"? It all seems a bit overdone. Abraham was silent. It's simple, Kiyoto interjected. We'll take some hostages and make our demands. If the demands aren't met, we'll kill the hostages. Win or lose, we'll all escape together to Japan. I have associates already who'll smuggle us in. That'll be the only promise we make to each other. That'll be the extent of it, we won't owe anything else to any other organization. Our ultimate target is Japan, the giant castle in the center of Japan, that gaping hole surrounded by trees and walls. Kiyoto claimed to have all the necessary money lined up. My father owns land in Kobe, giving out money is part of his duty as a parent, plus it'll be part of his reparations for my crime, he boasted.

Just like when he read the diaries he'd written, Yukinori was seized with nausea that felt strong enough to turn him inside out. It wasn't his hangover, or lack of sleep, or the marijuana. He was being poisoned by Kiyoto's words. These quiet words that had seemed to cleanse and purify his body were now boring holes in it, burrowing their way in, invading him. They were oxidizing him, rusting him, turning him into something cloudy, unclean, riddled with holes. But on the other hand, something was also resonating deep within him. It was exactly like the impulse he'd felt to destroy his diary. It strengthened his nausea. Yet, when he'd been seized with that impulse, he hadn't gone through with it, he hadn't destroyed his diary. He felt his hair stand on end like flame. Kiyoto was what he had to destroy. Whatever else he was, Kiyoto was false, conniving, a trickster. The one who needed expelling was him. Him or me, thought Yukinori, only one of us could live.

And even as he thought this, Yukinori nodded his assent to Kiyoto. Great, let's drink to our new comrade, exclaimed Kiyoto, and he ordered a round of Pisco sours. Abraham led the toast, shouting: give me the world or give me death!

The world or death. Him or me. Yukinori repeated this toast every fifteen minutes or so to himself, silently, in his heart. Every time, he felt an unpleasant sensation, as if he were viewing his feverish, frenzied self from afar. He felt water filling the space between him and this other self. And as he repeated the words, him or me, he realized it would be Kiyoto who'd survive. It was Kiyoto who'd framed the question in the first place. It was his logic it obeyed. Mermalada had used those words, too: it's either him or me, she'd said. Broken by these words, he wanted to stand before Mermalada again, but this time fully intact, free of impurities and holes and pockets of nothing, he wanted to confront her with his unmixed purity and this time he would be the one to break her. Kiyoto fed on hearts divided against each other and would therefore live forever. If he thought like Kiyoto, he'd be destroyed by his words. Yukinori intended to write these thoughts down in his diary. In Spanish or Japanese, it no longer mattered.

After that, Yukinori was forced to live in a cardboard cell separated from the "Dōjō" for three days as a test of his loyalty. The boys who kept watch over him, trained to keep their eyes devoid of emotion, spoke not a word to him, leaving Yukinori to make do with the conversations of the other slum dwellers as he wandered the streets. Whenever they caught sight of him, their lips would purse and they'd shrink back like little birds from his questions no matter how unassumingly he asked them, so to find anything out he had to melt into his surroundings, into the walls and dirt, like a ninja. Then he'd write the information he gathered down in his notebooks. The conversations he overheard were frequently concerned with the countless sects crowded into this city bounded by chain link. There was an organization plotting to turn the world on its head for every shanty in the town, from underground cabals plotting revolution to new religions striving toward worldwide salvation, and while all were suspicious and hostile toward the government, they were even more so toward each other, and the hatred gathering within the fences grew ever stronger. As he recorded his findings, he realized that it was this hatred itself that Kiyoto aimed to foment. He nursed the paranoia and hostility that grew within him as he wandered the streets, ignored by the fellow cardboard city residents who'd been told to shun him, and found himself playing more and more into Kiyoto's plans. Thinking that if he didn't solidify his thoughts into words he'd be molded completely into the shape Kiyoto had in mind for him, he consolidated his antagonism by tracing the process of its flowering as he'd written it down during his three day incarceration, and, satisfied by this knowledge of how much of what he did and felt were part of Kiyoto's plan, he drifted off to sleep on the final evening of his loyalty test.

Yukinori opened his eyes to find something stickier and hotter than human skin sliding over his face and down his entire body, making it hard to breathe. He heard a sound like liquid rising violently to a boil. Before he could think of what it could be, smoke rolled into the room and filled it, wrapping itself around Yukinori's body. Coughing violently, he crawled across the floor trying not to breathe in the smoke, and then the cardboard walls around him broke apart and folded down on him, the leaves forming the roof blowing upward, carried by the hot blast, and he could see flames dancing in the wind like waving hair. "They got me," he cried in Japanese, and he reached for the bag containing his diary notebooks, only to find a brown envelope lying beside it with the words TREASON DIARY Magic Markered in Japanese across its face, so he grabbed that too and ran into the street, heading toward the gate and yelling *Fuck, it's a trap* over and over to himself as he fled. A sound like a tree snapping shattered the air in front of him, and as the hot, close breath of the fire caressed his face, he smelled his hair begin to smolder and felt sweat begin to run down his skin as if his very flesh was melting and running down his body, and he pressed his eyes shut and covered his face with his hands. The slick feel of the skin beneath his fingers made him think he'd turned to wax and that this wax was catching fire and dripping through his fingers. He made a break for the river, which seemed to give off coolness amid the heat. To his right a man yelled, *save my house, put out the fire on the second floor*, and when he turned to look, he saw a column of flame rising like a pillar. The fire must have started there and spread, he thought. Flames danced across the tops of the cardboard buildings as fast as a person could run. He knew if he faltered he'd be overtaken. Yukinori broke ranks with the others fleeing around him, and, climbing over and stepping on the fallen, he ran for the fence and clawed his way up and over it. He didn't stop running once he hit the riverbed and instead kept going until he reached the sludgy, putrid river itself and jumped in. Fighting the current, he waded across to the far shore, and, finally, after making sure the incinerating wind couldn't reach him, he collapsed. All along the shore were others who'd fallen to the ground like he had, as well as those who stood and wept as they watched the fire, their faces stained red and sooty black by its light. Feeling his singed hair and clothes and the blistered backs of his hand, Yukinori stared vacantly at the flames as if watching a firework display. Flames bloomed as the fire burned like orchids or hibiscus flowers. Even amid all the red, he could make out shimmering threads of lemon yellow and jacaranda violet, the delicate green of dragonfly wings and the various colors of twilight.

A hand clapped on his shoulder and snapped him out of his flame-induced trance. Kiyoto was laughing. Something cold slipped down Yukinori's spine, raising goose bumps. It looks like something not of this world, said Kiyoto in the tone of someone struggling to suppress his excitement. His hair was scorched and shriveled, his blackened face slick with mud and soot. And not just Kiyoto, but Yukinori too, and everyone else gathered on the riverbank, all their faces were wet. He didn't know if it was river water or fluid from burst blisters or blood, but he smeared his finger in it and sniffed and licked it. It was sweat. He hadn't noticed himself sweating at all, he even felt a little chilled standing there where the fire's heat no longer reached him.

So you rescued it, I should thank you, said Kiyoto, indicating the brown envelope still clutched in Yukinori's hand. I almost went back in to retrieve it myself.

Why did a fire break out while I was incarcerated, asked Yukinori in a low voice.

Why ask me? As if I'd know such a thing.

So it was a coincidence this envelope shows up right when I'm trying to escape?

And for that I give thanks. If it hadn't, it would just be ash by now.

Who put it there? The others?

I don't know. I couldn't have banked on you rescuing it, could I?

If it was so important, what was it doing there?

I couldn't have it discovered, there's some bad shit written in there.

Yukinori pulled one of the notebooks out and flipped back the front cover to read in the glare of the fire. The first page bore the heading TREASON DIARY I: TURN AWAY FROM THE SELF THAT RULES THIS WORLD. On the next page he read a poem cursing a nameless god. The narrating "I," who'd been betrayed by this "unclean god," becomes himself a "god of this stinking world/enclosed in concrete," and then the "hate and pain/of the people I rule/will curse and kill" this unclean god. Reflexively, Yukinori vowed never to write poetry. It was all lies, poetry. Yet, looking at the shape of it on the page, the short lines running across the top half leaving a white expanse below, he felt anxious, as if it were his own lower half that had been cut away. The poem's words seemed to infiltrate his body through this wound. Turning the page again, he found not another poem, but something more like footnotes. The further he progressed into the diary, the denser the words on the page became, as if driven by an increasingly pressing need to obliterate entirely the white space from the pages.

Yukinori felt his heart start racing, and he closed the notebook. He was afraid if he didn't he'd get sucked in and have to read it all the way to the end. As if reading his mind, Kiyoto told him he could take it with him and read it. After all, you saved it from the fire, he said. Actually, I want you to read it. Perhaps I wrote it just to be read by you, now that I think of it. As a souvenir of my time in the juvenile detention center. I plan to publish it when we complete our mission in Japan.

Yukinori felt something crackle in his chest the way the fire crackled on the far shore. This guy knew I was keeping a diary during my incarceration. My writing was all a part of his plan. He's showing me his diary now to ridicule me, as if to say that everything I write has already been written. He knew I wouldn't be able keep my hands off anything written in Japanese that wasn't my own, he planned the whole thing. Yukinori felt as if Kiyoto had seen through him entirely, had even seen the things he'd written in his diary before they met.

You can't possibly be thinking that I set this fire just to make you read my diary, said Kiyoto, staring at Yukinori as he pondered his suppositions, and while his lips were smiling, his voice was deadly serious. These slum dwellers are an important resource. Why would I senselessly kill them before I could use them? Didn't you see that guy screaming his head off back there while you were running away? The fire was set to spite him. The second story on his building could be used to send signals to the outside, so the story is that he'd been communicating with government intelligence and helping out with their sweeps of underground activists. So it was payback for that, or maybe the work of a different government snitch who'd found himself out of a job, I don't know. But what does it matter? The important thing is you reading the diary.

After that Yukinori washed up at Kiyoto's apartment near the university, borrowed some clothes and went back home. When he flipped on the light, Mermalada sprang from the bed and assaulted him with a voice like scraping metal and a look in her eyes like a shooting flare: you've gone too far, there's no taking this back now. I told you if you chose that creep over me I'd be gone for good, and, as if she'd prepared for this scene beforehand, she started to rip up all the letters Yukinori had written to her into tiny pieces like tearing bread into crumbs. These were the letters she'd said she'd wanted even to eat, every time she received them, the envelopes he'd paid for with his laboring flesh, the stamps he'd licked, the words his hands had put to paper. Yukinori simply watched silently from where he stood by the potted plants, bathed in the early morning sun coming through the window. Mermalada cried as she tore the letters apart. How could you do this when you know I understand how you feel, she whispered, her voice shaking, her nose snuffling. Yukinori realized that Mermalada felt the same unsettled feeling that Yukinori did when he came into contact with Kiyoto, but a hundred or two hundred times worse. Yukinori knew he was different from Kiyoto. His heart swelled with the desire not to lose her. Yet he remained frozen where he stood, enveloped in particles of orange light. Still muttering to herself, Mermalada finally left the apartment.

Over the next four days Yukinori read to the end of the three notebooks of Kiyoto's diary. It seemed both just like and completely different from his own. The first part was filled with naïve musings on the definition of "self" and "humanity," interspersed with large amounts of poetry, but gradually the focus shifted toward a more generalized, socially conscious perspective. In one of the notebooks, there was a daily series of "THOUGHTS ON JAPAN FROM THE OUTSIDE IN," which attempted to interpret the incident he'd perpetrated through its context. It started as an analysis of his home life and his dissatisfaction with the education system, but soon he came to see it as performing a kind of social critique, and the analysis became a fevered call for revolution. It was in these pages that Yukinori saw Kiyoto's ideas about "broken people" first begin to take shape. He wrote that while the impetus behind his crime was correct, its target was not, and this process of redirecting his actions toward a more appropriate object seemed to serve as expiation for his wrongdoing, as a kind of self-justification. But what didn't come up was any mention of Peru. About halfway through the diary, Kiyoto finally described his crime directly. It took the form of a series of confessions recounting the incident accompanied by explanations for why it happened. Written in a studiously conversational style, each version differed slightly in its delineation of motive and in the details of the crime itself, but none failed to give some sort of clear causal explanation, and while Yukinori felt refreshed and comforted by this, as if swimming through a river of clear, cold water, he also felt a growing irritation as he sensed these accounts drifting farther and farther away from the incident itself as they retold and reframed it. He found the phrase WORDS ALWAYS BETRAY scribbled in the margin of one of the pages. Near the end, increasingly large gaps began to appear between the dates of the entries, and sometimes they sounded more like excerpts from a novel than a diary. This novel appeared to tell the story of a group of dispossessed people who'd had their voices taken from them banding together to convert their pent-up anger into energy and take back their stolen words through terrorism. As he kept reading, though, Yukinori noticed that the words structuring the diary were themselves stolen from other sources. Whenever footnote-like treatments of some book or other would appear, the subsequent entries would suddenly change, aping these new ideas.

Yukinori felt as if bits of Kiyoto's flesh were lodging themselves within his body and he wanted to dislodge them, rip them out. He was angry at himself for sucking these slick words down so easily and clinging to their comforts so tenaciously. He knew that words begat words. It was a fallacy to think they could ever be stolen or taken back. Kiyoto didn't really believe that he'd be taking back his words by publishing these diaries. It was just a plan to render words themselves extinct. Yukinori was gripped again by a strong urge to kill Kiyoto, to prevent this coming loneliness at all costs. And again he wondered if this was not just one more trap carefully laid for him. Was Kiyoto trying to manipulate Yukinori into killing him?

As if reading his mind once more, when Yukinori came to return the diaries, Kiyoto told him in Japanese that he had no ulterior motives for having him read them. I just wanted to give you an idea for where I was coming from, before you join me in our present action. From now on, there'll be no more cogitating about hidden meanings, no more room for hesitation, just one concerted movement, full speed ahead. I'm only this confident because I'm not alone, I have other comrades supporting me. The Red Shining Path has expressed interest in using me. They're pursuing a red and shining path to bring about a miracle. Did you know that the Path's founder comes from a noble family that goes back hundreds of years? Anyway, it's obvious that MARTA's attempt to free its leader will end in failure. Worst case, they'll all be killed. But we'll get away, you see? We're going to pose as hostages. I want you to prepare yourself to get a little banged up. Though our lives mean less to them than theirs do anyway. So why should we help them? I want to make this little cookie-cutter cell self-destruct. If it were to succeed, all that would happen would be the destruction of a few cookie-cutter cells on the other side. So was there any need for me to come all the way to Peru? There wasn't, was there? But I'd heard from the Path that you were living here, so I decided to come. I thought it might be worth it to pick you up and bring you back with me. Though I have to say it's been hard putting up with the people here, you know?

Yukinori just nodded. It all felt like lies. Did he even know the Red Shining Path? It seemed patently obvious that he was lying about coming to Peru to meet him. All Kiyoto'd been thinking when he came here was that there'd be outcasts to reach out to, that Peru itself was a broken country that was outcast itself. Or rather, it had decided it had been broken and used words borne of hate and anger to make the rest of the world see it as broken too. Yukinori didn't believe any of Kiyoto's words. And it wasn't because words always betray, either. It was because Kiyoto himself didn't believe in words. Kiyoto had never been betrayed by words. You can't believe the words of someone who didn't believe in them himself.

Yet Yukinori remembered tasting the pleasure of purification more than once in Kiyoto's words. He'd felt the poison leave his body as he listened to the clumsy, halting Spanish coming from Kiyoto's mouth, words that formed a discourse as cookie-cutter as any he decried. Yukinori always found himself defenseless in the face of it. Yukinori felt forbidden from ever keeping his diary again. He knew that if he resumed his writing he'd end up arriving where Kiyoto was now, that Kiyoto was seducing him, saying go ahead and write, go ahead and turn into me. It drove him crazy. It was he who prevented his own writing.

Kiyoto told him he was starting his recruitment drive for the action scheduled to take place seven months hence, and he brought Yukinori along with him as he visited the refugees from the burned-out riverside settlement who'd gathered in Plaza San Martín. Some displaced residents had found new homes in other slums, but those who couldn't wound up in the Plaza. Blue plastic tents erected by sympathizers encrusted the Plaza like barnacles, and even the "Dōjō" found new life, using one of these tents as a base for plying new refugees with alcohol and shady rituals like those previously performed on Yukinori.

In order to devote all of his energy to these recruitment activities, Yukinori packed his bags and moved into a separate blue tent dubbed the "Dōjō Annex." He did so to prevent himself from thinking, to prevent himself from writing. Whenever he allowed himself the smallest room to think, to remember Mermalada, to confront himself, he was seized with the urge to bury a knife into something soft. As his body filled with Kiyoto's empty words, everything around him seemed to grow more and more hateful. He became slavishly obedient, and the feeling of his body possessed by someone else's will, no matter how fleeting, closed any gap through which his thoughts could leak. As if marking time until an alarm went off and freed him, Yukinori transformed himself into a robot, and his body as he moved it felt like so much meat.

Fire struck the new tent city a month after it had struck the old shantytown. This time it was day and it remained small, so no one died, but it sparked a rumor that the five-star hotels facing the Plaza had conspired with government intelligence to burn them out. The refugees rolled up their tents and moved to the sandy plateau in the mountains on the far side of the Rímac the next day. There was already a major slum in that area, sprawling along one side of a major highway leading to the countryside, so Yukinori and the others ended up "settling" the higher slope on the opposite side. At first there were just tents, but soon there appeared homes built of cardboard and plywood. The settlers stole electricity from a nearby pole and water from the slum down below. More people started to move in, and within three weeks the makeshift city grew big enough that the roads winding between the shelters bore names again. And amid all this activity, Yukinori concentrated on his training and self-indoctrination, on this process of automating his being.

Three months later, this new village was obliterated once more. Unseasonable rain fell hard and reduced the cardboard houses to mush, and landslides wiped out the plywood ones as well, changing the composition of the ground itself so that nothing could be rebuilt. The residents evacuated for a time in a large shelter in the lower slum, but as soon as the rain stopped they were chased out, accused of stealing water. Left with no other choice, the refugees returned once more to the burned-out ruins on the Rímac riverbed. There was already a small group of squatters who'd created their own little community there. Work began to rebuild the chain link city, and just as the future was looking bright for this project, it was time for the MARTA members to move deep into the Amazon basin on the far side of the Andes and begin the final stage of their paramilitary training.

Yukinori still felt warm, lemon-colored light bathe his body. Slowly opening his eyelids, his eyes were pierced by the sun shining in through the window. The hostages were shuffling wordlessly around the room for their morning exercise. Fine particles of dust danced in the shafts of light behind them. He could hear shouts filtering up from where the MARTA members were playing soccer down below. Yukinori was still alive. No one else had noticed that the air reeked, filled with this smell of iron or explosives, whichever. Yukinori observed the sunlight going in and out of the room through the windowpane. During the time it took for the particles of light to enter, bounce off the carpet, then go back out the window, the smell just grew thicker. It seemed that the explosion could happen at any time.

Yukinori's job was to spy on the hostages. Having infiltrated the Japanese Ambassador's Residence dressed as waiters during the celebration of the Emperor's birthday taking place there on the twenty-seventh of December, Yukinori and Kiyoto shed their white uniforms and blended in with the other guests during the confusion following rockets being launched into the Residence's rear garden, pretending to be herded along with them by the masked guerillas who poured through the hole blasted in the fence, and as negotiations drew to a standstill, they were able to insinuate themselves into the society the hostages created and eventually caught wind of the action the government forces were plotting just outside the Residence walls, but Yukinori did nothing to prevent Kiyoto from spreading misinformation about it to the MARTA members. There was no reason for MARTA to trust them in the first place, after all, and he wasn't even sure the real information was true anyway.

Yukinori had transformed completely into a battle robot. He'd come to see himself this way as he trained deep within the Amazon jungle alongside Kiyoto and the thirteen other members of the team. A battle robot needs no words. He'd sent Mermalada his diary, telling her that in her hands she held the words that formed Yukinori Akimizu's soul, and that even though they'd never meet again, he'd be with her, and that he prayed she felt the same way about him: these were his final words. Any that escaped his lips thereafter would be nothing more than so many robotic components. As he'd entered the jungle and sweat flowed from his body in the humid air that felt heavier than water, as his blood was sucked by mosquitoes and leeches, as diarrhea from living on nuts streamed from him, as muscles emerged from deep within his body, all the unnecessary words stored up inside him flowed free, borne along with his excretions to be swallowed by the Amazon, leaving him at peace. He'd had nothing more to tell.

But now these words began to move within him once more. As the smell of iron or explosives drifted up from the eight holes carved into his body and from the space below the Residence floor, Yukinori was once again seized with shock. He felt himself become a bomb, felt the Residence begin to bleed. He heard the Residence cry out, heard Miss Michiko's moans, felt himself swallowing Kiyoto's words and shitting them uncontrollably from his anus, heard tense whispers amid the particles of light, he wanted to write this all down, this was the story he wanted told. That he wanted understood. Or rather, that he wanted someone to offer to understand, that he wanted to understand himself. Why was no one else noticing the smell as he did, it was pitiful, painful, a puzzle. With every movement of the air around him he hallucinated an explosion, and he attempted to fill in the blanks between Miss Michiko's stabbing and the massacre about to ensue, he wanted to think it all through, wanted to write it all down, but the words that came to him transformed instead into a choking iron smell and colors made of flames, shards of Japanese mixing into Spanish until he saw a vision of his father's flesh stuck in pieces to the ruins around him, of he and Miss Michiko and Kiyoto wrapped in threads spun from blood, falling. These visions and sensations collided into one another and Yukinori couldn't piece together any relation between them.

The light flickered in the wind. The wind was the beating of birds' wings. There were inky-black wings glittering iridescent blue and orange as they danced outside the window. Perhaps the birds had come to suck the nectar from the red, flame-shaped flowers of the vine that twined around the iron window frame. A fluting bird-call rang out from where one of them perched. He felt the floor swell beneath him like a rising wave. Intense heat burst upward, strong enough to melt people like wax. Then a rushing blast of air, followed by an eardrum-battering roar that shook the building. The hostages who'd been walking around hit the floor, their hands covering their heads. Several angry voices could be heard below, but the bombs kept exploding and soon there was the sound of gunfire, cutting them off. Soldiers entered the second story from an unexpected direction and shouted something at the hostages, who squirmed across the floor like crushed ants in the direction the soldiers indicated. The soldier at the head of the group began exchanging gunfire from a hiding place near the door and suddenly his neck snapped back as if broken, and he fell face up on the floor. The other soldiers dragged him away. Another soldier descended the staircase and plugged a bullet into Mary's forehead where she lay at the bottom glaring up at him, both her legs blown off and shitting herself. Reaching for Kisaragi as she wriggled her upper body, her lower half pinned beneath an oak desk, Abraham suddenly had his throat slit wide by a knife the size and shape of a rubber tree leaf, and the fountain of blood that erupted continued flowing even after the battle had ended and all the hostages were evacuated, filling the bathtub-size hole blasted into the ground beneath him to overflowing.

And Yukinori and Kiyoto seemed to be everywhere at once yet nowhere to be found, not in the rust-colored pool of Abraham's blood, nor in the group of hostages striking jubilant poses and exchanging handshakes outside the Residence walls, not among the shadowy figures quietly splitting off from the rest of the hostages, nor in the group of men in khaki uniforms leaving through the tunnels that had been dug beneath the Residential grounds to facilitate the attack. There was even a critically injured soldier who'd reported seeing two hostages killing each other amid the confusion, but he too eventually died. The official dead remained numbered at just fifteen: two government soldiers and thirteen MARTA guerillas.

A *Milonga* for the Melted Moon (1999)

They say it doesn't exist, this city that glows like a flow of molten silver. Long ago, before the first words were heard, these plains stretched in all directions without end, and they say there fell rain like golden honey and snow like grains of silver. Clouds of crumpled silverleaf would appear in the clear blue sky and the sunlight, confused, would refract and light the sky even brighter, and then the silver would dance down, the daylight outshining even the plains that stretched below, untouched by any shadows thrown by boulders or tall-standing trees. The silver would split the sunlight more and more finely as it fell thick enough that everything below turned silver-white at once: the grass, the trees, the stones, the water. A glittering desert formed as the silverfall grew deeper, and, just as rivers of sand form amid dunes, the silver began to flow toward the sea, grains of it rubbing together as they tumbled until the friction melted it into a shining liquid. Soon these silver rivers flowed into those formed by the golden honey rain and their tributaries of liquid crystal, and as rivers begat more rivers, they widened until their shores pushed beyond the horizon and the river grew large as an ocean, large as a sky, flowing languorous as liquid candy. The untroubled surface of the great river reflected the sky without the slightest distortion, a perfect mirror. The sun as it shone on the river received its light reflected back and shone a doubly bright platinum. And as the pale light from the heavens met the denser light thrown back by the river, shadowed rifts formed in the sky, rifts shaped like knives, like fish, like birds, like people.

The rifts shaped like people gathered in the sky and were reflected in the river, and they say that this was start of the city. And this is also why they say it doesn't really exist. What looks like a city are simply shadows formed by fluctuating light. And the source of this light is no longer traceable. The river reflects the light, reflects the breath of the people. It reflects the birds as they fly, the fish as they swim. It reflects me as a man, it reflects me as a woman. It reflects you, it reflects him, it reflects her, it reflects a skylark. It reflects me and I become him, it reflects him and he becomes you, it reflects you and you become a swallow. You and I both, as we walk this earth, are nothing more than shadow sculptures carved from light. Everyone here is just light thrown by the city in the sky as it shines in the night. This city is so filled with light the night shines like the midday sun, the silver from the sky as it falls on the surface of the river builds up and combines with the new light falling from the sky, the proof is in the way the light comes not just from the sky but from the ground beneath our feet: no shadows trouble the surfaces of this city. Instead they hang suspended, unmoored from the ground, and eventually turn back into birds, back into people.

Then, one copper-colored midday near the end of summer, you appeared. The city at noon is extremely bright, and the cloudless sky above turns a blue so pure it starts to look black; some days stars appear. When night falls, the numberless stars shine like hot, crushed-crystal sand, and their light pierces like so many needles thinner than threads of silk, rendering us unable to raise our eyelids. Eyes shut and ears open, we can hear the streams of falling light vibrate like the strings of a guitar, play an arpeggio as they pour through the empty sky like molten metal from a cauldron only to coalesce again, turn back into silvery light once more as they reach the surface of the earth and flow into the river that continues on its course as a sound like

the tangled songs of violins and *bandoneones* plays across
its surface. But we all know that the stars, too, are merely
heavenly reflections of the silver on the surface of the river.
Everything here wavers like the voice of a violin, only really
visible in silhouette, dizzying all who come here from afar.
And yet you are the only thing I've ever seen that seemed
truly distorted, as if constantly reflected in water.

You were wearing a shirt striped with white and pale
blue. That morning our soccer team had just won their
game, so everyone was running around, frenzied; everyone was wearing striped shirts like yours, and everyone
was clamoring to shout from the top of the lookout tower
and spray amber-colored beer over the crowds below:
"*Viva!*" Young men gathered at the base of the coquettish
angel who stepped off the top of the tower with her wings
spread, prepared for either takeoff or a tumbling descent,
and they kissed her breasts and danced merrily, their arms
slung around her hips. Perhaps under the impression that
they could fly too, some of them tumbled from the tower to
smash like ripe mangoes on the ground below. The traffic
in the roundabout encircling the tower drew to a halt, and
some drivers leapt from their cars as if driven mad by the
sun and waved flags striped the same blue and white as
everyone's shirts, while others spun their tires against the
gravel in a kind of waltz, or extended their hands out their
car windows to interlace their fingers with those whose soft
hands similarly extended from the cars beside them.

But I found myself alone, set carefully outside the
fray as if made of fine china. I was the only gloomy one.
Everyone else's voices and faces melted into each other
like butter, but I found myself completely intact, able to
pick out the songs of the darting little birds, discern the
ripe passionfruit from the unripe, distinguish the smell
of hogshead soup from that of soup boiled from chicken
feet. And so I was the only one to notice you as you stood
beneath the hundred-year-old jacaranda tree blooming
in the central plaza and scooped red meat from a wedge

of melon with a spoon, a tiny flag that matched the others' tucked behind your left ear, skin the color of toasted wheat showing through your beer-drenched shirt, a red handkerchief stuffed carelessly into your breast pocket, a knife in a sheath tooled with a complex pattern of foliage hanging from your hip, your feet slid into two right shoes.

The figure you cut blurred as you stood there surrounded by all the others. No matter how hard I tried to focus, your edges refused to resolve. At first glance you looked just like everyone else, but as I watched, you seemed somehow separate from the crowd's din. Watching you I thought, *here was a person with whom I'd be willing to escape the closed circle of my everyday.* And this thought made my skin fragment and bubble, made me feel as if I were giving off steam. At the same time, I felt like I already knew you. Like I'd seen you countless times before. Your hips and the knife that hung from them seemed familiar. Every time I fall in love, it's with the same person. The time we spend together always ends up a repetition. I was your captive even before you first called my name, first touched your fingers to my skin. My heart hurt as presentiment gripped it, and I felt a certain sadness as it did.

The plaza rustled with a sound like the leaves of all the trees around us whispering at once. The breeze scrambled the sound of the soccer fans' celebration into an oceanic roar. Never taking your eyes from mine, you briefly mimed wearing the rind of your melon atop your head of long, black, wavy hair before throwing it away, and then you were walking toward me, smiling only with your eyes, your head held immobile, stalking me boldly like an animal. I couldn't tell if the wetness on my skin was from sweat or from the windborne spray of the fountain at whose edge I stood as I panicked and turned my face to the right, keeping your image in the corner of my left eye as you drew closer. You turned to your own right in response, disappearing from my field of vision with a squeak of your obviously new shoes. I turned my face farther to the right to see where you went. My neck corkscrewing like a crane's, I watched you march away from me as if keeping in step with an unseen line of soldiers.

I'd just resigned myself to my disappointment at your leaving when I heard the loud, sudden sound of gravel crunching beneath shoes to my left and turned to find you approaching, already almost close enough to touch. My skin quivered nervously, suddenly sensitive to the slightest breeze, to the soft breath of birds. The din of the crowds, the rustling of the leaves, all the sounds around me blended together and caressed my body like a banana-shaped mass. I sensed soft heat gathering at my pelvis, movements in the air around me, footsteps that sounded like whispers—but then, at the very moment the surface of my body surged in anticipation of the feel of your breath upon it, you passed right by me, leaving me adrift in your melon and *maté*-scented wake. The right side of my body tightened as the cold spray from the fountain hit it, and all the energy left me at once as I curled forward, my knees cracking, and sat back down on the fountain's edge, suffused with equal parts relief and despair. I gazed after your retreating head, heedlessly caressing each flowing strand of your hair with my eyes as it shimmered blue-black as the night sky. Imagining this hair as a series of dark waves I felt compelled to part, I was closing my eyes and preparing to let out a deep sigh when you turned back again, prompting me to rise to my feet like a cresting wave myself. It would have been better if I had just continued gazing at the far jacaranda tree as if able to gaze right through you, but my body's response had already precluded that excuse and I was left with no way to escape as you made your third approach.

Bearing down upon me, you slipped into my pale blue eyes without a splash. *Kathung:* my body filled with the sound of your submergence. You swam in my eyes like a thin, silver-bodied fish, and it tickled so that I exhaled sharply, neither quite laughing nor sighing. I shivered at the chill of the liquid in my eyes, goosebumps rising on my skin. You examined these bumps one by one as they arose, then at last raised your eyes to meet mine and laughed. Droplets of moisture seemed to rise like a sweet mist from your entire body and my body, in turn, began to moisten in response, grow sticky. I looked away, turned my gaze toward the sun. I squinted into the silvery, faintly reddish light and this light became concentrated within my contracting pupils, bouncing back on itself within them. Strength returned to my eyes and I turned back to look at you again, wanting to burn you with my gaze. The laughter disappeared from your lips, your eyes narrowed, and you circled me, your body close enough to brush my skin, your feet barely moving, and you withdrew an orange blossom from your pocket and tossed it to me. I don't know if it was your scent or the blossom's, but I found myself engulfed in a sweet perfume that seemed to melt me, dissolve my will, dissolve my bones, make standing seem ridiculous, make keeping my eyes open seem unbearable. The air undulated as you moved, producing a breeze that was hardly a breeze at all, and the golden, downy hair along my arms felt this breeze as an embrace. Your warmth penetrated to my very bones. The breath that escaped my mouth mingled with yours and riffled my downy hair again. Even as I asked myself why it would be so, I felt everything solid within me melt, turn liquid, threaten to overflow my body: there was nothing I could do. And even as my lower body buckled and I felt myself collapsing toward the earth once more, I heard your voice like a cello's lowest register murmur something into my ear. Into only my ear. You spoke and the words echoed in the hollow of my body.

You collapsed like a wave retreating, clutching at my knees as you went down, drawing shallow grooves down my pants with your knifelike nails painted glittering green, until you lay completely prone upon the ground. Your eyes filled and turned transparent, swelling like a drop of water at the lip of a faucet, stopped by the lashes that edged your eyelids like the points of a crown, making it look as if your very eyes were liquefying. Your skin shone pure white from where your dress, the color of a ripe tomato, revealed it. This skin looked so delicate that to touch it would be to wound it, it seemed filled with liquid about to over-flow, and even though I moved to support you, my hands refused to reach out; instead I bent to look you in the eye, brought my mouth to your ear once more to whisper my words as if filling you with breath to reinflate what had wilted within you.

"Please don't ask my name, it's rude." Your voice wavered in the air as if it would disappear like smoke if I weren't careful.

"I won't. Even if I did, I'd just forget it. I've met people like you so many times before." Your voice trembled like a flute's song, and you refused to look directly at me.

"I've seen you many times before as well. Not people like you, but you; it was really you."

"When, I wonder? I can almost remember, but not quite." The warmth of your lips passed through your breath to touch my ear.

"That makes sense. I didn't meet you, I just saw you. I saw you practicing that dance of yours on the roof of your apartment building, that dance that looks like the move-ment of waves: I'd watch you from my room on the other side of the river."

"You came from the other side of the river? We can't see the other side from here, but you can see us from there? I know nothing of that side of the river." Your eyes glinted silver like the river, reflecting the shine of mine.

"It's exactly like this side. Even I find it hard to tell whether I've really crossed the river, if I really am in the city on the far shore."

"Is this the first time you've come?"

"No, I've come and gone countless times before. For my work. I've crossed back and forth too many times, sometimes I lose track of where I really come from, where

I was born, whether I've mixed my cities up. Watching you dance on your rooftop became a way for me to keep track. The city where the real you lives is the one I wasn't born in."

"How can you see this city from the other side when we can't see the other side from here? It's impossible to imagine anyone being able to see across that river."

"We can't see across it all the time. Only on windy days; your city appears with the sunset. An image like a shadow borne by the wind. On cold, dry evenings when the setting sun's light burns red and the wind blows strong, the streets of your city appear overlain across mine. Sometimes the streets of my city disappear completely, and all I can see are the streets and buildings of yours; I get lost in them. The roof of your building lines up perfectly with my apartment looking west." The outline of your body as you dance limned in apricot light overlaps with mine as I watch you.

"That doesn't happen over here." It seemed as if you were being given kindnesses withheld from me, and I felt a twinge of jealousy, "And besides, there's the thought of you peeping on me."

"I don't peep! Your figure simply flies into my room. Though I admit I welcome it. I put a record on and dance with you even though you lack substance, lack skin to touch, lack smell. I've danced with you so many times." You withdrew the red handkerchief from your pocket and wiped your brow with it.

"It's just a one-way thing then." Against my intentions, your spirits seemed to fall.

"I only wanted to surprise you. It's fun to be surprised, isn't it? Though whenever you surprise someone, it turns into a one-way thing." My lips as I spoke brushed against your earlobe. The tiny hairs there fluttered with my breath. I extended the tip of my tongue a tiny bit and brushed them with it.

"Could you tell just now when I licked your tiny hairs? Does your ear as I touch it feel connected to your eyes as they see me? Can you believe that all these parts go together, that they are all a part of you? That's what it means to be surprised, to be taken apart." And as you said this to me, my nerves as they clustered at my ear like ants swarming something sweet tried to reverse their course, tried to gather instead at my eyes but were unable to. My flesh suddenly felt stiff and cold and I filled with unease, so I traced a path across my skin from my earlobe to my eyelid with the pad of my fingertip. I could feel them connected by the surface of my skin, but when I thought about whether they connected deep inside, I became profoundly uncertain. I was suddenly outraged to have been asked to think about such upsetting things and began to run my mouth without thinking.

"It's just because you refuse to really touch me that I feel this way!"

Your eyes undulated again like the surface of water, and this undulating spread across your entire body, smearing its edges. And then, as if inadvertently, I brushed you with my arm. I looked up into the dazzling sky filled with bronze sunlight and rubbed my eyes, then looked back at you. I always fall in love with this kind of person, I thought, and this time would be my last. But what kind of person was this exactly? I knew it was the kind of person you were, but when I tried to think of others besides you, my head would fill with a maelstrom of ashen grey that squirmed in all directions, leaving me muddled and confused.

"I'd never worried about such things before. I didn't mind that it was all just repetition. What's so different about you? I feel sure that things with you will be no different than with anyone before."

"There's no helping it. It's the river's fault your memory's unclear. Everyone's memories in this city end up flowing into the river. Those who raised me told me. In the city on the far shore, they'd say, the people go to sleep and then from between the houses memories flow like grey soup, you can see them run down into the river. Your mind and the river are connected. Your memories run and mix with other things. That's the reason why your ears and eyes don't connect: a river lies between them."

"But what about you? You said the city on the other side is just the same as this one."

"I don't know. But maybe if I watched my city from here at night I'd see the same thing happen."

"But I told you. You can't see your city from here." Your voice had grown as thin as spider's silk.

"Well, then let's go to the other side together. It might answer your questions if we did, and besides, I've become the kind of person who can't stay in one place for any length of time. So let's go."

You looked at me with those eyes the same emerald green as a lake I was sure I'd seen somewhere in the north, your gaze unblinking, penetrating deeper and deeper into mine, nodding your assent. I felt as though the harder you looked at me the more definite my outline became. You poured too much concentration into your gaze, though, and you began to forget who or where you were, only remembering that if you failed to grasp this moment it would never come again, and then you struggled to your feet but grew dizzy and fell back down. I reached for you, supported your back and hips, pulled you up as if lifting a giant squid into my arms and carried you to lay you out on a bench in the shade of the stout-trunked jacaranda tree. Your limbs were warm and flexible, sticking to my arms and legs like tentacles. Thinking you were about to say something, I stared hard at your lips, smooth as cherry skins, but all that emerged when they parted was breath and the sight of tiny teeth like kernels of white corn. To prevent being overcome with the compulsion to dive between these lips, I bought another red-fleshed, quartered melon from the booth that stood in the shade of the nearby chestnut tree and slipped its flesh between them instead, cutting it from the rind with my knife.

The overripe smell of the red-fleshed melon thickened like slowly dripping honey with every step you took toward me as you walked back from the booth. You brought the knife in your right hand toward the melon in your left hand, seeming about to cut into the flesh from your palm, but you cut into the red flesh of the melon instead and placed it in my mouth. The sweet, smooth smell filled my nose and even seemed to reach my eyes, and as I stared at the pink flesh of your palm crossing my vision, I had a feeling like I was eating a secret of yours, something I'd been unable to see before, something I wasn't supposed to know. I swallowed the fruit of your secret shame. I felt it in my chest and around my hips as the fruit from your palm turned quickly into blood within my reclining body; I felt it turn into flesh, into power. But even though it was I who should have been consuming you, instead I felt myself taken over. I became an extension of you and so there was no longer any need for us to talk, but you put voice to your words anyway, asking, "Can you stand? If you can stand, then we need to hurry, we need to get a car." "I want one the color of strawberries," I answered. "We'll get one as swift as a swallow," you replied as you stood me up. I thought you were going to hail a taxi from the road in front of us, but instead you walked me to the supermarket parking lot and found an open car the color of wine to heft me into, and then, after punching the code into the pad below the steering wheel, we were off, the shining breeze blowing through my hair.

The magenta sportscar flew down the road like a swallow, like a low-flying aircraft. It raced through the streets as if swimming. In the passenger's seat, your golden hair streamed behind us like a scarf, and as you stroked it in an attempt to bring it under control, you began to speak. You asked which I preferred, swimming or flying. "Swimming," I answered, but you didn't wait for my answer, you just kept talking. "Flying and swimming, they're just alike," you said.

"Fish and birds look alike, too. Just turn their scales into feathers, their fins into wings, and fish become birds.

I think birds as they fly through the sky feel a lot like fish do as they swim through the water. Birds swim through the sky, fish fly through the water."

"I want to fly through the water."

"I want to swim through the sky."

"You want to play bird and fish when we get to the river?"

"We really are alike," you said with a smile like ripe fruit, and then you sang in the high voice of a violin: *the swallows live for only a summer, they fly to us from skies afar, pulled by the heat of desire.* I pressed the accelerator hard beneath my foot and joined in with my low *bandoneón* tones. Our voices intertwined in a duet like the cries of ecstasy that sound as a brother and sister consummate an incestuous union. You rose up from the passenger seat to stand with your left hand gripping the windshield's frame and your right arm extending outward, flapping lightly, mimicking a wing. I glanced quickly up at you from the driver's seat and saw sunlight silhouette your slender body, transform it into the black body of a swallow sliding through the air. You sang like a bird. You sang.

"Just as birds and fish look alike, a famous writer once said that dueling had much in common with dancing."

I looked at you as you squinted ahead down the road.

"That makes sense. Dance's origins are in duels. Like the 'dance of knives,' right?"

You took a pair of black sunglasses from the glove compartment and put them on, then looked at me.

"My intuition tells me that someone good at dancing would be good at fighting. But I wouldn't say that every good fighter was necessarily a good dancer."

"And you?"

"I'm a skillful dancer, so I'm also a skillful fighter. You're a professional dancer yourself, so I'd wager you'd be good in a fight too."

"Do you fight?"

My right hand tapped the leather sheath hanging heavily from my hip.

"I'm not the one who fights. He's the one."

I didn't want to look at the knife in its leather sheath so I looked up into the sun instead, but that only made me dizzy and I fell back into my seat. A pattern of lines like a tangle of passion vine appeared before my eyes. It was the same kind of vine that was tooled into the leather of your sheath. I had no way to relax; it seemed I could do nothing to escape those vines.

"Whenever I think about knives, everything around me seems to darken."

"Me too. It's because a knife shines too brightly. Do you know how a knife is forged? Light from all over the world is gathered and then the smith pounds it into shape, concentrating it, binding it together. It doesn't have a constant form, it's something human eyes can never really see."

"Knives are used to hypnotize, aren't they?"

"A condition for becoming a knifefighter is the ability to resist their spell."

"So you're a professional knifefighter," I said, but even as I did, I failed to sense the ill-starred foreboding one associates with a man who's killed countless times before.

"That's all in the past now. I had to wield my knife for myself instead of for a client once. As soon as you do that, you're no longer a professional."

"So you failed at your job?'

"No, I gave it up."

Why—, I started to ask, but when I opened my mouth no sound emerged. There was something in my throat that wasn't words. A mass that tasted of metal. That smelled of it. Clanged like iron in my throat. I remembered the many lovers in my past who'd been killed in duels. Knives had pierced their bodies and they'd given off a knife's metal smell, bled its metal color as they fell. The knives they'd clutched in their hands, these empty things unable to fulfill any human desire were always handed to me and then I'd bury them beneath the floorboards of my café. Whenever I'm near a knife I feel as though it's going to swallow not just the light but me as well. Of course, not all my former lovers have been knifefighters. It's just that those are the only ones I remember.

When we arrived at the riverside docks, you got out of the car and walked toward the marina. But before you'd even reached the ticket booth, you stopped in your tracks and stroked the handrail where a mermaid had been carved into it, your face darkening with displeasure, and then you turned on your heel and came back. "It's no good?" I asked, and you nodded.

"It's just as I suspected. Our pursuer has already caught up with us. That mermaid wasn't there before. It's a sign. A warning." I squinted at the mermaid as the light reflecting off the river silhouetted the handrail, turning it black. It was difficult to make out. I suspected that the little mermaid had actually always been there, but I kept silent.

"He's playing some kind of game with us. It looks like he intends to chase us down."

"So we have to watch our backs."

"Indeed. But in times like these the best defense may be to just avoid a flawed offense. It's out of our way, but I think the best course may be to follow the shore north to the city where the river narrows, then cross over on a bridge."

"Should we switch clothes to confuse the enemy?" As soon as the word *enemy* crossed my lips I suddenly felt like we were desperate fugitives, wrongdoings amassing in our wake.

You agreed, and so I shed my clothes, even my underwear, and handed them to you. Your delicate frame and narrow shoulders slipped easily into my tomato-red summer dress that fluttered so in the breeze; it looked good on you. It had always been a little big on me, gapping away from my body in various places, but you filled it out perfectly.

You seemed repulsed by my sweaty shirt and jeans, so

we went to the marketplace and shoplifted a white cotton shirt and some pants of flaxen hemp. As you buttoned up the shirt with nothing on beneath it, your body as I glimpsed it wriggling beneath the cloth made me think of internal organs pulsing and twitching beneath the translucent shell of a shrimp or pupa. You gathered your hair into a bun and tucked it under a tweed cap, then took the sunglasses off my face to wear yourself; merrily, you spread light brown foundation across my jaw to hide my beard, painted my lips, and stuck a straw hat on my head. The last step was handing you my knife in its sheath. You seemed suddenly nervous as you took it.

You placed the carefully sheathed knife in my hand and it immediately felt so heavy I was afraid it would sink me right to the ground. The sheath's leather, still warm with the heat of your body, exuded an animal smell as if it were a living, breathing thing, making my heart race. Complex tangles of passion vine decorated not only the sheath but the knife's handle as well. One of the vine's flowers had a clock's face set into it. I figured the hands must move a tick for every man it killed. An ominous feeling filled me as I traced the vines with my finger; I suddenly knew that the next person to move the hands would be me. I'd stab you and advance the clock. I felt like I'd been given a mission.

"I've never used a knife before," I said, but my words sounded like lies to my ears.

"What do you mean? It's easy. A knife longs to be held. Once you do, it begins to move on its own. It has stabbed countless men this way. The more men's lives a knife has claimed, the more efficient its movements become."

"Have you stabbed so many men?"

You laughed softly in response.

"You'll find out when you use it. As soon as you grip that handle, the faces of all the men who've killed while gripping it will appear before you."

You started to withdraw the blade from the sheath, but then hesitated.

"Grip the handle while it's still in the sheath. As long as it's sheathed it'll remain docile. Like a blindfolded bull."

I covered your right hand with my palm and guided your fingers with mine into the correct position on the knife's handle. Your grip strengthened as the tip of your index finger stroked the detailing on the handle again and again. The white of your hand flushed the color of roses.

"If an assassin ends up stabbing me, use this knife to avenge me."

My spirits rose higher and higher as I hung the knife in its sheath from my hip and turned to face you. As we gazed at each other's bodies, now neither fully male nor female, something materialized between us, a certain feeling of privilege, of transcendence, like permission granted to commit whatever acts may be necessary to continue on our path. As people who'd just transformed into men and women who never were, we had the right to do whatever we wished. However heinous, no act of ours could ever be evil; however profane, we could desecrate nothing.

As the two of us raced north along the riverside, we threw lit fireworks into rings of dancing children. We doused soccer fans in paint, white and pale blue. We'd bite lit cigarettes between our teeth, puffing smoke like locomotives without inhaling until the fire nearly reached our lips, then spit the fiery butts at passersby. We'd spin our tires against the gravel and announce to people, "Tonight the moon has fallen onto Avenida Callao, go run and see!" and then we'd race away. In our last act, we performed a ritual we'd imagined as little children, making limes into bombs and throwing them into used bookstores. In celebration we made a shoeshine boy shine our car, then toasted sparkling wine as the sun transformed its polished crimson body into a sizzling griddle. I having become you and you having become me, we cursed each other, slithered against each other, threw each other to the ground, sang a dual aria of our own devising, I in the role of the macho man, you in the role of the willful woman. Our cries resounded loud enough to crack the hard blue sky, a chorus declaiming, "I'm *loco!* I'm *loca!* You're *loco!* You're *loca!*" Then we'd fall to the earth and tangle our limbs into a dance; I would bite your shoulder, you would stomp my foot. We would compete to see who could spit the farthest up into the sky. My spit would fall on you, yours on me. Our saliva dried up and so we stopped. I wanted us to break each other's bones with resounding cracks, but something told me that that would be a pleasure signaling the beginning of the end, and so I kept this desire to myself.

The two of us stretched our bodies across the hood of the car like drying laundry and our breathing was the only sound we heard. From time to time there came a skylark's cry. We'd had so much fun we nearly passed out. But as much fun as we'd had, there still seemed to be something missing; suddenly, a sense of emptiness arose that refused to heal. My eyes were filled with so much light that I began to lose track of who I was. But I wanted even more light, wanted to get even dizzier. I wanted to be near you, near the dazzle of you so bright it almost made my eyes explode. I worried that if my body didn't give off light I'd disappear. Sadly, no matter how hard we played we never sweated, so when we lay beneath the sun our bodies were never wet, they never shone. I licked your skin where I could find it, but it quickly dried. Near your wit's end, you bought some golden beer for us to shower on each other, but in the time it took to gulp down what remained it had all evaporated. The cooling breeze dried everything: the hair running down the nape of your neck, your chocolate eyebrows, your coffee bean mouth, so full from top to bottom and narrow from side to side. I dreamed so many times as I dozed atop that sportscar's hood of kissing those pink-tinged, brownish lips with my unremarkable ones, but as dry as they were I was afraid it would be like rubbing paper against a stone, that nothing would pass between us, and so I never did. My throat became so dry that the back of it began to hurt, and the pain solidified into a mass like the pit of a peach, like the metallic mass from before. Lying there next to you, I felt two emotions at once: the light, airy feeling that arises between two freshly minted lovers and the desperate ardor of a couple who've reached the final stages of their love, who have just one option left. I felt bereft, about to weep.

Soon all the two of us could do was sigh. Your throat began to glisten and blush, and so I nuzzled it, licked it. It tasted sweet yet sour, and I felt the power start to leave my body. The reason why we'd had so much fun, too much in fact, was that we were having a seven-year relationship in the span of a day; if things had occurred normally we would have simply met today, then built our love slowly, feeling as if we were living within a miracle year after year until eventually we grew apart, and then, when you could no longer stand it, you'd betray me with another and we'd split up—but instead, it all was happening at once. You were in pain and wanted to cry but couldn't. It was too dry, there were no tears left. But I knew if I peeled away your pure white skin I'd see what flowed within you, the fluid that shone so, reflecting even the faintest light, and so I didn't worry.

Even though I knew I'd fallen in love like this so many times before, it seemed to me that I'd never previously felt so filled with emotion; I tried to recall the faces of my former lovers but all their faces turned into yours, my only memory was of meeting you by the fountain. But as I thought of you and tried to recall all that came before, what came to mind were emotionless memories of the knives my former lovers had held as they'd been killed, or the hands of the ones who'd simply disappeared. I'd touched those hands and they'd touched me, but my skin no longer remembered the feeling. I'd consumed your flesh, you'd become a part of me, I was more connected to you than I'd ever been with anyone else, and yet it still didn't seem quite real; was it because I had no specific memories of you to recall, or was it because our skin was too dry, preventing us from really sharing anything between us? As I tried my hardest to remember, my memories kept splitting: did you resemble most the lover before my last or the one I'd repressed within my memory, the one who'd tried to commit love suicide with me but ended up dying alone? Were you my father, who died when I was eleven, or were you my older brother, or a younger one by a different father whom my mother had hidden from me? Confusion begat confusion. Perhaps you were my everything.

"Maybe it would be better if our pursuer hurried up and killed us right away."

The taste of oranges filled my throat, and I couldn't decide if it was the taste of loneliness or simply sorrow; it was congealing into yet another hardened mass, narrowing my breath.

"There's no need to hurry things."

I ran my hand through your hair and it fell away smoothly, like sand made of light.

"But the way things are going, I'll just do the same thing I always do."

"What is it you do?"

"I don't know, that's why I'm frustrated. I don't understand our relationship."

"I've been watching you on your roof as you practiced your sunset dance since you were twelve. I watched as you eventually grew conscious of your body's weight and became an adult; you began to dance at the café at the end of the row, under the rose-hued lights."

"You came to my café?" Your pupils widened, turning your irises cobalt.

"While I was in your city, I went nearly every night."

"So that's why I remember you. That makes sense." I felt expansive.

"No, that's not it. I always visited the bar disguised as an old man."

"A precautionary measure?"

"Precisely. The day before yesterday, I transformed myself into an old man a mere 130 centimeters tall."

"The day before yesterday? You didn't visit the bar yesterday?"

"Yesterday I watched the soccer game," I said, stroking the soft space between your eyebrows where your skin furrowed. "But I could also say I was watching you and still be telling the truth."

"I wish you'd stop talking in riddles."

"You really don't remember?"

I closed my eyes. I took a deep breath. I hadn't watched the soccer game. I had no memory of being with you. I shook my head.

"When you are so uncertain, I become uneasy too. Is this you really the same you I watched before?"

I felt like I was being carried away by I knew not what.

"Take me somewhere I can swim," I asked in a voice that was not my own. "All my memories are in the river. I want to submerge myself in them."

"I understand. Let's go. Let's swim in the river like birds."

Your chest flexing in stages as if part of a mechanical body, you pulled me to my feet. I imagined that if I touched you there, that place where your strength hardened your body, and if you touched my body in turn where it could harden, where it grew strong, then we could both be strong, together; but instead you simply climbed back in the car.

They say the only thing in this city able to keep a consistent form is this river that wets the hands dipped into it, that turns them transparent, silvery. All along the riverside live the people born in this city, people who dance and sing and play instruments, who make music impossible to separate from the sound of the river itself, this river too wide to see across to its other shore, this river that rumbles through its rocky bed with a sound like a hollow tree trunk being pounded. The music and the sound of the river whip the people into a frenzy, a frenzy that draws blood. Blood that flows a shining white. Where does the blood flow?

What sound does it make? Wanting to know, even tourists come. The musicians warn them not to go into the river. The water is dirty, they say, and the dirt never washes off. To those who come from outside the city so warned, this mirror-skinned river that shines like silver looks dull as lead instead, so polluted its riverbed cannot be seen. But as soon as anyone drinks the water here or breathes the city's air, they become infused with silver from the inside out. This is how outsiders become townspeople. The wet walls of our very organs glitter with the river's silver.

You stopped the car when we'd reached the enormous park that lay just north of the city. We walked through the grass that grew along the riverside and sat at the tables set up in the shade of the trees. Newsboys wandered through the umbrellas and benches, declaiming newspaper headlines announcing the soccer team's victory as if singing them. A middle-aged man wearing only one shoe shouted "*Viva! Viva!*" while brandishing a tiny "open car" flag from a taxi with both hands. A group of young men and women leapt and danced about, their naked torsos painted in stripes of white and pale blue. Men stinking of alcohol approached, leeringly entreating me: "Hey, c'mere, *milongita . . .*" A street musician tipped his violin so its strings ran parallel to the river's flow, playing as if the river were his real instrument. The reflected light from the river limned the edges of everyone's bodies so sharply that they looked as though the slightest touch would split their flesh to the bone. Except you: your form wavered still, as if behind water. I'd said I wanted to go swimming, but as I watched your body undulate before me I was overcome by the feeling that I was already submerged, looking up at you from the riverbed. And maybe this was why every sound around me—the rumble of the river, like the sound of the heavens crumbling bit by bit; the music that so resembled it; the shouting of the crowds; the gravel crunching in three-four time beneath car wheels—reached my ears as if through water, muffled and echoing. You threw your arms about my waist, your muscles crushing me tight against you, and you said something I couldn't hear even as your breath blew right in my ear. I nodded and smiled as you continued speaking. The only thing I could hear clearly was the approaching wind. Looking toward its source, I saw a young boy with a wisteria basket hanging from his arm that overflowed with blue blossoms. The boy was singing, advertising his wares in a voice like the blowing wind. Listening to him, the breeze ruffling my hair, I felt my spirits rise.

I called out to the boy: "Hey, *chiquilín!*" The golden-eyed *chiquilín* stopped before me. The seat of his denim shorts had been ripped and now was patched as if to hide his precocious development, but what made his legs look truly unnatural was the fact that he wore left shoes on both his feet. When I pointed this out, he replied, "Both my feet are shaped like left feet. Big toes sprout from the right side of each. So all my shoes are left shoes, and my socks too, and my tights." I asked him to remove his shoes and show me, but he stubbornly refused.

"Why do you have two left feet?"

"It's my parents' fault."

"Oh, they're . . . closely related?"

"No, not that. My mother slept around on my father, so he grew a cuckold's horns and I ended up with hooves."

"Why did *you* have to grow hooves?"

"Because long ago, my mother slept with me as well."

"I see. So you were cuckolded too. Did your father sprout horns then?"

"My mother said that when my father's horn turned into a real horn, she lost her use for him."

"So your feet got this way because they turned into hooves?"

"After a while. I walked on them until they split back into toes, but they both ended up as left feet."

"How old are you?"

"A thousand years."

"Exactly?" My eyes widened in surprise.

"Exactly," he said, laughing bashfully. I found myself blushing a little myself.

Feeling left out, I broke into the conversation, asking, "What is it you're selling?" He replied, "I have bouquets of voices."

"Here, I'll take one," you replied, handing the *chiquilín* three bills. He told us he was going to sing "Prelude for the Year 3001" for us, but your expression clouded and you said, "Enough with the future. Sing something with some history to it."

And so, taking on the persona of a wanton woman, the boy began to sing "A *Milonga* for the Melted Moon." His voice seemed to contain the hoarse voices of multitudes, men and women alike. I knew the song. It told the story of the *chiquilín* himself. How hooves sprouted from his feet, how his father found out about his affair with his mother, how horns sprouted long and hard from his father's forehead and crotch, how his father used the horns to kill his mother, how his father went to the printer's shop where he worked and stuck his head into the paper-cutting machine, killing himself. An orphan now, *chiquilín,* you vowed never to grow up and sliced off that which protruded from your body. You lived on as an eternal boy, never quite a man, never quite a woman. You made your living singing in your pure, eternally unblemished voice, but in the end you were still only a child and could only earn so much. You could never make enough to eat, so when the *maté* you drank finally dried up you came here, joined the other musicians in feasting on the light the river reflected and the dancing girls in drinking its silver water; you all ended up drunk, dancing together. But even as you danced, you were never more than waist-high to them; the dancing girls were always kind to you, this being who was neither man nor woman, but who'd lived too long and done too much to be a child. You'd drunk enough silver riverwater that your body shone bright as a moon all night, the eyes of the city always on you. You became the city's center. You danced with the girls, surrounded by it. The city spun around you. It spun: *yira, yira, yira.*

The *chiquilín*'s song came to an end and in an attempt to express the emotion rising within me, I kissed his forehead. But that somehow seemed inadequate, so next I pressed my lips hard against his. His moonlit eyes wide open all the while, he just stood and let me. The *chiquilín*'s lips when mine left them shone wetly, a pale shade of rose madder. With these lips, he began to speak.

"You were born in this city, weren't you? Only women born here can understand my song."

"You seem to be like me. You seem to have my memories."

"Do you sell anything else? Don't you have anything else in that basket of yours?" Burning with sudden emotion, I interrupted again.

"I have a bouquet of blue eyes."

He withdrew from his wisteria basket a clutch of long stems topped with large, round balls like lollipops. Each sphere was an eye the color of the legendary lake that lay in the unexplored regions of the north. You salivated at the sight of these spheres that shone wetly as if freshly sucked. Seeing the hunger in your eyes, I thought for a moment and then bought you the blue-eyed bouquet. Squinting as if dazzled by brightness, I received the bouquet from the *chiquilín* in exchange for five bills and then, before I handed them over to you, said, "All of these eyes are my eyes. These are the eyes I used to watch you dance. By giving you my eyes, I'm giving you back your past. You'll remember if you know me from before, you'll remember who you are, you'll remember everything."

"That's a lie! These eyes are mine!" shouted the *chiquilín* suddenly. As if anticipating something you were about to say, the *chiquilín* burst into tears and threw himself at my feet, looking up at me from below.

"You don't remember, but exactly four years ago today you came to me even though I danced here, drinking the light of the moon. You had no one else either; you were a wanton woman, a *yira*. The sight of the two of us dancing together is burned into the eyes of this bouquet. Suck on these eyes and you'll remember."

You licked your lips and reached out to take one of the eyes. The bouquet shook and the eyes brushed against each other, jingling faintly like bells. I tickled your side, preventing you from grabbing the eye you reached for. You glared at me for a second with hatred-reddened eyes of your own, but soon enough their gaze returned to the *chiquilín*. Bereft of companions, I wanted to shout at you, tell you that you and I were the couple, not you and he. Keeping me in the periphery of your vision, you spoke to the elderly child.

"I'll never forget you. I'll keep this bouquet with me always. If I could just keep remembering you, I can keep from doing the same things I've always done."

"It relieves me so to hear you say that. I've lived this way too long. I've been singing the story engraved in those eyes and now I'm so, so tired. If you take care of these eyes for me then I can disappear at last. I just ask that from time to time you caress your body with the bouquet. Put my eyes in your mouth, caress them with your tongue. That way I'll be able to touch you still. Don't leave me all alone again, please."

"I promise. And keep watch over me, too, all right?" You'd once said that those who bore the same reef-hued eyes belonged together, and now you stared at these light blue eyes with tear-filled, light blue eyes of your own. Realizing that if it weren't for me you'd never have exchanged words with this wizened brat, I was crushed and hung my head. And as I did, I caught sight of my feet. Sucking in my breath, I quickly shifted my gaze to the *chiquilín*'s. It was he and I who were alike, not you and he. You'd made a mistake; this love too would be yet another repetition.

He was looking at the *chiquilín* and I with sympathy in his gaze. Yet he was the one all the eyes in my hand stared at.

"Well, now I'm going to disappear. I leave you everything I have left."

And with that, the *chiquilín* slipped the knife from the sheath at my side, and, after pressing it briefly against the pad of his fingertip to confirm its sharpness, plunged it into one honey-colored eye before I had a chance to stop him. For a moment I couldn't see what had happened. The blade dazzled my eyes, and just imagining it entering his eye, a sharp pain lanced through the back of mine, darkening it. By the time my eyes adjusted to the brightness and the blade, the knife had already penetrated the entire eyeball, slicing easily as if through gelatin. A thick, syrupy fluid that was not quite clear and not quite silver ran down the knife's handle, and I swallowed my own saliva hard. Ten centimeters in, the knife had reached the point that it could gouge, and the eyeball emerged skewered on the blade like a sea turtle egg. Exposed to the air, its color turned from that of a cat's eye marble to that of the sky. After gouging out his other eye, he faced me with his syrup-seeping sockets and sightlessly fumbled his eyeballs from his hands into mine, speaking in a voice filled with intense emotion.

"Now I am bound to you more strongly than that man. There's nothing left for you to do." The *chiquilín* winked at me with one of his ruined eyes. I couldn't stop myself from wanting to lick the fluid that ran from his sockets like liquid candy.

The child had smashed his eyes for you, but when his eyelids closed, clear fluid ran from beneath them. It glittered with the light of the tangerine sunset that the river reflected. Transparent semicircles like scales filled it, refracting the light. He walked toward the riverside, the sound of his passage dry, as if he were an insect jumping through grass. The fluid still flowed, leaving a trail like a slug's behind him. The child seemed to shrink as the fluid poured down. Thin creases appeared on the nape of his neck, sucking in the light from the river even as it illuminated them, darkening the area around him. A black mist gathered at his feet. But as you followed after him, all you seemed to see was his shine.

Liquid, sweet as candy, covered your entire body, made you glitter like an ice sculpture. I couldn't help but follow, but you shone so brightly it was hard to look at you directly; I became afraid I'd lose you. With only your voice like the blowing wind to guide me, I reached out to touch you. "*Mentira, mentira, verás que todo es mentira*," you sang, "I'll be reborn in 3001 and around I'll go again: *yira, yira, yira.*" Lost in the light that danced down around us, I felt an overwhelming empathy with you and tried to sing along, reaching my hand toward you, but I stumbled and fell to the ground. Your body, now a mass of melted glass, fell too.

The boy collapsed soundlessly at the river's edge. When I ran to him, I saw only the boy's shriveled, blackened skin and a turgid flow of colorless fluid. His mouth, now just fleshless lips, still dripped with the remnants of his song: "*Yira, yira . . .*" I touched my finger to his colorless blood and sniffed it. The odor was so raw it turned my stomach. I brought my finger to your raspberry lips and I heard you swallow in anticipation.

The fluid ran slowly down the backside of his finger, light from the reddening sky transforming it into grenadine as it flowed in a string to the ground. Returning to myself, I quickly put the finger in my mouth, but instead of sweet it tasted faintly salty. There was no change in my memory, not even when I scrambled to put one of my newly acquired eyes in my mouth as well. Disappointed, I looked over at the *chiquilín* and found that his body had turned transparent and lost its voice, that he was now a pale, silvery puddle trickling slowly into the river. The *chiquilín* had died, and the body he'd formed from the riverwater he'd drunk was returning to its source. The blood I'd tasted had been concentrated riverwater. I could hear the river flow within my body with a sound like violin strings being rubbed, and I felt as if I were transforming into the river myself. Hurriedly shedding my clothes, I dove in.

I was suddenly displaced, bereft. Doubts overwhelmed me: why was I here, what was I doing? I stood
and watched as the evening light turned your tears opal-
escent, as your naked body dove into the river like a bird
taking flight. It occurred to me that I was always watching
things—perhaps you had always been just a trick of the
light carried to me by the wind; perhaps instead of being
excluded from your company, I'd always been alone. Last
night I snuck into your room as you watched the soccer
game on television, intending to stab you with my knife,
but of course I couldn't do it, in the end all I did was steal
a red handkerchief as I retreated—but perhaps all this too
had been just tricks of the light, things I dreamt in my room
in the city on the river's far shore. I felt as though I were
playing a leading role in a game our pursuer was playing
with us, that my very existence depended on our pursuer's
gaze. Indeed, this feeling became a certainty; I was sure
our pursuer was hidden somewhere even now, watching
my every move. And in fact, hadn't there been a mermaid
etched into that metal handrail back there?

But there was no one around that I could see. The
breeze brought only the sounds of a far-off flute and
passing cars. I slowly shed my clothes. The cheap dress
looked faded under the sunset, the color of persimmons,
and its passage over my shoulders left a cold, dry, fluttering echo on my skin and sounded like velvet being rubbed,
like the song of a *bandoneón*. Shedding my shoes as well, I
heard another sound, this one like knocking on a wooden
door. I was muttering to myself, but it sounded like a bass
line. I waded slowly into the river to its rhythm.

The light split and danced within the river, and it was
brighter there than on land at noon. When the sky darkens,
the stars that appear are formed of light the river reflects.
Or perhaps it is the star's light that flows down into the
river. The truth is, no one can recall the light's true source.
It is simply said that just as sand heated by the sun all day
stays warm even at night, these grains of silver so bathed in

light retain it still and thus the river and stars and people are formed.

His skin now scaled, the *chiquilín* swam past me. His shape remained unclear. But I could tell it was him because of the lack of eyes. The river teemed with others like him, silver-scaled creatures not quite mermaids, not quite people. Indeed, the translucent, silver water itself was fish. Silver fish, large and small, formed the water's substance. When they died, these fish melted into a liquid that filled the spaces between those that still retained their shape. The liquid moved as the fish swam, and this was how the river flowed. There was no upstream or downstream, just movement; the river flowed in whatever direction it wished, rumbling as it went. The multitudes of sounds it contained reverberated across the entire surface of my skin, from the subtlest susurrus undetectable from the shore to the all-too-familiar rumbling that we'd grown so sick of—the sound of a lover peeling an orange; of the breath inhaled by a skylark just before it sings; of thunderclouds as they gather; of my cries as a baby, and my mother's irritated outbursts in response; of my parents moaning on their shabby mattress; of blades crossed, metal scraping metal; of my whispers into the ear of a man I'm only pretending to love; of velvet sighing; of footsteps across a hardwood floor; of a door creaking; of light cutting through the silver curtain of the sky. I heard murmurings, too, "*Yira, yira,*" "*Mano a mano,*" the sounds of memories that had poured into the river, numberless and endlessly repeating. I realized that to be in the river was to hear these sounds forever, and I was overcome with a terror that seemed to crush my pelvis—I had to escape this shadowed netherworld while I still retained my shape, before I rotted and melted too. I struggled, but the river's current was too strong, rendering me immobile. The memories of the dead twined around me, starting with the *chiquilín*'s. I realized that following him had been a mistake. Perhaps the *chiquilín* had been a devil all along.

Unable to swim, you needed to be saved and of course

I would be the one to do it. It was a struggle searching for you in this cloudy river that stank and tasted of rotting fish. The light refracted unpredictably in the water, forming shapes I mistook for you again and again. When I finally found you, you were undulating like a jellyfish, adrift but heading nowhere. I thought perhaps you'd hear me through the water so I called out in a loud voice, but you just stared blankly, uncomprehending. I brought my legs together and rippled my body like a dolphin to reach you, and then swam the same way back toward the surface once I'd secured you in my arms.

When you appeared before me, slicing through the water like a glittering knife through flesh, you were a merman. Scales of every color in the rainbow covered your lower body and your long hair waved like kelp. Absorbed in this vision, I reached my arms around your neck and clung to you. But as I did, I heard the *chiquilín*'s voice behind me, calling out for me to stay, freezing me. I could hear it singing: *Please don't leave me all alone.* Thinking that if I turned to look I'd be lost forever, I shut my eyelids tight and thought of only you. I told myself I had to accept you now that I'd nearly led us both to a watery grave; it was only fair. And as I did, I recovered some of the feelings I'd had when we'd first fallen in love.

But once it came time to haul you out of the river and onto the shore, you seemed angry at my rescuing you. "Why do you have to do such needless things," you murmured, "I was about to remember everything."

"I didn't want you to forget me." We both flopped onto the grassy shore like landed fish, gasping for breath.

"That would be all right. All my memories go in the river, so I'm sure I'd remember you again somewhere along the way." But your voice had lost its reproachful tone.

"You don't need to attack me any longer. Just look at me." I turned my head to gaze at yours as you looked up at the sky.

"I'll look you up and down like a dancing girl at a

café would do," you replied, and stared down at the space between my toes.

"I would like it if we could dance again together at your café."

"In that case, I'll disguise myself as you and watch you dance." And then you laughed like you had a secret. Your long lashes and the creases at the edges of your eyes formed darkened hollows that filled me with an emotion so sweet it threatened to melt my insides. I withdrew the red handkerchief from the pocket of my discarded pants and handed it to you.

"Use this to dry yourself. I borrowed it from your room last night."

"You visited me to steal it?"

"I was going to stab you, but not for the handkerchief."

"So you accepted a job to kill me even though you knew me?"

"I didn't know it was you until I saw you."

"I wonder why someone would want me killed."

"I never ask my clients why."

"Who is this 'client'?" There were doubtless many who I'd forgotten, who hated me. But it was possible I'd gotten wrapped up in something far more serious—I just couldn't remember.

"I could never tell you that. I'm still that much of a professional."

"So you say even as you betray your mission. When did you come to my apartment?"

"While the soccer game was on. It was on your television and you were sitting on your sofa, watching. Or sleeping, now that I think of it."

"I'd never have had the soccer game on. That was someone else's house."

"But isn't this handkerchief yours? Well, no matter. Maybe I'm misremembering." I was getting confused.

Even as I listened to you tell me this, I didn't think I'd discovered why I thought I'd seen you before. I began to realize that nothing you remembered from your past could ever explain my déjà vu. The reason why I felt like my time with you was a repetition and yet that you were also somehow unique had nothing to do with whether I'd met you before. And as you realized that you were as bound by memory as I was and that your comprehension of things was no less constrained than mine, I grew to love you even more. I touched your long hair. You sniffed the red handkerchief and then brought your nose to my naked stomach, saying, "They smell the same." You licked at the droplets that remained around my navel. I let out a sigh from somewhere deep within me. There were still some trapped in the downy hair along my side and in my pubic hair; it surely looked to you like spun silver. You began to lick each droplet with your tongue, one by one.

The droplets on my tongue tasted sweet yet sour, like dew licked off berries. The kind of berries used to make jam. Berries I once fought my way through thickets to gather. Touched with morning dew, lit by light from I knew not where, these berries would shine like gold. The dew was part of the light. I wanted to taste it, and I painted your body again and again with riverwater. Droplets ran down the nape of your neck and across your chest to drip from your pinkish nipples; they ran across your stomach and the breadth of your hips to pool at your thighs. Countless droplets ran over each other and dried, forming scales along your legs. The process seemed to tickle and agitate you, and you let out a hoarse, breathy cry as you dribbled riverwater to lick off my body as well.

It was difficult to distinguish your cinnamon skin from the deepening orange of the sky, and you seemed to melt into the air even as my own skin remained resolutely conspicuous, a luminous white that refused to blend with the orange. You were my last, and if you disappeared, so would my final chance to love again. I felt left behind. But as I watched, the orange shaded slowly into a purpled red, and as it grew bluer and bluer, it turned the deep violet hue of jacaranda blooms, fading into the color of the river. You were painted this same color, as was I; I rejoiced in our common shine. But even so, we shone hardly bright enough to dazzle the eye. I no longer felt lonely, but my anxiety had yet to disappear.

Those along the riverside gathered like ants beneath the streetlights and began to dance. From time to time their singing voices would reach us like far-off thunder. The sound of the musician's guitar was like the sound of the wind as it rustled the leaves and cleansed the branches of the trees. I put my ear to your stomach, using it as a wall against these sounds. As I did, the sound of the river grew stronger. Countless pink scars dappled the tawny flesh of your side like raindrops. I traced them with my fingertip. You laughed and told me, "I've acquired one for every year I've been alive." And so I counted them.

"There are twenty-eight scars."

"You must have miscounted. If you include the little ones, there are three hundred and twenty-nine." You turned to show me your dappled back that looked like paint corroded by running water.

"So you're three hundred and twenty-nine years old?"

"Yes. And you're three hundred and twenty-six."

"I don't believe I've lived so long as that."

"It only seems long. Compared to the *chiquilín*, you're still quite young."

"In the river, he called out to stop me from leaving. It frightened me."

I listened hard to the sound of the river.

"I heard singing too. *Mano a mano*, it said."

"Is that you and I, you think? Five by five, *mano a mano*?" Your eyes filled with liquid, seemed about to overflow with a sound like a sparrow's song. Looking into their darkness, I was dizzied by the countless grains of silver that swam within them. I wanted to kiss them, drink from them. And then bite down.

"I want to add us together and get ten."

You brought your head toward mine. I mistimed my approach and ended up sucking on your lips before I intended to. Your lips felt expectant, waiting, taken a little by surprise, and I pressed my tongue through them.

Your tongue tasted like a mango's flesh, slippery and sweet and a little bitter. You wrapped your arms around my body a split second before I could bring my arms around yours. You kept beating me to my every move, and we ended up in a clumsy embrace. My right arm wrapped around you neck while my other hand explored your hips, and then went lower.

My right arm wrapped around your hips and my left hand caressed the back of your head. Your buttocks felt like the skin of a pear, firm and slightly rough.

You brought your body on top of mine, and I looked up at you as my lips sought yours. Your legs tangled in mine, forcing them to open wide. Your hand had descended at some point and now grabbed hold of me.

I couldn't take any more at that point, and I stopped, separating my lips from yours, and said to you as I looked into your flushed, wet eyes, "How is it that we fell in love, I wonder."

Your eyes had absorbed the purple light and swam with sapphire liquid.

"I was just minding my own business and suddenly I was in love with you. It's strange. Did you slip me an aphrodisiac? Was it in the melon you fed me? Did you put something in it?"

"All we needed to begin was for our eyes to meet. I'd waited so many years for it to happen. I'd looked at you so long, trying to catch your eye, but you never looked back. And now today, this day when everything seems so mad, your gaze met mine as if by accident. I hid from you by spending the night in the branches of that jacaranda tree, the pollen from its blooms showering down on me just as the sunlight and the fountain's mist rained down on you." Your dark, wet eyes were like a deer's.

"I remember that. But I'm so distracted. I feel like I'm being kept alive just for you." Your skin was like a screen, absorbing the light that fell upon it, making it flicker languidly.

"That's the same as saying you live only for your own sake."

"Touch me here," you said, indicating your navel. I slipped a finger into the hole. "Wait, not there," you said, and then pointed to your solar plexus. "Here," you said, and my finger explored the spaces between your bones. "Not there either," you sighed. "I don't know where my center is. Everything I want to know is there, I'm certain."

"It's here," I said, my finger inserted partway into your exposed vagina.

"It's true, that seems like a center. But I want to find my midpoint from side to side, not just head to toe," you replied. I licked my finger.

The air began to chill, and mist arose from the ground around us. The light's rays grew visible within it. They split in all directions, clashing with a sound like breaking glass, and this sound fought with the velvety *bandoneón* rumble of the river, tangling and disentangling itself as it did. My skin trembled. You stood and brought me to my feet, and we carried our clothes with us as we headed back to the car.

I helped you into the car as if carrying you from behind. My naked body as it slid over yours felt like it was rubbing against velvet, and I sighed involuntarily. As I turned in my seat to shut the driver's side door, you embraced me from behind. The warm, soft scent of honeysuckle arose from where we touched.

A crescent moon appeared low in the sky and absorbed the pale, bluish light from the river until it shone sharp and bright. Stars began to twinkle too, refracting the light into an arpeggio. But indigo still filled the air, and even as everything grew bright as midday, nothing shone so bright that its light threatened to exceed its edges. Light fell across the left side of your face as you sat in the passenger seat,

your lashes splitting it into shadowy zigzags as your mois-
tened, pale green eyes absorbed it. When you looked back
at me, was my face silhouetted, backlit and outlined by
tiny glowing hairs? As you wet your lips slightly with your
tongue, they grew shiny as jelly, and those enormous eyes
of yours, their whites so large they betrayed every flicker of
your gaze, now grew dark, their pupils widening. I turned
my head toward you slightly, and then, after a moment's
pause, I turned back forward only to feel you close enough
to me that the downy hairs along our jaws nearly brushed.
Raising your jaw and letting your lips part slightly, your
wet teeth shone a bluish white, enticing me until our
pleated, blood-engorged lips met. Each tiny crease along
their surfaces meshed perfectly, as did the warmth of our
bodies, the rhythm of our blood's pumping, the melodi-
ous breathing of our pores, everything in sync, nothing in
excess. We slipped beneath each other's tongues. We licked
each other's gums. We explored the slick inner surfaces of
each other's cheeks.

I paused a moment to take a breather, then dove back
into your lips. They were suffused with a taste I recognized,
a familiar smell—and I, who had been so scared of repetition, now quietly succumbed. A pale, heart-shaped breath
escaped your mouth. Moonlight gathered within it.

Beside each other in our seats, our bodies dovetailed
perfectly, from the soft skin of our breasts to our long,
long limbs and the warmth of our lower bodies, and we
shared everything between us: our warmth, the rhythm of
our heartbeats, the sound of our smooth, sweat-free skin
sliding. You watched me with your bottomless eyes that
seemed to overflow with night.

As if to regain dominance, you mounted me, staring
unblinkingly into my eyes all the while.

You teased the points of my breasts with your tongue
where the light that limned them seemed to concentrate.

You traced the edges of my body if testing their limits,
gazing at them, touching them, biting them, licking them,

sniffing them, slapping them. My body hardened to its very core, no longer animal or vegetable but mineral, my outline sharpening as a familiar scent filled my nostrils, a wavering smell like burning grass; blue-tinged, milky light poured over your skin and flowed across my stomach.

The soft, heavy feeling between us seemed to clarify your boundaries like light and comfort you, but I felt as if there was still a space between us and remained unsatisfied. *I feel like this car's too small, it's forcing us together, it annoys me,* I whispered as I reached behind my back to grip you where you arched up to bathe in the light of the moon.

You left the car with nothing covering your naked skin and leaned against the hood. Your voice blended into the rumble of the river, ruffling the nearby grassy plain. Your breath enveloped me, slightly wetting my skin. Steam arose from between you and I, and we became the water, mist rising off our surface, became the river that rumbled like a tree trunk being beaten, became the riverside alive with grass that rustled in the wind. Lying face up across the front of the car, our every crease and fold opened to each other as we slid together. You'd become the moonlight, the starlight, the riverlight; you'd become the grassy plains filled with rising mist; we'd become like mucous membranes exposed and superimposed. Soon we would exceed that boundary too, and our flesh would meet directly, our blood and fluids mixing unimpeded. *I want to go that far. I want to.* I murmured this into your chest and your hoarsely whispered answer filled my head: *I will become you.* Your heartbeat was my heartbeat; my chest hurt, constricted.

As I reached my climax, I was suddenly overcome with the desire to throw it all away. We should tie our bodies to the car, pitch it into the river and disappear into the darkness of its depths, I thought. I despaired of there ever being a future for you and me. Yet there you were, unthinking, bathed in moonlight as satisfaction filled you. Unaware that something had changed forever in that instant, you stroked my hair just as you had before. You no longer had the power to leave this city, I thought. I wanted to wash your fluids from my body. I wanted to demand that you give back the fluids of mine on yours. I came to a decision. Either I would die, or you, or both of us together; those were the only options left. Why did you have to be me too? I was alone: this I knew for certain.

You brushed my hand away and got back in the car. Your body trembled unceasingly. The moisture our skin had accrued evaporated, the air swallowing it, disappearing under exposure to the shine of the moon, of the stars, of this river that flowed with a sound that was somehow round, like a bouncing, multicolored ball. I tried to talk to you, but you replied with only sighs. Suddenly, I turned on the ignition and looked at you again.

"Don't look at me."

"You look at me like I'm a dancing girl."

"You seem to think you can see through me somehow, but I assure you, it's all your own delusion, an effect of the too-bright light. It's all just trickery. You're hardly something grand yourself."

"True enough. I'm just a puppet of the knife."

At the word *knife*, my body responded, and I stroked its leather sheath. It emitted a scent like an animal's hide. I wanted more than anything to slip the knife from it and slide it into your flesh. I'd be the one to stab, I thought. I felt as if I'd done so countless times before. My hand remembered, as did the knife. Yet you just looked at me, a smile on your face so bright it seemed able to make all the flowers of the world bloom at once. I felt about to weep, surer more than ever that we must be split apart. Stabbing was the only way. I pointed the blade at you, but it seemed as though even a breeze so slight it barely shook the pollen from a mimosa flower would be able to point it back at me.

Realizing I could no longer control my actions, I left the car, saying as did, "Your aphrodisiac's worn off." You tried to coax me back, but I was intent to avoid this terrible situation, and I pulled on my underwear, my white shirt and flaxen pants, spitting, "You're quite the vain one, aren't you," as I walked away. Shaking off your arm and words as you tried to make me stay, I walked to the highway that ran along the riverside and flagged a black taxi to take me back to my café.

Pulling on not the hibiscus-colored dress you'd left behind but my dirty shirt and pants from before, I rushed to follow you in the car. Its intense red met the night's blue light and fluctuated bewitchingly. I followed the river's southern flow, driving along its edge. The road, the sky, the river: all were bluish white, as if I were swimming through water, flying through air. The wind bathed my face like a free flow of water. I was gripped by the impulse to drive into the river. I felt as if I could drive right through to its far shore. We could have driven together across this ocean-wide river, I thought, we could have driven through the city that glittered like a mirror along its opposite side, we could have made it all the way to the tropical north, and as I thought about these things, I was gripped with fierce regret. They say that in the tropics of the north, the rain falls like light, wetting the skin of the men and women there without them having to go the river, unlike here. The air is hot as fire, turning everyone the color of roasted cocoa beans, producing a scent that attracts everything: insects, animals, those of the opposite sex, those of the same. When they dance, their sweat turns to steam beneath the light and rises to the heavens, soon to descend again as rain. Pieces of the sun and moon fall with it, but this causes no problem, since these too just rise again as well. Mysterious darkness yawns black and deep at the feet of these women and men, like holes that trail them wherever they walk. The southerners, unfamiliar with such things, say that if one touches you, it emits a poison that eventually makes you disappear. If you even just approach one too closely, the southerners say, your equilibrium upends, you'll grow dizzy, lose consciousness. Wandering into the jungle in such a state, you'd be sure to mistake the river there for the ground and fall right in. No one knows where this river flows, this river like the earth itself turned liquid; green trees grow plentifully within its earth-colored water, coloring it in places shades of emerald and pale green, while dirty yellow grains of gold churn along the bottom and mix into the mud, invisible to human eyes. Houses are built along this river, and people live there, harvest crops, search for gold, dance. From time to time the water rises and wipes them out, leaving behind vast, dried-out ghost towns filled with clouds of golden dust when it subsides. They say if you lose your way amid them and eat a passionfruit from the vines that grow there, you must throw its seeds into the river. If you throw it to the ground instead and take a nap, within hours you will awaken entangled in vines growing over you faster than a hummingbird wing, strangling your breath from your body. As the sun descends, the black holes at the feet of the people and everything else merge to become the nightfall, and within the hot steam of the rain forest all bodies grow wet with darkness.

I grew uneasy as I drove, feeling false, like a prop in a play, and I reached over to touch the red dress I'd draped over the back of the passenger seat. Dry and slick, it slid down easily to pool in the seat. I knew then that I could never escape the city on the shore of this river just by crossing to its other side, that I'd never reach the northern tropics.

Riding in the enclosed body of the taxi, I remembered how my hair had streamed in the wind beneath the midday sun as I'd ridden with you in the red sportscar, and my lungs began to constrict. No doubt you drove now too, cold wind whipping your expressionless face, a blurred purple mass hurtling fast as a flying swallow, sure only of yourself and the steering wheel you gripped, my scarlet dress pooling in the seat beside you, deflated and empty; no doubt it seemed as if it had never been worn by anyone at all, that it had always been lifeless, vacant all along. I suddenly loved you again, intensely. It made me angry, but I couldn't stop. My teeth ground with loneliness.

The moon tumbled into the river. I followed suit, tumbling too. I was committing love suicide with the moon. The clock in the car read exactly midnight.

The crowds had largely left the main streets of the town. But as I stopped my car and ventured into the smaller ones, I found them again, twitching like dying insects amid a milky mist that hung in the air, neither smoke nor steam, parted by a neon flow of liquid fire, pink and red. The women leaned against the buildings conversing as the men languished drunkenly on the ground like soft stones.

This arrangement remained consistent even inside the café decorated all in crimson neon save the letters spelling *La Esquina Rosada* in white. The languishing men in their stupors slid toward sleep, tossing and turning intermittently and muttering. Everyone wore the same shirt I did, stripes of white and pale blue around a laughing sun, or at least carried a little flag bearing this design. Except you: you were wearing a glittering, deep green dress as you gazed levelly from your barstool at the door as I came in. You hopped to your feet as lightly as hopping on the surface of the moon, your expression studiously blank, and a cry arose from the regulars who'd been waiting for you to dance: "*Viva!*" You held a bouquet of blue eyes in your right hand; you kissed one then held them aloft, grinning at me all the while. I advanced a few steps toward you.

I walked slowly toward you too: three steps. You twined your fingers into those extended sharply from my hand. You stalked around me like a cat, never letting go. A sound arose, a slow stomping on heavy wood. I turned suddenly, a moment before you thought I would. A long, deep sigh like a squeezed *bandoneón* trailed through the air. I caught your eyes with mine; I tried to crush them. You resisted, tried to pry mine open. At some point you'd gotten hold of both my hands, and now you spread my arms like eagle's wings. My chest, exposed, was crushed against yours. I continued to murmur my *bandoneón* sigh, like velvet ripping. I deceived you again and slipped from your grasp, turning my back to you as I walked unblinkingly away.

I hurried to look you in the face again, but you studiously turned your eyes from mine and kept walking. You reached the counter and ordered a whiskey. Blending my footsteps into the bass line of the music, I slunk stealthily to the back wall of the café and picked out one of the wide-brimmed felt fedoras hanging there, tipping it to shadow my eyes as I returned to the counter to present you with a pale blue rose I'd plucked from a glass on the counter's edge. You downed your whiskey in one gulp and looked up, sighing with a soulful expression on your face, and then turned swiftly toward me, your shoulders hunched and neck extended, gazing into my eyes as if able to see through me to my very bones. I looked down, hiding my eyes with the fedora's brim. You merely hunched your body even lower, searching out my eyes from below.

And that's when I saw your eyes glitter like knives, and suddenly I was in your arms as you leaned against your stool, arms that crushed my lower body hard against you as you leaned me over to press your lips to mine. My head nearly touching the ground, my arms clutched your head as if suctioned there, and the tip of your nose slipped down my body, tracing a line from my lips between my breasts to reach my navel. All at once, a scream rang out from beneath the stool, not the squeak of grinding teeth nor the squeal of twisting metal but the cry of a stringed instrument, and you brought me with you as we stood back up and, still locked in embrace, began to spin. We spun, you and I, together.

No, it wasn't us that spun. It was this whiskey-soaked café, this entire town. We were the center, everyone's eyes turned toward us.

You brought one of your legs between mine, forcing

me to raise one to accommodate it and let myself be overcome, to fall before you. You cradled me in your arms as I
descended, only to bring me back up to split my legs with
yours once more. I let them tangle with yours, let them
move as if independent from the knees down, let them
leap and twirl. We spun once more. And that was when,
finding my moment, I slipped your knife from the sheath
that hung at your hip.

The blade was soundless, slicing through the light
that fell upon it, suffusing the air with bloodlust. The ill-
omened atmosphere raised goosebumps across your skin,
but I knew what was to happen even as I watched them cast
tiny shadows all along the white of your arms. I made no
move to take the knife from your grasp. You feinted as if to
stab me, but at the last moment it was your lips and skin
that reached me, not the blade. We were fused, you and I,
our skin just shy of dissolving to transform us into a single,
heated mass as we embraced, as we gave in to the spinning of the city. Our legs twisted together, tangled, meshed,
made a dry sound against the wooden floor as we collapsed.

I crashed to the floor like a cresting wave.

I fell atop you.

I turned the blade of the knife toward you as you fell,
sure of myself again. You'd left me no choice from the
moment you'd shown up at my café. We could never share
the same space again. I thought about the knives that slept
beneath the café's floorboards. I was a professional dancer,
after all.

I never took my eyes off the point of the blade even as
we fell. I knew all too well what the knife desired. I twisted
slightly to the side, and the blade sliced harmlessly through
the empty space to the right of my torso. I rolled immediately to pin your wrist and the knife it held between my
side and elbow. I used my weight to trying to loosen your
grip, grinding against your hand, but it was all in vain. For
the knife had already been snatched from your fingers by
an enormous man.

This rough-looking character had been sitting at the counter since I'd returned to my café, glaring at a stuffed mermaid he'd set in on the counter in front of him as he downed grappa after grappa without even removing his hat. He was wrapped in curious clothes that seemed made of endless layers of thin black cloth, and his unidentifiable face was obscured by a wide-brimmed leather hat. He rose for the first time when your body fell on mine to pluck the knife from my hand as easily as picking a flower. You rose to your feet and looked into the man's face. As you did, the skin of your own face convulsed, paling blue as the rose you'd given me. The man just stood there as you gazed upon him. Then, slapping the blade absently against the palm of one hand, he returned to his seat. A drunkard bumped into him along the way, but he fell to the ground with an ostentatious clatter seemingly of his own accord, gaping at the other customers as if asking them what happened. Silence spread throughout the café, and soon the only sound to be heard was the music filtering in from the streets outside. You followed after the man involuntarily, as did I.

As soon as he'd sat down on his stool, he looked you up and down and slapped the handle of the knife into your palm. He fixed his eyes on mine and spoke.

"My name is Réal. Of the northern Réals." He smiled a little then, looking back and forth between us. Seen close up, his high cheekbones and narrow, knife-slit eyes made his face look aboriginal or East Asian. But his kinky hair and rounded nose indicated that he might instead be black. I felt as if I knew this man with dark brown skin. You started to say something, but he stopped you. "You don't have to give me your name. I already know it. I've followed every move you've made," he said, his voice both clear and hoarse.

I looked him up and down, this man who grew like an enormous tree from the counter. There was something different about him. This town was filled with black-clad men in wide-brimmed leather hats with faces that seemed both Asian and black. Yet this one seemed somehow strange.

"I have a message from Mister T. Ango: 'You did your job well yesterday,'" he said, nodding toward you, and then he turned to me. "He also said to give you this," he continued, indicating the stuffed mermaid on the counter.

Hearing the name, I remembered something from long ago. A man of that name had been my lover, and at some point he'd gone overseas, or was put in jail, or at any rate left, and I'd taken up with another man. But I couldn't put together how my T. Ango could be related to the man in black sitting before me now.

"If you wish, I can lend you any blade you like for this final job. What do you say?"

"This one will be fine," I said, stroking the knife in the sheath at my side. I felt noble light envelope my body. A cold, blue-white flame rose behind me to the back of my head, and I could see it engulf her as well.

"That knife has already been dirtied, hasn't it?" The man indicated her with a flick of his eyes. "A dirtied knife brings bad fortune."

You looked at me. I felt a chasm open in my chest.

"It was a splendid item, don't get me wrong. Hard, pure, with a top-notch shine." The man spoke these words in a respectful tone. You nodded deeply. Before you kill me, you'll exclude me. I felt my wandering, homeless hatred finally find its center, felt it prepare to explode.

The man stroked a knife that hung from a sheath at his own side.

"We cannot brook betrayal. But this is not the time for punishment. A knife risks its light to fight. It depends on purity. You know I'm right." You nodded deeply once again. I watched the two of you. But you and he just watched each other. It occurred to me that neither I, nor the city, nor the river would ever be satisfied until both of you were destroyed.

I turned my back wordlessly and walked toward the

door. I heard the shrill, false timbre of her voice as she called out, "Are you going to walk away from my challenge?" I ignored her, just kept walking. A sound rang out, high heels running across the wooden floor. Carefully judging the timing, I turned around quickly as she bent forward to slip the knife from my possession again. I struck her between her shoulder blades, near her spine. She fell, moaning, and the knife remained in its sheath.

"I don't think that man is a stranger. If I don't kill him, I think I might disappear."

The wooden door closed tight. You were gone. I'd been betrayed. Not by you but by some unknowable entity. The floorboards reverberated with heavy footfalls as the man followed after you. As he passed by my prone body, he said, "You could never kill him. You can never kill anyone, and you can never leave this city. And neither can he."

"We both have killed countless times before."

"It only seemed that way. It's all been nothing more than woven light. I'm the only one who can truly kill."

The wooden door closed tight again. My body filled with smoke that stank like char and blocked my breath, and I rose to my feet to follow after as well. Even though as I did, I imagined my own death, pierced fore and aft simultaneously, inserting myself into the space between you as you dueled.

But there turned out to be no room for that. The thick, intimate space between you repelled me. You'd both shed your shirts and wrapped them around your left hands to use as shields as you faced each other, every nerve on your bodies bristling. From time to time, a knife would slice through the space between you at the speed of light. There was no one else around. Sourceless, blue-white light cut through the mist. You and the man were bathed in flickering light that illuminated in flashes your faces, your glittering blades. The knives gathered the light to them and made it dance, shining sliver like fish swimming through water, cutting through the air in all directions. Both you and the man had disappeared. The knives were all that remained, two masses formed from light. When they crossed, sparks flew, reaching even to where I stood watching. The only sounds I heard were the squeak of shoes against asphalt, the metallic scrape of knives clashing, the heavy breath of two men rendered invisible by the blinding brightness of their blades.

The duel lasted for hours, evolving finally into less an exchange of slashes than of glares, but still dawn refused to break. Dizzy, I lost track of how long the duel had lasted. I lost track of who it was I'd known first, who it was I loved, you or he. But then, the man lunged at you, his entire body suffused with power and the smell of sweat that ebbed and flowed around him like a tide, bringing his left hand within striking distance of your nose, and that was when I noticed the pitch black shadow at his feet and realized that he was a different sort of being than you and I; I lunged to stop you, to embrace you even as you stabbed at the man's left hand with all the strength left in your body, but his right arm had already unswervingly extended like a column of sun-burnished flesh to reach its destination: your right eye. So the one who cried out like a northern rain forest bird was you. Bringing both hands to your face, you ran, catlike, to press yourself into a gap between two buildings. The man's left hand flapped from his wrist, nearly severed by your blade and connected only by a thin strip of skin, and he brought the knife in his right hand to cut it off completely, muttering, "That does it," as he ground it into the dirt with his heel before chasing after you, yelling, "This isn't over!" in a shattered voice as he did.

But he didn't have to chase you far. You collapsed, falling from the shadowed alcove where you tried to hide, exposing yourself to the blue-white light once more. Your entire body was covered in the thick, syrup-like liquid that ran from your eye, not quite silver and not quite clear, filled with semicircles like scales that refracted the light with a sound like glass orbs colliding. I ran to where you lay, murmuring the words, "*Mano a mano,*" again and again. The man walked over to stand beside us. "He was a strong one," said the man in a voice that trembled as if overcome with emotion. I looked up at him. The end of his right arm glittered like a jewel. The knife it held was engraved from handle to blade-tip with fine patterns like hairline fractures or tiny hairs, like skin completely covered with tattoos. The delicacy of its patterning exceeded your knife immeasurably, splitting the light into a complex array that gathered at your feet, creating a lacquer-shiny, jet black shadow to oppose it. Gazing upon this, my first shadow, I was captivated. It had a gloss to it, and a heft; it looked as if a pleasant dampness would greet my finger if I touched it, and I wanted to, desperately. As I watched light cut across the edge of its velvety darkness, I heard music, a scale playing softly that pressed me to the ground, felling me through my ears.

"Just go to sleep," said the man as he bent down toward me, his voice strained. "I did not emerge unscathed either."

He pulled his left sleeve back to show me the stump at the end of his arm. Blood, redder than lips, gushed from the cleanly shorn surface as if from a pump. I stared at it blankly for a while, then shook off my stupor and ripped a sleeve from my dress to wrap the wound. But he pulled away, tearing off a piece of black cloth from his own clothes to staunch the flow. Absorbing the blood, the cloth turned the same rich, glossy black as the shadow at his feet. Looking at it, I realized that I was witnessing something impossible, that this man was made of different stuff than you and I, denser, more intense, and I understood at last that unlike him we could never escape this city or this river, a realization that filled me with loneliness, drained the strength from my spine. You were my loneliness incarnate, and as I felt it coalesce once more to block the breath in my throat like a pit in a peach, I knew the only one able to dissolve it now was gone. Looking down at where you lay, I saw the silver fluid within you had almost drained completely, flowing back into the river in a little stream.

"I won't forget you or your knife. I promise you that," said the man, addressing you.

"And neither will I," I said. There was no mistake; I'd loved you today. I'd touched you and you'd touched me. I'd heard your voice like music, tasted happiness great enough to take the fear from dying.

"It's too bad. Now that he's dead, it's the end for you as well." The man looked at me sorrowfully.

"I know. I'll leave the city alone."

"Don't you understand? When he dies, so does the light inside you. Once I block his light, there's no more reflection, no more of anything. When I kill, it's the end for real."

The man stood before me. The shadow thrown by his enormous, treelike body engulfed me completely. Ecstasy coursed through my core, making my spine tingle. I was feeling my first shadow: hot in the center, its surface cool, pleasant, like being submerged in water. No, that wasn't it—it didn't feel like the river had the first time I'd jumped in. The shadow was exactly as warm and exactly as cool as I was myself. We were connected, the shadow and I. I was a part of it.

"I want you to take me away from this city." I was starting to fade.

"Please understand. It's impossible. Even if you remained alive, you could never leave. I'm blocking the light, burying you along with the city," the man seemed to laugh as he said this. Particles of darkness invaded my body, tickling as they penetrated. Or, rather, it was my body itself that was fragmenting, dissolving into the dark.

"Hold this and sleep in peace."

The man set the stuffed mermaid on my chest. As I raised my arms to embrace it, I realized I was gripping something in my right hand. Unable to see anything within the darkness of your shadow, I traced its form with the fingers of my left hand as I held it in front of my uncomprehending eyes before recognizing it at last as your knife.

I had lost the strength in my right arm already, and the knife lay on my chest. The mermaid fell away. My chest grew hard and strong, a muscled plateau. I tried to see the man, but my right eye ached, blinded. I imagined the silvery fluid that ran from it as it flowed beyond the shadow's edge. I tried again to look up at the man. All I saw was darkness, all I heard was a sound like the wingbeat of an enormous bird. Occasionally I would see a tiny flash of light but that was it. Where had you gone? I was sure that I had really touched you. That I had really kissed you. The echo of your lips on mine was all I had now, and it was enough. Something flashed again. I reached my left hand up to grab it. Complex, refracted light needled my left eye. It glittered silver, a knife covered in fine engravings as if tattooed. I could hear the light. It sounded like velvet ripping, like a hollow tree trunk pounded, like plucked strings, like singing: *yira yira yira.* My left hand lost its strength and fell, dropping the knife. It rocked back and forth, clattering as if against a wooden floor. I was all that remained here, and I was alone.

In memory of Antonio Agri

Afterword: The Politics of Impossible Transformation

The first short story in this collection, "Paper Woman," opens with an extended meditation on the nature of literature. The protagonist, who shares his name with the author, laments that people no longer read novels "as if printing the words on the interiors of their bodies." For the Tomoyuki Hoshino of the story, this unwillingness defeats the purpose of literature for both the reader and the writer. Literature, he explains, is "an art that wavers, like a heat shimmer, between joy at the prospect of becoming something else and despair at knowing that such a transformation is ultimately impossible."

By his own account, "Paper Woman" was the first short story (as opposed to novella) Hoshino wrote after making his debut in 1998 with the Bungei Prize–winning *The Last Sigh* (*Saigo no tōiki*), and the musings embedded within it ring Rosetta-like, providing a key for decoding the themes he pursues in a body of work characterized by otherwise wildly divergent experiments in style and form. The drive to become something other than oneself is both an aesthetic and ethical demand for Hoshino, articulating a definition of writing as art and of this art's purpose among other modes of human expression and activity. The figures, images, and situations that recur within his works dramatize moments of transformation that act not only as resonant incidents within the stories but as instances of metafictional commentary on the activity of writing that produced them. Hoshino invites his reader to follow him in this process of becoming other, of rendering otherness inhabitable without flattening or domesticating it. The promise is joyful, but also demanding—not only is the reader expected to be willing to "print" these words within her or his body, but the joy of transformation is indivisible from the despair felt when the attempt to transform inevitably reaches its limit. To inhabit these stories is to inhabit a space that, while ephemeral and illusory (a mirage, a heat shimmer), nonetheless marks the reader with evidence of this passage between joy and its opposite. "One could say that a novel's words trace the pattern of scars left by the struggle between these two feelings," explains the fictional "Hoshino" of "Paper Woman," but as the rest of the stories in this collection demonstrate, it is an apt description of the experience of reading the literature of the real Hoshino as well.

Modern Japanese Literature's "End," Hoshino's Beginning

Hoshino made his literary debut at thirty-two, relatively late in life (at least by the standards of the youth-obsessed Japanese publishing world) and at a time when some of the most influential voices in the critical establishment were busy declaring Japanese literature to be over. Most famous of these was Kōjin Karatani, the author of the now-standard *The Origins of Modern Japanese Literature* (1980; English translation 1993). Having defined the beginnings of modern Japanese literature in this examination of the early Meiji Era (1868–1912) politics of confessional "naturalism," Karatani declared the "end" of modern Japanese literature in a 2004 essay published in the journal *Waseda Bungaku*, the text of a speech he'd been giving for a few years previous and which he subsequently expanded into a book the following year.

In *Origins*, Karatani demonstrates how turn-of-the-nineteenth-century "modern" confessional literature played an important, and troublingly complicit, role in articulating a newly defined sense of Japanese subjectivity amid the Meiji government's assertion of itself as an imperial power commensurate with its European colonial peers. In "The 'End' of Modern Literature," he argues that during the course of the 1990s and 2000s, the status of Japanese literature eroded to the point that it can no longer play such a role, for good or for ill, in the creation of what it means to be Japanese. Literature has moved steadily out of the mainstream culture and become bound to the articulation of minority voices or the output of "subcultures," like otaku fandoms centered on manga, animation, or other mass cultural forms. In other words, modern literature's implication in "mainstream" Japanese history, its power to advance (or resist) expansionist pre-war colonial policies or post–World War II capitalist development has reached its terminus in the present neoliberal order that has wrested literature from its privileged space within national consciousness and reduced it to just another commodity that articulates nothing beyond the price consumers are willing to spend on it. Literature has "completed its purpose," Karatani declares, and is now indistinguishable from any other commodity in a global marketplace. It therefore may reach beyond the boundaries of the Japan-as-nation (as is the case with otaku-targeted "light" literature, which is popular with the international otaku community), but this very property also limits its influence to market segments corresponding not with a "mainstream" Japan but to various subcultures and special interests within it.[1]

Karatani's claims are continuous with the larger flow of left-leaning cultural criticism in Japan, which came out of a post–World War II moment of intense critical reflection on the legacy of Japanese imperial fascism that led to the tragedies and horrors committed in the name of the Emperor during the war. Writers such as Kenzaburō Ōe and Kenji Nakagami are celebrated within this body of

---

1 Karatani Kōjin, "Kindai bungaku no owari (The End of Modern Literature)," *Waseda Bungaku* (May 2004), 4–29. Translation of this and other passages is mine unless otherwise noted.

work for their openly political fiction, which challenged the status quo by exposing these elements of the past and militating against their continued, if disavowed, presence within the rapid capitalistic expansion of the 1960s and 1970s. Much literary criticism coming out of this discourse prizes literature insofar as it articulates a countercultural consciousness that opposes and attempts to remake the mainstream national culture of Japan. This brand of reading literature politically frequently focuses on issues defined by the idea of Japan as a unique nation—analyses of the Emperor system, for example, or "unique" features of the Japanese family or social system. Karatani's interventions in the 1980s and 1990s focus on how the modern nation-state form that was instituted in the late 1800s affected the way people thought of themselves as individuals and as members of a nation, tracing this history through an analysis of canonical literature and its role in shaping that discourse. Indeed, he and his contemporaries show how the concept of "canonical" or "pure" literature itself emerged at the same time the idea of literature as a "national" art form did, in the process demonstrating how implicated modern literature has been in systems of power as a nationally mediated mode of cultural legitimacy. And in the case of Karatani's close association with and promotion of Nakagami in the 1970s and 1980s, this critical effort helped to add a vital and oppositional political voice to the postwar literary edifice by exhorting the countercultural power of his writings, effectively changing the nature of Japan's literary canon by helping add a writer like him to it.

There is a limit to this way of defining the political potential of literature, however. Due to its emphasis on the nation as the governing unit of politics and culture, opposition registers within this kind of analysis solely through its relation to the mainstream. The Meiji Period is interesting for Karatani, for example, because it is a historical moment that installed certain writers and certain kinds of writing as "modern" and "Japanese," and he sees in this moment the possibility for *other* kinds of writing to have been installed this way instead. It was a moment of unfulfilled possibility, when different alternative national literatures could have won out and affected the then-emergent discourses on Japanese-ness and perhaps resulted in a different Japan. The despair articulated in his declaration of modern Japanese literature's "end" in 2004 finds its root in Karatani's perception that it is no longer through national literature, however alternative, that this kind of political change can be effected. Karatani urges his audience to no longer "think through literature"; rather, they should "separate from literature, and then think" of effective ways to combat the deleterious effects of global capital.

Ironically, the same *Waseda Bungaku* issue that begins with Karatani's essay asserting the end of literature's sociopolitical relevance ends with the results of a survey of literary figures who have been asked for their thoughts on two hot-button political issues of 2004: the deployment of Japanese armed forces to aid the UN force in Iraq and a possible revision to the Japanese constitution that would render them a conventional military rather than the Self-Defense Force they have been since the end of the American Occupation in 1952. Hoshino was one of the literary figures who responded substantially (as opposed to Haruki Murakami, for example, who sent a fax stating that "as a matter of principle" he "does not respond to surveys"), and within this response, one can see how a contemporary writer might address the issues raised by Karatani's rather dispiriting essay.

Indeed, Hoshino's opening sentence reads like a direct response to Karatani's closing one. "My fundamental stance," he writes, "is that to apprehend the issues arising at the meta-level from such an inquiry—that is, how is it that these issues have taken the form of questions like 'Should the Self-Defense Force be deployed abroad?' or 'Should the Constitution be revised?', and what is the mentality of those (myself included) who accept such questions at face value?—I must think through them by writing fiction."[2] He goes on to distinguish between these meta-level inquiries and his immediate personal reactions ("I have a website where I can write freely about those"),[3] which he claims are formed as much out of his lack of knowledge of the fundamental issues involved as anything else. As an individual, he is against both the deployment of Self-Defense Forces to Iraq and the revision of the Constitution because neither question seems to have been formulated with regard to the fundamental issues lying beneath them. What is a military? What role should it play, if any? What is the history of the Constitution's creation and how has that affected subsequent Japanese history? For Hoshino, these vital questions fall by the wayside as the public sphere grows obsessed with questions of deployment and revision in isolation.

So what is literature's role in pursuing underlying issues of the age? Hoshino takes the opportunity offered by the survey to offer an answer: "Fiction is neither a medium from which to expect immediacy nor a method for effecting change to the social system in an easily observable form; at best, it signifies little more than the driving of a tiny wedge. And yet, the tiny fissure so created also signifies the sole impediment left to the total shutdown of time and space."[4]

In this sense, Hoshino's answer to Karatani's challenge seems to be that fiction cannot be reduced to its historical implication in the mainstream articulation of Japanese national subjectivity. To do so would be to expect from it the ability to directly change the social system in

---

2 *Waseda Bungaku*, 158.

3 He keeps a blog at hoshinot.asablo.jp/blog/, posts from which have been translated into English by Shiori Yamazaki, Brent Lue, Adrienne Carey Hurley, Francis Guérin, and myself for publication on the PM Press website (www.pmpress.org).

4 *Waseda Bungaku*, 158.

easily observable ways and constantly be disappointed. Karatani suggests that neoliberalism has robbed literature of its power to affect the mainstream and therefore we must "separate" from it to change society, but Hoshino here implies that the ascription of this power to literature arises from mistaking literature's historical positioning within larger power structures for something inherent in literature itself.

Hoshino's literary endeavors are not simply an extension of the more forthright political musings found in his essays and on his website, but are instead explorations taking advantage of a medium that allows a fundamentally different type of questioning to take place. The importance of writing fiction for Hoshino lies not in the sheer number of people who might read it or in whether the "right" people approve or argue about it, but because it allows the possibility for both author and reader to inhabit a different world—a different time and space—from the one conventionally available to us. A novelist's words chip away at this conventional world and a "tiny fissure" opens up, allowing those stifled by the closed circuits formed by the routines and regimes of everyday life to breathe a different, freer air. And in this sense, to read Hoshino is to read a literature unafraid to be "minor"—that in fact finds its purpose there. Whereas Karatani dismisses the rise of "minority" literature in postwar America as the beginning of the "end" of modern literature there ("Starting in the 1970s, black, and then Asian-American, women writers and the like began to emerge. And indeed, their endeavors were literary, but not the kind of thing that could affect society as a whole."), Hoshino asserts literature's ability to allow readers and writers to inhabit minor or otherwise excluded or unthinkable positions as precisely what allows literature to affect "society as a whole"—one story, one reader, one word, one fissure at a time.[5]

---

5 *Waseda Bungaku*, 7.

Literature as Transformation: Between Ilusión and Realidad

It would not be too bold to say that every story in this collection narrates a transformational movement, and usually more than one (or one that takes place on several levels at once). Some are explicitly such, like the quest to "become paper" undertaken by the title character in "Paper Woman," or the passages between modes of gendered embodiment experienced by the two protagonists of "Air." Others are more metaphorical, embedded within narratives told in a more or less realist mode, such as the Japanese protagonist's attempts to shed his First World privilege and become a revolutionary Latin American guerrilla in "Chino" or the testing of the limits of one member of a couple's ability to see the world from the other's point of view found in "We, the Children of Cats." And in some stories, like "A *Milonga* for the Melted Moon," not only the characters but the entire world of the story exist in a state of constant, dreamlike flux, the prose gliding freely between points of view and frames of reference in an uncanny re-creation of the titular Latin American dance (as well as paying homage to the magical realism found in Latin America's literary tradition, which is similarly preoccupied with shapeshifting and synesthesia). These transformative movements run along lines of unexpected affinity and longing, and may be said to be one of the major "fissures" Hoshino's writing opens up in the surface of the everyday, and thus constitutes a major part of its meaning and politics.

Hoshino's works frequently explore alternative versions of the everyday world. "Treason Diary," for example, is recognizably inspired by a series of incidents that made the news in Japan and internationally during the late 1990s. The two young men with violent pasts in the story are based on the perpetrators of two famous incidents that gripped the Japanese public sphere at that time and lead to a panic about depraved acts committed by the younger generation (even as the overall rate of juvenile crime was trending downward). First is the 1997 Shônen A (or "Boy A") Incident, in which a fourteen-year-old boy was found to have committed a series of attacks on younger children, resulting in two deaths and one major injury; his use of a baroque pseudonym to sign the letter he left with the decapitated head of one victim and those he later sent to the media and police, as well as the extensive diaries that were found in his room after his arrest and published in the mainstream press, make him an obvious basis for the character of Kiyoto. The subsequent "Butterfly Knife Incident," in which a young boy killed his English teacher at school with a knife that resembled one used in a popular television drama at the time, resembles the situation of the narrator, Yukinori. The details of the incidents differ in ways large and small from how they are portrayed in the story, however, marking Hoshino's critical distance from (rather than sensationalist replication of) the media narratives he plays upon. Further, he places both boys in Peru, allowing their stories to play out in a context removed from the national media narratives their real-life counterparts find their stories embedded within—and frequently distorted to suit, especially in the sense that within Japan, these narratives of savagely criminal youth were marshaled by the state to justify revisions to the Juvenile Law that lowered the age of possible criminal prosecution of minors from sixteen to fourteen in 2000, then to "around twelve" in 2008.

Hoshino further distances his narrative from conventional understandings of juvenile crime as individual or generational monstrosity by allowing his young offenders to pursue a path not of successful or unsuccessful assimilation back into Japanese society, but political resistance. The attack on the Japanese Ambassador's Residence that forms the climax of "Treason Diary" connects these Japanese figures of juvenile crime to the real-life siege of the Residence in Peru by members of the Túpac Amaru Revolutionary Movement, or MRTA, from December 17,

1996, to April 22, 1997. Hoshino thus creates an alternative version of the world that allows him to make connections between simultaneous media "incidents" that are rendered otherwise unthinkable by the way they were presented to the public at the time. Conventional accounts of juvenile crimes emphasized the grotesque particulars of the crimes and thus created a sense of these young men as bearers of "unimaginable" forms of consciousness. Their narratives were thus politically neutralized, unable to signify anything beyond a sense of growing, inscrutable menace from a generation that had been "indulged" by a system of laws that fostered anonymous rehabilitation rather than public punishment. On the other hand, the siege of the Ambassador's Residence in Peru was presented as an act of terrorism motivated by the radical but obscure politics of the MRTA that callously put innocent Japanese lives in danger, a media narrative that disallowed any consideration of the MRTA's position or the possible legitimacy of their struggle against the totalitarian policies favoring the very rich that characterized the regime of Peru's then-president, Alberto Fujimori. This allowed the eventual storming of the Residence by government troops to be framed as a justified and even happy outcome, the violence of the situation placed on the shoulders of the resistance fighters even as they were executed without trial and, in some cases, after their voluntary surrender.

But Hoshino's project is not to straightforwardly "correct" conventional media narratives about current events. Instead, his alternative worlds, with their uncannily simultaneous proximity and distance from "real life" (for example, his renaming MRTA "MARTA," his setting of revolutionary action at "Santo Domingo University" rather than the real National University of San Marcos in Lima, and so on), exude an dreamlike atmosphere that condenses and plays out in alternative form various elements of the news stories that constitute the average person's perception of the "reality" lying beyond the borders

of immediate experience. This makes both these conden-
sations and the "news" and "incidents" they index seem
equally unreal, equally the product of dreamwork and
imagination. The reader is thus encouraged to read the
story-behind-the-story, to ask "meta-level" questions about
why these stories are told the way they are and what other
ways these stories might be told. What might juvenile crim-
inals from a First World nation like Japan have in common
with revolutionaries in Latin America? What does it mean
to think of both as "broken" (*hajikareta*, which can also
be translated as "bounced out" or "cast off"), a term that
evokes the violence of a crazy-making world system that
"breaks" people psychologically and materially by coding
as personal failings the effects of the institutionalized dis-
empowerment of specific groups—the young, the poor, the
rural, the indigenous, the migrant, the dispossessed?

This approach also animates "Sand Planet," which is
based on Hoshino's own experience working as a newspaper reporter in the late 1980s. Hoshino's beat as a reporter
was the Urawa region north of Tokyo where "Sand Planet"
is set, and, like "Treason Diary," well-known news events
like the 1998 Wakayama Poison Curry Incident and the
1999 Columbine high school shooting incident in the
United States form a paratextual landscape against which
the fictional incidents within the narrative unfold. "Sand
Planet" also incorporates the very real history of Japan
encouraging the migration of poor or unemployed rural
people to the Dominican Republic in the immediate
postwar period, letting this history inform its portrayal of
the growing numbers of homeless people in present-day
Japan. The migration was a ploy on Japan's part to rid itself
of its unemployed (and, as Hoshino implies in the story,
potentially revolutionary) population after the devastation
of World War II decimated the economy; it was part of a
broader immigration of Japanese people into Latin America
at this time, including to Brazil and Peru (though those two
countries had prewar histories of government-sponsored

Japanese immigration, unlike the Dominican Republic).[6] This little-known moment in Japanese postwar history is folded into the story in layers, disrupting the stultifying day-to-day travails of a beat reporter as it emerges in a variety of forms—poetry, memory, performance, hallucination, haunting. Correspondingly, these forms break up the very surface of the text itself, changes in typeface, indentation and the like creating jagged interventions into the smooth, conventional realism of the narrative present. This throws the reader off-balance, creating a seeming dichotomy between reality and dream that implies, by the end, that the truth lies in the latter rather than the former, or, more precisely, in the space of interaction between the two. As with "Treason Diary," "Sand Planet" forces the reader to reconsider the foundations of everyday reality and the narratives conventionally used to give it meaning. As the protagonist tries to write an article about the school poisonings through conventional journalistic means, he finds himself constantly dissatisfied: "it seemed like lies slipped in no matter how he tried to write it." The dream-like encounter with the old man in the forest catalyzes the protagonist's renewed search for a truth that can knit together the disparate incidents happening around him and create meaning more profound than the "lies" found on the surface of the facts.

Saying that fiction is the only medium through which a tiny crack in the everyday can be opened up is not quite the same thing as saying that it is only in fantasy that truth lies. Hoshino's stories are often joyous explorations of the alternative spaces that can open up through fantasy and dream, but this joy is as frequently as not leavened with a melancholy ambiguity, a realization of a certain limit within the process of transformation. The stories in this

---

6 For a good history of the Japanese immigration to the Dominican Republic, see Oscar Horst and Katsuhiro Asagiri, "The Odyssey of Japanese Colonists in the Dominican Republic," *Geographical Review* 90, no. 3, (July 2000): 335–58.

collection almost always end with their protagonists either stranded in a space between two states of being or disappearing completely. Even *"Milonga,"* which takes place entirely within a world of flux, ends with the intrusion of a character representing the "real" (named, not coincidentally, "Réal," echoing the protagonist's journey "beyond Ilusión to a village called Realidad" in "Chino"). The real within that story is signified by Réal being the only character who throws a true shadow, a shadow that blocks the fluidity of identity and existence literalized within the story as the silver fluid flowing in the veins of both protagonists that binds them to the river they travel along. The implication is that this silver fluid is the light reflected by that river's shining surface in concentrated form, and an identity created through reflection cannot exist alone; as the title of the story implies, the characters exist as partners in dance, itself a transformation of music into visible movement. So it is appropriate that the dissolution of identity at the end is portrayed not as pain or nothingness, but as an experience of isolation: "I was all that remained here, and I was alone." Tellingly, the journey to the village of Realidad described in "Chino" also ends in an encounter with profound isolation, as the protagonist finds himself refused in his attempts to connect with Maki, who herself exists in a state of self-imposed isolation due to the violence that severed the connection between her and the surrounding villagers.

Hoshino uses a variety of metaphors for the transience of the everyday. In "Sand Planet," for example, the protagonist floats in a pool and feels a sudden disconnection from anything real:

> *I'm on a set somewhere, surrounded by manufactured oceans, manufactured plains. That's all nature actually is to me, just a series of sensations recreated in rooms. Even my own self is just a recreation, an illusion. Everything I touch and know to be myself is just*

the product of a brain that's no more than just another illusion itself. Not the grand illusion of life's endless cycle. This self of mine is no everlasting soul able to pass through cycles of reincarnation—it's the empty shell made and remade with every cycle, an infinite illusion.

The Buddhist nature of these meditations on the "cycles of reincarnation" is overt, but of a piece with the world made of reflected light in "*Milonga*" and with the passages between illusion and reality found in the other stories in the collection as well. It is less a moment of Hoshino showing his hand (and thus indicating that one should read all of his works through a Buddhist lens, for example) than him employing a variety of modes through which to explore the organizing paradox at the heart of his fiction. This paradox states that the world is made of fabrications and illusions that are more fluid than they may at first seem, but also states that there are truths that lie behind these fluctuations, truths that are not precisely transcendent but rather something more like conditions of possibility for that very fluidity.

Therefore, the idea that there are parts of life that are eternal and others that are ephemeral does not translate into a traditional metaphysics that locates truth in the transcendent and distortion in the contingent. The "meta-level" questions opened up by the medium of fiction for Hoshino concern themselves not with transcendent truths but with the way the *interactions* between different modes of representing reality produce a kind of truth that emerges as phantasmagoric irruption. Hoshino's stories produce these irruptions through a variety of techniques: the creation of alternative versions of "incidents" produced within the contemporary media; the folding together of histories conventionally held apart; the disruption of the literary text itself, such as the disorienting switches between first-person narrators in "Air" and "*Milonga*" or the various discursive variations found in "Sand Planet"; and a profligately allusive approach to literary creation that forces the reader to actively translate between various modes of writing and the literary traditions they draw upon: the Latin American magical realism of García Márquez, the confrontational political early fiction of Kenzaburō Ōe, the rewriting of the Japanese literary tradition from a minority position found in Kenji Nakagami and the Resident Korean author Yang-ji Lee, the gamesmanship and intellectual rigor of Borges and Nabokov, the rich folkloric archive of Japan, and so on.

When Hoshino himself speaks of his writing, he phrases it as a balancing act between building upon the work of those who inspire him and expressing something that he only reluctantly calls a distinct "identity." In a published conversation with fellow author Rieko Matsuura (*The Apprenticeship of Big Toe P,* 1994; English translation 2009), Hoshino puts it this way:

> Before the postmodern age [of 1980s Japan], the idea that if something wasn't original it was worth nothing was very strong. And within this environment that was telling me "Express the uniqueness within yourself!", that seemed to value originality above all, I found myself at every turn faced with the fact that to express what I wanted to express, I needed to borrow from things that already existed— this happened to me all the time, even as a child. When I made a friend, we'd become very close. I'd be influenced by my friend to an inordinate degree, until we almost became the same person. Indeed, I'm secretly rather good at imitations (*laughs*). And perhaps that part of me comes out strongly in my fiction. . . . But after [the postmodern 1980s], in the '90s, everything changed again: I'd accrued more life experiences at an individual level, and that '80s way of thinking, that, *whatever you do is fine* type of thinking, I noticed that it was a view held most strongly by the already privileged. Those most blind

> to the privilege supporting them were the ones most
> loudly proclaiming, "Interiority and identity are just
> illusions!" and minorities and the like who were
> already suffering from being deprived of identity
> were doubly deprived, and even identity arising
> from one's very minority status was suppressed
> or forbidden from serious consideration. And so,
> I began to feel a need to break with the postmod-
> ernism that had previously freed me. . . . I had no
> intention of returning to the cult of originality, but
> I did want to capture a sort of loose form of identity,
> an identity that was not an identity, something that
> was not necessarily coherent and was always already
> in constant flux—and I thought that through fiction,
> I could express this sort of thing.[7]

Here Hoshino demonstrates both his commitment to a politics of transformation and his acknowledgment of its risk. Every story in this collection describes a shift in identity of some sort, either a literal one or a shift in a character's perception; indeed, one could say that Hoshino's fiction asks if there's a real difference between the two. The flux of consciousness and a constantly changing identity may be two ways of saying the same thing, and by taking that as a premise rather than an endpoint, Hoshino asks the reader to go further than the exposure of identity as illusion that characterizes the typical "postmodern" literature that he speaks of in the above quotation. For it is not enough to simply say that identity or consciousness is an illusion and leave it at that—Hoshino's world is not a free-for-all without consequences.

Instead, his idea of recombining borrowed elements to create his fiction resembles something more like the "task of the translator" as laid out by Walter Benjamin (it is worth noting that Hoshino, after quitting his job at

---

7 *Bungei*, (Kawade Shobō, Spring 2006), 58–59.

the newspaper, spent the early 1990s living off and on in Mexico and then, upon his permanent return to Japan, became a translator himself, creating subtitles for Spanish-language films shown in Japan). "It is the task of translator," writes Benjamin, "to release in his own language that pure language which is exiled among alien tongues, to liberate the language imprisoned in a work in his re-creation of that work."[8] Benjamin's over-arching point is that translation is not an imitation of an original but a re-creation of it from the ground up within a new language and context, which means that it must recapture on its own terms the initial impetus that made the original something that had to be written in the first place. The resulting work, the translation, is the "afterlife" of the original, produced through the interaction between the translator as a kind of ultimate reader of the original and the original itself, a process of ideal reading that resembles that described in Hoshino's "Paper Woman" as a wavering between the euphoria of becoming other and the despair at one's inevitable failure to do so; the resulting work is the pattern of scars left by the words the author-as-translator printed on the interior of his or her body.

Hoshino's fiction may thus be seen most precisely, perhaps, as an act of translation, a meeting of disparate "originals" borrowed from various literary traditions, real-life incidents, personal experiences, etc., that produces through their interaction something like the "pure" language Benjamin writes of, identifiable within the texts themselves as transformational desire.

The plot of "Paper Woman" illuminates this in its allusion to the legend of "Earless Hōichi" in the game played between Paper and the narrator. "Earless Hōichi" is a legend known best as it was retold by Lafcadio Hearn in

---

8 Walter Benjamin, "The Task of the Translator," in *Walter Benjamin: Selected Writings Volume 1, 1913–1926*, eds. Marcus Bullock and Michael W. Jennings, trans. Harry Zohn, (Cambridge, MA: Harvard University Press, 1996), 261.

Kwaidan, a collection of "Stories and Studies of Strange Things" published in 1904. Hearn is a complex figure in the English and Japanese language literary worlds, spending his time refining a talent for translating local legends and "weird" stories into atmospheric prose wherever he found himself (New Orleans, the Philippines, etc.). But it was when he moved to Japan near the end of his life that he found the material for his most lastingly popular works, the collections of adapted Japanese tales that circulated first in their original English and, after being translated back into Japanese after his death, in Japan. Hearn's versions of these stories, including "Earless Hōichi," persist as their most well known versions in Japan; Masaki Kobayashi adapted "Hōichi" and three other Hearn tales to make his 1965 film *Kwaidan,* which in turn inspired, at least in part, Peter Greenaway's 1996 film *The Pillow Book,* the "British movie" Hoshino slyly alludes to in "Paper Woman."[9]

Hoshino's retelling of "Earless Hōichi" in "Paper Woman" may also allude to Hearn's translation process as reported after his death by his widow, Setsu Koizumi, in her memoirs.[10] She describes Hearn asking her to act out parts of the legends he was adapting, "studying her every gesture, insisting on the exact intonation of every word."[11] A similar act of bodily "translation" forms the center of "Paper Woman," the titular character's desire to become paper meshing (at least at first) with the narrator's writing process, until they are inseparable. And the story of Earless Hōichi is itself a story about storytelling: Hōichi is a blind *biwa* minstrel, famed for the quality of his musical retellings of old legends. He is summoned one night to sing ballads retelling the famed sea battle in the straits

---

9 See *Kwaidan: Stories and Studies of Strange Things,* (New York: Dover, 1968).

10 See Yoji Hasegawa, *A Walk in Kumamoto: The Life and Times of Setsu Koizumi, Lafcadio Hearn's Japanese Wife,* (Kent: Global Oriental, 1997); this text includes a translation of Koizumi's memoir, *Reminiscences.*

11 From Oscar Lewis's introduction to *Kwaidan,* xii.

of Shimonoseki that culminated in the death of the boy Emperor Antoku that marked the end of Japan's classical period; soon it becomes clear that these summons have been issued by the spirits of the warriors who died in that battle. To protect him from this dangerous bewitchment, the priest of the temple where Hōichi lives orders him to be stripped and a holy sutra inked upon his naked body, which will render him invisible to the unholy spirits of the dead. And when the spirits come for him that night, he is indeed invisible—save for his ears, which the priest's acolytes had mistakenly left untouched by their brushes. The spirits grab these ears and rip them from Hōichi's body, freeing him from the bewitchment. He goes on to attain great fame as a performer whose singing entrances even the dead, but he can never shake his new name, borne from the scars that were the price of this fame: "Earless Hōichi."

Blind and then earless, Hōichi's body is an ideal conduit for the stories of the dead, enough so that the dead themselves attempt to claim him so that they can hear their own exploits recounted back to them. The priest wrests Hōichi's body from their clutches by inscribing it with words of his own, words that bind Hōichi to the temple instead of the cemetery. Caught between these two realms, Hōichi is both bridge and boundary, his body marking the divide between them even as it provides the way for the stories of the dead to inhabit the world of the living when he sings. Similarly, in "Paper Woman," Paper longs to transform her body into an ideal inscriptive surface, yet every inscription becomes troubled by impermanence, dissolving into its disarticulated constituent parts only to recombine and dissolve again, endlessly. Her body is a vessel for a desire that seems to demand its own dissolution even as it seeks to provide an ideal surface for the self-expression of others. This desire is the "loose" identity Hoshino speaks of—a desire to shed one's qualities and become other, which is always frustrated by the way this otherness becomes a new quality, a new identity. And so the grounding for the politics of identity one can read into Hoshino's work seems located here, in the desire itself, and not in the completion of this or that process of transformation—this is where the joy resides, and the despair, but also the political edge.

Inhabiting Unconditional Possibility: The Mermaid as Revolutionary

This collection begins and ends with stories that use one of Hoshino's favorite recurring figures: the mermaid. In "Paper Woman," the initial conversation between the fictional Hoshino and Paper gets off to a rocky start, but finds its footing when "Hoshino" mentions that he has written a story called "The Mermaid Myth." Paper recounts her own past as the girlfriend of a boy with a mermaid fetish, which led her to grow her hair out and dress in costume for him. The culmination of this conversation shifts the discussion to a slightly different register, as Paper mulls over why mermaids make such compelling figures: "It's the impossibility. But it's also a gender issue, I'd say. These days there are all sorts of people who are neither man nor woman, or who are mixed racially, and it seems like it wouldn't be too huge a leap to think about humans mixing with animals, or even mixing with plants and trees. We can imagine these things precisely because of the times we live in. Mermaids are simply ahead of their time. It makes their sorrow all the more palpable."

In the last novella in this collection, "A *Milonga* for the Melted Moon," this mixing becomes as literal as it can, with the two protagonists made of light not only mirroring each other but constantly trading qualities (clothing, gender, voice). Hoshino switches the first person narration fluidly from one to the other until it becomes almost impossible to distinguish between them, forcing the reader into a moment-by-moment registering of sensation from within the space where they bleed together. But this euphoric rush

of constant transformation and interpenetrating identities is haunted throughout by the emblem of the real in
the form of a mermaid—seen early on as a carving into a
railing signifying Réal's ominous approach and then at the
end as a doll carried by Réal and placed on the body of one
of the protagonists as he extinguishes her in his shadow.

But beyond the literal use of mermaid imagery in
these stories (and in his novels, such as *The Last Sigh*, with
its swimming revolutionary protagonist, and 2000's *Open
Your Eyes, the Mermaids Sing,* to name just two), one can
see how the mermaid provides a conceptual model for
the transformational, revolutionary desire Hoshino's
fiction articulates in general. As the quotation from "Paper
Woman" illustrates, the mermaid is a figure caught between
two modes of being—not quite human, not quite fish; able
to inhabit both the land and the sea, but completely at
home in neither place. In this sense, all of the main characters in the stories in this collection are mermaids of one
sort or another, caught up in a flight from the "real" circumstances of his or her life and attempting to imaginatively
move beyond them, to become other in some way and
ending up in an ambiguous place of mitigated, incomplete
transformation.

For example, Joe, the narrator of "The No Fathers
Club," takes part in the communal imaginative leap of
first No Ball Soccer and then the titular No Fathers Club
in order to open up his stultifying everyday existence and
rediscover his "passion." And it works—he enters into a
series of intense relationships, first with Yōsuke, then
Kurumi, and above all with his new "father made of air."
But this endeavor is enabled by a shared commitment to
imagine a father—a necessarily doubled and incomplete
commitment, as there is a careful parsing of these young
people both from those around them who still have fathers
and take their existence for granted and from the father-
less who lack the nerve to create them from a whole cloth.
What unites club members is not the imaginary fathers

but the commit to imagining them, and the uneasy vacilla-
tions between Joe believing in his imaginary father and his
understanding that his father is imaginary become more
jarring as father becomes more real, culminating in the
crisis point signified by the father slapping him during
an argument. Moments like these abound in Hoshino's
work—moments when the boundary between the real and
the imaginary becomes suddenly blurred for the reader
as well as the characters in the story. Did Joe imagine the
slap and the resulting injury? Did he slap himself? And yet,
asking these kinds of questions seems to violate the experience of the story in the same way that the No Fathers Club
member who asks about the circumstances of Kurumi's
anecdote about her father educating her about sex violated the rules of the club. Unwittingly, the reader, too, has
become a member of the No Fathers Club at this point and,
like Joe, is slapped into consciousness of this fact.

And so, at the end of the story, as Joe attempts to rec-
oncile the two realities he's been inhabiting (with father
and without), the reader is also torn between taking his
side in abandoning the fantasy of the imagined father
and feeling this abandonment as a kind of fundamental
betrayal, as Kurumi evidently does. During their final confrontation, it becomes clear that what disturbs Kurumi is
not that Joe is willing to abandon their shared fantasy but
that he misunderstands the quality that allowed it to be
shared—the commitment to the act of fantasizing itself.
The "thinness" of Joe's desire at the end consists less of his
inability or unwillingness to believe that his imaginary
father is real but his self-serving willingness to abandon
his father once he fulfills Joe's immediate need for him. As
she puts it: "All you ever really wanted was to say goodbye
to your father. He disappeared before you could do that,
so you forced him to come back and let you perform some
sort of farewell ceremony with him. Now that's done, so
you don't have any use for him anymore and you feel like
you're your 'own man.'"

Here, the story reveals its thematic continuity with seemingly dissimilar stories like "Chino." "The No Fathers Club" ends with Joe realizing too late that the process of imagination by which he created his father affected more than him alone. It created a community that included those with whom he entered into the fantasy, including not only Kurumi and other members of the club but the imaginary father himself. In "Chino," the fictional "Tomoyuki Hoshino" fantasizes that he can escape the burden of First World ennui by taking on the glamour of the revolutionary, but finds out through his encounter with Maki that this rather self-serving fantasy also has consequences. To become other than oneself is not a simple process of escape via an alternate identity. The ethical component of Hoshino's work demands that this process never veer into simple appropriation. Taking on the identity of another risks becoming a process not of liberatory community building but touristic exploitation. In "The No Fathers Club," Joe helps to create a community of alternate fatherhood with the other club members, and when he abandons this, he reduces his participation in the community to a symptom of his individual lack of normative self-sufficiency, itself just another fantastical narrative, as Kurumi points out: "And what, exactly, is a self-sufficient individual?"

Fantasy, in Hoshino's world, always involves more than one person and always has consequences and ethical limits. "Sand Planet" spells this out perhaps the most explicitly, showing Yoshinobu fantasizing the connection between the school poisoning incident, the inhabitation of green zones by large numbers of homeless people, and the postwar experiment with Latin American immigration as a way to get at a "truth" more meaningful than the "lies" that keep these stories isolated from each other. Hoshino as author encourages us as readers to contemplate these things in conjunction, thus allowing these conventionally disparate narratives and phenomena to resonate in unexpected ways. But the story also dramatizes the potential violence of interposing oneself into these histories and forcing one's personal investment in them to stand as their ultimate "truth." Contemplating the old man performing his show alone in the woods, Yoshinobu thinks about these "words that wanted so badly to be said but refused so violently to be told." And at the very end of the novella, Yoshinobu violates this stricture when he publishes his own version of the story in the newspaper. The culmination of becoming other in the story takes place as Yoshinobu performs the old man's show alone in the woods, saying the words without imposing them on anyone else; and it is directly after that, when he sees that the children he forced into the fabricated "truth" he wove into his newspaper article have begun to tell their own story, that he realizes the violent appropriation and imposition his article represents.

But Hoshino does not mean his work to simply be a set of cautionary tales warning his readers of the dangers of appropriation. Far from it—the opening of fissures in time and space he sees as the purpose of fiction consists of allowing for this "looseness" of identity, providing the medium for the imaginative leaps that allow us to inhabit states of being beyond our own. But there is always a risk in this endeavor, one that constitutes his critique of the postmodernism he also finds so liberating. The risk is that in becoming other, one tames it, turns it unitary and static and simply a function of one's previous self. The flux of identity should not be considered simply a serial inhabitation of various static identities; this is the position of the tourist, the appropriator, the egotist unaware of his or her privilege. Instead, to become other is to attempt to become a part of the fluidity of the alternate position, to recognize that this will always be an incomplete process, but that this makes it no less necessary as a politics of being. Elsewhere in the conversation with Rieko Matsuura, Hoshino mentions that he has always admired the groundbreaking cycle of novellas on the theme of female-female desire she wrote called *Natural Woman*: "Just as you attempted to show in *Natural Woman*, I wanted to show the same sort of minor quality. I am a man, so I attempted to think of it as a man, tried to write on the theme of the 'Natural Man,' if you will. And the result of this is to write as an *Un*natural Man, to expand the purview to becoming catlike, or plantlike."[12]

This discussion was sparked by Matsuura explaining that her favorite of Hoshino's stories is "We, the Children of Cats," particularly the way the two main characters question what makes a natural woman or man. Matsuura emphasizes the way the story opens up gendered expectations that gain their coercive force from being thought of as natural, such as the expectation that the couple, now that they're married, should be trying to have a child. Hoshino sets up the story as an array of different ways this issue plays itself out through the situations of the different characters. Masako is afraid that she may physically be unable to have children, while the narrator is afraid of his own "unnatural" manhood, since he can't imagine having a child at all. Masako's friends Kasumi and Ryū are in the midst of a negotiation of surrogate parenthood, Kasumi unsettled by the circumvention of coupledom and marriage this demands and Ryū seeming to celebrate the very unnaturalness of his position as a gay man who wants a child to raise alone, hoping to replicate this unnaturalness into the future through his arranging to have a child this way. But, as Hoshino's comments hint, there is a range of perfectly natural but inhuman modes of reproduction and family-making in the story as well: the propagation of plants through the cultivation of cuttings in the kitchen, as well as the adoption of the couple by Soccer, the stray cat, who slips in and out of the apartment on his own terms. How do the human and inhuman reflect and inform each other? Can the catlike or plantlike be modes of community

---

12 *Bungei*, 54–55.

and reproduction that are as natural as (or more natural than) those debated by the humans in the story?

In "Air," the most recent of the stories included in this collection, the question of identity as something that can be alternately "loose" or constricting comes to the fore. The experience of otherness undergone by Tsubasa and Hina disrupts their gender and sexual identities, leading both to think of themselves as suddenly belonging to a "sexual minority" of some sort. But when they attend the Tokyo Gay and Lesbian Pride Parade, they feel alienated by the way the parade presents identity as fully formed and coherent, which is not how they are experiencing their own senses of difference from the norm. Hoshino allows them to find each other at the parade, and their signs of difference, the phantasmatic bodies that had been sensed only secretly, now become mutually sensed, summoned into existence like an erotic version of the game of No Ball Soccer that begins "The No Fathers Club." In their communion, they summon an alternate body that encompasses both of them, joining them in a way that again resonates with the human yet moves beyond it: flesh and blood transformed into air, a phallus hollowed out, now a conduit of song and breath. And the story ends on a hopeful note, its protagonists disappearing from a "real" existence that would force them back apart into the female/male, gay/straight, majority/minority binaries they have opened their bodies to escape.

But whether the categories that Hoshino renders fluid divide genders, races, classes, nationalities, or even species, they retain their political charge from the play of fluidity against the power relations that work to fix these categories into rigid permanence. Hoshino's fiction shows an affinity for flux that works against conventional narrative coherence, but this is a necessary part of his project—the structures that "shut down" time and space in our everyday lives take the form of narratives that justify the exercise of state power by demonizing dissidence, that code compulsory heterosexuality as "natural," that assume the nation-state to be the default unit of identity and cultural difference, and so on. Hoshino's fictions create openings and resist closure, a textual analog to the in-between-ness that emerges as the emblem of ethical being in figures like the mermaid. They force the reader to become other as well, to inhabit this in-between space of transformation that resolves into neither tourism nor projection.

Which is not to say that nationally inflected Japanese identity does not concern him. Indeed, stories like "Sand Planet" place such issues in the forefront through the use of images that overtly invert and subvert the symbols of the Japanese state. The song sung by Misao, the old man in the woods, replaces the word *kimi* in the real anthem, which signifies the Emperor, with the word *kimin* (棄民), which literally means "the abandoned" or "thrown-away," and which I translate as "the Forsaken." The image of the Japanese flag dyed red literalizes, as the character Yayoi mentions, a real Meiji-era martial song taught to school children that uses the image of the flag's white field dyed red with the blood of enemies. By reintroducing this image into the supposedly pacifist, demilitarized postwar atmosphere of Japan, the implication is that Japan, as a nation, is still built upon the blood of those it sacrifices to fuel its prosperity, be they Japanese or not (while also opening the question of whether, when Misao returns to Japan brandishing this flag, he is even exactly "Japanese" himself anymore).

And Misao's adoption of the persona of "Urashima Tarō" in his performance alludes to one of the oldest folk tales in Japan, included in an eighth century text, the *Nihongi,* and passed down in various versions ever since. The tale tells of a fisherman named Urashima who catches a magic turtle and spares its life, whereupon it transforms into a beautiful goddess. They fall in love and she brings him to the world of the gods, high in the sky (later versions relocate this world to the Palace of the Dragon King, located beneath the sea). After a while, though, he grows homesick for the mortal world and decides to return, despite the divine beings' entreaties for him to stay. When he does return, he finds that time runs differently in the divine world and years and years have gone by; in desperation, he opens a box that his goddess-wife had given him as a keepsake but cautioned him not to open. It turns out that she herself is in the box, but because he's opened it, she drifts away, marooning him forever in a former home that no longer remembers him. "When he dried his tears, he sang about her far, cloud-girdled realm," the tale ends, "But the clouds hid her paradise from him and left him nothing but his grief."[13]

Misao's retelling of the story of his migration to the Dominican Republic and return to Japan uses this tale as a template, but again inverts it. The "divine kingdom" of the Dominican Republic and the pastoral prosperity promised to the poor farmers enticed to move there turns out to be a salt-sown wasteland, and then the representatives of the divine Japanese Emperor (the Japanese word for ambassador, *taishi* [大使], is one horizontal stroke from the word for angel, *tenshi* [天使]) refuse the settlers reentry as well, leaving him abandoned to lament in the woods. Hoshino writes the word "Urashima" not with the conventional character for *ura* 浦 (which, incidentally, is also the *ura* in Urawa, the area where the old man performs his show in the woods), but a homophonous character, 裏, that means "backside." This reinforces the idea that Japan and the Dominican Republic are on opposite sides of the earth, and the irony of the embedded retellings of the story of their relation is the interchangeability of which island is the true "backside" of the earth. When Misao returns to Japan, he finds himself excluded and doubly dispossessed, and he longs to return to the place he now feels more at home: the island to which at first he felt he'd been

---

13 This version of the tale is translated as "Urashima the Fisherman" by Royall Tyler in his *Japanese Tales* (New York: Pantheon, 1987), 154–56.

exiled. This fits into the larger metaphoric structure of the novella whereby the images of death recycled into new life continually undermine the existing structures that stand for established power and fixed identity. The emphasis on rocks breaking down into sand and then cultivated into fertile soil works against, to take one example, the image of the moss-covered boulder symbolizing the eternal nature of the Emperor and the Japanese state found in the national anthem.

It seems important, though, to remember that even in "Sand Planet," Misao does not *identify* as suddenly Dominican, but rather as part of a larger collectivity of *kimin*: the forsaken, the dispossessed, the discarded. Hoshino distinguishes himself from the kind of opposition to the nation-state that inadvertently reinforces its centrality, which is why it differs from Karatani's notion of an oppositional—yet still national—political literature. As in "Treason Diary" and "Chino," the divisions between First World and Third World are presented in "Sand Planet" as two sides of the same coin (like the "lighter-than-air aluminum one-yen coin" that the protagonist of "Chino" longs to distance himself from even as it "buoys" his travels), but the emphasis is on the in-between spaces of passage between these positions. "Sand Planet" dramatizes this in moments like the performance in the woods that reads like a moment of pure witness to Misao's travels and travails between two sides of the world, or the fantastical penetration of the earth dreamed by Yoshinobu that unites Japan and the island of Hispaniola along the same axis, a root driven into the ground that suddenly transforms into a route, a conduit for connection (this also echoes the phallus-as-flute in "Air"). In "Treason Diary," Yukinori attempts to write and rewrite a new self in the Spanish-language diaries he keeps, using the "invisible third hand" of his non-native Spanish. And in "Chino," the protagonist ends up in neither Ilusión nor Realidad, but facedown in the dirt (and in inadvertent sexual union with it, recalling

"Sand Planet") somewhere between the two, his embarrassing erection bespeaking of his still-present desire toward revolution, even as he acquiesces to the impossibility of joining the guerillas.

Perhaps it is more accurate to think of this dynamic in Hoshino's literary vision less as impossible transformation and more as non-linear transformation. His stories follow a logic of *what if*—what if I were human, what if I were not? What if I were a cat? A fish? A bird? But, as I have said, the transformations that result from these conditional premises (if I were Japanese, I would do this; if I were a guerrilla, I would do that) are left incomplete—there is always the possibility, or maybe even the necessity, of never staying for long within the parameters of the new condition. Rather, Hoshino keeps multiple incompatible possibilities open within his narratives (I am Japanese, I am a guerrilla, I am a Chino), resisting the kind of narrative closure that would leave his characters (and readers) in one place or another. The medium of fiction allows for this open-endedness, this wavering movement between mutually exclusive *what if*s. It is, perhaps, the true basis of change, of revolution, for him: this space between incompatible possibilities, between conditions. It is a space of the unconditional, where possibility emerges at its purest.

To inhabit this space is to be neither fish nor fowl—a bird swimming through air, a fish flying through water. Benjamin's theory of translation again resonates, providing a key for understanding Hoshino's interest in allusion and adaptation as a mode of creating this space of pure possibility. The "pure language" Benjamin speaks of is similarly unconditional, a fleetingly glimpsed realm where the conditions imposed by two languages melt away and the meaning that emerges belongs to neither, yet both. The desire to inhabit this space drives Hoshino's fictional production and defines its political potential, as it is impossible to remain in the space of the majority while filled with such desire. It drives toward constant multiplicity, constant flight into the endlessly proliferating minor worlds excluded by the parameters of the major. In each instance, of course, this flight is fraught with anxiety and an acknowledgment of the impossibility of completely overcoming one's origins. But the desire persists, like a phantom limb or phantasmatic phallus (or tiny wedge?), opening up the everyday and allowing for an experience of otherness that leads to an inability to return to the previous status quo. And at its most successful, Hoshino's fiction produces a similar complex of revolutionary desire in the reader as well.

Brian Bergstrom
July 2011

Acknowledgments

Brian Bergstrom

I would like to thank Thomas Lamarre, Anne McKnight, Norma Field, Christine Lamarre, Maria Krasinski, Ramsey Kanaan, the endlessly vivacious ATJ Team (Brent Lue, Olivier Marin, Vinci Ting, Jayda Fogel, Irene Kim) and, above all, Adrienne Carey Hurley, who introduced me to Hoshino and his works and helped facilitate this project from conception to publication. I would also like to offer special thanks to Angela Covalt, who allowed me to consult her previous partial translation of "Sand Planet" during my work on that novella; any errors are, of course, mine alone.

Finally, I would like to dedicate this translation project to Cheryl Rudd, Akira "Ron" Takemoto, and the memory of Steve Rumsey.

Lucy Fraser

My translation was originally published online by the Japanese Literature Publishing and Promotion Center, which provides wonderful opportunities for emerging translators. I would like to thank Alfred Birnbaum and Elizabeth Floyd for their inspiring and insightful editing.

ABOUT PM PRESS

PM Press was founded at the end of 2007
by a small collection of folks with decades of
publishing, media, and organizing experience.
PM Press co-conspirators have published and
distributed hundreds of books, pamphlets,
CDs, and DVDs. Members of PM have founded enduring book fairs,
spearheaded victorious tenant organizing campaigns, and worked
closely with bookstores, academic conferences, and even rock bands
to deliver political and challenging ideas to all walks of life. We're old
enough to know what we're doing and young enough to know what's at
stake.

We seek to create radical and stimulating fiction and non-fiction books,
pamphlets, T-shirts, visual and audio materials to entertain, educate
and inspire you. We aim to distribute these through every available
channel with every available technology — whether that means you are
seeing anarchist classics at our bookfair stalls; reading our latest vegan
cookbook at the café; downloading geeky fiction e-books; or digging
new music and timely videos from our website.

PM Press is always on the lookout for talented and skilled volunteers,
artists, activists and writers to work with. If you have a great idea for a
project or can contribute in some way, please get in touch.

PM Press
PO Box 23912
Oakland, CA 94623
www.pmpress.org

FRIENDS OF PM PRESS

These are indisputably momentous times—the financial system is melting down globally and the Empire is stumbling. Now more than ever there is a vital need for radical ideas.

In the four years since its founding—and on a mere shoestring—PM Press has risen to the formidable challenge of publishing and distributing knowledge and entertainment for the struggles ahead. With over 175 releases to date, we have published an impressive and stimulating array of literature, art, music, politics, and culture. Using every available medium, we've succeeded in connecting those hungry for ideas and information to those putting them into practice.

Friends of PM allows you to directly help impact, amplify, and revitalize the discourse and actions of radical writers, filmmakers, and artists. It provides us with a stable foundation from which we can build upon our early successes and provides a much-needed subsidy for the materials that can't necessarily pay their own way. You can help make that happen—and receive every new title automatically delivered to your door once a month—by joining as a Friend of PM Press. And, we'll throw in a free T-shirt when you sign up.

Here are your options:

- **$25 a month** Get all books and pamphlets plus 50% discount on all webstore purchases

- **$40 a month** Get all PM Press releases (including CDs and DVDs) plus 50% discount on all webstore purchases

- **$100 a month** Superstar—Everything plus PM merchandise, free downloads, and 50% discount on all webstore purchases

For those who can't afford $25 or more a month, we're introducing **Sustainer Rates** at $15, $10 and $5. Sustainers get a free PM Press T-shirt and a 50% discount on all purchases from our website.

Your Visa or Mastercard will be billed once a month, until you tell us to stop. Or until our efforts succeed in bringing the revolution around. Or the financial meltdown of Capital makes plastic redundant. Whichever comes first.

Lonely Hearts Killer

Tomoyuki Hoshino

ISBN: 978-1-60486-084-9
$15.95   232 pages

What happens when a popular and young emperor suddenly dies, and the only person available to succeed him is his sister? How can people in an island country survive as climate change and martial law are eroding more and more opportunities for local sustainability and mutual aid? And what can be done to challenge the rise of a new authoritarian political leadership at a time when the general public is obsessed with fears related to personal and national "security"? These and other provocative questions provide the backdrop for this powerhouse novel about young adults embroiled in what appear to be more private matters—friendships, sex, a love suicide, and struggles to cope with grief and work.

PM Press is proud to bring you this first English translation of a full-length novel by the award-winning author Tomoyuki Hoshino.

Since his literary debut in 1997, Tomoyuki Hoshino has published twelve books on subjects ranging from "terrorism" to queer/trans community formations; from the exploitation of migrant workers to journalistic ethics; and from the Japanese emperor system to neoliberalism. He is also well known in Japan for his nonfiction essays on politics, society, the arts, and sports, particularly soccer. He maintains a website and blog at http://www.hoshinot.jp/.

"A major novel by Tomoyuki Hoshino, one of the most compelling and challenging writers in Japan today, Lonely Hearts Killer *deftly weaves a path between geopolitical events and individual experience, forcing a personal confrontation with the political brutality of the postmodern era. Adrienne Hurley's brilliant translation captures the nuance and wit of Hoshino's exploration of depths that rise to the surface in the violent acts of contemporary youth."*
— Thomas LaMarre, William Dawson Professor of East Asian Studies, McGill University

"Since his debut, Hoshino has used as the core of his writing a unique sense of the unreality of things, allowing him to illuminate otherwise hidden realities within Japanese society. And as he continues to write from this tricky position, it goes without saying that he produces work upon work of extraordinary beauty and power."
— Yuko Tsushima, award-winning Japanese novelist

Calling All Heroes:
A Manual for Taking Power

Paco Ignacio Taibo II

ISBN: 978-1-60486-205-8
$12.00   128 pages

The euphoric idealism of grassroots reform
and the tragic reality of revolutionary failure
are at the center of this speculative novel
that opens with a real historical event. On
October 2, 1968, 10 days before the Summer
Olympics in Mexico, the Mexican government responds to a student
demonstration in Tlatelolco by firing into the crowd, killing more
than 200 students and civilians and wounding hundreds more. The
Tlatelolco massacre was erased from the official record as easily as
authorities washing the blood from the streets, and no one was ever
held accountable.

It is two years later and Nestor, a journalist and participant in the fateful
events, lies recovering in the hospital from a knife wound. His fevered
imagination leads him in the collection of facts and memories of the
movement and its assassination in the company of figures from his
childhood. Nestor calls on the heroes of his youth—Sherlock Holmes,
Doc Holliday, Wyatt Earp, and D'Artagnan among them—to join him
in launching a new reform movement conceived by his intensely active
imagination.

*"Taibo's writing is witty, provocative, finely nuanced and well worth the
challenge."*
— *Publishers Weekly*

*"I am his number one fan. . . I can always lose myself in one of his novels
because of their intelligence and humor. My secret wish is to become one
of the characters in his fiction, all of them drawn from the wit and wisdom
of popular imagination. Yet make no mistake, Paco Taibo—sociologist
and historian—is recovering the political history of Mexico to offer a vital,
compelling vision of our reality."*
— Laura Esquivel, author of *Like Water for Chocolate*

*"The real enchantment of Mr. Taibo's storytelling lies in the wild and
melancholy tangle of life he sees everywhere."*
— *New York Times Book Review*

Fire on the Mountain

Terry Bisson
with an introduction
by Mumia Abu-Jamal

ISBN: 978-1-60486-087-0
$15.95   208 pages

It's 1959 in socialist Virginia. The Deep South
is an independent Black nation called Nova
Africa. The second Mars expedition is about
to touch down on the red planet. And a
pregnant scientist is climbing the Blue Ridge in search of her great-great
grandfather, a teenage slave who fought with John Brown and Harriet
Tubman's guerrilla army.

Long unavailable in the US, published in France as *Nova Africa*, *Fire on
the Mountain* is the story of what might have happened if John Brown's
raid on Harper's Ferry had succeeded—and the Civil War had been
started not by the slave owners but the abolitionists.

*"History revisioned, turned inside out… Bisson's wild and wonderful
imagination has taken some strange turns to arrive at such a destination."*
— Madison Smartt Bell, Anisfield-Wolf Award winner and author of
Devil's Dream

*"You don't forget Bisson's characters, even well after you've finished his
books. His* Fire on the Mountain *does for the Civil War what Philip K.
Dick's* The Man in the High Castle *did for World War Two."*
— George Alec Effinger, winner of the Hugo and Nebula awards for
Shrödinger's Kitten, and author of the Marîd Audran trilogy.

*"A talent for evoking the joyful, vertiginous experiences of a world at
fundamental turning points."*
— *Publishers Weekly*

"Few works have moved me as deeply, as thoroughly, as Terry Bisson's Fire
on the Mountain… *With this single poignant story, Bisson molds a world
as sweet as banana cream pies, and as briny as hot tears."*
— Mumia Abu-Jamal, prisoner and author of *Live From Death Row*, from
the Introduction.

Sensation

Nick Mamatas
ISBN: 978-1-60486-354-3
$14.95   208 pages

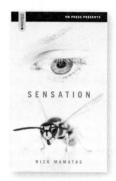

Love. Politics. Parasitic manipulation. Julia Hernandez left her husband, shot a real-estate developer out to gentrify Brooklyn, and then vanished without a trace. Well, perhaps one or two traces were left . . . With different personal and consumption habits, Julia has slipped out of the world she knew and into the Simulacrum—a place between the cracks of our existence from which human history is both guided and thwarted by the conflict between a species of anarchist wasp and a collective of hyperintelligent spiders. When Julia's ex-husband Raymond spots her in a grocery store he doesn't usually patronize, he's drawn into an underworld of radical political gestures and Internet organizing looking to overthrow a ruling class it knows nothing about—and Julia is the new media sensation of both this world and the Simulacrum.

Told ultimately from the collective point of view of another species, Sensation plays with the elements of the Simulacrum we all already live in: media reports, businessspeak, blog entries, text messages, psychological evaluation forms, and the always fraught and kindly lies lovers tell one another.

"Nick Mamatas continues his reign as the sharpest, funniest, most insightful and political purveyor of post-pulp pleasures going. He is the People's Commissar of Awesome."
— China Miéville, award-winning author of *Kraken* and *The City and the City*

"Nick Mamatas' brilliant comic novel, Sensation, *reads like an incantation that both vilifies and celebrates the complex absurdity of the modern world."*
— Lucius Shepard, winner of the Hugo, Nebula, and World Fantasy awards.

*"The Majestic Plural, or Royal We, is well known—*Sensation *introduces the Arachnid Plural, the we of spiders, the ones that live inside you. The spiders care about you—deeply—and want to use you in a millennial war against certain parasitic wasps. No, I was wrong. The spiders only want to help. So let them in."*
— Zachary Mason, the *New York Times* best-selling author of *The Lost Books of the Odyssey*

Vida

Marge Piercy

ISBN: 978-1-60486-487-8
$20.00   416 pages

Originally published in 1979, *Vida* is Marge
Piercy's classic bookend to the Sixties.
Vida is full of the pleasures and pains, the
experiments, disasters, and victories of an
extraordinary band of people. At the center
of the novel stands Vida Asch. She has
lived underground for almost a decade. Back in the '60s she was a
political star of the exuberant antiwar movement—a red-haired beauty
photographed for the pages of *Life* magazine—charismatic, passionate,
and totally sure she would prevail. Now, a decade later, Vida is on the
run, her star-quality replaced by stubborn courage. She comes briefly to
rest in a safe house on Cape Cod. To her surprise and annoyance, she
finds another person in the house, a fugitive, Joel, ten years younger
than she, a kid who dropped into the underground out of the army. As
they spend the next days together, Vida finds herself warming toward a
man for the first time in years, knowing all too well the dangers.

As counterpoint to the underground '70s, Marge Piercy tells the
extraordinary tale of the optimistic '60s, the thousands of people
who were members of SAW (Students Against the War) and of the
handful who formed a fierce group called the Little Red Wagon. Piercy's
characters make vivid and comprehensible the desperation, the
courage, and the blind rage of a time when "action" could appear to
some to be a more rational choice than the vote.

A new introduction by Marge Piercy situates the book, and the author,
in the times from which they emerged.

*"Real people inhabit its pages and real suspense carries the story along...
'Vida' of course means life and she personifies it."*
— Chicago Tribune

*"A fully controlled, tightly structured dramatic narrative of such artful
intensity that it leads the reader on at almost every page."*
— New York Times Book Review

*"Marge Piercy tells us exactly how it was in the lofts of the Left as the 1960s
turned into the '70s. This is the way everybody sounded. This is the way
everybody behaved.* Vida *bears witness."*
— New York Times

"Very exciting. Marge Piercy's characters are complex and very human."
— Margaret Atwood

Dance the Eagle to Sleep: A Novel

Marge Piercy

ISBN: 978-1-60486-456-4
$17.95   208 pages

Originally published in 1970, Marge Piercy's second novel follows the lives of four teenagers, in a near future society, as they rebel against a military draft and "the system." The occupation of Franklin High School begins, and with it, the open rebellion of America's youth against their channeled, unrewarding lives and the self-serving, plastic society that directs them. From the disillusionment and alienation of the young at the center of the revolt, to their attempts to build a visionary new society, the nationwide following they gain and the brutally complete repression that inevitably follows, this is a future fiction without a drop of fantasy. As driving, violent, and nuanced today as it was 40 years ago, this anniversary edition includes a new introduction by the author reflecting unapologetically on the novel and the times from which it emerged.

"Dance the Eagle to Sleep *is a vision, not an argument… It is brilliant. Miss Piercy was a published poet before she resorted to the novel, exploiting its didactic aspect, and her prose crackles, depolarizes, sends shivers leaping across the synaptic cleft. The 'eagle' is America, bald and all but extinct. The 'dance' is performed by the tribal young, the self-designated 'Indians,' after their council meetings, to celebrate their bodies and their escape from the cannibalizing 'system.' The eagle isn't danced to sleep; it sends bombers to devastate the communes of the young… What a frightening, marvelous book!"*
— New York Times

"*It's so good I don't even know how to write a coherent blurb. It tore me apart. It's one of the first really honest books this country has ever produced. In lesser hands it would've been just another propaganda pamphlet, but in Marge Piercy's it's an all-out honest-to-God novel, humanity and love hollering from every sentence and the best set of characters since, shit I dunno,* Moby Dick *or something. At a time when nearly every other novelist is cashing in on masturbation fantasies, the superhip college bullshit stored up in their brains, even on the revolution itself, here is somebody with the guts to go into the deepest core of herself, her time, her history, and risk more than anybody else has so far, just out of a love for the truth and a need to tell it. It's about fucking time.*"
— Thomas Pynchon, author of *Gravity's Rainbow*

Byzantium Endures: The First Volume of the Colonel Pyat Quartet

Michael Moorcock
with an introduction by Alan Wall

ISBN: 978-1-60486-491-5
$22.00   400 pages

Meet Maxim Arturovitch Pyatnitski, also
known as Pyat. Tsarist rebel, Nazi thug,
continental conman, and reactionary counterspy: the dark and
dangerous anti-hero of Michael Moorcock's most controversial work.

Published in 1981 to great critical acclaim—then condemned to the
shadows and unavailable in the U.S. for thirty years—*Byzantium Endures*,
the first of the Pyat Quartet, is not a book for the faint-hearted. It's the
story of a cocaine addict, sexual adventurer, and obsessive anti-Semite
whose epic journey from Leningrad to London connects him with
scoundrels and heroes from Trotsky to Makhno, and whose career
echoes that of the 20th century's descent into Fascism and total war.

This is Moorcock at his audacious, iconoclastic best: a grand sweeping
overview of the events of the last century, as revealed in the secret
journals of modern literature's most proudly unredeemable outlaw.
This authoritative U.S. edition presents the author's final cut, restoring
previously forbidden passages and deleted scenes.

*"What is extraordinary about this novel. . . is the largeness of the design.
Moorcock has the bravura of a nineteenth-century novelist: he takes risks,
he uses fiction as if it were a divining rod for the age's most significant
concerns. Here, in* Byzantium Endures, *he has taken possession of the
early twentieth century, of a strange, dead civilization and recast them in a
form which is highly charged without ceasing to be credible."*
— Peter Ackroyd, *Sunday Times*

*"A tour de force, and an extraordinary one. Mr. Moorcock has created in
Pyatnitski a wholly sympathetic and highly complicated rogue. . . There is
much vigorous action here, along with a depth and an intellectuality, and
humor and color and wit as well."*
— *The New Yorker*

*"Clearly the foundation on which a gigantic literary edifice will, in due course,
be erected. While others build fictional molehills, Mr. Moorcock makes
plans for great shimmering pyramids. But the footings of this particular
edifice are intriguing and audacious enough to leave one hungry for more."*
— John Naughton, *Listener*

The Wild Girls

Ursula K. Le Guin

ISBN: 978-1-60486-403-8
$12.00   112 pages

Ursula K. Le Guin is the one modern science fiction author who truly needs no introduction. In the forty years since *The Left Hand of Darkness*, her works have changed not only the face but the tone and the agenda of SF, introducing themes of gender, race, socialism, and anarchism, all the while thrilling readers with trips to strange (and strangely familiar) new worlds. She is our exemplar of what fantastic literature can and should be about.

Her Nebula winner *The Wild Girls*, newly revised and presented here in book form for the first time, tells of two captive "dirt children" in a society of sword and silk, whose determination to enter "that possible even when unattainable space in which there is room for justice" leads to a violent and loving end.

Plus: Le Guin's scandalous and scorching *Harper's* essay, "Staying Awake While We Read," (also collected here for the first time) which demolishes the pretensions of corporate publishing and the basic assumptions of capitalism as well. And of course our Outspoken Interview which promises to reveal the hidden dimensions of America's best-known SF author. And delivers.

"Idiosyncratic and convincing, Le Guin's characters have a long afterlife."
— *Publishers Weekly*

"Her worlds are haunting psychological visions molded with firm artistry."
— *The Library Journal*

"If you want excess and risk and intelligence, try Le Guin."
— *The San Francisco Chronicle*

"Her characters are complex and haunting, and her writing is remarkable for its sinewy grace."
— *Time*

"She wields her pen with a moral and psychological sophistication rarely seen. What she really does is write fables: splendidly intricate and hugely imaginative tales about such mundane concerns as life, death, love, and sex."
— *Newsweek*

The Great Big Beautiful Tomorrow

Cory Doctorow

ISBN: 978-1-60486-404-5
$12.00   144 pages

Cory Doctorow burst on the SF scene in 2000 like a rocket, inspiring awe in readers (and envy in other writers) with his bestselling novels and stories, which he insisted on giving away via Creative Commons. Meanwhile, as coeditor of the wildly popular Boing Boing, he became the radical new voice of the Web, boldly arguing for internet freedom from corporate control.

Doctorow's activism and artistry are both on display in this Outspoken Author edition. The crown jewel is his novella "The Great Big Beautiful Tomorrow," the high velocity adventures of a trans-human teenager in a toxic post-Disney dystopia, battling wireheads and wumpuses (and having fun doing it!) until he meets the "meat girl" of his dreams, and is forced to choose between immortality and sex.

Plus a live transcription of Cory's historic address to the 2010 World SF Convention, "Creativity vs. Copyright," dramatically presenting his controversial case for open-source in both information and art. Also included is an international Outspoken Interview in which Doctorow reveals the surprising sources of his genius.

"Doctorow uses science fiction as a kind of cultural WD-40, loosening hinges and dissolving adhesions to peer into some of society's unlighted corners."
— New York Times

"Utterly contemporary and deeply peculiar—a hard combination to beat (or, these days, to find)."
— William Gibson, author of *Neuromancer*

"Everything comes under Doctorow's microscope, and he manages to be both up to date and off the cuff in the best possible way."
— Locus

"One of the genre's fresh new talents, one of the few who seamlessly mixes the future with the bizarre."
— Rocky Mountain News

"Doctorow shows us life from the point-of-view of the plugged-in generation and makes it feel like a totally alien world."
— Montreal Gazette

Send My Love and a Molotov Cocktail: Stories of Crime, Love and Rebellion

Edited by Gary Phillips
and Andrea Gibbons

ISBN: 978-1-60486-096-2
$19.95   368 pages

An incendiary mixture of genres and voices,
this collection of short stories compiles a
unique set of work that revolves around riots, revolts, and revolution.
From the turbulent days of unionism in the streets of New York City
during the Great Depression to a group of old women who meet at their
local café to plan a radical act that will change the world forever, these
original and once out-of-print stories capture the various ways people
rise up to challenge the status quo and change up the relationships
of power. Ideal for any fan of noir, science fiction, and revolution and
mayhem, this collection includes works from Sara Paretsky, Paco
Ignacio Taibo II, Cory Doctorow, Kim Stanley Robinson, and Summer
Brenner.

Full list of contributors:

Summer Brenner

Rick Dakan

Barry Graham

Penny Mickelbury

Gary Phillips

Luis Rodriguez

Benjamin Whitmer

Michael Moorcock

Larry Fondation

Cory Doctorow

Andrea Gibbons

John A. Imani

Sara Paretsky

Kim Stanley Robinson

Paco Ignacio Taibo II

Ken Wishnia

Michael Skeet

Tim Wohlforth